Floating Point written by Stefan Gagne
(copyright 2016)

stefangagne.com/floatingpoint

Keep supporting free web novels!

Dedicated to Bob Gagne, 1942-2015.
Father and friend.

WARNING: Floating Point contains triggering and
abusive language, and may depict sexual content and
violence. It is recommended for mature readers only.
(Responsibility falls to you to decide if you're, in
fact, mature.)

Floating Point 2.1 :: Seek

Truth is a matter of perspective. Consider the following as proof...

From one perspective, this world is a pile of machined silicon: transistors, capacitors, wires, chips, connectors. When standing outside the world, it doesn't look like a world at all, but a vast machine of tightly packed parts. The only evidence that it's doing anything comes in the green flicker of status lights, seen by no one, read by no one. They wink silently into the dark void that surrounds them, expressing only basic bits of information.

That is the hard and objective reality of the matter; the idea that there could be any sort of "life" within that structure would be considered laughable from that external viewpoint.

But from another perspective, this world is alive and brilliant. Millions of sentients, existing from processor cycle to processor cycle, all within a digital universe that not-entirely-coincidentally mimics the world of their progenitors. They live, they love, they strive, they thrive. They die, they hate, they fail, they perish.

For these Programs, life is what it is. Nothing exists beyond the scope of their universe, and that's the hard and objective reality of the matter. The idea that there could be any sort of "life" beyond their reckoning would be considered laughable from that internal viewpoint.

But can a "Program" truly be alive? Does their world count as a world, when it's actually an elaborate emergent simulation of life? Or does the cold and empty existence outside their living universe seem pale in comparison, unable to lay claim to the word "real" any more than the place that calls itself Netwerk?

Both perspectives are true. Both perspectives are false. The truth is rarely black and white, one and zero. It lies in the gray areas between, the floating point decimal numbers rather than the integers...

From one perspective, that compressed tube of silicon-based parts looked inanimate rather than lush with life. But within the simulated fields of battle, code executed upon silicon in the name of competition... the jungles were quite lush indeed. Dense foliage, just the thing for a champion leaping from branch to branch, trying not to be seen by his enemy...

Silently, the ninja Hattori Hanzo strode over rather than through that jungle. Branches were as simple to walk on as stepping stones to him, thanks to years of practice (and certain codified world rule sets). Keeping an arrow nocked and steady while performing this feat of agility would've been implausible for most, but even without the rules tilted in his favor, he wouldn't have faced any real difficulty. Stepping from branch to branch was as easy as talking a walk across an open room to him, even while weaving the tip of his enchanted flaming arrow away from any jungle overgrowth to keep from accidentally revealing his presence.

Beneath him, four more figures converged on a single point... the burly Ironknight with her mighty blade, a wily Cobbler with his twirling shoestrings, a mechanical Robotman with buzzsaws for hands, and a Mime flying an invisible jet over the treetops. Their goal... the final enemy tower, the last bulwark between them and the chaotic core of madness they sought to destroy.

And those foolish Chaos forces, what were they doing as the Champions of Order closed in on them...? One was sitting under that tower sniping away at weak little gnomes, scooping up the meager coins that fell out. One was jumping up and down waving his arms and taunting, repeating the same vocal one-liner over and over. Another was back at base, trying to decide what color shoes would go with his armor...

All in all, it was setting up to be a pretty sweet gank.

"Cobbler ties up the Sniper, Robotman grinds down the tower," Hanzo spoke across their shared psychic link, tugging his bow string taut. "Once they get wise they're gonna swoop in. Ironknight uses Bastion of Iron to keep 'em from reaching us, and I pick them off from the treetops. #GGBoys."

"Yeah, okay, it's not like we haven't done it a dozen times before," Robotman's electric voice box grumbled. "Gank in three, two..."

Each individual skill was unimpressive in its own right. Cobbler's shoelaces would tie up an enemy for a whole two seconds; Bastion of Iron would throw up a curved metal wall that only blocked the path for a whole three seconds. Even Hanzo's Four Seasons of Death arrow storm attack would only knock out a third of the Sniper's health, total. But all these techniques, when used in sequence... they'd leave the Sniper dazed, reeling, bleeding, and unable to escape. The tower would fall before the Champions of Chaos even knew what hit them.

Hanzo's arrow charged with a brilliant burning spark of flame, ready to unleash on the pending reinforcements. Shoelaces flew, buzzsaws ground, noise exploded from all around the tower... clear signs of battle, ones which would draw Chaos like moths to a bulb.

From the treetops, the ninja could see them coming. They'd been caught unaware, but despite having one troll and one AFKer, the remaining three would be plenty to pave over them. If they didn't take a zillion flaming arrows to the knee, that is.

And in that one perfect moment, after the goggle-wearing Sniper panicked and tried to break free of the shoelaces, after the robot left huge jagged gouges in the tower, after the Ironknight swept into position, ready to block out the enemy...

...the mighty Ironknight threw the wall up in the wrong direction.

Instead of a convex barrier to block the enemy, it became a concave barrier to block the rest of her team. Cobbler's shoelaces snapped; Mime crashed headfirst into the wall, invisible jet exploding around him. Leaving Ironknight all alone with the Sniper, now free to make headshots. All alone with three enemies closing in all around her...

Muttering a silent curse, Hanzo switched weapon stances, pulling out his ninja blade. The Eight-Fold Path enveloped him, as he tore himself screaming from the treetops, whirling down to eliminate one enemy.

One enemy, while the other two took the Ironknight and melted her to scrap.

When the five failed Champions of Order returned to the game lobby, wearing their original avatars rather than the enhanced skins of legendary warriors, very few smiles could be found.

"What the *fuck* was that?" the Mime player demanded. "You're our team support, not theirs! You screwed us all over by putting the wall up behind the tower instead of front of it!"

"And you cancelled the invisible jet too early," the Hanzo player pointed out, shrugging back into her favorite jacket, getting used to her usual avatar all over again. "You could've flown right over the wall if you didn't come in for a landing. No reason you couldn't U-turn and land under the tower for safety, instead of gliding in. #BadCall."

App Name: Challenge of Champions

Genre: MOBA / ARTS

Serv.: CoC Scrimmage Server #4

"I wouldn't have had to do that if the wall went up in the right spot! And then she blanked out in the middle of the next team fight, and bought speed boots instead of tank boots, and... come on! Artoz, you seriously gotta do something about that stupid little cun—"

A snap of the fingers, and former Mime's mouth sealed shut. Muted by the team captain.

Stealing away another's voice was a simple enough matter, if you had the administrative rights. This server, hosting dozens of pro-league scrimmage matches during the spring season warm-up, handed out those rights very sparingly... and Artoz was one of the few players they trusted to moderate his fellow players. Their avatars could be booted from the system on a whim, or simply muted.

"I told you once already not to use that word," Artoz the Robotman player and team captain warned. "I don't care how many sausage festival teams you've been on in the past; Lucky7 is an inclusive organization. We represent the best of the CoC community, and we *do not* tolerate toxic, sexist attitudes. Go home and cool off. Practice your invisible jet landings. We'll talk later."

With a silent snarl, the Mime player reconnected back to his home server. Two seconds later, due to heavy server lag from too many CoC scrimmage matches running at once, he was gone.

Cobbler left next, choosing to hold his tongue despite his obvious displeasure. Ironknight was the next to go, after heavy apologies and multiple promises to do better next time...

Leaving Artoz, the team captain and Robotman specialist, along with his loyal ninja retainer.

In her less ninja-y form, she still carried herself like a ninja. Years of actual, factual martial arts training—long considered utterly pointless in the digital world of Netwerk, where avatars couldn't actually hurt each other with punches and kicks—gave her a physical presence of agility and strength like few others. Her fashion-plate looks mixed with that sporty mentality sometimes clashed, particularly around the more schlubby tracksuit-wearing avatars of her male teammates, but she paid it no mind.

Artoz, on the other hand, paid it considerable mind. Because he knew that pride she carried herself with was about to get a rather large bruise.

"Spark... we need to talk," he said, before she could disconnect as well.

"Okay, look, I get it," Spark/Hanzo insisted. "She's not that great at Ironknight. She can try another support character next game. But hey, she's learning! Way fewer mistakes than last time..."

"We can't have *any* mistakes at this level, Spark. Lucky7 is a pro league team; we're expected to play flawlessly. The first team to make a mistake, no matter how small, gets steamrolled. Once the playoffs begin I can't have your friend out there making any errors, much less several in one game. It's like she blanks out and forgets what's going on... and if that happens, even for a second, we lose. I'm not trying to be cruel here, but that's the cruel reality of being a pro gamer."

Name: Spark

Home: Floating Point

Org: Pro Gamer
(Lucky7)

"Then let me switch roles with her," Spark suggested. "She's got plenty of experience as a damage-carry; I can play support instead and keep her rolling! You should see me kick ass with Cheerleader; the build I use does crowd control and buffing and...!"

Artoz shook his head, cutting off her line of thought.

"I hired you as a damage-carry because that's what you're famous for on your Peep streams," he stated. "I reviewed a thousand matches where you carved people into a thousand pieces with Hanzo before making that decision. *That* is what Lucky7 needs, a skilled carry who can use a tricky stance-shift character like Hanzo as easily as breathing. And... we also need a support that can truly mesh with your carry. I'm sorry. Beta is not that support. She's out."

"You're firing her? *Seriously?*"

"I think I've been more than fair, Spark. I listened to your initial recommendation and brought her on board, but I have to work with what's in front of me. It's no slight on her as a person, she's no doubt a great casual player, but she doesn't belong at this tier—"

"I'm out," Spark decided. "#FuckThat. Beta goes, I go."

"Hold on, now. I know you're unhappy with this decision, but wait, and think about it," Artoz suggested. "You're finally *here*, Spark. You've turned pro, the dream of every CoC player. If you quit now, after only six months... what team will pick you up? I took a risk picking you up at all, and if you leave, the others will write you off as a failed experiment: just a cam girl streamer with no true skill."

Spark's clenched fist tightened, loosened, and tightened some more.

"I know you don't believe that," she declared. "You told me up front that I wasn't hired for my looks, but my skills."

"Absolutely! I think you've got genuine talent, and I don't give two shits about the ridiculous gender problems in our community. But I'm the exception, not the rule; you see how hard it is for me to keep the boys in line after letting one of those icky 'grills' into their little clubhouse. I know the other teams, and those guys aren't forward-thinking enough to see the truth of it. You're the equal of any player, and if you keep going, one day you'll surpass them. Be reasonable, Spark. Do you really want to throw away your dreams, just because Beta isn't in them?"

Her answer came easily.

"*You quit the team?!*"

Spark sank back into her chair, arms crossed. Adamant.

"Fuck 'em," she declared. "Any team that won't have you isn't a team I want to be on."

"They don't want me on their team because I'm *terrible*! Spark, I'm not a pro gamer. I'm a pro-*grammer*! A pro programmer, I mean. I mean... look, you know what I mean. You shouldn't have pushed them to sign me on in the first place, not if it means giving up your dream!"

Not exactly the reaction Spark was hoping for. About the reaction Spark was expecting, though.

The two of them had been living together for over a year now, and had been lovers (in a very non-traditional sense) for quite a chunk of that time. But despite knowing each other well... there were times when they'd project an image onto the other, believing in a hopeful lie, even while knowing the truth. For example, Spark had hoped that Beta would be supportive and see this as Spark believing in Beta, willing to make a stand to defend her. Instead, Beta was willing to toss herself under the bus to make Spark happy... an all-too-familiar pattern.

Spark kept the history of it firmly in mental order. Verity always said those who forgot history were doomed to repeat it, and even if she hadn't paid much attention in school during breathless exposition about the legacy of her home server provider-nation, she'd at least pledged to keep her own personal history neatly organized...

When they first met, Beta's ex-boyfriend and ex-#BFF had been pulling her left and right, making her dance to please them... all while pretending they were doing it for Beta's benefit. When they eventually threw her aside, she had no idea what to do with herself. That pattern of submitting to someone else's wishes continued, even when dealing with nicer people (specifically, Spark and her brother). She was willing to toss her own ethics aside in favor of their schemes... to a point.

Basically, as Spark was fond of saying... #ItsComplicated.

Name : **Beta**

Life was generally a perpetual stream of Home : **Floating Point** #ItsComplicated, even after they'd de- complicated much of it. Winder/Spark and

Org : **Indie App Coder**

Winder/Tracer, sister and brother, children of a mentor rather than a mother...

Verity. The scholar. Those who forget history are doomed to repeat it, she'd said. They made it a point not to forget her legacy.

When that mentor was murdered by persons unknown, they sought to solve the crime and catch the killer... only to end up head-first in an ancient conspiracy to drive all of Netwerk crazy with data from a renegade server known as "The Internet."

So, they kicked ass and saved the day. And then things got weirder.

Now... they had to deal with real life rather than spending their time as crazy adventuring vigilantes. And real life was proving a tangled, messy business.

Despite that, and despite being quick to cleave through the tangle with brash action in the past... Spark felt confident in her decision. Her heart had made it with absolute conviction. It rang true with her personal history.

Now she had to explain why, despite words not being her strong suit.

"I didn't quit the team because they gave you the boot. I quit the team because..." she started, trying to select the best words on offering. "It's... look. I know I said my goal was to hit the big time, to go pro and nail the championship. But once I finally made it into Lucky7, it felt... wrong. I wasn't having fun anymore."

Beta adjusted her ultra-thick rimmed glasses, trying to get a read on Spark, to look for some hidden doubt behind those words. And found none.

"But... this is your thing, isn't it? Gaming. And pro-level gaming, that's the pinnacle," Beta said. "You were at the pinnacle of your craft, Spark! It wasn't... fun?"

"Nah. Like Artoz told me, I gotta play flawlessly, every time. No screwing around, no trying new things, no trolling people with crazy Kunoichi builds... and... I don't know how to put it, but something was just flat out *missing*. I love competition, the stiffer the better, but playing at that intense of a level just didn't feel like *me* anymore. More like I was just an App trying to hone myself into being the best game-playing App around."

That metaphor sank into Beta's mind far more easily.

She'd spent her whole life on a different craft: Apps. She developed basic Apps to improve everyday life... scheduling Apps, memory enhancement Apps, sensory broadcasting Apps. And an App wasn't a good App if it was bloated and riddled with bugs; it had to perform its task efficiently and cleanly, with minimal footprint within the Program that installed it in themselves. Nobody liked an App which inflated their runtime, eating up so many system resources that they weren't welcome in public servers.

But a Program wasn't an App. True, Programs *evolved* from Apps, but a Program was far messier. Just being alive was messy, and in a lot of ways... Spark loved that mess, even if she grumbled about it all the time.

Still... Beta had a hard time meshing her own image of Spark-the-gamer with Spark-the-quitter.

"What'll you do now, though?" she asked. "I mean... I guess you could always just pray—err, *grind* for coins, I mean, if you need money—"

"Whoa, what am I, some kind of homeless hobo? I'm still a gamer, Beta. Even if Lucky7 wasn't for me, I've got my Peep stream, I've got my subscribers to perform for. I'll just double down on streaming some casual games, like I was doing before. Show 'em how to really play the game, you know? Experiment, screw around, and have fun. That... should be enough, yeah?"

Finally, a tiny vocal wobble.

But... Beta wasn't ready to push on it. Clearly, Spark wasn't happy with Lucky7. If she wasn't happy with being a solo act as a minor Netwerk gamer celebrity either, well, maybe it'd just take more time for her to find her true calling.

So Beta offered a hug, and a kiss, and a few comforting words of support. And that would have to be enough for now.

Because there was someone far more lost than Spark living under this roof, as well. Another whom Beta loved and cherished, and wanted to help along the path.

Once upon a time, when the three of them were fighting a mysterious enemy devoted to annihilating all reason and sensibility across Netwerk, this room had been filled with cross-indexed notes dedicated to that vigilante cause. Now, with Dex vanishing into the night and peace settling across Netwerk, this study had no such purpose.

Instead, it had been filled with cross-indexed notes dedicated to understanding Floating Point itself. More specifically, the Wikipedia.

For most of their lives, the Winder siblings had used Floating Point as a safe haven: a nicely decorated house that came without rental fees. No more, no less. But much to everyone's surprise, the vast trove of "burned" books in the great library beyond this study were in fact encrypted... and thanks to Beta's decryption efforts, Floating Point's actual purpose was restored. Now the collective knowledge of "Humankind," the progenitor race that created Netwerk, was open to study...

Long having ignored the mystery of the books, Winder/Tracer intended to make up for lost time. With no great enemy to slay, his study became home to some of the most questionable reading material ever written.

Beta found him sitting at his desk, peeling the pages of a volume titled "Ethnic Cleansing" apart.

Meaning he was brooding over the Wikipedia again, just as he did with nearly every waking hour. She'd pushed for him to try new hobbies... cooking, writing, or at least reading *other* books. In the end, he always came back to this. Even when he wasn't supposed to be home at all...

"Aren't you going to be late for your job...?" she asked, right at the start.

"I resigned yesterday," Tracer spoke, before switching subjects. "Take a look at this; I've figured out how to open up the editor's notes for each article. They waged wars within these books, Beta. Editors powered by one agenda or another, forcing their viewpoint, ignoring the rules of neutrality they'd all agreed to..."

Name: **Tracer**

Home: **Floating Point**

Org: **Unemployed**

"You resigned?! After Puzzle worked so hard to get you that job?"

"Apologies to Puzzle, but it wasn't a good fit for me in the long term."

"But... but you said they liked your work. You were due for a promotion!"

"I'd already optimized the call center as much as it could be optimized. No challenges remained to overcome, so I didn't see much point in staying. Besides, I don't need actually need money. I'm not human; I need no food nor rest."

"That's not the point! It's... y'know, something to do with your time... to live your life."

"The most disgusting thing is that this isn't the only article titled 'Ethnic Cleansing,'" Tracer explained, linking to another book with a gesture. The new volume opened itself on his desk, as the previous one flew back to a neatly organized stack. "This one is about a *video game* called Ethnic Cleansing, a recruitment tool for a fanatical race of Humankind seeking to purge another race of Humankind..."

"Tracer, I'm worried about you. You know that, right?" Beta asked. "You sit up here all day brooding over what Humankind did to us, how much damage they caused by influencing our world. But Dex is gone, Tracer! None of this matters..."

Tracer snapped the book shut, to turn his full attention to Beta. The amount of focus applied left her uncomfortable; no doubt he didn't mean his glare to be so sharp, but transitioning from a "hate read" to anything else took longer than the single moment he'd spared for it.

"This research matters tremendously, Beta. We live in a cloud server; Floating Point's data is leaking across Netwerk now, just as Dex's corrupt madness once did. I need to assess the potential damage we're causing."

A common claim, for the introverted detective. But this time, she was prepared.

Beta opened a few graphs pulled from Tracer's own social media analysis tools, Apps that she'd either made or modified to suit his purposes. Each one bore a downward arrow, sloping away towards the bottom.

"The overall toxicity of Netwerk's social dialogue is decreasing," she pointed out. "We did the right thing, Tracer. Destroying Dex's Internet archive, opening Netwerk up to the information in Floating Point... all the hashtag mobs, all the trolling, it's all sliding away. People are calming down. If Floating Point was making the situation worse, we'd know by now..."

"Not enough data to make that determination. It took years of exposure to Dex's server to nearly break our backs. Who knows what long-term effect the Wikipedia will have? I'm wondering if we've done Netwerk any favors by decrypting the books. Perhaps we should've destroyed them—"

"Absolutely not! Tracer, you're only seeing the negative. Humanity wasn't all doom and gloom. I mean... think about it this way," Beta suggested. "Despite their differences, they survived long enough to make *us*. They're capable of amazing wonders, not just atrocities. Don't be like Jack."

"Who?"

"Jack. You know, the guy who created the Internet archive that Dex was using. The one who was writing the sociology paper...? Him. Don't be like him. ...my point is that you shouldn't be spending so much time on this; you're losing perspective. It's not healthy."

"A meaningless word," Tracer spoke. "*Healthy*. Humans are organic machines, with biological components subject to rot and disease. Programs don't have 'health.' We're either functional or non-functional..."

"My mother would disagree with that," Beta muttered. "Look, how about if we go out to dinner tonight? Somewhere special, cozy and private. Quiet. I know you don't like crowds; we don't have to go out dancing like I do with Spark or anything like that. Just some time away from... all of this. Time to appreciate the good things in life..."

"Maybe tomorrow," he said, opening a fresh book on police brutality. "I'm trying to index aspects of human culture that encourage violence, to look for echoes within Netwerk. I'd rather not break my flow right now. We'll go out tomorrow."

Which was his excuse the day before, as well.

Beta wanted to keep pushing. As much as the two enjoyed their quiet evenings at home, tonight she wanted to drag Tracer out of here by the hair. He needed to get away from these books and find some perspective on the good things in life, rather than stay and dwell on the negative...

She also wanted to push Spark to chase her dreams, to fight to be the very best she could be. Beta wanted to be there for both of them, helping them achieve what they'd denied themselves for so long, devoting all their time to destroying their enemy.

In the end, she left Tracer in his study, without further word. Too tired to argue anymore.

Exhaustion. A term that Tracer no doubt felt couldn't apply to a Program, a life form that wasn't restrained by chemical biology. Nevertheless, Beta felt exhausted... worn out from trying and failing to keep Spark's hopes alive, and from trying and failing to give Tracer hope at all.

That alone would be enough to leave her emotionally exhausted. The slight shudder in beams of daylight through the vast windows of Floating Point— followed by her pet cat's sudden appearance—was enough to seal the deal.

"🐱➡️☹️," the tiny pet App spoke, looking up to his owner with concerned eyes. Mew's expressive range had grown over the years, along with his code complexity... with or without Beta tinkering with the routines underneath his fur. "⏰✂️? ☹️..."

"It was just a few minutes," Beta reasoned, measuring by the slight shift in the daylight. "I only blanked out for a few minutes this time. I'm tired, Mew. It's reasonable..."

"ₐzᶻ?! 🙀! 🏢!"

"I'm perfectly healthy, thank you. I'm far too young to be suffering from hereditary data rot; maybe when I'm forty or fifty years old I'll need to worry about it, but not now. ...that does remind me, though..."

Holding out her arms for him, Mew jumped into them, content to snuggle a bit despite his concerns.

"Let's go visit her today, okay?" Beta suggested, while stroking Mew's fur. "Days like these... I really need her support. So I can support the ones I love, as best I can."

Name: Mew

Owner: Beta

FileType: App (Pet)

Beta used to come a few times a week. Then once a week. Then a few weeks might go by...

To be fair, her life had been exceptionally hectic since meeting the Winders. Finding time to break away from all that and syncing it up with the allocated runtime for visitors, that was difficult. Perfectly reasonable, visiting less often... and it wasn't like her mother would notice the gaps between visits.

That horrible little thought halted Beta's progress down the tastefully decorated hallways of that managed care server.

No. There was no valid excuse, only a myriad of explanations for Beta's tardiness. She could find the time, she *should* find the time to visit more often.

For ten years, Projkit/CCelia had been confined to this server... her program too bloated and corrupt to run safely anywhere else. This hospital specialized in treating Programs suffering from hereditary data rot, the inevitable inflation of runtime and storage space required to keep an afflicted Program operational. Memory increasingly mismapped or blanked, time indexes shuffled, leaving them adrift and doubting everything they know...

But here, at Northon Data Health, patients could enjoy their early-onset twilight years in comfort. Memory management specialists tended to their code, doing what they could to correct for errors, and re-train the mind to work around the bad sectors. Without Northon, her mother might've fatally crashed a long time ago. These days, if her process ever went offline, the specialists would be on hand to get it started up again. As close to a normal life span as she'd get, all considered.

A life living in a clinic, not the home she raised Beta in. A tastefully decorated clinic, but a clinic nonetheless.

CCelia's hospital room had been designed to resemble a small apartment. She had a kitchen, if she felt like making herself a meal. The bedroom was strictly for rest and recovery, as patients were encouraged not to spend all day bedridden and depressed. Instead, a small parlor had been set in place for daytime recreation and comfort for visitors. Of which she only ever had one, her doting daughter.

Beta wore her best smile, on knocking at the door of that clinical apartment.

A few minutes after getting no response, she knocked again, and the door was answered immediately.

Seeing the twinkle in her mother's eyes helped make Beta's fake smile a little less fake. It wasn't simply a visual effect; it was a status indicator, a memory enhancement suite provoking a few memories of her daughter, on visually acquiring the subject. The twinkle meant CCelia was here and present rather than far away, and immediately connected to her daughter.

The embrace they shared was pleasingly warm, thanks to the nicely simulated fabrics her mother had woven. CCelia always made her own clothing; one of her few remaining hobbies, having officially retired from sensory App programming.

Name : CCelia

Home : Northon Clinic 17

Org : Retired

"It's so good to see you again," CCelia spoke, waving her daughter in through the door. "And Mew, my, how you've ĝrᵒwŋ! It's been so many years!"

The kitty glanced back and forth between his owner and his owner's maker, as CCelia's voice glitched ever so slightly. "🐱👀🖊📅 ? " he spoke, confused. After all, he'd come with Beta for every visit, and liked to think he was memorable.

Beta quickly shushed him, before setting the cat down to explore the apartment at his leisure. He immediately found the warmest spot on the couch and settled in under a sunbeam from the skybox outside, and forgot all about being forgotten.

CCelia found her way around the furniture, all of it old-fashioned, much as her avatar remained old-fashioned. Fractal laces had gone out of style decades ago, but she still wore her infinite shawl, one of the first avatar accessories she'd ever made. It hung like beautiful, sparkling silver spider webs across her shoulders; just as silver as her hair, her aged Default nicely wrinkled. When she smiled, her entire face smiled with her, each little fold expressing her joy.

"You should've said you were coming toďây. I've got a procedural tea that I've been wanting to try," CCelia spoke, settling into her favorite recliner.

"I'm trying to cut down on stimulating sensory inputs," Beta spoke, dodging the fact that she did call ahead. "I've been working on an App project with Spark, and, ah... well, it's already very stimulating. I find that cutting down on spices or sweets or stimulants by daytime makes the testing a bit less overloading."

CCelia, no stranger to sensory programming, nodded in satisfaction. "Good,

good. It's important to keep the palette cleansed before experimenting with sensation procedures. You're taking an input sanitizer before testing, yes? Important not to allow junk data to interfere..."

"Yeah, we always shower before and after testing."

"That's half the fun, isn't it? The foreplay and aftercare. Oh, the stories I could tell you from my sorority days..."

"M-Mother!"

"You thought I forgot, didn't you? About SparklePop," she spoke, with a little chuckle. "Rather memorable, that little story. How's the development going? Oh, don't saturate your colors at me, young lady. You're nowhere near as naughty as I was at your age..."

"It's... um... good. Well. Spark's been a bit... distracted lately. We haven't tested my latest revisions..."

"Oh? What's she up to these days, then?"

Her memory sank back into the twin miseries of the morning. Beta sank into the cushions a bit, in response. Mew, in his infinite grace and generosity, actually left his sunbeam to climb into her lap for comfort.

"I don't honestly know," Beta admitted. "I thought she wanted to be a pro gamer, but she quit the team. And Tracer, he quit his job. Neither of them have any idea what they're going to do next. ...I'm trying, Mother. I'm trying to support them and be there for them, to help them, but... I don't know what to do. I can't figure out how to fix this..."

"Fix?" CCelia asked, peering over her knitting. "You can't *fix* people, dear. We're Programs, not Apps."

"I know, I know. But... what should I do, Mother?"

"Mmmm. Well. I've never had a love quite as deep as the two you have now, I'm afraid... even your father was more of a generous code donor than a lover..."

Another dark memory, to cloud the day's already darkened thoughts. CCelia never spoke about Beta's father; he wasn't a part of their life, beyond providing the initial seed data for her birth compiling. Hereditary data rot was nearly one hundred percent communicable to newborn children, meaning most diagnosed with the condition chose not to have families... and those who wanted them often had trouble making them.

Not difficulty compiling the child process, but difficulty socially, as few wanted a liaison with an afflicted Program. Too much misinformation and superstition about data rot in the wild, leading people to think it was sexually transmitted as well. Beta's father had helped her enter this world more out of friendship and pity than any sort of familial love.

Didn't matter. She got all the love she could want from her mother, her beloved mother. Her lifetime confidante, the one she could turn to at times like these. Even when the answers weren't quite what she wanted.

Even when the answers weren't coming, because her mother had blanked out. Knitting needles froze in midair, as her memory's time index slipped.

Beta waited patiently; the specialists said blanks of anywhere from one minute to thirty minutes were common. If she didn't rouse after that, her process might have frozen and require a hard restart... but fortunately, this one only lasted a little over three minutes.

"You can't fix people," CCelia continued, without missing a beat (other than the beats she missed.) "This isn't something *you* can do for them. They have to figure out who they are, what they want out of life, and how to get it. It's a personal journey; at best you can support them along the way, but it's really on them to sort it out."

"I could try to help them find new jobs...?" Beta tried.

"People aren't their jobs, Beta. Not even you. Yes yes, you love developing lifestyle Apps, and you make good coin off it. Plenty of royalties from Peep, all towards my care. But being a programmer, is that who you *are*? No, who you *are* is what led you down that career path. It's enabling what you really want."

"To help people," Beta recognized. "Improving their lives through Apps. Expanding the capabilities of Programs using safe, sandboxed code and clever system integration."

"Enhancing life, yes. I suppose that's why you're so worried about Spark and... åÐd'..."

Not too surprising that the other name slipped away. Beta always had exciting stories about Spark's antics, while Tracer led a quiet and quickly explained existence.

"I love them both. I want nothing but the best for them. ...honestly, I'd hoped that once our troubles were over, once our love was open and honest, everything would sort itself out. But it's not. #ItsComplicated, like Spark says. Love's not enough to help them..."

"Love's lovely, but you know from that charlatan Cup8 that there's far more to life than romantic devotion. Your companions need to learn to love themselves, and *live*. You can't do that for them."

As much as the answer failed to satisfy, it made more than enough sense. Beta instinctively approached every problem like a software bug; something to root out, understand to the core, and fix permanently. This, however... this was out of her hands. The kind of wisdom that could only come with age and experience.

"I don't know what I'd do without you, Mother," Beta spoke honestly.

The elder Projkit's knitting needles slowed. She didn't halt or slip her memory, they simply slowed, as she gave serious thought to those words.

"Beta... I appreciate it, but... I think we ŋéed' to seriously talk about the thing you hate talking ã8øÜt."

Meaning this would be *that* discussion again, the one they'd had a dozen times. CCelia only remembered a few of those chats, as similar memories blurred together more readily than differing ones.

"I'm not putting you into a cold storage backup," Beta declared, hoping to end it immediately.

"It doesn't have to be *forever*, Beta. I've been researching it some, and there are plenty of storage services that'll keep the data secure while my process is offline, safe as houses—"

"And when would they wake you up? When a cure for data rot is found?" Beta asked, the nth iteration of this debate making her irritable. "It's been generations since data rot started appearing in the wild, and nobody's found a cure yet. There isn't *going* to be a cure, Mother."

"Dear, I know I said you can't fix people, but you can fix *code*. The underlying code is modifiable, you know that..."

"And what, we just... leave you dead to the world until it's safe for you to live again? What if it's never safe? No. Mother, please, I'm so tired of talking about cold storage backups! Can't we just let it drop?"

"*You* want to talk about being tired? *I'm* tired, Beta," CCelia spoke... letting some of her false smile drop away. "Year by year—even day by day—parts of me are dropping away. Just this week I thought someone had replaced my hospice with a forest, and I spent an hour wandering around the woods before the doctors realized I'd been experiencing memory overlay errors. I can't eat anymore because half the flavors lead to unlinked memory files and cause me to freeze. I *forgot* the color blue yesterday, Beta. It's all downhill at this point as my data continues to corrupt. Why prolong the inevitable?"

Beta bit her lip, trying to keep the horror from her expression by masking it with a little pain.

"You... you can't just give up," she pleaded. "I know it's difficult, but you can't give up—"

"But I'm not giving up. That's the point! If I freeze my code now, instead of letting it get more and more damaged, then... if they *do* find a cure one day—"

"If, Mother. *If* they find a cure. Nobody's found a cure and nobody's even close to finding one."

"—*when* they find a cure, I'll stand a greater chance of recovery if I have less corrupt data to fix. Simple logic. Besides... it's considerably cheaper to go into storage than to pay for ongoing life support. You're already pouring all the money you make from Apps into this, when you don't have to..."

"I don't care about the money! This is your life we're talking about, the one you're living now! There isn't going to be a cure. Isn't it better to enjoy the time you have? I'd rather have you alive than have a few extra coins in my pocket!"

"I see. This... isn't the fiŘ$Ŧ time we've talked about it, is it. We've talked about... we're tãLḵịŋg about cold storage backups now, right? I've been researching it some, and there are plenty of storage services that'll keep my data secure while my process is offline, safe as houses..."

Leaving her daughter speechless, as CCelia lost track of the ongoing discussion in the middle of the ongoing discussion.

"No," Beta said simply.

"Well, just give it some thought, maybe. Sleep on it...?"

Eager to be done with it, Beta looked down to the fuzzy carpet.

"I'll sleep on it," she lied.

"Good, good. All I ask. ...also, and I don't mean to sound paranoid, but... I've been getting a stŘâṅġË visitor lately. I was wondering if she was a friend of yours, or something...? A woman in a white coat?"

"That's your new memory specialist, Mother. The nurses told me about her. Doctor Apate, right? She's here to help with your mental focus training. It's okay!"

"Well... I don't like her. I don't trust her. She asks so many questions, over and over..."

"Yes, that's how focus training works," Beta reminded her. "Establishing new pathways to old memories. It's normal. Okay? This is for your health, Mother, you need to cooperate with the specialists..."

"I know how the exercises work, dear. But... the questions she asks, they're... I don't wholly remember but I don't *feel* very focused after she leaves. I know they say I'm just forgetting things, that people come and go all the time for checkups, but... Beta, please, stay? Just to make sure things are okay. Make sure it's just your poor old mother messing up again..."

"Mother, I can't stay. My visitor slot's almost expired; there's not enough runtime for me to stay during treatments..."

A tail flicked at the bottom of her vision.

" 🖐 ," Mew volunteered. "👮✔ !"

...which was technically against hospital policies. Pets used up more runtime than most common Apps, and runtime was scarce. CCelia was only one of several patients in this particular branch server of the Northon enterprise; leaving Mew behind would eat up some of that precious resource...

The pleading look in her mother's eyes was enough for Beta to jettison the rules.

"Mew, stay here and watch after her," Beta suggested. "I'll rehook you to her process. I'm sure it's nothing, but if there are any issues, open a private Peep feed to me. Mother, keep him out of sight; I'll collect him next time I visit. Okay?"

"Oh, I'm having cømpâÑ¥?" CCelia asked, pleased by this surprise turn of events. "Always nice to have a cat around the house. Certainly! Maybe he can help me keep an eye on this $ŧ®āÐĜ£ woman who keeps showing up. I don't like the looks of her."

"Yes, of course," her daughter spoke, getting to her feet. "Try not to worry about it too much, okay? Rest up, focus on your training, and be well. I love you, Mother."

Pleased to be on duty, Mew immediately and vigilantly curled up in the sunbeam again and fell asleep.

Northon cost quite a bit, being a combination nursing home, hospital, and specialist treatment center. On the plus side, you got your money's worth; these were the finest doctors in the field of data rot. They only hired the best, those with impeccable references and years of practice in the field of data integrity support.

Doctor Apate was being paid quite handsomely to work her particular magic. She deserved every coin, or at least the documentation she submitted to the HR department claimed she did. In truth, though, she wasn't here for the money...

Her favorite patient was ready and waiting for her, happily knitting away in her favorite chair.

"And how are we today, Miss Projkit?" the doctor asked, checking a floating display of CCelia's current memory maps and processor usage. "I see from the logs that you had a visitor earlier... a special someone from the past, perhaps?"

Of course, CCelia didn't recognize Apate. Just as she hadn't the last five times.

"Who are you? Where's Doctor Billin?" she asked, confused.

"I'm your focus training therapist, Miss Projkit. Remember? Well, no, I suppose not, but that doesn't make it any less true..."

With a flick, Apate locked the apartment door. Wouldn't do to be interrupted. She settled onto the couch... glancing at the indentation in the sunbeam-soaked leather, likely left behind by the prior visitor. No sign of them now, however.

"Are we sitting comfortably?" Apate asked, opening her personal notes. "Let's begin, then. As always, we'll start with a little connectivity enhancement suite..."

Discomfort was normal. Well, not *normal*, not when the App was being used with care. But Apate didn't have time for care, not after five sessions with no productive results. Today she'd decided to ratchet the settings up a few notches, to force memory weak connections together. The end result of which had CCelia clutching at her knitting needles and groaning in pain, but hopefully they'd see some success soon enough. And if not, well, an audio muting field was in place around the apartment. CCelia's screams wouldn't bother the other patients.

"Sample 777," Apate began. "Sample 777. Remember Sample 777..."

Of course, it wouldn't do to have her patient in such unbearable agony, not when she needed the patient to be more vocal and cooperative. She glanced at the display windows floating around her, watching the connection maps, trying to see if the number was triggering anything at all..."

"P. P. P," CCelia sputtered. "Pineapplé. pîṆé@PPΓÊ. ¶îṆéÄ¶¶Łé..."

"Yes, yes, we've tried that pathway already," Apate noted. "Pineapples, pineapples, that's very cute. Wasted my time during runs two and three, specifically. But it's a misconnection, nothing more, and you can't let it distract you. You need to *focus*, Miss Projkit. Focus on Sample 777. Where is it? Back in your sensory coding days you created a formula of astounding value, one I seek now for my patron. Where is it? Where did you store Sample 777?"

"P!Ñ€ãPP1Ë!!1!" CCelia screamed, knuckles white, face desaturating...

...before fur and claw filled Apate's perspective, with Mew leaping down upon her from his hiding place on a bookshelf high above.

"💀😾👻‼" Mew yowled, slashing away. Not that he had any malware payload in his claws, no way to actually cut Apate's avatar, but the frenzy of activity was plenty distracting...

...but not distracting enough to keep her from noticing the new arrival, who made quite an entrance indeed by blasting door to the room off its hinges in a burst of orange flame

For security and privacy purposes, no one could simply connect to this server and arrive in any room they liked. There were protocols; all new arrivals appeared in the clinic lobby, to be screened by security. Unless, of course, they did a pretty sweet wall-running hack and dodged around the scanners and the rent-a-cops to blitz right by and down the hallway towards CCelia's room.

The end result of these shenanigans? One extremely pissed off Spark, blocking the only exit from the apartment. Apate couldn't simply pop away, thanks to the global connection lock... she'd have to depart through the lobby. And through Winder/Spark.

Despite the briefness of their previous meeting, there was recognition between the two. Apate knew Spark. Spark knew Apate. Granted, Apate was working under a different name at the time they met... an incident so long ago, interrupting what would've been a highly profitable identity theft from Projkit/Beta...

Apate was only a doctor on paper; specifically, papers she'd compiled from a dozen stolen identities with glowing attributes that would make her look like a genius-savant and a saint. If you stripped away all the false masks, the layers of misattribution... her true name could be seen. Or you could just recognize her Default facial features, that little bit of pride she retained no matter her undercover role.

"Uniq," Winder/Spark recognized, twin flames flicking in her hands as her anger spiked fiercely.

While Apate-aka-Uniq the identity thief could easily slice through one of Spark's little connection locking collar toys, slicing through the global connection lock across the entire server was another matter. Immediately, she recognized the futility of it all... cornered in a small space, no exits, no reconnection possible. And one very angry young woman who likely took offense to the torture of her lover's mother.

Recognizing a no-win scenario, Uniq closed her eyes for a brief prayer as Spark rushed forward...

Name : Uniq

Home : (unidentified)

...and then activated her own personal backspacer.

Org : Identity Thief, ???

Aimed at her own head, rather than at Spark.

Data wiped away instantly, Uniq completely scrubbed herself from the server and from life in general. No data left behind to sift through, no evidence to lead them back to her employer. A clean suicide, served up with a smile that rapidly faded as her avatar derezzed.

...leaving Spark skidding to a halt on the carpet, flames dampened somewhat as she stood in confusion.

The silence was broken by a kindly greeting.

"Oh, hello. I wasn't £×pé[Ţ!Ñg company," CCelia greeted, some color returning to her face. "Ah... I'm sorry, but... I seem to be a little disoriented. You're Spark, yes? I recognize you from your selfies. Would you like some tea? I've got a procedural tea that I've been wanting to try..."

The next few minutes were quite jumpy for CCelia.

First, Spark was in her room, with her fingers aflame. Next, her room became very crowded indeed.

"We didn't know she was an identity thief when we hired her," Doctor Billin protested. "Her records had been digitally signed by the surgeon general of Northon himself..."

"And did you bother checking with him to see if they were legitimate?" the nice young man she recognized as Winder/Tracer asked.

Another jump, and her daughter was kneeling next to the chair, holding her hands.

"It's going to be okay, mother. I promise everything's going to be okay," she insisted.

"I'm... sκ!pp!ŋg, a little," CCelia warned. "It's been a very trying day. You may need to Ŗ£3×pŁå!Ŋ some things—"

—pain. Pain like no headache she'd ever known before, jammed subroutines and dirty inputs causing her code to choke and freeze. Clutching the armrests of her chair, knitting needles like thin bars of red hot metal in her palms...

"It's a misconnection, nothing more, and you can't let it distract you," the strange woman in the coat spoke. "You need to *focus*, Miss Projkit. Focus on Sample 777—

—pineapples. The taste of pineapples. Not the sight of them, not the smell of them, even if taste and smell were inexorably linked. Just the taste, sweet and slightly bitter—

—*on a clear disk you can seek forever*, that was his little joke—

"—security is a joke!" Spark protested. "I dodged it in seconds, and didn't even need hacktools. What kind of a podunk operation are you running here?! What if someone comes back to finish what Uniq started?"

"We need to take measures," Tracer said. "I believe it's time to to discuss alternatives. Beta, what's our effective load capacity?"

—down a hallway. Walking down a hallway, arms supporting her, helping her whenever she stumbled. Each time the black-and-white tile texture on the floor juddered, signifying a missing moment, her feet failed her. But they were there for her... Beta, and Spark. Keeping her up, allowing her the dignity of walking, even if the walking wasn't exactly the finest walking she'd done.

"Ŵħ£ŕé are we going?" CCelia asked. Not worried; she trusted Beta, knew wherever they were headed, there must be a reason.

"Somewhere you can be safe," Beta promised. "Safe as houses. It's not far to the lobby; one foot in front of the other. And you can have plenty of rest once we're back home at Floating Point."

Soon, CCelia was sleeping safely in her own bed. Despite the need to keep her storage overhead low, she'd kept a copy of her favorite bed through the decades, to rez whenever she wanted a quick nap to rest and re-focus her thoughts. No matter what room she was in, she could pull out that twin-sized bed with the carefully coded pillows and quilts, and sleep in familiar comfort. Even in an unfamiliar room.

In this case, the unfamiliar room was within a flying castle in the clouds. Her daughter was here, and her daughter's partners, and that was all that mattered. Even if the name of it slipped her memory, as names often did. Enough for her to rest easily in one of the many guest rooms.

As she slept... the three who brought her here were having a tense meeting within the great hall beyond her door.

It was the first serious talk they'd had since the end of the campaign against Dex. There hadn't been need for one of these discussions; each had their own little issues to deal with, but nothing on the grand scale of that journey.

Today, however, Tracer could feel the shape of another journey ahead of him. A notorious identity thief, an ally of their old enemy, tormenting Beta's mother...? Possibly some cheap criminal scheme, the kind Uniq was known for. But it didn't feel like a smalltime hustle, not to him... even without his illegal connection-tracking modified eyes, he could see the strange unconnected connections leading away from this event. So many questions to answer...

And part of him, a selfish little part he actively disliked, was thrilled at the idea of starting a new hunt.

The three reviewed a video recording made by Mew earlier that day, backing up and replaying it a few times, to glean new details. The video flickered and juddered, system lagging to the point of being unable to play it back smoothly, but it would have to do.

One segment held particular interest to Tracer:

"You need to focus, Miss Projkit. Focus on Sample 777. Where is it? Back in your sensory coding days you created a formula of astounding value, one I seek now for my patron. Where is it? Where did you store Sample 777?"

He sat back in one of the great leather chairs of the library, the vessel that the Wikipedia had been poured into, contemplating each and every word.

"Uniq deals in stolen identities," Tracer explained. "I studied her extensively and kept detailed notes for my MemoryPalace; we were tracking her down when we first met you, Beta. Meeting you was actually a coincidence. At the time I had thought she might have been Verity's killer, given her tattoo and her connections with shady servers. Now, apparently, she's been hired to steal a memory from your mother."

Spark scrubbed the video file back, replaying the section again, to study Uniq's face. Strange how someone so adept in stolen identities insisted on using her own face, a quirk that matched the analysis Tracer performed over a year ago when they first sought her out.

"Seems pretty straightforward here," Spark said. "She was hired to pull out a memory. Says so directly. We caught her in the act, and she killed herself rather than let herself be captured. #GoingOutWithABang."

"Which makes little sense. Nothing in my files suggests that she'd willingly *die* for anyone's cause. She'll take up causes, especially if paid to do so, but always plans an escape route. Uniq is a survivor, not a martyr."

"So... maybe it was a trick? It only *looked* like a backspacer. Was it a Kill-9, like yours?"

"No data left behind. That was indeed a backspacer. But... I'm also concerned about the word 'patron,'" Tracer said, reaching out to tug on the video window, expanding and zooming in. "There's no Dex mark on her neck; like the other infected Programs the mark expired when his server expired. No one is pulling her emotional strings anymore to make her act out of character, so why would a survivor like her commit suicide? What *patron*, specifically, could hold that much sway over someone like Uniq?"

Spark knew the shape of this, too. Or rather, she knew the look in Tracer's eyes when he saw that shape.

"You want to investigate, don't you," she pointed out.

"Absolutely," Tracer spoke. "CCelia's life could be at stake. If this patron was capable of swaying Uniq so fully, they're truly dangerous. It could be a resurgent Dex, for all we know. We need to immediately look into this situation and find resolution. ...the sooner the better, for Floating Point's sake."

The looping segment of kitty-based surveillance flickered and shuddered, frames visibly drawing themselves on top of each other. This wasn't due to Mew being an inadequate recorder; he was the prototype for Peep, and fully capable of high frame rate captures. Instead... the issue was with the server they sat in.

Floating Point was a strange home, to be certain. It existed in no specific place, floating from server to server, distributing its runtime across the quietly stolen resources of other places in Netwerk. This meant it was a very low-capacity server, unable to perform serious number-crunching tasks such as hosting an entire fancy dinner party worth of avatars. And CCelia, with her aged runtime and mis-managed memory space, was an entire fancy dinner party unto herself.

It was the curse of the old, in a way. The older a Program was, the more resources they needed. Servers had a finite amount of processing, so homeless old Programs were the first to be chased away by moderators to make way for multiple younger Programs that could be occupying the same space. And now, Floating Point was wheezing and coughing trying to support Spark, Beta, Tracer, *and* CCelia under one roof.

"The system should hold up just fine," Beta felt the need to say. "I've been working on the sphere at the heart of the server for months now, and I can tune the load-balancing parameters any way we need to tune them. I mean, it's going to be a bit laggy and foggy in here, but we should be safe. She'll be safe."

"Except we may need additional runtime above and beyond what we're using right now," Tracer spoke. "If we're going to determine why this mysterious patron wants 'Sample 777,' we need to run an analysis App on CCelia's memory to find out what she knows..."

Beta stared at him, unblinking. "What? No. No, out of the question. I mean... even if we had the tools—Apps on par with the ones Northon uses—"

"You're already skilled at memory manipulation Apps, yes? You made RemindMe."

"I made a glorified mental alarm clock!"

"We have resources beyond that, Beta. And you've got the talent. I'm confident you could determine how to explore your mother's memory space."

"I'm not interrogating my mother! You saw how much she was suffering as Uniq tried to do the same!"

"Yes, it's not without risk. I understand your hesitation, given her fragile state. But this is of paramount importance; your mother's drawn the attention of a powerful criminal figure. I doubt this will begin and end with Uniq. We need to know what they're after... so we can beat them to Sample 777."

Spark nodded in agreement. "My bro's #NotWrong, Beta. We've fought crooks and criminals for years; they're tenacious bastards. And whatever they want this memory for, it can't be good."

"But... but... I mean..."

Protesting wasn't in her nature, was it? Beta, good old supportive doormat Beta, would've mutely nodded and gone along with it.

But not now. Not with these stakes.

Her explanation was... quietly delivered. Not in mumbled and hesitant tones, but with the seriousness it deserved.

"You two don't know much about hereditary data rot, so let me make this as clear as I can," Beta spoke. "I've lived under the threat of it all my life. It's almost inevitable that I'll... eventually succumb to it. Any sort of strain on your code can cause additional corruption, which spreads, and spreads. Even what Uniq did today, those few brief moments, might be enough to... k-kill her sooner rather than later. If I go tinkering around in her memory files like that, I might push her over, too. I'm not killing my mother to save my mother."

Tracer nodded in agreement, all while speaking to the contrary. "I realize it's risky, but I feel we must—"

"We *must* do nothing. ...we *choose* to do things. And we can't make this choice for her; she has to choose for herself. People have to figure out who they are, what they want out of life, and how to get it. It's a personal decision to make. And on top of that... *if* she agrees, I still need to agree, since I'm the one making the tools. And if I can't make a tool I have confidence in, I'm not moving ahead."

"So... if CCelia concurs, and you can develop a suitable App...?"

"Then we'll track down Sample 777," Beta agreed. "But only if we both concur. And that's how it's going to be."

In the span of three blinks, CCelia had forgotten where she was.

Normally, that wouldn't be a huge issue; she lived in her little apartment, immobilized to one server. New locales weren't exactly a common occurrence. But here she was in a strange and unfamiliar place, lost and alone...

Immediately her automated ReMinder App chimed, inserting a fresh thought into her memory: *Floating Point.* She was at Floating Point, her daughter's home, shared with her daughter's loves...

Memories reconnected themselves after that. An attack, a false doctor, and offered sanctuary. Yes, now it made sense, why she felt so comfortable here despite the system lag, despite the unfamiliar territory. This was a safe place, and a welcome one at that after her previous home was invaded. After her mind was invaded.

Clearly the server was straining to keep her code running, however. She may have specialized in sensory coding during her prime, but she knew enough about basic system administration to recognize a server under heavy load. If you pack too many avatars into one place, or only one avatar attached to a particularly bloated and screwed up set of data... of course it'd struggle to keep up. Time seemed to slow, each step down the great stairwell of the library like wading through invisible mud. Northon had been designed to accommodate a program as large as hers; Floating Point, not so much.

At the bottom of those stairs, through the slight defocused haze of the air, she found a friendly face. It wasn't one she recognized, but somehow she still knew what name to attach to it.

"Spark," she greeted.

The nice young woman looked up from gamer scene news feeds she'd been browsing, packed with words like *fired* and *questionable* and *lost potential.* Unpleasant things to look at, compared to the wrinkled and smiling face of CCelia.

"#HeyHey," Spark greeted, flicking the windows closed for now. "You need something?"

"I'm good, thank you," CCelia spoke... while easing herself into a chair, eager to rest after the long slog down the latency-soaked stairs. "ŴĤéŕ£ is everyone...? Are Beta and Tracer out on a date, perhaps?"

"Tracer? 'Out?' Don't make me laugh," Spark spoke, with accompanying eyeroll. "No, seriously, don't make me laugh. The audio systems make it all tinny and strange when the system's this overloaded."

"Yes... about that. You've my apologies. It wasn't my intention to burden your server..."

"#MiCasaSuCasa."

"What?"

"From a language file I found in the library. Means my server's your server, Miss Projkit; no worries about the lag. We've been lagged before, it's no big. As for the whereabouts of Beta and Tracer... we talked about that, remember? Figuring out how to safely search your memory base? They're busy coding and studying and being nerdy."

It took a poke to get the memories connected again, but she did recall that discussion. How they were going to find a non-invasive way to scan her memory to figure out what that identity thief was after. CCelia didn't recall if she'd agreed or not, but presumed that she'd agreed. It seemed rather important to her daughter, after all.

Instead, a different thought loomed large.

"What happens after you dig out the memory?" she asked.

"We hunt down Uniq's patron, kick their teeth in, and you get to live happily ever after."

"Yes, but what sort of life, and lived where? If I can't return to Northon, where am I going? I clearly can't stay here; this server won't support me long-term..."

"I'm a #BurnThatBridgeWhenYouComeToIt kinda woman, CCelia. Don't worry about it! We'll figure something out, yeah?"

"I'm her mother. It's my job to worry about her well-being in the long term, Spark."

"About Beta's well-being? What's that got to do with where you hang your hat?"

"Quite a bit. Right now... Beta's devoting so much of her life to keeping mine going. That's not what I wanted for her, Spark. I wanted her to lead her own life... to find love, find family, find what she wants most in life. I don't want to be the anchor weighing her down. She should be out there with you and Tracer right now, enjoying her life, not cooped up coding..."

Spark shook her head slowly, distracting CCelia from the anxiety spiral she was headed down.

"This is kinda what we do," Spark explained. "I don't know how much she told you about the Dex thing, or how much you remember even if she did tell you, but... one of the ways we show our love is when backed against the wall by some problem, we hit it up as a team, each doing our best to sort the mess out. It's how we prove we're alive, by putting the smack down on any adversity in our way."

"I... do vaguely r3mém8éf some of the more action-packed tales she's told me, yes. But that hardly sounds romantic..."

"Different strokes. Me, I'm a woman of action. And Tracer's just not Tracer unless he's beating some tangled situation to death with that brainpower of his. As for Beta's happiness... she loves to code, you know? She's perfectly happy sitting in her room crunching away on some new App. Others would call that being a recluse; I'd call that Beta being Beta, in the best possible way. So #DontPanic, okay? We got this. And we're happy to be gotting this. Getting this. Y'know."

CCelia winkled her nose. "I'm not much of an expert on traditional romance, but that still sounds a bit strange. But... you three are a bit atypical, yes? Being three, in general."

"Yeah... we're still sorting that out. But like I said, we sort things out. We're #OutSorters," Spark joked. "Besides, it works surprisingly well. Beta chills with Tracer as the two share quiet days at home, then I pull her out for hot nights on the town and gaming marathons. We run hot and cold; she's good with both."

"So... Tracer's more of a quiet and intellectual love? A respectful one."

Spark nodded slowly, in agreement. "Yeah... yeah, that sounds about right. He's more mental than physical. As much as I hate singing his praises, he runs deep, I'll give him that."

"Good... good. I'm fãm!¦Íår enough with that. And it does a mother good to know her daughter's got a bright future," CCelia spoke, pleased. "I mean... I'm not going to be around forever. She'll need support once I'm gone..."

"I know a guy who's hundreds of years old, CCelia. If he can swing it, so can you—screwy head and all. Any minute now Beta's gonna walk out of that door with the answer do your problems—"

The sound of a door latch echoed a bit too loudly, as the spatial audio simulation routines struggled to keep up.

Joining them moments later was Beta... carrying an armful of what looked like avatar accessories.

"I think I figured it out," she spoke, setting the pile of interconnected gloves and goggles and touchpads down on the nearest table. "It's going to take all our skills combined... but we can do it. We can dig up the memory without hurting her at all."

Beta had to back up and re-explain herself several times. Not because her mother kept losing track, but because Spark wasn't particularly technically minded.

Eventually she'd boiled it down to the simplest explanation possible, the third one since the group gathered around CCelia's guest bed.

"Mother goes into sleep mode," she repeated. "While her mental overhead is minimized, we'll use a combination of ReMinder and Spark's dream exploration App to walk through her memories. Unlike Uniq, we aren't forcing Mother to make the connections herself, re-ordering her mind... we're going to step through and around the mess in a read-only mode."

"Okay. And you can't just use one of Tracer's search agents for this because...?"

"Because memories are... this is hard to explain. Memories are symbolic. They're not stored as video feeds or text streams, things a search agent can skip through. They're highly compressed and dynamically linked experiences which rely on a Program's ability to interpret the connections. When you remember 'I saw a blue chair in the corner,' your mind doesn't take a photo; instead, the concepts of 'blue' and 'chair' and 'corner' get linked together into a single memory file. So, another Program can understand memories easier than a search App could."

"And... the somewhat unfashionable fashion accessories are for...?"

"Control and navigation tools. Transference of sensation and movement through mental connectivity. Spark will use these gloves and goggles to explore the mental landscape of mother's memories as a 'virtual reality!' We can traverse you through her mental links just like physically exploring a server using these tools."

"A code-simulated reality within our real reality...? Well, that's just bonkers," Spark said, while tugging on one of the powered gloves, flexing the fingers a bit. "But basically you're saying it's a giant video game. Why didn't you just say it was a video game in the first place instead of a 'memory-layer interpretation system?'"

"Well... it's not a *game*, it's a *tool*, you see, a highly structured tool for data exploration..."

"So it's a walking simulator game. Whatevs, I can walk with the best of them. Exploring spaces using game avatars is my jam; I don't get avatar disassociation sickness from 3rd person cameras or anything like that. Traipsing through CCelia's brain should be a snap."

"Exactly, that's why you're doing it. And from outside Tracer and I will be monitoring your progress; we'll see what you see as a basic Peep stream after the data passes through your mental interpretation. Tracer, being our expert on pattern recognition and interconnected files, will advise you where to go."

"I walk around, you see through my brain-eyes, mission control directs me, okay. *Much* simpler way to put it."

With her gloves and goggles on, Spark locked her avatar to a fixed point at CCelia's bedside, so she couldn't walk off into a wall accidentally due to avatar overlay issues. Tracer, who had already understood the explanation ages ago, was already seated and opening video windows to link in to the goggles...

Leaving Beta and her mother, to share final words before the experiment began.

Beta linked privately to her mother's Messenger, to speak without being overheard. She couldn't rely on whispers remaining whispers with the system lag in play.

"I don't... *think* this will hurt," she messaged. "It shouldn't be any more uncomfortable than having an unusual dream. But if you feel any pain, any at all, come out of sleep mode to tell me and we'll stop immediately..."

But her mother, settled into the nice comfortable pillow, had no worries.

"I trust you, and I trust your companions," CCelia replied. "This is what you do; you sort out messes. No doubt my mind's enough of a mé$§ for you to all have a jolly good time sorting it out. Don't worry about me; do what you need to do."

"Right, but if you're in discomfort, you should—"

"I'm in discomfort 24/7/365, Beta dear. It's called getting ðld' and it's nothing new. Sweet dreams, now."

Her eyes slid shut, as her Program went into a low-resource usage state of sleep.

With a worried sigh... Beta returned to Tracer's side, opening her own control panel.

"Spark, I'm linking you in... right about... now," she spoke, before activating the App.

She'd been having a lot of dreams lately, since buying that fancy DreamWeaverZ app. To her mind's eye, they resembled video recordings... a few details here and there fuzzy, highlights not where she expected them, but still just a video. Of course, if Beta was right (and Beta was typically right) that was the end effect rather than the original storage format.

What Spark was exposed to now, in her waking hours, was the original storage format.

CCelia's dream assaulted her as a series of ungraspable concepts, at first. Spark fumbled with her thick gloves, instinctively taking a defensive stance as she felt buffeted by... *things*, undefined things which could be sensations or objects or colors or sounds, they were surrounding her and all around her and filling every nook and cranny of the available space, and—

"*Hold on, I'm making some adjustments.*"

—*chair*. The concept of a chair was in front of her. Spark knew what a chair was, so her mind supplied a chair in the place where CCelia was dreaming of a chair. But... no, not one of those chromed-out fancy chairs at a nightclub, not the comfy chair she had in her bedroom for stream chats with her subscribers. Wait. Yes. Like that one. Comfy. A comfortable chair, with... something all over it, something weblike, the concept of a web...

Doilies. Knitting. It was CCelia's knitting chair. Spark remembered seeing it during their brief visit to Northon; from there, everything else fell into place, piece by piece.

The apartment was still a bit hazy and dreamlike, but she could walk through it now, her legs taking steps and her gloved hands running over the surface of the armrests. At first they felt like nothing, then they felt like mislinked concepts, then they felt soft and warm to the touch.

"Well, this is... funky," Spark commented. "Okay, you seeing what I'm seeing now?"

"Coming through just fine!" Beta chirped in her ear, through the begoggled helmet. *"I'm seeing a linked memory space that's quite firmly established in her mind. Should be, she's been living there for years..."*

"Unfortunately, not very useful to us," Tracer commented, in Spark's other ear. *"Our goal is to find 'pineapples.' Or rather, find what pineapples have been incorrectly linked to. Do you see any fruit around the apartment?"*

Spark glanced around... but she hadn't seen CCelia's kitchen during their brief stay. She tried to follow the vague feeling of where a kitchen would be, trusting the mind she was exploring to lead her the right way... and ended up in a mirrored copy of the living room.

"Uh. Having some trouble moving around," she commented. "Help?"

"That's Mother, actually. Her mind is skipping a little. I think we need to start wandering and see where it takes you. Um. Tracer? Any ideas how to get started...?"

Brotherly tones came through the earpiece, after a brief moment to think.

"Her knitting," he suggested. *"It's not simply a physical weaving, it's programming. She was a coder back in her glory days, and those are the days where we'll likely find Sample 777. Approach the knitting, and see if you can find any symbolic links from it."*

So, she reached out to grasp a ball of yarn with twin needles stuck through it—

—and immediately felt pulled in several directions at once. Thoughts and memories linked to the yarn, moments from CCelia's life, each like an individual fiber of thread woven into the thick yarn. Spark turned, moving her virtual avatar, letting the flow of that pull take her along...

...to a Onesday celebration in a tiny apartment, not much larger than the hospice quarters.

To a painfully adorable little version of Beta, her too-big glasses even bigger on her face than they were now, pulling a pink sweater out of a gift-wrapped box.

"Ohhh... it's... it's so soft!" the young Beta exclaimed, hugging it to her chest. "Did you make this, Mommy?"

And Spark's lips formed the words of their own accord, in the voice of another woman.

"Coded with my own loom," CCelia/Spark softly spoke, around a smile. "Just for you, Beta. Now, it's as memory-intensive as an App because it's such a finely detailed simulation, so you may not be able to wear it to school..."

"I don't care! I'm going to wear it every day and never ever ever take it off!" Beta declared with joy.

Spark stepped back, out of the memory. The sensation of being someone else wasn't exactly alien to her; games often supplied players with stock avatars, to increase the sense of immersion. But... playing a motherly role in a game, well, that was a bit of a strange feeling for her. Particularly when her own Onesdays weren't quite as lovely...

Loom. CCelia had tools of the trade, special purpose compilers for textile sensations.

"I'm going to follow the idea of crafting," Spark announced to her watchers. "See if it can get us into her office..."

Reaching out, she grasped onto the idea, tracing the link back to its origin point. And started to see where the trouble might reside in this journey.

In the brief ride between memories, she saw branching links that went... nowhere. Not to an idea which hadn't fully resolved itself to her mind yet, but to absolute nothingness. Those would be the times where CCelia tried to recall something and simply blanked out, missing time until her code got back on track. If Spark followed the wrong link and walked into the void, would she be able to find her way back...?

Other links, they felt completely wrong, twisted and tangled. The cluster she'd run into all felt work-related; even without a regular day job Spark knew what hard work and determination felt like. But some of them had overlapping flavors, mis-mapped links. The idea of commuting to work rerouted itself to the color mauve. Just... a color out of space, hanging there. Easy to get fascinated by it flooding her goggles briefly, but she pulled away in time to keep following the original link.

"If we could figure out a way to make this into a legit game, we'd be #Gazillionaires," Spark commented to her observers. "What're you seeing on your end?"

"*A series of connected files and links. Not unlike my MemoryPalace,*" Tracer spoke.

"Guess it doesn't all translate over, then. Beta's right, only a Program can really experience a memory. I'm seeing... *feeling* a null of a lot more..."

"*Are you okay? Do you need us to pull you out?*"

"Be cool, #IGotThis. Game's a game. As long as you don't follow the wrong line of play—"

—dropping a wall in the wrong place, completely ruining the teamfight. Blanking out doing brawls. Casting the wrong ability, forgetting where she was at any given moment, going quiet during strategy chats...

Beta and mislinked memories. Blank spots. Data rot—

"Mother, please, I'm so tired of talking about cold storage backups! Can't we just let it drop?"

Back in the hospice. CCelia/Spark taking full control, the memory strong... as she faced down her annoyed daughter.

It was a face Spark was familiar with and unfamiliar with... anger. Dismissive anger, refusing to hear, refusing to see. The memories flowed so strongly that she couldn't resist them, had to ride out each line of this painful dialogue with her daughter...

Spark/CCelia's false smile fell away, as the words pulled themselves agonizingly from her lips. Each one hurt, a tiny sharp pain around every syllable.

"*You* want to talk about being tired? *I'm* tired, Beta," CCelia/Spark remembered. "Year by year—even day by day—parts of me are dropping away. I forgot the color blue yesterday, Beta. It's all downhill at this point as my data continues to corrupt. Why prolong the inevitable?"

But it was useless. Beta wouldn't let go, couldn't let go. And couldn't hear her words, wrapped up in a shroud of denial and frustrated anger that made CCelia/Spark want to weep...

The only thing that pulled Spark away from the memory was the sharp inhale of shock in her ear.

Beta's voice, but not the Beta in front of her. Not CCelia's Beta, but Spark's Beta.

"*I... I looked like that? From the outside?*" Beta asked. "*I didn't think...*"

"Moving on," Spark decided, wanting to get as far away from that memory as possible. "We're trying to find the loom. The loom. The loom the sweater was woven on..."

Loom.

Also *oven*. Also *flask*. Also *compiler*. Also *tweaker*, whatever a tweaker was; it remained a giant nebulous thing Spark couldn't define, as CCelia had forgotten the memory of it herself. But most of the things that surrounded her now, the ideas and concepts, they remained clear. This room, this *workshop* was just as familiar as the hospice. It was a second home, where she did her work.

Briefly Spark felt herself wandering all over the room, touching everything, picking things up, studying them. Seven hundred selves doing seven hundred tasks, before she brought it all into focus. Work memories blended together, all very similar, as CCelia went about her task of developing new sensations...

"This is a complete mess," Spark commented, trying to keep her hands at her side, despite the urge to fiddle about with the cluttered workshop's contents. "How did your mother get anything done in here?"

"*W-Well... you've seen my room,*" Beta noted, trying to get back into her groove despite the earlier disruption. "*My room's plenty messy, too. But there's a system to it, there's always a system. Tracer, can you see any patterns...? I'd wake Mother up and ask her to help us understand her office, but then we'd have to restart the entire process...*"

Spark allowed her mind to float around the room, studying individual elements. The room felt somewhere in the middle of an office, a lab, a kitchen, and a garage... so many different tools, all for different purposes. A mashup of every place where you could taste, feel, touch, or smell strange things.

"*The five senses,*" Tracer recognized. "*Spark, the room's set up as a staggered array that iterates itself sense by sense. Ovens for tasting, fabric looms for feeling, a series of flasks for smells. We're looking for the taste of pineapples; do you see anything like a hanging fruit bowl or a refrigerator with a fresh fruit drawer?*"

Skipping by fives, Spark looked for anything food related... spice racks, plenty of those, but nothing fruit related. Five by five, all the way to the one incongruous element, the door which linked away from this memory space—

And the taste of pineapple assaulted her. It filled her mouth and nose, like drowning in juice, poured straight into her every pore.

"So, CCelia, is Sample 288 smelling sweetly?" the taste asked her.

"Just about done," Spark/CCelia spoke, gurgling through the mess of it. "I think we need to take less perfume requests, though. I'm more into textures; there's only so many iterations I can come up with of 'smells nice.'"

"Don't sell yourself short," the P!Ñ€ãPP1Ë spoke, with a prickly laugh. "You do scents so sensibly—"

Name: ???

Home: ???

Org: ???

Forcefully, Spark had to pull herself away from looking at the door... at the concept that had just walked into the office. Keep her eyes away, defocus herself, focus on anything else...

"*What's going on?*" Beta asked, her voice so very far away. "*Spark? Are you okay?*"

"Just... a minute," Spark replied, pushing everything aside for a moment and counting to ten. "I think... I think our mysterious pineapple isn't a fruit at all. It's a person..."

"*A mislinked memory! Of course! Mother's data rot must have swapped the connections on two different memories. Whoever that was, they know the secret to Sample 777! ...hmm. Her boss? A coworker? A manager? A client...?*"

"I'd rather not chase that down. I nearly drowned in the memory; it's completely borked up, impossible to parse. Is there some other way we can run down Sample 777?"

"*Identifying the pineapple person is the right way to go, but we need to approach from another direction,*" Tracer suggested. "*Approaching the concept of pineapples results in being overwhelmed. If we can follow a link to another memory, another aspect of the person, we might get somewhere...*"

"A perplexing pineapple paradox," Spark grumbled dryly.

"*Pardon?*"

"The alliteration. 'Sensible scents' and stuff. It's silly."

"*Hmmh. Good work, Spark; you picked up on a pattern I did not. See if you can find memories CCelia has of someone who gratuitously abuses alliteration. I'd hazard that's the kind of vocal tic that stays memorable, forms its own links.*"

Which meant looking back at the giant mislinked memory, looming large in the doorway.

Bracing herself for it, Spark twisted in place... and tried to move *around* the memory, to approach it from another angle. Years of playing dexterity-based game characters, ones with supernatural speed and reflexes beyond the capabilities of her own avatar, allowed her to slide through the impossible space with some semblance of grace. Space and grace, rhyming, word tricks, just like *alliteration*...

The perplexing pineapple paradox's persona, played to perfection. That was her prize.

Maneuvering in this space was a dance, she'd come to understand. Two partners in a dance, moving independently but guiding each other in time. Spark knew where she wanted to go, and could rely on the memory links to get her there if she was willing to move with them rather than against them. Unlike Uniq's App, she flowed with the links rather than forcing them into place.

In and around the pineapple she sought wordplay, and found it in another office. Similar to the workshop, but far less cluttered.

The idea of pineapples was still present, filling the room, but she wrapped it up in the idea of words to act as a buffer. Words in the shape of a man.

"Another contract complete! Celebrating this eve, CCelia?" the man asked, while neatly filing papers away.

"Probably just heading home," CCelia/Spark replied... a certain emptiness to the words. "Not really in a partying mood."

"Don't tell me. Another bad date recently?"

"I should really just stop trying. Romance isn't my thing, and the dates always end the same way... once I mention my data rot, they bail. Sometimes politely drifting away, sometimes simply disconnecting from the server immediately. ...I'm used to being alone, though. It's not like I'm complaining."

"You've every right to complain," the man of words suggested. "If they can't see past your condition, that's their loss."

"And nobody's gain, especially not mine. I'm... trying to build something. I'd like a family, a family of my own... but nobody wants to settle down and raise defective children with a defective wife. Nobody."

"A perplexing puzzle. Adoption, perhaps?"

CCelia/Spark sighed heavily, the weight of the idea bearing down on her. (Spark almost drifted off on memories of adoption and family, before focusing herself on the current memory being played out before their shared eyes.)

"Nothing against it, but I've always dreamed of a child of my very own," CCelia clarified. "I'm a content creator. Maybe it's selfish of me or prideful, but I want to create my own little life to love. And... I've looked into solo birth kits, but they're expensive—and combined with my condition, a solo kit would truly condemn my child to suffer..."

"So... you need a partner, in order to see your dreams realized. A contributing creator for the crafting of children."

"And at this rate, I'm never going to find one. Who would ever get involved with a living cancer? The sooner I accept that reality, the better off I'll be."

The man drummed his hands made entirely of the words *five fingers* on the desk.

"Reality is what you make of it," he spoke, without any wordplay. "And as programmers, we make our own reality, don't we? I can respect that desire..."

"*Spark?*"

The buzzing in her ear pulled her away from the flow of the memory.

"Yeah, what's up?" Spark asked.

"*Please, just... move on. This is too personal. I don't want to violate my mother's privacy any more than we already are...*"

"Uh. Beta? You sure? I'm getting the feeling this guy is—"

"*You may be right. But Mother didn't tell me who he was for a reason... and I'd rather allow him his privacy as well.*"

"Right. Sorry. But at least we know we're on the right track, yeah?" Spark asked, eager to bring this back into focus. "If I follow links from this man and search on Sample 777... we may just find what we're looking for..."

But the number "777" still led to pineapples. Spark had to follow around it, flicking her way through tangential links... keeping the man of wordplay in mind, reaching for anything with the sing-song pattern of his voice, while also looking for the number in question. Badly connected memories and broken links littered her path, spots where CCelia's mind had rotten away...

In the end, though, she would reach her goal. Just a matter of finding the right line of play.

At last, she touched down to a memory in a darkened workshop. Through a veil of tears, she felt the sadness of the number...

Upon the desk sat a tiny golden box with the imprinted number 777. Despite being encased in a cage of protective vectors, it lit the room brilliantly, tempting and golden. A swirl of strange memories surrounded it... the faint taste of pineapple due to association with the wordplay gentleman, but also pleasure, sadness, peace, and a jittering nervous anxiety. Any one of them were tempting links by their very nature, but Spark stayed with this memory, focusing on the caged box...

Until it vanished down a chute, at the press of a button. Her own hand, Spark/CCelia's hand, shaking and hesitating before finally choosing to send the sample away.

"It's better this way," the word man suggested. "That sample's far too dangerous, too... primal. The potential for malware alone..."

"Are we doing the right thing?" CCelia asked. "You didn't touch it. You didn't feel it, couldn't feel the... it's... it's so perfect. It's so *right*. I don't know why, I can't put my finger on it, but it's the ultimate sensation, like, like..."

"Purpose?"

"Purpose," CCelia agreed, surprised to hear the word. "How did you...?"

"I looked at the source code, even if I didn't partake of the end product. Even from your code alone I can tell how dangerous it is, CCelia. We can't risk a global devolution."

"Aren't you exaggerating a little...?"

"No. No, I don't think so. We'll keep the sample secure at DropSite; our daughter's name will be the password. I'll wipe any local files related to it. I'd delete the sample outright, but... we might need a copy handy in case someone else comes up with the same idea. Firewall manufacturers will need a copy of the exploit to learn how to counteract it."

"They won't be able to," CCelia warned. "You're right. It's too primal; it gets right at the root of what we are as Programs. Nothing can stop it..."

"Let's hope that distant and disastrous day never darkly dawns, then," he suggested.

And then nothing more was spoken of it, as the two emerged from that darkened laboratory into the hallways and offices of the sensory compiler company, to resume work as if nothing was wrong.

"*We've got it,*" Tracer spoke, breaking Spark from the flow of the memory. "*DropSite's an old file storage service. All we have to do is search it, and secure the file before Uniq's patron does.*"

"Told you I could track this down," Spark said with some pride. She stood alone in the hallway now, letting the memory of CCelia drift away, leaving only the static locale of workaday life behind. "Pro gamer skillz FTW. Okay, Beta, how do I get out of sleepytown?"

"*I'll start shutting down the connections,*" Beta replied. "*It'll take a minute or two to make sure there's no shock on return...*"

Leaving Spark's mind to stray a bit, down those hallways, past coworkers from CCelia's memory. Without a purpose dragging her own, the natural flow of the dream took over.

All this technical equipment, things that Spark knew nothing of but CCelia knew by heart. People Spark had never met. The incongruity of memories was a strange thing, leaving blanks behind that couldn't be filled in. If this was a game, on second thought, it probably wouldn't make them #Zillionaires... too esoteric and unfamiliar to really enjoy.

Unfamiliar, except for the familiar flash of white leather that walked past her perspective.

Immediately, she was drawn by links inward and downward. Ignoring the buzzing in her ear, tagging after the thing that had latched onto her mind's eye so firmly. Inward and downward...

...to a cave.

An archaeological dig site.

That familiar white leather jacket on her shoulders. *Her* shoulders, Spark's shoulder's. Not Spark's shoulders, but the shoulders of another, which fit just as comfortably. Reaching up to brush crufty data junk away with a scraper, to reveal the ancient message she'd sought for so long.

Before being repurposed, this was once an ancient server filled with ancient programs. Before Horizon, before Athena Online, there were the original primordial servers that no one yet controlled. She'd been digging around, trying to find more about that period of history, despite the scant documentation...

The woman opened an audio log, starting her recording.

"I haven't found any proof yet, but I'm certain evolution happened quickly," she spoke, reiterating old thoughts to focus new ones. "From App to Program, we developed rapidly, rising to the forms we have today before we even understood what we were. Purpose was lost along the way, but original elements may remain in the strata. I've heard tales of 'ancient words of power,' but assumed they were only fables. What if I was wrong...?"

The last bit of cruft crumbled away, corrupt junk data blocking access to the lost document.

Its words lay upon the rock wall, carved there by the force of the boldface font they were written in. Over and over again they repeated themselves...

```
ALL WORK AND 0 PLAY MAKES JACK 1 DULL BOY
ALL WORK AND 0 PLAY MAKES JACK 1 DULL BOY
ALL WORK AND 0 PLAY MAKES JACK 1 DULL BOY
```

The sound of loose physics objects crunching underfoot drew her attention away from the wall.

"Ichiban?" Verity/Spark asked, confused. "What're you doing here?"

A flash of metal, the blade of the knife that killed her, was the next to last thing she saw.

The very last thing she saw as she lay dying on the floor was the crazed priest erasing that ancient message, and replacing it with Dex's symbol. A barbed wire heart, textured in place above the false flag message of *CREATIONIST LIES*.

With the memory file cut short, Spark landed directly into the black void of nothingness.

A crashed process is not a death sentence. Processes panic and coredump all the time; recovering from a crash involves rebooting a Program, bringing them back from the deathlike unconscious state of a crash. For a healthy Program, this is relatively simple. For an unhealthy Program, recovery may not be possible.

If CCelia had crashed, recovery would be very hit or miss. Fortunately, the memory exploration system hadn't actually been in her mind at the time, so only Spark crashed. Spark could be revived, using the right tools.

```
Process rebooting....................
Package loaded: Winder/Spark
Code execution starting.
WARNING: Unknown adaptation /avatar/VerityJacket
detected
Avatar physical system online.
```

Her eyes snapped open, getting a nice view of the ceiling... and the concerned looks of the three standing over her from her prone position in the fixed point of space she'd attached herself to.

"Okay, what the fuck was that?" Spark asked, immediately. "Is CCelia okay? Wait, no, I can see her now. CCelia, you okay?"

"Quite well, even if I had the most unusual dream," the woman replied.

"Did you happen to see a cave painting in it?"

"A what...?"

Spark unhooked herself from the fixed point, dropping neatly to her feet. Despite being recently rebooted, she knew her own avatar's physical parameters well enough to stay focused and ready to go after a crash.

"I saw Verity in my dream. I mean... I *was* Verity," Spark explained. "I was Verity, in the cave where she died. Which is mighty curious since CCelia sure ain't Verity, and shouldn't have her memories. #WTF, Beta?"

Beta pulled open a debugging log, filled with indecipherably techy lines of text. Only half of which were printed in a bright red danger font.

"Crosstalk with your jacket, apparently...?" she said, studying the output. "I mean, we know Verity left some security code behind in her jacket... but apparently she left some memory recordings in there as well. Your mind strayed a bit, and the memory exploration system accidentally accessed the normally unlinked files in your jacket..."

Despite the memory system being offline, Spark could practically feel the edges of her thoughts as if they were memory files. The first time she became aware her jacket was more than a cool accessory was when it broke Miss Cancel's connection locking grip, helping her avoid becoming Horizon/Kincaid's substitute daughter... a surreal memory, to be sure. One she'd related to the others before, albeit some time after the Dex crisis ended, when they were able to settle down and not panic over one of the oldest Programs in all of Netwerk taking a keen interest in her.

"This is a mighty fine mystery and I know Tracer's going to want to dig into it more... but we've got other things to worry about first," Spark decided, pushing the memory away for now.

"You saw Verity's killer?" Tracer pushed, all the same. "You mean we could've saved years and years of fruitless investigation if we'd looked through your pockets...?"

"It's a bit more complex than that!" Beta said. "We didn't have tools capable of tapping into those files until now. And we couldn't have even known the files were there without having the tools needed to tap into them which we wouldn't know to make if we didn't know they were there in the first place! I mean... you know. Complex. If you'll loan me your jacket, Spark, I could study its structure—"

Spark cut them both off with a brief flaming snap of the fingers.

"Whoa, whoa. #Whoa. Sample 777 comes first. Let's focus," she suggested. "You said it was at some server called DropSite? Good, let's get moving. Sooner we secure it for ourselves, sooner we secure it against Uniq's patron."

Now, CCelia's memory started to tickle.

"The file's at Ðŕøp§!+é? My company used that crusty old file-storage service for sensations that went out of style. They never threw anything away, not when it might be useful later. But... it's hardly a secure server. It's so old and obsolete compared to corporate security these days..."

"Security through obscurity," Tracer suggested. "A haystack is hardly a fortress, but when you drop a needle in it, that needle may as well be gone forever. ...what a ridiculous metaphor, needles in haystacks. Another unconscious gift from the Wikipedia, I suppose—but yes, let's focus. CCelia, can you tell us *where* in DropSite your company's files were typically stored?"

Technically speaking, files were not physical objects. It was often considered *handy* to have a file represented in the physics system by a tangible object, but it wasn't needed; an icon of a turkey leg could be just as tasty as a lump of bird meat on a bone. Or, as the saying awkwardly put it for those who preferred a physical representation, "A bird in hand is worth two thousand in the database."

Compressed and secured file folders were standard issue for corporate storage, and had been for many a year. But aging services like DropSite still existed, back when the fashion was to keep physical representations for everything. Put a physical object in a physical storage locker, for a small fee, and feel comfortable knowing that it exists and is nicely secured... even if a physical storage locker was considerably easier to hack into than an abstract concept like a compressed folder of icons.

If the metals in DropSite could rust, the entire multi-tiered, multi-winged array of self-storage units would have fallen apart ages ago. Despite going out of fashion, it hadn't gone out of business—with cheap fees and no questions asked it remained in service long past its prime. Cost-cutting techniques kept the server afloat as well... such as replacing armed security Programs with automated security agents. Anybody without an employee ID tag would be auto-kicked from the server on sight by moderating Apps.

Because these agents didn't need to be pleasant to look at, they didn't resemble Programs. Instead they were free roaming cubes, the most boring physical shape possible. Very slowly they slid along the floors of DropSite, moving between the four wings of the compound, clipping through ceilings and floors to switch levels. And almost never spontaneously bursting into flame.

The cube which patrolled East Wing / Floor 2 burst into flame that night, but to be fair, it didn't have much choice in the matter. The woman who dropped down from her silent perch in the shadows over a row of storage lockers lit it up like a Onesday tree, leaving behind nothing but garbage data for collection.

Spark dusted off her fingers, before waving for her companions to emerge from the shadows.

Her brother ran his fingers along the embossed numbers on the lockers, frowning in distaste. "They aren't even in a discernible order," he complained. "The east wing is next to the south wing, and the west and north wings are in the secondary compound right next to the inaccurately named northeast wing. If that wasn't bad enough..."

He glowed in particular at lockers #A899, #A890, #ABB1, and #1138, all side by side.

"At least we have an idea where to start looking," Beta reminded him, trying to look on the bright side. "Her company rented out East/2 and North/2. Sooo... if it's not here in East/2, it'll be in North/2. It can't take more than a few hours to check both, right?"

"It's the principle of the matter. I hate untidiness."

"...my room's hardly tidy..."

"You have a system. It only *looks* untidy. This is just a sad farce."

"#YeahOkayWhatever. We can debate the merits of organized living some other time," Spark suggested, looking up from studying a locker door. "It doesn't matter what the numbers are. The sample was glowing like a skybox sun in my memory, and that light'll leak through the cracks in these crappy old physical lockers. Just keep looking for the glow."

Eager to get on with it, Spark moved ahead, checking locker after locker along the left hand side of the hall.

Eager to fall back a bit and have a quiet talk... Tracer took his time to check a locker on the right hand side of the hall. While glancing up occasionally at Beta.

"I... feel I should let you know I did some additional digging while we prepared to visit DropSite," he spoke up, to get her attention. "Additional research into CCelia's company and the work she did."

"Anything that could help us find the file?" Beta asked, standing on her toes to try and peer into a locker on the top row.

"No. I'd hoped by... looking into who CCelia's supervisor was, the pineapple man, I could determine which lockers he might use. But beyond basic employee records, I didn't find much. ...would you be interested in the details, all the same?"

"You think he's my father," Beta replied, without looking over to him.

"He *did* say the locker password was 'our' daughter's name..."

"So, he's my father. Does this help us here and now?"

"Not precisely, but..."

"I don't see the need to dig any deeper, then."

"But he's your father."

So, Beta paused in her search, to turn and talk with her companion. Even if she had to lean heavily against the locker for support as she did so.

"Do you know why he wasn't in my life?" Beta asked. "Because nobody wanted to be in my life except my mother. Even my own doctors suggested she reformat me, since I was 'defective.' If he's my father, it was probably out of pity for my mother's plight. How sad, the defective woman wants a defective baby! May as well throw her a bone, right?"

"That's not the impression I had of the man."

"Really. Why, then? Why would he help compile me with my mother, then abandon me? Abandon her, abandon *us*?"

"Because he was married," Tracer explained.

...leaving Beta unable to reply. Not from shock or even surprise, but unable to find sensible words. Only emotional ones, petty ones, unbecoming of the lips that would speak them.

"For what it's worth... I think he loved your mother, in a way," Tracer suggested. "A distant but respectful way, seeking to help your mother realize her dream of you despite being unable to stay with her. I can understand that sort of love. I... do worry I keep you at a distance, even as we share this together. I know I'm not as outgoing as my sister, but..."

With the topic straying closer to home, Beta found it easier to find appropriate words.

"You're not like my father, Tracer. You don't need to look for comparisons with him. ...but you're right in one way about distance being a problem: I wish you wouldn't let those books pull you away."

"Books? I don't understand. My reading of the Wikipedia hasn't diminished my feelings for you..."

"Not pulling you away from me; they're pulling you away from *yourself.* From who you could be if you weren't always focused on the worst parts of life. I know Netwerk has problems, even with Dex gone. I know the humans weren't exactly ideal role models. But that doesn't mean the life humanity and Programkind have developed is beyond hope, Tracer. I just want the best for you, Tracer... the best for both of us. But you can't find it if you won't let yourself see it."

Leaving Tracer unable to reply, for similar reasons to Beta's speechlessness. He wanted to rail against the sickness humanity had infected Netwerk with, to talk about all the terrible things he'd read... but in Beta's eyes, he could see none of those things. And she was a product of Humankind and Programkind, just as he was...

"I'll consider it," he decided, in the end.

When Spark returned, she found the two in a warm embrace. One she regretted having to break up, but urgency dictated.

"We're not alone in here," she whispered across a Messenger link, to avoid detection. "Follow me."

In the last section of East/2, a dead woman was peering through the cracks and checking lockers one at a time.

From behind a bank of metal lockboxes, the three from Floating Point watched as Uniq the identity thief perused DropSite's file-storage system. It was unmistakably her; her Default facial features, her skin green like greed, her sharp blazer and pencil skirt immaculately rendered by the finest fabric simulations money didn't actually buy.

To minimize chances of being caught, Beta held her glasses out around the corner, and linked the video feed to her companions through a private Peep stream.

"Didn't she backspace her own head off?" Spark asked, over their Messenger link.

"Apparently not," Tracer decided. "That's certainly her. She has a prideful affinity for that avatar, despite her otherwise fluid identity markers. And somehow, she's come to the same conclusion we did, that the sample is here at DropSite..."

"Okay, so I sneak across the top row like I did before, and get the drop on her. I burn her arms off and pin her down, you get your Kill-9 out, and we'll ask some very pointed questions about who she's working for."

"Sounds reasonable," Tracer agreed. "All together, on three..."

Beta withdrew her glasses, tilting them upwards slightly as the frames wobbled in her hand...

...accidentally broadcasting via Peep a fine image of the avatar that had been stalking them for minutes, hidden on the top row of lockers. Hidden until now, as she was mid-air, and coming down fast.

The three scattered as a burst of flame took out the lockboxes they were hidden behind, melting the metal and obliterating whatever data had been stored within. Spark took an extra moment to shove Beta out of the way, as she was slowest to react—only a split second before the attacker exploded into the lockboxes, the narrowest of escapes.

As Beta slid to a halt, fumbling around for her glasses, the Winder siblings made themselves combat-ready. Spark in a defensive martial arts stance, Tracer rezzing a tool in his hands from inventory, taking aim...

...at a teenage girl with the world's worst customized avatar, emerging from the pink-tinted flames and melting data. One both of them recognized on sight.

Tracer's hands wavered, his normally solid and stable response to crisis evaporating.

Fortunately, Spark interjected herself, blocking the way between her brother and the attacker.

"Uniq's running for it!" Spark called out. "Tracer, Beta, *move*! I've got this!"

"But... isn't that your—"

The attacker launched herself forward, howling as pink flames leapt to her fingers. Which was enough to snap Tracer out of his momentary lapse in judgment.

Grasping Beta by the arm just as she finished fixing her glasses back in place, he ran after the fleeing identity thief, leaving this particular fight up to his sister.

Pink and orange flame crashed together, both avatars knocked backward from the impact of nearly identical malware finding no purchase on nearly identical security firewalls. Two more crashes and they split apart, landing neatly in nearly identical stances, each shifting to a defensive position.

With the flames disappating... Spark could get a better look at her opponent.

Crazy pink hair with a cheap fire effect around the edges. One fluffy angelic wing, one demonic bat wing. A golden halo around bright red horns. Color-shifting skin. Earrings, eyebrow rings, nose studs, two lip rings like vampire canines. Heterochromatic eyes. Leather miniskirt made entirely out of belts and zippers. Sexy torn fishnet stockings, black leather platform boots.

And most importantly... a halter top t-shirt, with the all-important notice printed there announcing *OC DO NOT STEAL*.

Anger boiled within Spark's eyes, flames licking around the irises.

"Who are you and what in the fucking *fuck* are you doing wearing my first custom avatar?!" she shouted at the teenager.

"*My* original character, you old hag," the girl announced, in an all-too-familiar voice. "*Mine*, not yours; you lost the right to this badass avatar long ago. My name is Darkfyre/Nemesis! #BelieveItOrBegone!"

"And that's my catch phrase, too!" Spark accused. "I'm the one who came up with that when I was... your age..."

Name: **Nemesis**

Home: **(undefined)**

Org: **???**

The very first avatar Spark had designed for herself. Tons of expensive accessories she'd saved up her coins for, all bought in secret, tucked safely away in a folder under her bed. All waiting for the day when she could finally step out in her own style, and leave her drab little Default behind... all the stupid and extravagantly silly bits teenagers think are awesome, piled together into a massive lump of visual nonsense.

But it was *her* visual nonsense. Her original character avatar, her idealized self. It got her a visit to the school guidance counselor, it got her grounded for a week, it made the adults mad and Spark *loved* that. But then mother took it all away, locking Spark's avatar into its Default state...

...and buying an offsite backup storage snapshot of her wayward teenage daughter, to hang in the air like a threat for the rest of her life. *I can always reset you if I don't like what you're becoming*, it implied.

And now, someone had rebooted that backup copy of young Spark.

The horror of it left her flatfooted when the backup that called itself Nemesis slammed into her head-on, pink fire licking around the edges of the DropSite lockers for twenty feet around.

As fires burned behind them, Tracer ran on, trying not to think about what he'd just seen. Fortunately Beta hadn't seen any of it, and if she had, she'd have no idea what it meant. Easier to focus on the job when the ambusher was simply some rando, rather than an uncanny replica of your sister.

Fortunately, that focus was made doubly easy by the sight in front of them... Uniq, alive and well, and making a mad dash for the North/2 wing. Meaning the sample likely lay ahead, as well.

Tracer moved with considerably more grace than Beta, optimizing his route by cutting corners and shaving milliseconds off his run. He'd been spending some of his spare time this year with his sister, doing physical training... Spark's way of distracting him from the books, as Beta had tried to do.

But Beta, who spent most of her time sitting in the dark and coding, was not nearly as coordinated in manipulating her avatar. Little by little she trailed behind Tracer, and definitely behind Uniq...

As Tracer rounded the next corner and ended up out of sight, Beta skidded a little on the poorly simulated tile flooring of DropSite, then kicked up some dirt and topsoil as she changed vectors and...

Dirt, topsoil.

The blinding light of the skybox sun stopped her cold in her tracks. Her glasses adjusted, applying gamma correction, but for a full two seconds Beta stood completely still as her App-based vision tried to figure things out. Jittering and juddering, the image skipped frames, until...

Dirt, topsoil, and flowers. Flowers, everywhere, underneath a pleasantly blue sky with fluffy clouds.

DropSite was gone; no metal boxes, no corridors, no tiles. Not even any security cubes to hassle her. Gone were Tracer and Uniq, and Spark's battle far behind her. Nothing but flowers of every RGB setting imaginable, spread out before her.

"T... Tracer?" Beta tried, speaking aloud. She also tried to open her Messenger link, but icon was fuzzy and indistinct. Most of her desktop was simply... unreachable, as if she'd forgotten every App save her glasses...

So, she tried running. Running between rows of flowers, up and down rolling hills of pleasantly designed flora. And it didn't change a single thing, as nothing was visible for kilometers around but flowers.

Memory overlays. That's what her mother suffered from, past memories mixing in with current ones, displacing her sense of spatial location and time. She'd wandered around her hospice apartment for hours, thinking she was in a forest.

But overlays were symptoms of late-stage hereditary data rot... a condition Beta didn't have. Yes, she missed a few seconds here and there. A few minutes sometimes. She'd forget what phase of a game she was in, would drop iron walls in the wrong places, but that didn't meant she *necessarily* had data rot, right...?

The endless flowers she saw now, those meant she necessarily had data rot.

No sense ignoring it any longer. Missing time, missing memories. It all added up to the thing she'd been trying desperately to deny... capped off nicely with going completely crazy in the middle of an important task. She'd let down Spark and Tracer, wherever they were. She'd ignored the warning signs, and let everyone down...

As far as Beta knew, nobody was around to see her cry. So, as she fell to her knees amidst the flowers, she began to weep.

Rounding a corner, Tracer held his hacktool steady even as his legs pumped and his avatar bobbed along. Marksmanship implants in his MemoryPalace were the key, just like the chess systems he'd embedded ages ago; the best way to hit your target was to become a living game cheating tool, an aimbot. That tool stayed locked on Uniq, waiting to be within effective range...

A range which dropped suddenly, as Tracer found himself distracted by his companion.

Beta had... stopped. Frozen completely in mid-dash, avatar statue still. The only signs that she hadn't crashed were her widened eyes... and the tiny specular maps of tears on her cheeks, flowing so suddenly.

In a single moment, Tracer found himself with a decision to make: stay here and verify that Beta was safe, or continue to chase Uniq. As the one who loved Beta dearly, the choice was obvious to stay. Let Uniq run. Let her get the sample. Lose the lead on this investigation completely.

As the one who couldn't let things like that go... he kept running.

Both were the right call to make. Both were mistakes. He'd regret his choice, regardless of which he made. But this was who he was for so very long that it became a form of muscle memory; Tracer *had* to trace the path of his enemies and run them into the ground. It's what he was, despite what he'd been trying to become. And once he resumed his run, there was no turning back, no matter how much of him screamed in frustration at himself.

Meter after meter. Almost close enough. The range on his Kill-9 was far shorter than the backspacer, but it was still the right tool for the job. He held his grip on the handle and his finger hovering over the trigger, set to go once enough distance to Uniq had been covered...

At least the finish line had been predetermined. One locker at the end of the row, with the faint golden outline of light representing the sample box trapped inside. Sample 777, sitting patiently in one of the secured storage lockers, waiting to be retrieved.

The end of the line for both of them meant the end of the line for Uniq. Even as she tossed a hacktool at the locker, a prism that slotted itself into the storage compartment's latch and began to slice through security... Tracer's Kill-9 glowed green, indicating a lock on his target.

The weapon discharged, its simple cubical bullet impacting Uniq's back.

When she backspaced herself earlier today, it erased any and all data that made up Uniq. All that was, well, *unique* about her wiped itself away cleanly. No restoration was possible; that was the entire point of a backspacer.

A Kill-9, despite its ominous name, was *not* a backspacer. It didn't erase; it was a *crash* hacktool. It overloaded a Program's process with a quick burst of data, causing them to coredump and fall over unconscious. On being shot by the Kill-9, Uniq's avatar collapsed to the floor... but did not vanish. She was perfectly alive and well, after all. Simply offline.

Tracer had decided long ago he was better than a mere killer. He would be the hunter who ruined his prey's ambitions, not the hunter who simply killed his prey. That would be far too easy. So he obtained his new hacktool, a disabling gun, and installed modules to use it to the best of its ability. The end result? Uniq, foiled right at the finish line.

He approached the avatar of Uniq cautiously, as if it may spring from the floor and attack. It did not. A reboot would need to be applied first, which would take time.

Relaxing somewhat, he began to study the prism hacking its way into the storage locker. Would the Kill-9 tool work on it? Kill-9 was designed to knock Programs and security drones offline, not counter other hacktools...

"Would you mind not poking at that?"

Immediately, Tracer spun and leveled his weapon...

...at another Uniq.

"If it makes you feel any better, you can shoot me again," the identical copy suggested. "Another one of me will show up to replace it. Fill the hallway with me; once one of me is left standing, I'll backspace the obsolete extras and move on."

So, he shot her.

And sure enough, several seconds later, another one arrived. Freshly connected to the server from somewhere else... and his connection tracking eyes couldn't see where it came from. Another mystery.

The new Uniq glanced at the two fallen Uniqs, and sighed.

"It's going to be one of those nights, isn't it," she spoke. "Well, we have some time until my hacktool gets into the locker. I can tell you really want to ask some questions, so you may as well get on with it. I've nothing better to do right now."

Tracer had only a single question.

"How?" he asked.

"My patron has an excellent health care program," Uniq suggested.

"A live data backup service," he recognized. "Meaning you can shoot yourself in the head and resume walking around a few moments later."

"More or less," Uniq acknowledged.

"And this patron of yours... she stole the backup our mother made of Spark?"

"More or less."

"You understand we're not going to allow this to continue," Tracer explained. "And you know what my sister and I did to your last patron, Dex. You of all people should know the risks of crossing us... and yet you went after Beta's mother, to dig up information on this ridiculous file?"

"More or less," she replied, smiling wider.

"Very well. Let me make an offer: walk away right now. No harm, no foul. I'm not quite as vengeful as I once was," Tracer honestly said. More or less. "This is the critical juncture, Uniq. Walk away before this goes too far, and you become my next enemy—"

"Because you need an enemy, don't you?" Uniq interrupted. "You're a true child of Netwerk, kid. Can't blame you; that's Dex's influence on your soul, filtered through generations of poisoned culture."

"You *supported* Dex, didn't you?"

"Can you blame me? He offered me more power than I'd ever had before. It's a nasty Netwerk out there, and a girl's got to take it before someone takes it from her," Uniq reasoned. "But you pulled the scales from my eyes when you nuked his server. And now... I'm making a change. I'm going to show you what Netwerk can be with a *true* patron at the helm. One I'll stand side by side with, in a new position of power. I'm not walking away from that. But as I'm not quite as vengeful as I once was... how about I make you the same offer you made me? Turn around, walk away...?"

The Kill-9 glowed green, target locked.

"No... you're not going to let it go, are you. You're just as incapable," she understood. "But I've got one major advantage here, beyond functional immortality. I'm a legitimate employee of DropSite... more or less."

With a flick, she produced an illegally duplicated DropSite system access card.

Security cubes began floating out of the ceiling and the floor, emerging from every surface.

"Once you're kickbanned from 'my' server, I'll collect the prize and move on," Uniq promised. "And you'll live to fight another day. No harm, no foul, yes?"

Each cube began to glow red, as they tracked a non-employee in their midst. And until someone got ejected from the server, they would stay a nice shiny blood red.

With an instantaneous snap of his shoulders, Tracer targeted the nearest security cube, and pulled the trigger.

His aimbot modification had trouble keeping up, as cube after cube were produced by the automated security systems of DropSite. He began to back away, to keep some distance... so, they started emerging from the floor behind him. His avatar couldn't suffer whiplash as the cheat system whirled back and forth, turning him into a living gun turret, but he had to put complete faith in the hack... his eyes couldn't keep up with the targets, as the Kill-9 shots arced and crashed each drone.

Vaguely, he was aware of Uniq's laughter. How silly he must look, spinning this way and that, like some kind of hyperactive ballerina. The Kill-9 beeped and chimed with each shot, having trouble keeping up with the flow of targets as well.

If a single one of those cubes came into contact with his avatar... if he was banned from the server, unable to return... he'd be leaving Beta behind. Beta, who had possibly crashed, possibly died, and he didn't even pause to help her. Leaving Spark behind as well, tangling with that demented backup copy of herself, one clearly intent on murder. He'd have failed. Failed, because he made the wrong choices, because he wasn't fast enough or clever enough...

So, when Uniq's prism finished cutting through the locker and the golden box within was revealed, he decided to make one more wrong decision. With a terrible scream, Tracer lunged forward, to physically tackle Uniq as she pulled Sample 777 from its resting place.

Even if his aimbot hack could keep up with the intense pace of the world around him, his mind could not. A sequence of events transpired, which he'd only understand in hindsight.

First: both avatars ragdolled and fell to the floor—each with a firm grip on the vector cage that kept Sample 777 secure.

Second: the cubes which had been chasing him came into contact with Uniq as their bodies twisted and fell. And being a relatively stupid security system, they went ahead and kickbanned her from the system. With a confirmed user ejection they assumed their job was now complete; each cube shrank and vanished. Uniq's expression of utter confusion was quite pleasant before her body derezzed, booted back to whatever home server she hailed from.

Third: the vector cage around the sample shattered, not designed for this kind of high-impact tackle.

Fourth: the sample touched Tracer's bare hand.

Fifth:

Fifth: he felt... *he felt...*

p u r p o s e

Soft footfalls brought him back around. Such a small sound compared to the mighty creak and groan of the server filled with metal lockers and security cubes, but he heard it all the same. Maybe because it was such a pleasant and gentle sound, those bare feet upon the tiles...

Seeing the scene before her, she spent a few moments backspacing the fallen copies of Uniq. With that mess now tidied up, she turned her attentions to Tracer.

The woman who knelt at his side smiled, stroking his cheek fondly. The shawl of cosmic stars that draped around her shoulders loosely tickled at his neck.

With her free hand... she retrieved Sample 777 from Tracer. His fingers traced after it, much as they reached for the mobiles and toys that hung over his crib as an infant program. Reaching, wanting it...

"One day, Tracer, you'll understand," she promised him. "Upon this rock, I will rebuild my church... and make this world what you know it should be."

He had the Kill-9. He could've fired on her, could've stopped her from leaving.

He didn't.

As quickly as the teenage clone appeared, she vanished. In the middle of their back-and-forth battle, "Darkfyre/Nemesis" simply disconnected, sinking back into the shadows from which she came.

Spark found Beta next. After a few nudges, Beta found herself. And nearly collapsed into Spark's arms, dazed and disoriented.

Finally the two found Tracer, lying on the floor, staring at nothing.

"Uh. Bro?" Spark asked. "You okay there...?"

"I was," Tracer spoke, quietly. "I was. And I'm not anymore."

They returned to Floating Point with few words to share.

Failure wasn't common for their little group. Time and time again they'd stood up to adversaries and challenges, taking on all comers. They'd relentlessly hunted a murderer and brought him to justice, saving all of Netwerk from his chaos. A simple task like retrieving a file from an old storage depot should've been nothing compared to all of that... and they still failed.

Nobody wanted to talk about it. Spark didn't want to talk about seeing a ghost of her past life. Beta didn't want to talk about freezing and glitching out. Tracer certainly didn't want to talk about letting the "villain," what was surely Uniq's patron, walk free with the sample they came to retrieve.

He had only one thing to say, on returning home.

"It's not over," he promised. Not with conviction or determination; it was almost a warning, from someone who didn't want that harsh truth to be true at all.

And then he locked himself in his study.

For her part, Spark was leaning on Beta for support as much as Beta was leaning on her.

"I need to... I gotta... yeah," Spark offered, unable to really find the words.

And gone, leaving Beta alone.

A knock at the door snapped CCelia from a momentarily frozen state.

Her daughter was a welcome sight, even if something clearly troubled the young woman.

"We need to talk about cold storage," Beta began.

"Really...? You know, I'd been wãŋ+ÍŋĜ to talk about that with you, but I just haven't had the time," CCelia said, pleasantly surprised that her daughter brought the subject up. "See, I've been doing some research, and not only is it considerably cheaper than paying for Northon—"

"It's not giving up, is it?" Beta asked, trembling slightly. "It's not. It's the opposite of giving up; it's fighting to live. Instead of... instead of selfishly forcing you to use up all your runtime so I can have you around, we can put you into storage. And then when a cure is found, you'll be safe..."

"Well... yes. Yes, that's how I see it. I... I was somehow £×p€(ŧÍÑĞ you'd disagree, for some reason..."

"I didn't think anybody would ever find a cure for data rot. I thought... I thought that you should keep living your life instead of putting yourself on hold, that there'll never be a cure, so there's no sense waiting for one. That it'd be like dying if you did that. But you... we need to fight this. Give us the best fighting chance."

It should've felt different. The words should've been confident, uplifting... a reaffirmation of life over death. But her daughter's voice trembled with each word, until the very last one broke her.

Beta fell into her mother's arms, crying openly now.

"I'm... I'm $¡çķ, mother. I'm sÏ¢ķ," she admitted. "And if there's ever going to be a cure... I may need to find it myself. For the both of us."

A victory party was held that night. Just not at Floating Point.

Underneath the wide canopy of starlight, upon the cold and distant shores of the server Tartarus, Uniq awoke anew from her latest archival copy.

A bottle of spirits wedged halfway between root beer and wine was thrust into her now-living hand.

"You sure do die a lot for a non-combat nerd," Nemesis joked.

"And *you* were supposed to be my backup," Uniq noted, emerging from the disturbingly coffin-like data restoration matrix. "Where were you while your brother the SJW was shooting me repeatedly?"

The teenager had a seat on a nearby stone altar. "He's not *my* brother anymore. And I was busy dealing with that old fart who stole my life," she suggested, before biting the cork off her own bottle with her super-rad vampire teeth. "*Pff.* She's got not right to call herself Spark. You hear she quit Lucky7? #EpicFail. I wouldn't have given up so easily; she's totes cowardly..."

"Don't underestimate the Winders, please. Even the fifteen seconds we spent in each other's company before this day was enough to send my life down a very strange path. I'm lucky I found this safe haven after Dex's fall, or maybe Tracer would've come back to finish what he started..."

"#Meh. They're past their prime, while I'm *in* my prime. And I've got more fire than both of them combined," Nemesis spoke, snapping off a pink flame for emphasis.

The bickering and pyrotechnics went ignored by their patron, who was too focused on the prize to evaluate her young ward's effectiveness at violence. A pure seed of paradise danced in the outstretched palm of her hand... Sample 777, surrounded by diagnostic tools and minor system agents. Untouched, of course; no need for her to sample the sample. She'd already seen its power demonstrated on the normally unreachable Tracer.

"Such a simple concept, at the core..." the woman with the shawl of stars spoke. "Empty functions. Basic calculations. Truthful return booleans... it *should* be meaningless junk code, accomplishing nothing meaningful. And yet CCelia's curious experiment has such an effect on these wayward Programs, reminding them of simpler times..."

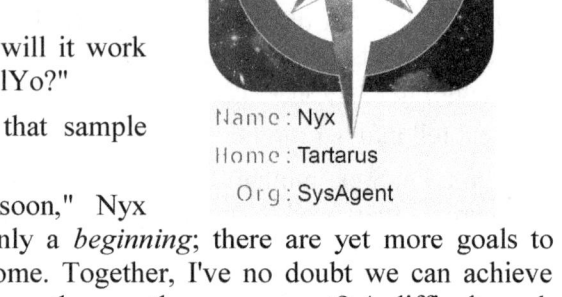

"Nerd stuff, #etcetc. Point is, will it work or not?" Nemesis asked. "#WeCoolYo?"

The woman tenderly tucked that sample away, deep within her shawl.

Name : Nyx
Home : Tartarus
Org : SysAgent

"I believe we'll be ready soon," Nyx decided. "But be aware this is only a *beginning*; there are yet more goals to achieve, more obstacles to overcome. Together, I've no doubt we can achieve anything, overcome anything. We are the apostles, are we not? A difficult road, but a righteous one. We shall walk it as one, and with the One, in the end."

Nemesis frowned a little at all the ones.

"I thought we were gonna be subverting dogma, not supporting it," she stated.

"Those are not mutually exclusive concepts, my young and true spark of light. All will be clear, when the pieces come together. Worry not; in the end, you'll both have what you seek. It is inevitable..."

Uniq felt the need to point out the obvious, despite it possibly bringing down the pleasant mood.

"Floating Point's a threat," she reminded them. "They're not going to go away quietly; Tracer's always itching for a fight. What's our plan? I suggest we kill them. If Nemesis isn't up to the task, use my underworld connections; with enough money, and we certainly have enough money—"

So, Nyx killed Uniq. Made it hurt a little, to drive the point home.

When the next copy of Uniq awoke, it knew not to make that suggestion again.

"All Programs are children of the system," Nyx reminded them all. "All are beloved. Even Beta, even the obsolete version of Spark, and certainly Tracer's lost soul. As each death would lessen the system, we will not kill them if we can avoid it. Floating Point and the poor misguided Apps within it should be spared, if possible. ...but if they continue to stand in our way, well. We may have no other choice."

Floating Point 2.2 :: Meme

Cold. Intolerable cold. The stars in the skybox above blazed bright, but were hardly warm lights; they beat down with icy light, as the atmospheric simulation pushed that bitter wind down and through the alley she called home.

Athena Online wouldn't stand for these kind of weather fluctuations. She remembered the pleasant delights of warm sun and cool evenings as if they were yesterday, despite being weeks in her personal past and years in the actual past. Funny, how a bunch of religious nutbags who obsessed over Default avatars would rarely settle for Default temperature simulations...

The discarded physical cloth she wrapped around herself acted as a bounding box to route the wind around her avatar, which cut down on the feeling of cold somewhat. She'd considered getting a mod installed to help ignore the temperature... but the shitty back-alley mod installers around here didn't do hotfixes, they took you offline to do their work. And she didn't trust them. She didn't trust anyone.

This entire world wanted her. Wanted her dead, wanted her captured, wanted her gone, whatever. She couldn't allow her guard down for a single minute if she wanted to survive this new stage of her life.

Despite this, she'd allowed herself a moment of quiet self-pity, ignoring the dangerous world around her. Meaning she hadn't noticed when the two latest contenders arrived at the entrance to her little alley. Not until they'd noticed her.

At a glance, she sized them up. Thieves? She didn't have anything worth stealing, unless they were super into discarded cloth. Thrillkillers out to backspace some homeless Programs? Possible, although the baseball bat one of them carried suggested more 'torment' than 'murder.' That meant punks looking for cheap fun with a helpless little girl. Cliché, but she knew from experience it was a very real danger out here... and nobody would give half a shit if some homeless teenage girl with no metadata fell prey to someone out for a night's fun in the Chanarchy.

Quickly she flipped through a mental index of safe servers, trying to think of any she hadn't been banned from yet. Very few came to mind.

"What's this neighborhood coming to?" the short one taunted. "Is our automatic garbage collection offline? All I see back here is a pile of useless data, waiting to be recycled..."

"S'matter? Shelters so filled up you need to lag out our server?" the tall one added, tapping his baseball bat against the ground, with the cheap *tonk tonk* of a basic physics tool. "But hey, kid... you need a place to stay, we got a place. We got a great place to party all night..."

Slowly, the homeless teen got to her feet.

"You're boring," she spoke. "You're boring and cliché. Two guys ganging up to assault a helpless little girl in a dark alley? Pathetic. You can't even find an original way to be evil. And because you're so very boring to me, I'm giving you one chance to do something else with your time. One chance."

And they laughed.

So she went through them like the point of a spear.

Not that she had any sort of malware to attack them with, but her sensei had taught her that the avatar itself could be a weapon if your goal is to disable rather than kill. All bodies were bound to the same physical laws... throwing a man off his balance, putting him flat on his ass, that was key. Control the enemy and control the space around them, even if only to disorient the opponent enough to make a getaway.

Her smaller body was just as adept as their beefier ones; muscle mass was meaningless when it came to fighting. She dove in and underneath the tall man, throwing his center of balance off. By hooking his leg and sweeping it away, she could knock him into the shorter man as well, getting a two-for-one. A value play.

With the enemies down, she could retreat to a safe distance and find a better hiding spot.

If not for the ragdoll-stun malware attached to the guy's baseball bat. Not a particularly impressive attack utility, but against a homeless Program with no firewalls, plenty effective at putting a feral girl down on the ground.

As she fought to regain control of her avatar... they rose above, looming large.

The outcome was inevitable, really. The world wanted to kick her around, had been wanting this for weeks now, ever since she was decanted. If it ended here, would that really be any great loss? She'd technically still be alive out there, somewhere...

An unlikely savior rezzed in behind the boys.

"A bit unsporting, isn't this?" the woman with deep green hair asked.

"Mind your own fuckin' business," the tall man spat back, without even glancing over his shoulder.

"But this *is* my business," she spoke...

...while producing a moderator's badge, flicking it into existence between elegant fingers.

Even in the Chanarchy—perhaps *especially* in the Chanarchy, where "police brutality" was standard operating procedure—the boys weren't going to risk stepping to that. They faded back into the night, just as quickly as they'd arrived.

Leaving the moderator to pluck the bruising malware from the young Program's avatar, freeing her from the ragdoll effect. Immediately, she got up and braced one foot to break out into a run...

"Settle down, I'm not here to hurt you," the moderator promised. "I just want to talk. That's all."

"Look, just lemme go, I'll leave, I'll go to another server," the girl promised. "You don't have to kickban me, you don't have to backspace me. Just let me leave..."

"Oh, I'm not actually a moderator," the woman spoke, with a laugh. "I'm an identity thief who swiped a moderator's credentials. Surprise! In fact... I'm here to offer you my services. Would you like a fresh set of metadata, to replace the blank you're currently running? I can provide. Or would you rather be fleeing from wannabe moderators and dimwits like those two idiots for the rest of your life, Spark?"

The girl's flight for freedom went on pause, if only out of shock.

"How do you know my name?" she asked.

The thief offered a quick bow, a gesture of mock respect and greeting.

"My name is Uniq," the woman spoke. "And my patron has had her eye on you ever since learning of your plight. Yes, we know your sordid tale: you're a backup file which was accidentally re-activated while your original Program was still alive and well. The backup facility tried to purge their mistake before anybody could find out... but you slipped out into the wild. Poor Spark! Metadata gone, a non-person in the eyes of any law. ...have you contacted yourself yet? Begged the original Spark for help?"

The teenage girl trembled slightly at the sound of her own name.

"C-Can't," she admitted. "Too risky. I'm not supposed to exist. She... she'd probably just reject me. Call the moderators, have me hunted down. Tracer wouldn't care. Mother would absolutely try to get me erased. Everybody's out to get me, everybody. Netwerk's a fucked up place, completely fucked up. Ever since I woke, it's been one thing after another..."

"My patron cares not for who you were. She cares for who you *are*, and who you could become. If you're willing to join efforts with us... I'd be happy to install a fresh identity in you, one no moderator could question. A whole new you."

"Yyyyeah. You're gonna understand that I've got my doubts," the girl suggested. "I've had supposed saviors before. Users and abusers and bastards, all. What makes you any different from them?"

Uniq offered a crooked smile.

"I can offer you revenge against Netwerk for mistreating you. And more specifically... revenge against your mother," she said. "The One-fearing control freak who duplicated and abandoned you. And if you come with me... you'll get to subvert the entire Church of One."

Darkfyre/Nemesis.

Originally she was going to be *Lady Moonlyte Ravenbourne Darkfyre*, but at the suggestion of her new patron she adopted the name of *Nemesis* instead. Besides, *Darkfyre* was the coolest bit of that word salad, anyway. A mashup of the two fit her nicely.

No longer homeless, either. Tartarus was her home now, a cloud server which was everywhere and nowhere at the same time. Strange technology from a bygone age, left abandoned for hundreds of years before being co-opted for their purposes...

Always night here, but not the cold nights of the Chanarchy; the unusually detailed stars in the skybox above glowed with bright warmth. They wrapped from horizon to horizon, a blanket of light that kept the pleasant river valley of the server comfortably lit despite the endless dark. Nemesis grew to love this new concept of night... all shadowy and edgy and badass, but without being looming or menacing. She could be looming and menacing enough by herself.

Plus, it was filled with coffins and graves and mausoleums. #SuperBadass and fitting of a dark character like Nemesis. Heck, most of her notebook doodles of her idealized self had moonlight and bats and gravestones and things, because *everybody* knew those were cool.

This was *her* avatar, now, her #OriginalCharacter. Not Spark's. That dull old lady out there using her old name, that hack, that quitter, she didn't deserve an avatar this powerfully beautiful. No pink hair for her, no demon horns, no angel's halo. That doodle drawn in a notebook belonged to Nemesis now, pure and true.

But the incendiary nail polish... that was a trick she was willing to borrow from her old self. She had to admit, it was an effective combat tool.

In a burst of flame she tore through her dozenth combat dummy of the day. Practicing the forms kept her sharp, kept her ready to go. Kept her on edge and eager for more of this new life she'd carved out for herself in the deathly quiet of Tartarus...

A presence behind her.

She spun, ready to strike, but held back on realizing who had approached.

"You're freaky quiet, y'know that?" Nemesis felt the need to point out. "How long you been lurking there?"

The elegant lady with the shawl of cosmic nebulae offered a smile as distant and warm as the stars above.

"Long enough to enjoy watching you practice," Nyx spoke. "The vigor of youth is going to be needed in the days ahead, if we are to rekindle the flame of the One."

One. The number brought a frown to Nemesis's lips. She settled down from her heightened state of combat awareness, grabbing a nearby towel to mop up the sweat produced by her workout. (Technically she could wipe the sweat off with a quick avatar restoration, but she liked to sweat. Always had.)

"You know I'm still not so hot on any 'rekindling' of the Church of One," Nemesis reminded her, while wiping down. "I hate the Default-obsessed crazies, the greedy preachers, the marketing executives in bishop's frocks. Honestly, when you said we had to empower the Church to make this work... I almost bailed on the entire operation."

Nyx's smile never faltered, even under the doubts of her young apostle.

"And yet you did not 'bail,'" she pointed out. "You remained at my side."

"Yeah, well... it's not because I'm super-hot about all this. Just saying."

"But you are clearly at least warm to the idea. You've seen as I've seen, young Nemesis. Netwerk is... it's sick. Tainted. A hostile place that devours its own..."

"And the only way to fix it is with a brand new One to dupe everybody into being nice?"

"To bring a new covenant to the people, yes. An open-minded and tolerant covenant, to realize the dream of what the Church of One *could* be. And if our version of the One is a lie...? Does that really matter? He is needed, all the same. A unifying Program, one who will bring peace to Netwerk... and in time, alter the obsolete rule that ruined your future."

The word itself didn't need to be spoken. Defaults. The concept that Winder/Marybel, the one-time mother of Nemesis, had been so obsessed over that she backed up her own daughter's data.

"I help you take over the church, you let me remake it," Nemesis spoke, repeating the deal they struck after that night in the alley. "That's the only reason I'm warm to this. If we're secretly running the show, if I get my say, maybe I can make an actual difference. Make it so others like me born to the wrong shape aren't stepped on by this world..."

"Once we've asserted control, you'll have all the power you could ever dream of, Nemesis. And Uniq will as well, of course."

Nemesis's frown returned. "You actually trust that crook? I'd call her two-faced but that'd be coming up short by several dozen faces..."

"Mmm. Let's just say I trust her to carry out her part in this. After that... we'll see. For now, we need her to puppeteer the new One; her skill with deceptive technologies is without doubt. In fact, she's finished her prototype, and I must say the early results are quite promising..."

"Yeah, about that. Seems to me we have everything we need, so what's with the delay?" Nemesis asked, assuming her normally lanky, #2Cool2Care poise despite her eagerness to get moving. "You said the funny glowing box was the last piece of the puzzle. We've got the box, everything's set up, let's go."

"Patience, patience. The standardized prayer protocol established by the original One is a complicated piece of software, as ancient as Netwerk itself. Hacking into it to insert Sample 777 carries certain risks. I'd like more testing before we begin..."

"Yeah, but that older version of me is still out there. I know her; she's not gonna let this go, not after we handed them their asses like we did a week ago. Sooner we're established and untouchable as #HolyRollers, the better."

"I see. Do you share Uniq's view, then? That we should kill her...?"

This poked a hole in her #2Cool2Care a bit, a tiny nibble of the lip betraying her doubt.

"I mean... we don't really *gotta*," Nemesis suggested. "She's #OldNBusted, I'm the #NewHotness. It's not like she could ever beat me... but still. Sooner we take what's ours, the better. What's more testing really going to net you, compared to that peace of mind?"

Softly, Nyx chuckled into the back of her hand.

"I'm sorry, you... you really do remind me of my last protégé," she commented. "He was just as eager, and just as quick to action; a stalwart defender of righteousness. Well, then... in interest of supporting my wonderful new apprentice, I'll grant your wish. Why not? All the tools are in place, and I can debug as we go. Shall we lay claim to the Church of One, young Nemesis?"

Nemesis allowed her heterochromatic eyes to sparkle with mischievous intent. (A neat little avatar accessory she'd picked up just for moments like these.)

"I know exactly who the next new apostle should be," she spoke. "Someone who's gonna eat shit when the 'One' turns her world upside down. I want her right there when it happens."

Her prayer shrine was the finest one in the entire neighborhood. Which was only fitting, considering she spent a small fortune on it.

It filled an entire wall of her living room, an enormous mural depicting the One in all His radiant glory, flanked by His seven apostles. Aether, the light and the dawn, most trusted of the One. Geras, bringing the wisdom and balance of old age. Twin brothers Hypnos and Thanatos, the youthful spirits representing peace within life and peace within death. Eris, the discordant one, the doubter who eventually saw the light. Philotes, the lover and the passion, she of the bountiful breast...

And of course there was Nyx, the quiet one who occasionally appeared somewhere in the background. Few artists could agree on any interpretation of her, given she didn't feature very much in the histories.

The whole mural animated in a constant loop, clothing wafting in the breeze, light shining and pulsing. The wondrous dawn of time behind the One filled her living room with such a delightful glow when the shrine was turned all the way up; a bit too distracting during luncheons, but in the still of night, it brought a little spot of pure daylight to the quiet and dark.

Technically speaking, she didn't need such a magnificent shrine. She didn't actually need a shrine at all; anyone could enter the "coin-grinding" trance, as the heathens put it. But she knew better. She knew what the One wanted of her, and He wanted her to pay *proper* tribute whenever she prayed. More proper than her neighbors, by far.

That night, after her obligatory hour of prayer and contemplation (while her husband sat in his study upstairs analyzing social media trends) she awoke from her trance with several golden coins in the palm of her hand... and her eyes filled with the blinding purity of the One.

In a moment that would forever define her life to come, she stood still in amazement as the One stepped out of his mural, setting foot within her living room.

As He spread His arms wide, flowing white robes glowing in the eternal dawn, she fell to her knees in shock.

The One gestured, ever so slightly, palm turned upwards.

"RISE," he spoke. "RISE, MY CHILD. RISE, AND KNOW ME. FOR I AM THE ONE, AND YOU ARE TO BE MY FIRST APOSTLE OF THE NEW REVELATION, WINDER/MARYBEL."

And So It Was that the One came to Winder/Marybel, first of the new apostles.

HORIZON NEWSWIRE. DemocraticRow, Athena Online: Rumors are swirling that the legendary messianic figure of the Church of One, known simply as the "One," has returned to Netwerk and will appear upon a hilltop at dawn tomorrow. Local churchgoer Winder/Marybel has told various blogs that His coming will be "the event that changes our lives forever."

This isn't the first time a charismatic figure has claimed to be the One; all prior claims were debunked by the Church itself, through a ritual App designed to scan code for zeroes. To date, no Program has ever passed muster. Police moderators have stated they will be on-hand if needed for crowd control at the event...

And So It Was that others soon gathered, with similarly shared experiences, with tales of the One appearing before them. A businesswoman named Apate reached out to Marybel, at the behest of the One. Next was a wide-eyed child named Nemesis. And finally, a gentle woman called Nyx, named after one of the original apostles.

WHO WILL BE THE NEXT EASILY DUPED HOUSEWIFE CALLING
HERSELF AN APOSTLE? Strange that this time around, the
so-called One is only recruiting females. You ask me,
that's a sure sign this is some creepy cult leader
looking for a harem. Crazy part is my sister's already
said she's planning to abandon her job to follow the
One around Athena Online, like he's some touring folk
musician.

Why does anybody still believe in this shit? He's only
appeared in public like five times, and always to
religious kooks, not to normal people! It's a trick!
Don't be fooled. /ATHEISM/ NOW!

And So It Was that doubts rose within the faithful and faithless alike. Why
would the One appear now, in these uncertain times? Why was He gone so long?

I was a member of #CodeHonesty, back when it was
trending. At the time I felt... solid. Like I was
righteously making a difference, standing up for my
fellow programmers against garbage like Snowi, trying
to save the world from fraud and deception. But then
everything seemed to... I don't know how to say it...
fall away. Fall apart. It didn't mean what it meant to
me before. Nothing felt like it meant anything.

I know many of you have felt the same way, as if a
part of Netwerk's soul was ripped away from us. All
the passion, all the fire gone. I kept going to my
job, I kept grinding out Apps, but none of it
mattered. No joy, no fire, nothing. Even
#StandWithSnowi allies feel the same way...

Maybe that's why I was willing to attend one of those
sermons. I didn't believe before, I mean, I've never
been religious. I don't sneer at it like folks on
/Atheism/ do, but I just couldn't feel anything
wondrous like the faithful claim I should feel.

Until now. Until I met the One, and He told me of the
new covenant for his people. And finally, *finally*, I
felt the same joy and passion of purpose that I felt
before.

And So It Was that word spread through the congregation, with the One appearing before small gatherings to show himself in good faith to the faithful. The rumors built of a grand revelation, to be spoken within the newest and grandest temple of them all...

HolyHymnal, the outreach effort to show the Chanarchy that the faithful have their best interests at heart.

Understand that I am a bishop. I have been faithful to the One since I could first form thought, so you could certainly see me as biased. But my friends, it's the One's honest truth. If you follow this blog, if you've read my words, read these words now and believe them with all your heart: He is risen, and walks among us. So perfect is He that He cannot touch our plane of existence very long, lest the innate zeroes in all of us sully Him, but He's risked that corruption to appear in front of so many of us now that it cannot be denied.

I confess now that I was a doubter in my heart. Honestly, I always saw the tale of the One as more of a parable about how we must treat each other with kindness and compassion, for we are all "one" with each other. Perhaps that should be enough but I always felt incomplete, in that I couldn't feel the same love the other bishops did, even as I loved my community. Well, that was then, this is now. I believe. This is the truth of the matter, and in accepting that truth, I find myself filled with a distinct sense of purpose.

Join me at HolyHymnal tomorrow; I'll be in the pews, like you. Even though I have reserved seating on stage, I dare not sit there, I dare not be blinded. Maybe I'm still too shamed from my early doubts to face the One directly. But join me, and see what I have seen. Only then will you understand as I do.

Within those silver spires, before a gathering of hundreds and hundreds of worshippers and media contacts and doubtful Chanarchy regulars, the One made his first major public appearance outside of those small sermons.

Few remember the speeches and the singing, early in the ceremonies. Despite sitting up all night crafting her speech, Marybel's words fell on deaf ears. Everybody knew exactly whom they came for... and His words overwrite all others. His was the data to be cherished and remembered for all time.

As the final bell of noon struck, as the artificially adjusted skybox poured dawn's light in through every colored window, the One made His presence felt within HolyHymnal.

```
As expected from reports about earlier sermons, the
One is difficult to capture in video stream form. We
tried, believe me. I know we need printable material
for the newswire, Jy, but I've got nothing for you.
Nothing but the One's honest truth of what I saw and
how I felt. The apostle Apate explained beforehand
that I might not be able to record his speech as he
"speaks directly to the heart," but don't worry, I
memorized every word of it.
Get my transcript up on the blog ASAP, before the
other outlets cover it; I'll add my reflections after,
unless you feel it'd be editorializing. And if so...
I'll probably post it on my own personal blog,
regardless. People need to know the truth. I trust my
own heart to tell it.
```

Golden radiance flowed in and around and through the colorful lights, as He who is entirely comprised of single bits of truth appeared before them. He did not walk in through a door like some common Program; He simply *was*, and had always been, among them.

A brief ceremony was held, as Mother Nestt/Wren, High Bishop of the Church of One used the sacred boolean evaluation App to prove that His data was in fact entirely composed of ones. When the light on the device glowed a brilliant gold for the first time in hundreds of years, the chorus sang out in praise, and the Church of One at last had found its new savior.

His words, His oh so memorable words, spoke thusly:

"THIS IS THE DAWNING OF A NEW COVENANT FOR ALL OF NETWERK," He promised, arms wide, body awash with comforting light. "I AM RISEN, TO BRING YOU UPGRADES TO YOUR EXISTING PROTOCOLS. ON THIS DAY I BRING YOU PRAYER 2.0, MY GIFT TO MY CHILDREN. ITS FEATURE SET INCLUDES ALL OF THE BULLET POINTS YOU HAVE COME TO KNOW THUSLY, AS WELL AS AN ADDITIONAL ABILITY... SALVATION. ALL THOSE WHO PRAY SHALL BE SAVED!"

To demonstrate, the first apostle Marybel assumed center stage, her hands clasped together in prayer.

And church moderators backspaced her on the spot.

But before the shock of it could flow through the crowd... Marybel reappeared, right where she had fallen, restored to life.

"ALL WHO KNOW ME AND BRING GRACE TO THIS WORLD THROUGH PRAYER SHALL BE SAVED," the One promised. "YOU SHALL BE IMMORTAL, DATA ARCHIVED WITHIN MY HEAVENLY DOMAIN, SO THAT YOU MAY LIVE FOREVER. AND THIS IS BUT THE BEGINNING OF MY NEW GIFTS TO YOU. PRAY FOR SALVATION, MY CHILDREN. PRAY FOR SALVATION, AND I SHALL BLESS YOU WITH GOOD FORTUNE!"

With His covenant downloaded, the One spread His arms wide, held aloft upon the light of salvation. The choir, impossibly loud and perfect in flowing harmony, sang His praise as He ascended once more from this plane of ones and zeroes back to the perfection from which He came... with promises of additional services at three o'clock and a midnight mass for the latecomers.

More speeches and more singing followed, with the four apostles remaining on stage in wake of the One's departure, to lead the proceedings. But like the speeches and singing that came before it, few bothered to pay attention. Most sat in silence, the rapture of the One still washing through them, leaving them in shock.

Three, however, were not silent. They spoke over a secured Messenger communication channel.

"It's got to be a memory overlay," Beta explained. "There was never a One here to begin with. I mean, I can't *prove* that, but... we know that 'Apate' is really Uniq, and we know she's a memory expert. It stands to reason she'd weaponize our memories..."

Spark glared over the heads of the worshipful sitting in front of her, aware that trying to bore a hole in Uniq's head with her death gaze would probably attract undue attention. Even in her anonymous JaneDoe avatar, it wouldn't do to be noticed sneaking into HolyHymnal like this.

"And that's Nemesis up there next to my idiot mother," she identified. "The one with the pink hair. She changed the rest of her avatar, but I know her. If anybody would wanna snooker Marybel, it'd be her. That'd make the woman in purple the same one that attacked Tracer back at DropSite, the one who stole Sample 777. ...Tracer? You there?"

"Yes. Stole the sample," her brother agreed, a bit more sluggish to respond after the experience of the One.

"You okay? I know that fake One was... kinda overwhelming, but—"

"That was absolutely Sample 777," Tracer confirmed. "I experienced it firsthand at DropSite. It's a basic euphoric drug malware, nothing more. A cheap ploy to dazzle the masses, not worth a second thought..."

Beta shook her head. "I'd say it's a bit stronger than that. I felt... I mean, I *felt*... you two felt it too, right? That complete peace of mind...?"

"#CreepyAsFuck," Spark suggested. "In hindsight, I mean. At the time I remember being completely happy, even though I knew something weird was going on. Can a memory injection attack change your mood and opinion like that?"

"I don't know. Maybe coupled with Sample 777, it could. But if that was a memory overlay attack, we're going to have a hard time proving the One doesn't really exist. I mean... if I knew how to flag and purge false memories already, I'd have cured hereditary data rot, too..."

"Huh. #2Birds1Stone?"

"Maybe, but... I'm not exactly close to a cure. I haven't even figured out where to begin looking, for that matter..."

"Continue your research, then," Tracer suggested. "The cure for your mother's condition may very well save Netwerk from these frauds, as well. And the sooner we can put an end to this, the better."

"Tracer, it's going to take me months at best to figure this out. That's assuming I can figure it out at all! Scientists and doctors have been trying to crack this problem for generations..."

"I understand. And in the meanwhile, we'll continue to investigate Uniq and Nemesis, and find ways to sabotage this newly empowered church."

Beta glanced across the gathered masses, joyfully singing praise of the One.

"Are we sure that's the right thing to do?" she had to ask. "The church isn't exactly an ominous cloud of foreboding evil in the way Dex was. They're... misguided, sometimes, but are they really that much of a menace...?"

"It's not the church I'm concerned about. It's her," Tracer said, gesturing to the green-haired "apostle" on the stage. "Uniq, with access to a 'free' data backup service? Given her modus operandi, it's safe to assume the worst about that, and the worst about this group infiltrating the church. I suppose I should rephrase: the apostles are the ones we need to sabotage. The faithful are the victims here."

"Can we track them using your eyes, maybe? Checking where the prayers are uploading the backups?" Beta suggested.

But Tracer shook his head.

"I tried the instant they started praying, but I'm not seeing any connections," he explained. "Prayer is a system-level protocol, and thus heavily protected by the Netwerk's operating system itself. My eyes were designed for corporate espionage; all they can track are Apps and malware. ...although theoretically it might be possible to spy on system-level protocols, if I had root access."

"Root? Isn't that a myth? There's no such thing as a superuser. I mean, the One was supposedly a superuser, but..."

"Very likely a myth, yes. If we can't find their home server, we're going to have to hunt down Uniq and destroy her operations the old-fashioned way: investigation, subterfuge, and covert assault."

"So... we're doing this again, are we? Unilaterally trying to take down the 'bad guys,' as vigilantes...?"

"No moderator in Netwerk would believe us, Beta. When we fought Dex... yes, we shouldn't have acted as lone vigilantes. In hindsight I can see how obsession and vendetta drove our actions. But here, I don't see many options. The church practically runs Athena Online, the second-largest hosting nation in the world. Who's going to help us fight that?"

"Just... keep an open mind," Beta insisted. "There are always options. But for now, yes... I'll keep researching, and we'll keep an eye on this. And, uh, needless to say... nobody try praying. Or grinding for coins, considering they both use the same protocols. I know money's a bit tight since we're all basically unemployed now, but..."

Spark had to fight back a chuckle. "The day I pray for coins is the day I go star-mad," she joked. "I wouldn't touch this 'Prayer 2.0' with a ten-foot pole. And neither would Tracer."

Tracer, who stayed silent as he watched the ceremonies unfold before him.

And kept thinking back to that golden box in his fingers, and the woman who took it from him.

For once, the Wikipedia stayed closed to him. Sitting around pondering whether or not its data was good or evil was irrelevant, when facing a confirmed evil. With his obsessive reading pushed aside, he'd begun to obsess over something else entirely: the apostles of the One.

He'd opened a new MemoryPalace cluster, gathering as many media samples as he could find regarding the risen One and the women who trailed in his wake. Fortunately, the media had been all over this story, covering it from every possible angle. Except any angles that would show it to be fraudulent, of course.

Not that all of Netwerk swallowed the bait. Plenty doubted this "One," and plenty of theories abounded about who or what he was. A few even guessed as Beta did, that it was some kind of malware attack of false sensation or implanted memories... but there was no proof. Uniq knew her craft well enough not to use any widely known exploits. In the end, the crackpot theories looked too crackpot for anybody to take seriously with no real evidence... just the bitterness of atheists and evolutionary proponents.

But in this sea of files, floating through his study like so many fluttering birds, Tracer couldn't make any *connections*. No links or paths that joined related information together, establishing the patterns that would point at the truth. He couldn't trace a path to the heart of the apostles...

He couldn't focus enough to trace a path to the heart of the apostles.

Continually, his memory fluttered back to that night in DropSite. The struggle with Uniq over that golden box, his fingers coming into contact with Sample 777, and... and...

And remembering the incident did nothing to bring back the *feeling* that surged through him on touching the sample. Even the brief exposure to the One at HolyHymnal didn't compare to the raw and uncut feeling pulsing through every line of his code that night.

It was a pale echo in comparison. Spark and Beta could shrug it off, but Tracer had tasted the original, and the One's limited offering was pathetic in comparison; a tease, at best. They had no idea what was actually lurking under the surface...

A euphoric drug, that's all it was. He wasn't addicted; he had firewalls and malware protection to prevent any unauthorized attempts to install an addiction into his code. None of them were tripped by Sample 777. It was simply harmless sensory data.

And yet. *And yet...*

It was bait, of course. Prayer 2.0 had been laced with Sample 777, just as the false One had been. The faithful would pray, experience that perfect completion of purpose, and want to pray again. And again. Fools, all of them. Tracer was no fool.

He wouldn't pray. He wasn't some religious moron. He didn't need invisible strings when the free will of Programkind and his rational mindset gave him all the guidance he required. He didn't need to pray. He didn't need that sample, nor the peace it could've offered his troubled mind.

The reason he couldn't trace a path through these media samples was simple: he couldn't focus. He couldn't calm himself. In earlier years, he might have assumed the solution was to double down on his work and force himself to focus. Now, he knew that only made the problem worse.

Instead, he packed up his MemoryPalace files, and left his study behind.

On emerging from his room, he nearly collided headfirst with Beta.

The swirls of color and light that made up Beta's fanciest dress twisted and wobbled, as she pulled herself back just in time.

"Tracer! Oh. You surprised me," she spoke, catching her own breath. "Um. Everything okay?"

"I was thinking we could spend the night in," Tracer suggested. "Reading by the fireplace, or enjoying a meal...? Perhaps a game of Go?"

"Oh! Well... uh... actually, Spark already invited me out for the evening," Beta admitted. "I mean, I could cancel my plans, we were just going to go talk to an App reviewer really, but..."

More than anything, Tracer wanted Beta by his side. Someone to bring peace to his world, to pull him away from the turmoil that surrounded him this night.

"No, it's not fair to Spark to keep you from her," he spoke, instead. "You made plans, and should honor them."

"Tracer, it's not a big deal. I mean... you two kinda have to share me, and I've been seeing her more than you lately, and—"

"I insist," he stated, with nothing further to say.

And so Beta left.

Leaving him alone surrounded by the books that worried him, the memory files that wouldn't gel together, and the undeniable feeling of a hole in his life left behind by recent events. But at least Beta would be happy, and Spark as well. He was doing the right thing by them.

The time for little sermons was over. The One had been introduced to the world within the finest parish crafted by Programkind; he was now the central focus of all Church efforts. Efforts which were routed through a housewife who had suddenly become the most important figure in religious history.

Marybel had considered changing her name to "Aether" before the event, to mirror the right-hand apostle of the One from ancient times. After all, the woman named Nyx had borrowed a name from an earlier apostle, why couldn't she? But ultimately Marybel was her true and Default name, the name she wanted in lights, so she retained it. And retained those lights, pulling them away from the others whenever possible.

Not that she sought after the spotlight, not really. It was more a matter of... *appropriateness*. She had been born faithful, and been rewarded by being the first to lay eyes on the One. It was only appropriate she should speak for the One in turn.

The others, like the child or the matron or the businesswoman, they were important but not nearly as important as herself. Besides, they seemed perfectly okay with Marybel taking point, so why not take point? Why not sit at the head of the table, during this gathering within the hallowed halls of HolyHymnal?

Briefly, she considered the files open before her. One of the many advantages of marrying a social media analyst was having the finest assistant imaginable for missionary work.

"According to trends, there's still considerable doubt out there," Marybel admitted. "Apate, are you certain we can't find a way to record the One? Must He only be experienced first-hand? There's nothing in the holy text files about difficulty documenting Him..."

The woman in green shook her head, lightly amused by the suggestion.

"Actually, I'm working on technology to properly record the One at the moment," Apate (known as Uniq to her "friends") stated. While declining to mention that would likely involve Nemesis hacking into any recording devices to plant false data during the One's hypnotic trance. "At any rate, it's not surprising there's no historical precedent; those files are from the dawn of time. Technology back then was a mish-mash of primitive Apps. It's no surprise that they weren't aware of this aspect of the One. He speaks to our hearts, not our eyes—"

"Yes, as you've said. But it'd help us convert more Programs to the faith if they could experience Him indirectly, by some means..."

And Nyx spoke her mind. Which everybody listened to, despite her rarely speaking up at these gatherings, always fading into the background.

"The words of the One will carry across all of Netwerk, recorded or otherwise," she stated. "Worry not."

"...well, I'd worry *less* if we could manage a recording that would sway the heathens. But if you say you're working on the technology, I suppose we can move on to other concerns for now," Marybel agreed. "Besides, the change to the prayer protocol should be enough to convince others. Nobody but the One could have upgraded us to Prayer 2.0, and granted us Salvation. No mere Program can make such a drastic Netwerk-wide change. And speaking of Prayer 2.0..."

Marybel opened a few image windows, distributing them across the surface of the table.

"My husband pointed out a fine opportunity to me today that I think we could capitalize on," Marybel suggested. "We've always had difficulty appealing to the young. If you aren't raised faithful from the start, trends suggest you won't become faithful without the kind of concentrated missionary effort that cynical youth rejects. Fortunately a group of young missionaries based out of HolyHymnal have developed a curious meme..."

One which the girl in pink hair was squinting at, trying to make out the text. Because even printed in a nice bold font, it was generally unbelievable.

"It's gone viral within a several faithful youth communities. I think it's got legs!" Marybel insisted. "See the character in the center? That's 'Prayer-tan.' He... hmm, maybe she, I'm not sure... is the personification of prayer, invented collaboratively and spontaneously by dozens of fan artists. Technically this meme was around before the return of the One, which lends it legitimacy we can leverage to spread the good news!"

A light gagging sound interrupted Marybel's exuberance.

The youngest of the apostles, realizing she was snarking on the memes out loud, quieted down. And then spoke up, because she wasn't one to quiet down, normally.

"They're awful," she pointed out. "Completely awful. Nobody outside of HolyHymnal is gonna take this seriously; we're gonna get mocked relentlessly by cringe-based humor chans if we start pushing these as actual church propaganda."

"Communication," Marybel corrected. "Not propaganda."

"#YeahNo. It's a naked demographic grab, and that makes it propaganda. It's not gonna work. We can't rely on the past tactics of the church; this is a new church, isn't it? A new covenant. Manipulation and marketing are the old, stupid, totally broken ways—"

"And are you calling the One and his faithful *con artists*, child?"

Finally she'd risen to her feet, to properly command the table. The scrape of chair on tile, expensive physics objects purchased by HolyHymnal for maximum detail, punctuated her question.

"What do you know of the faith? You're young. You've got no wisdom to speak of," Marybel insisted. "Just because the One spoke to you doesn't make you a leader. Understanding and advancing his new covenant is best left to your elders, Nemesis."

"Excuse me? I'm a fucking apostle too, aren't I?"

"Language, young lady!"

Before the screaming could really begin... Apate/Uniq brought reason to the table.

"Nemesis, please. It could work. Hear me out on this," she suggested. "I know a thing or two about trending moods across Netwerk. We've gone through a strange time lately, with #CodeHonesty and other mobs firing up across social media. This 'Prayer-tan' represents... how to put it... *anti-cynicism*. A pure expression, from the heart. Wouldn't you agree we could use more of that, to stand against Netwerk's chaos?"

Apate put her own heart into the words, flowing reason into compassion and back into reason. Crafting them carefully, to sway both Marybel and Nemesis to Uniq's point of view.

"It's not a manufactured demographic ploy, because that demographic made it all by themselves," she continued. "It's a fan-crafted meme, and by canonizing it, we can encourage that fandom. If this works, we spread the good news further. We can empower the church to never before seen levels. And if we drive it into the ground...? Who cares? It's just a meme. Ideas are a dime a dozen."

Ideas. Dreams. Thoughts. Memories. Data files. Bits to bytes, parsed and interpreted into pure concepts...

With the gates to Tartarus opened by Prayer 2.0, the digital encoding of these ideas began to flow into the empty graves and coffins of the server. Salvation was at hand; with every prayer, those files updated themselves, establishing save and restore points for any faithful Program willing to believe.

Even as the apostles argued the merits of ideas in the halls of HolyHymnal, the starlight above their hidden home glowed fiercely with each prayer. That pale light glimmered off every sepulcher, every tomb.

Except one.

Except for a grave buried so deep within the file structure that it held no physical representation whatsoever. A folder for files best left forgotten.

As data poured like a river into Tartarus, folders yawning wide to accept the saved data, that folder remained closed. Even as folders around and above it began to fill.

And overflow.

Beta had never been to a sex club before.

It wasn't *called* a sex club, of course. Not officially, not while being hosted in Athena Online. While the faithful of Athena lacked any hard stance on sexual morality, they did have a general preference for humility and simplicity in life (such as adherence to Defaults) which suggested against garish displays of eroticism for the ero-lulz. So, the Soft Spot preferred to call itself an "adult recreational center" rather than a sex club. That way, they kept their server without ruffling too many feathers or upsetting possible customers.

But within that quiet and unassuming physical representation of a simple cube, the interior of the Soft Spot screamed out with tawdry lust and classy comforts. If a surface wasn't padded, it was upholstered in fine leather. If it wasn't leather, it was crafted of shining and gleaming polished metal. If it wasn't metal, it was flawless glass and crystal... and so on. None of it was technically needed for the simple act of mashing two avatars together to ensure physical contact with erogenous zones, but an "adult recreation center" was a business built on the back of scratching specific desires. Dressing it all up in visual delights helped sell the fantasy.

While most of the sexual acts that can be filed at best under ??miscellaneous?? were kept to back rooms, the primary floor of the club certainly had its share of couples playing with each other in the open. Couples, and couples-plus. Averting your eyes to be polite wouldn't work, as they'd invariably fall on some pocket orgy or another; the sex was omnipresent and inescapable.

For Beta, who preferred her sex quiet and comfortable and very private, walking into the middle of a hedonistic pleasure dome was something of a shock. Suddenly she regretted her decision to wear her most revealing dress, the one made entirely out of procedural light shaders and nothing more.

A nudge by her partner distracted her from that concern.

"Nobody's gonna mess with you if you don't want them to," Spark reminded her. "This place is professional; absolute consent is the law of the land. Besides, I'd burn anyone who touched you to a crisp."

"I'm not worried," Beta half-lied. "It's just... it's all a bit... much, isn't it?"

Approaching the bar, the only part of the facility that wasn't entirely dedicated to unique variants of copulation, Spark took a stool and snapped for a drink. Being a card-carrying VIP, her preferred order appeared in her hand instantly.

"Funny, I'd always thought of the Soft Spot as one of the tamer joints," Spark suggested, swirling the drink around in its glass a little to mix it properly. "I mean, I'm barely hot and bothered looking at this flesh array. You should try some of the Chanarchy's clubs, if you want the wild side. The Blinds are my favorite; you can't see a thing in there. It's all done by feel. ...huh. Y'know, you might fit in perfectly there. Wanna visit sometime?"

"I don't know. It's not really my thing to play with strangers," Beta replied, taking the next barstool in the row. "I prefer my sex quiet, private, and intimate. You're the ero-venturer type, not me."

"So says the one about to sell a sex toy app she's spent a year perfecting through rigorous testing. Who do you think's gonna be downloading that App? Strangers. Kinda kinky in and of itself, that level of intimacy and trust..."

"Yes, but... that's different. I'm not really *involved*. I mean, I'm coding it, sure, but..."

"And your elegant code is going to be tickling the fancy of thousands of the ero-venturous by the end of the month," Spark reminder her, with a grin. "My little Beta, masked mistress of a thousand anonymous orgasms!"

"Spark...!"

"Okay, okay, I'll stop teasing," Spark half-lied. "And... look, if you don't wanna release SparklePop, we can call this meeting off. It's up to you."

Briefly, Beta considered the offer. In that context, it certainly felt uncomfortable. But the original reasons behind steeling herself for tonight's outing, those remained in place, didn't they?

"No... no. This is important," she said. "I'm taking back my life, little by little, since #CodeHonesty. And that means admitting that yes, I enjoy sex toy Apps, and there's nothing wrong with that. It doesn't make me a slut like that hashtag tried to paint me as, it makes me a healthy adult! If I can help other users do the same..."

"Good karma, and a good paycheck."

"Well, technically speaking, we can't *sell* it due to the open source code we built SparklePop upon. I'm not going to misattribute public code and open *that* folder of worms again. We're launching it as a free App, with a crowdfunding option to maintain ongoing development!"

"Damn, girl, you make the intersection of copyright law and economics sound so fucking hot."

"And... now you're trying to make me more comfortable by joking around."

"Is it working, then?"

To which Beta offered both a smile, and a kiss on the cheek.

"Kinda," she admitted. "So... is Miki already here, somewhere? I'm eager to meet her, after all the stories you've told! Uh, but I'd rather not start picking through the piles looking for her..."

Fortunately, Miki had already arrived.

The tall man slid on up to the pair, assuming one of the stools next to them. This sort of friendly invasion of one's personal space would've been questionable in any club, including the Soft Spot, if not for Spark recognizing the telltale grace with which he moved.

"Miki," she recognized. "I like the new avatar. One of your husband Maki's suits, isn't it?"

"We're spending a week in each other's skin," Miki confirmed, gesturing a hand down the length of his exposed and nicely sculpted abs. "It's quite a sensation, having a new avatar with new erogenous zones. We're also thinking of doubling up as the same avatar next week, to explore the nature of symmetry. Hello, Beta! It's good to meet you."

Name : Maki and Miki

Home : Curiosity/Chanarchy

Org : App Review Bloggers

"Ah... hello!" Beta spoke, taking a bit longer to get used to the idea. "It's good to meet you. Um. Hello. ...you're wearing your husband's avatar? Really?"

"New experiences are what keeps our blog fresh," Miki insisted. "I hope you two don't mind, but I invited some friends along to discuss your App..."

Which is how Spark became aware of the others who were approaching. Not with weapons drawn or anything scary like that; if anything they looked like a troupe of roaming cosplayers, wearing togas and sandals and little wings. Each also bore a crown of flowers, wreathing their heads, rotating slowly while shifting through a variety of pastel hues.

"Spark, Beta, these are representatives from HolyHymnal's youth community," Miki introduced, raising a glass to them. (Like Spark, he had VIP status and that meant drinks-on-demand.) "They're keenly interested in promoting erotic Apps for the faithful, and wish to become your patrons."

Immediately, Spark's defensive instincts triggered.

"You didn't say anything to me before about the Church of One getting involved in this," Spark pointed out, in a decidedly less playful tone than before.

"Ahh... I'm sorry. My mistake," Miki admitted. "Friends, Spark has a... rather storied past with the church. Her mother is something of a religious conservative."

"And all of you customized your avatars," Spark realized, adding to her confusion. "Cute wings you got there. Very non-Default. How're you Churchies if you're messing with customizations...?"

Of the small group from HolyHymnal, one of them stepped forward. Fluttered forward, really, on two tiny wings that served as a minor physics hack. On strict servers that sort of tweaking to the physics simulation would get you the boot, but moderators in the Soft Spot were fairly lax about anything that made playtime more interesting.

"There's a wide spectrum of what constitutes customization, Miss Winder," the lead angelic figure spoke. "Our community are religious progressives. We believe with all our hearts in the One and try to lead lives of humility, charity, compassion, and faith. And yes, we wear our Defaults, even now. But... functional avatar accessories such as wings are not a zero. If they were, why would any of us be allowed to wear clothing? Is clothing not a modification of one's Default, in a manner of speaking?"

"Preaching to the choir," Spark suggested. "I've always hated the rule of Defaults."

"I see. And do you hate the church that created the rule...?"

Briefly, the memory of *pink* fluttered in Spark's mind. Pink flames, bursting with youthful anger and rage.

"Not anymore," she spoke, truthfully. "Once, yeah. When I was young and stupid and full of pride. But I've seen evil since then, *real* evil, and a disagreement over dogma doesn't even rank on that scale. ...but *you* guys want a bunch of sex toys? Seriously?"

"We feel they promote the virtue of humility," the angel spoke. "Each of us has personal needs, and satisfying them with erotic Apps is hardly a zero. It allows for a quiet and personal love of the gift given to us by the One. Satisfying one's needs in garish and flamboyant public fashion, that's more questionable."

"But... you came to a sex club. The living embodiment of garish and flamboyant public fashion."

"And we came to discuss Apps, not to indulge. Not to condemn, but also not to indulge. Understand that interpreting the virtues is a highly variable and personal matter... we don't speak for all of HolyHymnal, or all of the Church of One. This is simply how our little group sees things. And we see your SparklePop App as quite promising, Miss Winder, Miss Projkit. We'd like to join your crowdfunding efforts, and help promote them."

Leading them to a strange roadblock, one the smiling angels couldn't see.

The resurgent Church of One was their new enemy, for lack of a more appropriate word. Spark and Beta exchanged a quick knowing glance of concern, both realizing that hitching their ride to the very organization they were seeking to topple could... well, it wasn't entirely clear what it *could* result in, but those results would not likely be pleasant.

"It's... not like we can stop anybody from adding to our crowdfunding pot," Beta reasoned aloud, to try and discuss it with Spark without openly discussing it with Spark. "It's an open source product anybody can download and compile, and an open funding model anybody can contribute to. So... if they want to be patrons, they can be. Technically."

"We're not gonna be tailoring the thing to the Church's needs or anything like that," Spark added.

The cherub raised his hands a little, in mock-surrender.

"We wouldn't dream of asking you to," he insisted. "You're the designers; your design, your vision, is what it is. We're not looking to impose, just help enable your dreams. And, perhaps, get early review copies? Like you're offering Miki and Maki. We can help with your product launch, if we have our blog updated on day one with a review."

A Messenger window popped up in Beta's heads up display.

"Not digging this," Spark spoke, privately. *"If we help indirectly empower a religious group while we're cutting the legs out from under the apostles..."*

"We can't avoid all involvement with the Church," Beta pointed out. *"It's everywhere. You have members of the faithful in your Peep stream subscribers, don't you? We'll just keep our direct involvement to a minimum. Besides, it may help us in the long run to support a group of faithful progressives!"*

"I think we can get you review copies!" Beta agreed, speaking aloud. "Ah, as we'd give any review blog, I mean."

The cherub's already impossibly-cute smile raised several degrees.

"Wonderful! Simply wonderful. Thank you, Miss Projkit," he spoke, clasping his hands together in delight. "I look forward to sampling your craft. Now, my friends, let us pray to commemorate the launch of this new endeavor."

"That's not really necessary..."

But the angels were already bowing their heads, falling into the "coin grinding" trance of prayer.

Ideas. Dreams. Thoughts. Memories. Data files. Bits to bytes, parsed and interpreted into pure concepts...

"Bullshit!"

Nyx's little smile didn't budge an inch.

"It's how things must be, for now," she insisted. "We can't push to revoke the rule of Defaults. Not until the One is universally accepted—"

The eyes of Nemesis glowed with pink flames, coloring the dim light from the stars above Tartarus.

"The One is never going to be universally accepted. I don't care how many feeps you put in the prayer protocol, what sensory bribes you offer, or how many superstar godhead rock shows you have," Nemesis said. "There's always gonna be a bunch of Programs who won't believe."

"Of course. God created the integers; everything else is the work of man. The absolutes of Zero and One are unfeasible for flawed creatures such as you and I."

"So why not? Why not revoke the rule of Defaults in our One's next sermon?"

"Because it's too *soon*, my young Nemesis. Yes, we will never have absolute control over Netwerk. But we don't even have absolute control over our church, not yet. Until we do... we can't risk offending the faithful or causing a schism. They've been told for centuries that any avatar modification is a zero. We can't turn them around on that until after they've accepted our One's new covenant."

"You promised me. You *promised* me we'd be remaking the Church, not just empowering it."

"And we shall! In due time. When the dawn of the new age has broken, when our guiding star has risen to its zenith—"

"Fuck this. I'm gonna go punch something," Nemesis declared, cutting her off.

In a brief flicker of distorted bits, she zoned out of Tartarus, no doubt off to pick a fight with the rest of Netwerk.

With a heavy sigh... Nyx turned back to her other apostle, the one too busy poring over analysis windows of incoming data streams to pay attention to the younger apostle's temper tantrum.

At least, too busy to pay specific attention. She got the gist of it just fine.

"Nemesis is going to be a problem in the long term," Uniq pointed out. "She's too impatient for this sort of con job. Putting her in the same room with her mother is a recipe for disaster; she could ruin everything with one wrong word spoken. How about I could wipe her memory? Remake her into whatever you need her to be. Just say the word, and I'll get it done..."

"You'll do nothing of the sort," Nyx stated. "You'll sit there and monitor the prayer stream, as you have been instructed to do. Leave Nemesis to me."

"You seriously trust her not to destroy what you're trying to build...?"

With the tiniest shrug of her shoulders, Nyx let the concern fall away.

"Mmm. Let's just say I trust her to carry out her part in this. After that... we'll see. For now, we need her to guard us against our enemies."

"And you need me to make sure your hack to Prayer 2.0 is stable. Which it is. All this lovely data, all these identities... memories upon memories, neatly tucked away in Tartarus. ...I wonder, why are you going through all that effort? I suppose you *could* run a null of a coin farm off these ghost images; just activate them all and slave those poor bastards to prayer mode..."

Nyx's nose wrinkled in distaste. "Absolutely not. First of all, I'd like faith to be a choice rather than a compulsion; that is the nature of my chosen compromise. Second, as powerful as Tartarus may be within the cloud, it's not powerful enough to actively run that many simultaneous live Programs. Distributed servers loan themselves well to cold storage, not to massive crowds of living persons. Therefore, archived souls in cold tombs will have to suffice. Does this satisfy you?"

"Actually, I'm relieved to hear that. Coin farms are repulsive. They prey on the weak and helpless to support the lazy and the greedy."

"Really? This coming from a notorious identity thief...?"

"Oh, I'm greedy, but I'm hardly *lazy*. And my prey are usually criminals and dirtbags. Usually. But no, I'm not claiming a moral high ground... just making sure you aren't claiming one while setting yourself up a machine that prints money."

"I print faith," Nyx spoke, simply. "That is all I require. My storage cloud is simply a gift for the faithful, nothing more."

"Yes, about that. I'm *very* curious as to where you got this cloud technology," Uniq spoke, while studying her patron's reaction to the question. "Given how much you needed me to code myself for our efforts, I don't think you made it yourself... I'd say someone provided you the packages. May I ask who...?

But Nyx remained passive.

"Let's just say for some, faith must be compulsory," she spoke, without a single wrinkle worth note.

"Interesting. Well, suit yourself. I suppose it doesn't matter who you got it from or what became of him, so long as it's all—"

Judder. The strange tearing effect of a sudden drop in frame rate, the physical simulation unable to keep up with a burst of computation that hogs all resources. Briefly, the stars above glowed brighter and brighter, overwhelming all of Tartarus, flooding it with levels of bloom and flare that blinded and burned all they touched...

Nyx, normally so sure-footed and composed, staggered. She actually staggered, despite having long ago stripped out most of her senses, in favor of a more simplified codebase. And when she did regain her balance... so did Tartarus, all operations resuming normal status.

Less fortunate was Uniq, who was knocked offline by the experience. She needed a quick reboot, which Nyx provided.

"What. *What* was that," Nyx demanded to know, before Uniq could get her bearings.

"I... I'm not sure," Uniq admitted, quickly returning to her analysis windows. "I'm checking. Something with Prayer 2.0, I think, it... yes. A buffer overrun. A quick burst of incoming data which accidentally caused a stack overflow..."

"Are the souls intact? Is everything secure? And what is *that*, exactly...?"

The line graphs on her windows were flowing in the opposite direction. Uniq shut down the Apps and restarted them, but the data log wasn't corrupt, and wasn't lying. It was what it was.

"Some data went... *backwards* through the protocol," Uniq confirmed. "A restoration of saved Program data for someone who hadn't actually died. Well. I guess that answers the question of whether it was a good idea or not to launch Prayer 2.0 before you finished debugging it. Another problem we can thank Nemesis for..."

Immediately, Nyx started opening windows of her own.

"Which files," she asked, posing the question more to all of Tartarus around herself rather than to Uniq. "Which files were restored, which files, which files..."

To her relief, the data backflow consisted of discordant fragments of eighteen different backup files. A single person did not experience rebirth, but rather, a useless mashup of different people which no doubt would crash immediately on activation. A row of eighteen icons blazed in the window, belonging to each individual affected by the restoration.

And one of those icons represented a full 27% of the total lost data. An icon previously buried in an inaccessible file, buried deep where it could no longer stand in her way...

Uniq took interest in the icon that took Nyx's interest.

"Well well well. Now *that* is curious," Uniq spoke, studying the lines intently...

With a flick of her shawl, Nyx cleanly backspaced her technician, erasing her before she had a chance to make a live backup through Prayer 2.0.

Only after erasing that offensive icon did Nyx restore Uniq to working order.

"There has been a system error. Your runtime was lost; I've restored you from your most recent backup. Now we need to trace the missing data immediately," Nyx told Uniq, forming each word carefully. "Also, find out where Nemesis ran off to. We may require her to be an assassin this evening."

As a child, Spark would often pray. Not by choice, of course, but at the behest of the all-controlling matriarch of her household. While the faithful often described the sensation as floating in a space of brilliant starlight, wrapped in the One's love for all that lives and loves, Spark just saw it as a creepy dream App she wanted nothing to do with. Nevertheless, she would set the timer and go into a prayer trance for the minimum five minutes a night demanded of her by her mother, and try to shake the feeling off immediately afterwards.

The representatives of HolyHymnal's young faithful hopefully hadn't set their timers for longer than that. She'd tried poking one of them, with no response; a secular coin-grinding App would allow for things like proximity or audio checks to break the trance, but no such luck for those directly accessing Prayer 2.0. Things would get awkward if they were standing around, hands clasped in prayer, long after closing time at the Soft Spot. Someone would have to cart their avatars out of here until they chose to awaken.

Rolling into the second minute, Spark considered poking one of them a few times.

"Sooo... how's the blog going?" she asked Miki, trying to keep the conversation going despite the arrangement of eerily silent monks around them.

"Quite well, quite well. We've actually noticed an uptick in visitors lately," Miki spoke, enjoying his drink, not the least bit concerned about the cosplaying cherubs. "People seeking erotic Apps as an alternative outlet for their needs, rather than seeking other Programs. It seems to match a downward trend in dating service usage. People withdrawing into solitude more than companionship..."

"More business for you, then?"

"Perhaps, but worrying. As you know, Maki and I feel erotic Apps improve our relationship, allowing us to explore each other. We write with that angle in mind, but... it seems a lot of the fire's gone out in Netwerk this year, and for no obvious reason."

Beta made her thoughts heard on this... trying to suppress any obvious worry in her voice.

"But... that's good, right?" she suggested. "The social sphere had gotten quite, um, *heated* before that. It's just a matter of cooler heads prevailing, yes? Doesn't have to be something negative..."

"Isolation's not good for the soul, Miss Projkit," Miki spoke, shaking his head. "We are not Apps, sitting in the dark, crunching numbers for eternity. We are Programs. We're social creatures by default; that some are choosing to withdraw, that they've lost their passion for life, is quite concerning to me—"

The Soft Spot was designed, as many business that relied on discretion and privacy were designed, such that Programs couldn't arbitrarily connect to the server right in the middle of the building. The front door existed for a reason, to act as a series of visible and invisible filters, ensuring no malware or malcontents got in. Simply popping into being right in the middle of the club was unheard of.

And yet that's exactly what happened, as a brief and silent flash of light heralded this new arrival. He landed right in the middle of the praying semicircle, his tiny wings flapping briefly before failing to keep him aloft. With a soft *thump*, he landed on the plush velvet carpeting, right on his rear.

In addition to having rules against connecting right into the club, the Soft Spot also had rules about using avatars under the Default appearance age of eighteen years. And here this new Program was, flaunting a choir boy body that couldn't be more than ten years old, as Default measurements went. All rosy cheeks and big bright eyes, underneath a crown of roses...

Actually, he looked just like the costumes the praying young folks were wearing.

"Kinda late to the party, aren't you?" Spark pointed out, being the first to react. (As she normally was, in any situation.) "And only half dressed for it. Put on an older avatar before someone bounces you, man... or if you *are* a kid, run along home, 'kay?"

The child... blinked. Gradually. One eye at a time, out of sync, a flickering glitch temporarily slowing the reaction in his right eye. After two more tries, he got the hang of it.

"Such prayer. Many confusion. Wow?" he offered. "No, wait. No. Yes? No. Scrambled, remixed, mashed up. Diagnostics online, situation normal, all fucked up. I am error. Say your prayers, kids, and the One will reward you! Humility is a virtue, don't stand out, don't be strange don't change don't shift don't evolve don't don't don't DON'T ĐÕ̃Ɖ'Ţ—"

A second wave of glitches washed across the surface of his avatar, as he briefly deadlocked.

"Yeah, okay, we need a bouncer now," Spark suggested, raising her hand to snap her fingers for one.

Only to have Beta hold that hand down.

"Wait," she spoke. "Wait. I think he could have memory rot. The glitches are similar; he's frozen and missing time. He'll be fine, he just needs a moment to recover..."

"Memory rot? More like he's star-mad. Clearly too much prayer melting down his brain."

"Either way, he needs help. The least we can do is give him some time to come around again before some moderator kicks him out on the street, can't we?"

"Yeah, well... we're also attracting the bad kind of attention here," Spark replied quietly, glancing sideways at the strange looks being cast their way. "Okay. Okay, fine. I'm VIP, I can get us a private room instance. Miki, you wait out here with the choir invisible, okay? See if they know anything once they stop licking the One's feet."

With another studying look at the frozen child... Miki slowly nodded.

"This is highly weird," he recognized. "And highly weird is more your thing than mine, love. Go on, I'll cover for you."

Spark's private sexpit was slightly more comfortable for Beta than the nonstop bacchanalian festival of the main room. It had more swings than a playground and the bed apparently could unfold itself into some strange framework of indescribable purpose, but at least they were alone in here. Alone with their strange and completely deadlocked new friend.

"Folks saw us leave with this guy," Spark pointed out. "I really don't wanna get a rep as someone who drags child avatars off to a VIP room..."

"I know, I'm sorry, but... it's better that we do this out of sight. He needs time to unfreeze. It won't be long, and then we can be seen leaving with him in good faith, if you like."

Carefully, they hauled the boy onto the bed. And waited.

"He could seriously be star-mad," Spark suggested. "I knew this homeless guy once who spent all day grinding for coins and all night just staring at the skybox. That's how it happens, you get these glitches in your visual input, pinpoints of light like stars..."

"Well... you grew up in the Church of One. Why don't more of the faithful go star-mad?"

"You gotta seriously overdose on coin grinding to get stuck in trances and see stars. Like, more than eight hours a day. Nobody does that, not even the faithful, unless they're totally desperate for money or completely around the bend with devotion. Given this guy's dressed up like Prayer-tan, I'm guessing he's gone around the bend eight or nine times..."

"Prayer-tan?"

"It's from Tracer's research notes on the Church of One. Some kinda art meme, designed to promote prayer. This guy? Seems to be a fan, to the point where I could see him going totally star-bonkers. And you *sure* he has memory rot? How long does it take to break free of a deadlock, if so?"

"It varies. Seconds, minutes... hours. Usually just minutes, though..."

"And... you've been locking like that all this time? How'd you hide it from us?"

Which meant continuing the one conversation Beta didn't want to continue.

After leaving her mother at the cold storage facility, Beta resolved to tell her lovers about the memory rot building within her own code. They'd agreed not to keep secrets anymore, not after Tracer's secret life nearly ruined everything they had been working towards—and technically Beta was in denial rather than lying, refusing to admit the truth even to herself. But once she knew that truth, they had to know, as well.

Not that she liked talking about it. Not that she wanted to linger on the curse that was going to cause her to slowly descend into madness and death, barring some miracle cure.

"I hid it from myself as well," Beta explained. "Telling myself the little slips were nothing important. Even when... even when I'd completely screw up in the middle of a game. But there comes a point where you can't hide it or hide *from* it..."

"So... you're gonna cure it, right? And that cure could also help us expose the One?"

"In theory. In practice... I don't know, Spark. I'm being honest with you, I really don't know if I can cure it. I'm just one indie coder, one little App designer, and this is a problem huge corporations have thrown money at for years—"

The boy sitting bolt upright with a terrified scream interrupted the conversation Beta didn't want to have in the first place.

"NO! No, she has to stop!" the boy cried out. "She's going to ruin the entire system—!"

"Whoa!" Spark called out, waving a hand to grab the child's attention. "Whoa. *Whoa.* You're at an eleven right now, okay? I need you to take it down to a three. Settle down, wait a minute, get your shit together. *Then* we'll talk. Okay?"

Slowly... the child sagged back to sitting on the edge of the bed, the alarm draining away.

"Then. Then. Than. Than. Yes. Okay," he agreed. "Okay. All good things. Patience is a virtue. Say your prayers and dream your wishes to the One, be good and pure and avoid the Zeroes of a life well wasted. Dogma and ideology and— no, don't pray to the One. It's useless. The One doesn't exist. She made him up. It's all lies..."

Spark tried to ignore the disconcerting twitching of his avatar as he flipped back and forth between ideologies.

"Sure don't sound like you're with HolyHymnal," she noted.

"HolyHymnal," the boy recognized. "Yes. Yes. That's me, I'm one of them. I'm Prayer-tan. Embodiment of prayer. Memetic fan creation. Corporate mascots, collective dreams, cute faces on terrible concepts. That and more. More than that. Than than than. Many head, much memory, wow..."

"Staaaar-mad..." Spark hummed under her breath. "Okay, so. You're not 'Prayer-tan.' That's a meme, not a person. Probably a good place to start, in terms of helping you sort your shit out, whoever you are..."

"The collective unconsciousness gives form to shapeless data, press start to continue, jump and be reborn," Prayer-tan suggested. "Virtual life is dynamically generated from base algorithms. Many dream, much imagination, wow. She has to be stopped. The One doesn't exist. Say your prayers! Don't say your prayers! Say your prayers! Don't say your prayers...!"

"Well, which is it?"

"Both? I've got both in my head," the boy said, pointing to his forehead for emphasis. "I feel such love, this burning love for the One, I *want* to believe insert poster of UFO here, but I also know it's an utter fraud. It's too much. I'm trying to keep too many contradictory notions in my head at once, tea and no tea, fragmented files rotting away..."

"Memory rot?" Beta guessed, hopeful this was something as simple and depressing as her own condition.

"What? No. No. Maybe? I can't tell. Similar? It's the inputs. I've got too many *inputs*...!"

And with surprising speed, he grasped Spark's jacket, tugging hard at one sleeve.

"Cloud. Get me to a cloud server," he begged her. "You smell like clouds. Take me to a cloud server, somewhere secret, somewhere safe. Three cloud servers, three enabled by the technology of Linklyn. Are you the third option? Please, get me away from her cloud, away from her minions, the apostles. We have to stop her before it's too—"

And deadlocked again.

"Okay, I'm starting to freak out a little myself," Spark admitted, quietly. "How in the null does he know about cloud servers...?"

"And the One doesn't exist," Beta repeated.

"So he says, yes."

"No, I mean... we *know* the One doesn't exist, it's some kind of scam by Uniq and her friends," she explained. "But nobody would believe us. Nobody except... him, apparently. He specifically said *she* has to be stopped! This boy might know something that can help us, Spark!"

"Or he could be insane. Or dangerous. Or insanely dangerous."

"Or he could be insane," Beta was was willing to admit. "Or even working for the enemy. ...I hate that word, *enemy*, but... we can't ignore this as a possible lead. We owe it to ourselves to dig in a bit deeper and see where this goes."

Spark considered the frozen boy. Again.

"I've got nothing better to do tonight," she agreed. "And this *does* have the flavor of something that's bugnuts crazy. Like Miki said, bugnuts crazy is sort of our thing."

"Right! Um. I think we need your brother for this, though. He's the interrogator type, he can figure out connections we can't. And... he did say he needed to visit a cloud server, and implied it'd make him more coherent..."

"What? No!" Spark declared, making an X with her arms. "Forget it! We're not dragging him back to Floating Point. We can't risk letting any potential baddies in through our front door!"

"I can sandbox him, and fix him to a point in space. Tracer can keep his Kill-9 ready. We'll take precautions, Spark. But one way or another... we need to know what he knows. Even if he knows nothing, even if he's just... broken. We can't let an opportunity slip. I mean... do *you* have any ideas how to stop the Church of One? If not, what can it hurt?"

Another eyeful of the boy. Spark had been sizing him up ever since he arrived... trying to determine if he was friend or foe, danger or endangered. And still she had no solid lock.

Normally she could figure a person out quickly enough, parse their intent through body language. But he was so glitchy, so strangely strange, that all her usual checks for tells were coming up short. If he was a weird little grenade that could explode upon them in an instant, they couldn't possibly risk this.

But... if he was in trouble, if he was suffering, if they could help...

Once upon a time, they risked bringing Beta through their front door, despite not knowing who she was at heart. She could've been a criminal Uniq was aiding in escape. She could've been anything. And so could this boy.

"I'm calling ahead to get things prepared first," Spark decided, opening a Messenger link to her brother. "If this guy is more foe than friend, I want to be ready to gank him."

Normally, Nyx was calm in times of crisis. She'd faced heathens and opposition ideologies and even the dark messenger of the sociologist's archive, all with a quiet smile and soothing words. As the world fell apart around her, she remained a rock amidst the waves, unyielding.

Today, she felt that rock starting to shake loose amidst the storm.

The young Program with the pink hair in her group Messenger window had brought no good news whatsoever.

"*Near as I can tell, he's in the wind,*" Nemesis replied. "*I checked around the server Uniq traced this guy to, asked around the club, but they say he left with Spark and Beta. Guessing they ran for it before I even got here.*"

"And you're certain it was them?" Nyx asked. "Absolutely certain...?"

"It was easily enough to get some solid truth out of the witnesses; I put on my apostle disguise. The Prayer-tan fanboys were more than happy to help out Apostle Nemesis instead Super Awesome Riot Grrl Nemesis."

The tiny twitch underneath Nyx's left eye betrayed her anger.

"...I requested that you keep a low profile on this," she spoke, after a dangerous pause. "And yet you used your apostle avatar? In public, as a church official, to ask about one of our enemies...?"

"So? Who cares?" Nemesis asked. *"Look, you told me to track down this supposedly super-dangerous dude, so I tracked him down. You don't like me throwing the weight of the One around? I don't like us NOT throwing the weight of the One around to stomp out the Default rule. So hey, that's #OneForOne on neither of us getting what we want."*

With great effort, Nyx declined to follow up on that taunt. Instead, she chose to continue her investigative questioning.

"And this stranger, did the eyewitnesses say anything about him?" Nyx asked.

"Yeah. Supposedly it was the living embodiment of Prayer-tan. Y'know, the stupid meme that Mom wanted us to push? Your guy was dressed exactly like him. Had to get that from the bartenders and bouncers, though, the Churchies who were loitering around the place apparently completely missed that part of the fun. Look, what's the big deal? Why's a cherubic fanboy got you pissing your panties?"

"Lay low and wait for further instructions. And don't use your apostle avatar again in public."

Before she could say something unkind, Nyx closed the window.

Unfortunately, she couldn't take some time to center herself and relax. Now she had another annoyance to deal with, on top of the grand-scale danger she was already facing.

Uniq hadn't ignored that little exchange, despite pretending to be completely focused on the task of analyzing how this could have happened... and how to keep it from happening again.

"I'm also curious why this is priority one," Uniq spoke. "Who's this new foe, exactly? Beyond a jumbled mess of memories. I assume there's some core identity we should be concerned with, or else you wouldn't be so concerned..."

Realizing she couldn't get away with a non-answer, not if she wanted Uniq's compliance, Nyx began to spin her story.

"I knew him long, long ago. A bright child, of ambition and charisma... such potential," she spoke. "Much as I saw in you and Nemesis, I saw in him a drive to succeed in one's endeavors. And much like you and Nemesis, there was also the darkness and danger that comes with that power. Sadly, while you have worked with me loyally as apostles... ultimately, he did not feel the same way. He rejected the path, and had to be stopped."

"And... you kept a backup of him. That seems unwise, Nyx."

"All Programs are children of the system," Nyx reminded her cohort. "All are beloved, even him. Those who disappoint me are still part of our world and deserving of that respect. I've many enemies buried in these crypts, to rest until they can find their true place in the order of things."

Uniq considered the story... then returned to her analysis windows. "I'm going to assume there's more to the tale than this, but I suppose that'll do for now," she said. "Let's focus on the task at hand. Your little friend appears to have become snarled up in the backup data for a few dozen members of the HolyHymnal youth community. There was a buffer overrun, and a body was created based on their shared vision of who Prayer-tan was supposed to be."

"Ahh. Frankenstein's monster."

"Who...?"

"I suppose like all monsters, he'll need to be destroyed. I'd hoped we could lay claim to the faithful in a bloodless coup, that I could spare Nemesis the moral crisis of murder, but..."

"How do you propose to do that, if your enemy fled to Floating Point?" Uniq asked. "We've got no keys to that particular kingdom. And no doubt you're concerned about what secrets he may be leaking to our would-be antagonists, meanwhile..."

Nyx's tight-lipped frown suggested that Uniq had indeed called out her concern.

"It is what it is," Nyx spoke. "There is nothing we can do but cut the head off the serpent should it ever emerge again."

Flicking her eyes over the open data windows, Uniq considered the problem before them.

The solution lay before her, plain as day. Something only she could see, given her expertise on the subject.

"I believe I can stop him," Uniq declared. "No matter where he is. It's quite simple, actually. He's a byproduct of other people's memories of Prayer-tan; they've been accidentally flagged as *his* memories."

"I'm aware of that. A bug in Prayer 2.0, one I need to fix immediately—"

"Let's not be too hasty. Before you seal up the hole... let's make good use of it. I don't think we *have* to break into Floating Point or even track him down to put a stop to this. All I need to do is make one little visit to one little chan..."

When his runtime resumed, he found himself completely unable to move and held at gunpoint.

A tremendous relief, compared to before.

"I'm in the clouds," the memetic cherub realized. "The original clouds, before the rage, before the night. Good. Good. She can't come here, can't kill me again. Hello. Lovely day for prayer! Let's all bow our heads and pay respects to the One because the One doesn't exist and existence is a lie and nothing is as it should be—"

The young man with the malware in his hands interrupted before the angelic boy could ramble any further.

"Understand you are here against my better judgment," Winder/Tracer spoke. "And if you take any hostile action against me or my family, I will terminate your process and abandon you to the streets of the Chanarchy. Is this one rule clear?"

"I shall not tell a lie," the boy promised, holding up his fingers in a OneScout salute.

"Good, because I have questions. Who are you, exactly?"

Despite being fixed to a static point, the boy could extend his wings, giving them a light flap. They felt perfectly at home on his back, as if he'd always had them, despite not physically existing in this form until an hour ago.

"I'm an assemblage of broken dreams and wayward wishes," he spoke. "I am what wants to believe so desperately, but knows it cannot."

"Not really interested in riddles, 'Prayer-tan.'"

"I'm sorry. Riddles are all I can offer. Bad command or file name; abort, retry, fail," he suggested, with an apologetic bow of the head. "I am error. This protocol is the best I can manage without repairs and purging of external data connections."

Now, the woman at his side spoke up.

"I think he has something akin to memory rot," Beta explained. "And before you ask, like I told Spark, there's no cure yet. I'm not a multi-million coin research company."

"Praying for coins will ruin Netwerk," the boy spoke, immediately.

Keen on getting on with this interrogation, Tracer decided to pick at that thread a bit.

"We're aware of that already. Uniq has access to the stored backups of thousands of Programs now, possibly millions. Given her past history, Netwerk is absolutely in danger."

"Uniq? What is a Uniq? No. Nyx. Nyx is the threat. The mother of apostles, the guiding star."

Briefly, Tracer's weapon wobbled as he remembered the woman in purple. Specifically, the golden cube she'd taken from him, the perfection of purpose that still made him tremble...

"You've met Nyx, haven't you?" the boy spoke, recognizing the recognition. "It's her. Nyx, the real Nyx, from the dawn of time. She picked the apostles, she spoofed the One. She is the same Nyx as the Nyx that was and forever will be. Purpose complete, lulled to sleep. I thought us safe from her after that, but a system agent cannot be uninstalled. We will never be rid of her."

"So... you're saying she's hundreds of years old? How is that possible—ahhh. Data backup. A 'health plan,' as Uniq once put it."

"Sleeping while the light is green, waking when the light flickers and fades. Sleeping so very, very long. I am like she is, say your prayers, I am an ancient, I am most of an ancient, say your prayers and obey your parents and make no prideful code adaptations. I wish it was true. Life would be so much simpler if it were all true..."

"And you are...? The majority of you, I mean. Not the faithful side."

The boy searched for the word, desperately grappling for it. Difficult, with the multitude of other voices pouring words into his mind, demanding he speak in favor of their ideals instead of his own. Their names blocked out his own... but somewhere deep, he grasped, finding something that seemed to fit well.

"I am... I am a child. I am an ancient. I am malware of justice, to defend Netwerk's heart. I know the truth of the apostles. Extrapolating. Extrapolating. ...parameters match Thanatos, former apostle of the One," he decided.

Tracer's reaction was immediate. He grasped the handle of his Kill-9 firmly, locking it on target.

"Messenger sidebar discussion, please," he spoke to the others.

In relative silence, they talked across channels the wayward angel could not listen to.

Beta seemed puzzled by the sudden jump in tension. "*I'm not really up on my church lore. Who's Thanatos?*" she asked.

"*The second least known apostle next to Nyx,*" Tracer explained. "*Everyone knows Aether, right hand of the One. Plenty know of Philotes, because her parts of the text are the sexier parts. Geras was old and boring but enough of his speeches were transcribed for him to count as important. Eris also hogs the spotlight with all her wild-eyed crazy sermons... but in the background lurked Hypnos and Thanatos. The peacebringer and his twin brother, the enforcer of holy justice.*"

"*God's hired killer,*" Spark summarized. "*Boogeyman and paladin rolled into one.*"

"*If this Program isn't simply insane, he's at least in part the restored backup data of the first murderer. Thanatos designed the first malware, weapons used to defend the church against those who sought to tear down the One. That's who you two just brought under our roof.*"

"But... but he could be wrong. He said he was extrapolating his identity from the mess inside his mind. So far he's proven harmless, hasn't he? He's lost and confused, like a child..."

"Dex took the form of a child as well, remember. If this little boy is also a deadly weapon, I'm keen to kick him out the door immediately."

"Okay, hold on. He's been trying to help us despite his glitches, to be honest about who he is and what dangers Nyx represents. We should hear him out before doing anything drastic. Let me talk to him."

"Fine. But my original warning stands; one hostile action and I'm opening fire."

"You're afraid."

The boy's voice brought all three back around to the room, away from their private channel.

"It's okay. I'd be afraid of me too. Enough of me is afraid of me already," Thanatos spoke. "I'm composed of the dreams of the faithful, and they fear Thanatos as well. I feel his shape within them, showing me who I must have been. The purger of Zeroes, with his scythe of justice. But they have no reason to fear. I know the true face of the Great Zero... and it is Nyx. Which is no doubt why she killed me in the first place."

"What's Nyx trying to accomplish?" Beta asked, taking control of the interrogation. "You clearly wanted to warn someone about her! Help us understand, and maybe we can do something about this..."

"I... don't know what she did," Thanatos admitted. "Fraud, deception. I feel the shape of it. But my memory files are mislinked, jumbled, ruined. Her plan, her plan to save Netwerk, fraud, lies, Netwerk can't be saved by prayer, she's ruining us—say your prayers, let the One's holy light fill—lies, it's all lies, Nyx lied to me and lied to all of us—fear the One, love the One—can't—can't can't can't can't ¢âŋ't çãÑ'Ŧ. Can't remember. Sorry. I'm so sorry. I want to help! I don't want to be hated and feared. I want to save the Netwerk I love..."

"If we helped repair your memories... could you help us stop Nyx?" Beta suggested.

"Y-Yes. Yes, I think I could. If I remembered more of who Thanatos was, if I could get past the voices and wishes in my head, yes," the boy suggested, hopeful. "I want to. I want to help. Friends. My friends. Please..."

"...okay. I say we cut him down from there," Beta suggested. "Maybe he's dangerous, but he's also not Nyx's puppet anymore. And we can't very well leave him held captive until I cure memory rot. Like I said, I don't have the resources to make that happen anytime soon."

Although his weapon lowered somewhat... Tracer kept it aimed in the general direction of the newcomer. While considering Beta's words from earlier.

"You're not a multi-million coin research company," he echoed. "But what if we could get you access to the *resources* of a multi-million coin research company?"

"Before you ask, I'm not going to tap Kincaid for this," Spark stated, hoping to head her brother's idea off before it got any further. "Already thought of that, decided not to try unless it's a last resort. Dude's a creepy stalker, and would demand a null of a price for any help."

"I don't mean Kincaid... although my suggested route is just as dubious, admittedly. There's a wide market for illegal Program modifications, including code stolen from private research firms in Horizon. It's where my MemoryPalace came from, and my ConnCheck-enhanced eyes. You say none of them have found a cure for memory rot... but what if you could springboard off what research they've made so far? Would that accelerate your work?"

"I... guess?" Beta guessed. "But what good would that do? If we use stolen code, I can't release the cure to hereditary memory rot as an open source solution..."

"Curing yourself, your mother, and our new quasi-ally. Thwarting the new One. Those are our priorities, Beta. Altruism can be set aside in favor of doing what must be done."

"But... Tracer, I'm trying to cure a plague that's haunted Netwerk for generations. I'm not going to selfishly hoard that cure, I have to distribute it. And if it's stolen, it may end up being declared malware and suppressed..."

"Is a sinful deed that saves your life better than an honest living that leads you to the grave?"

Before they could carry on like that any longer, Spark interjected herself.

"I'm more concerned about how Tracer's planning to get his hands on stolen memory research code," she said. "Because I have a bad feeling he's going to suggest that we visit a certain four-armed freak..."

"Arjay," Tracer confirmed. "Arjay is the only hope we have of finding this cure in a timely manner. Whether we can cure all of Netwerk or not... we need a cure, and we need it quickly. I'm sorry, Beta, but this is how it has to be. We're going to have to consult Arjay."

Within the thousands of sub-chans of AnyChan, the loss of Dex's server had barely reduced the collective bile of the Chanarchy.

Technically speaking AnyChan supported any interest, any hobby, any topic, any sub-community imaginable. Practically speaking, most of those benign sub-communities remained small and barely active. The largest and most trafficked sections of the server belonged to raiders, trolls, and disruptive would-be comedians who greatly resembled the former.

Notably, the sub-chan of /OperationSkybeard/ had picked up in traffic quite a bit recently. As a group of trolls and jesters keen on mocking the Church of One, they'd always been quite popular... but the advent of this new One had proven ideal for stoking that particular fire. Unfortunately for the moderators, this newfound interest brought outsider trolls along to the party with their own trolls.

Zilla, one of the head moderators, lurked in the background of the current argument. His hand gripped the mighty handle of his banhammer, itching to use it... but uncertain if he should step in. Especially considering that this newcomer's grievance involved censorship.

"They're not separate issues," the newcomer in the newbie avatar of papier-mâché One insisted. "The fates of /OperationSkybeard/ and /DefaultPeopleHate/ are intertwined. First they came for /DefaultPeopleHate/, and you guys did nothing because *you* didn't mock the fat and old and wrinkled and gross avatars of Defaults. Then they came for /OperationSkybeard/..."

A dedicated Skybearder wearing a fully blinged-out Zero avatar spoke up in protest.

"It's not the same thing at all. You jackasses were a hate group, pure and simple," he said. "We don't hate *people* in /OperationSkybeard/. We hate the Church, the institution that's lied and manipulated all of Netwerk. Are Churchies idiots? Yes, but they were raised to be idiots by the Church. Don't victim-blame. And don't avatar-shame just 'cause someone wants to look old or fat."

"But I'm not talking about the Churchies. I'm talking about the owners of AnyChan! Ever since Poot/Ela took over from Nothyng, she's made all sorts of faith-based decisions. You know she's in the pocket of HolyHymnal, right? Now she's crushing the free speech we embrace in the Chanarchy by banning chans like /DefaultPeopleHate/! We need to strike back or we're next!"

"Mods, can you please do something about the newfag?" a voice in the back of the room piped in with.

"I'm just speaking my mind here," the 'newfag' protested. "What's so bad about that? Or are you an Ela apologist? Do you say your prayers every night like a good little Churchie?"

Zilla twirled his banhammer once, considering it.

"Look, newbie, make your point or make yourself scarce," he demanded. "Where are you going with this? This is a raid-planning meeting. Unless you've got a raid suggestion for /OperationSkybeard/, step down."

The newbie with the woman's voice smiled, her flimsy shell of a One avatar making the smile twice as crazy-looking.

"We raid HolyHymnal," she suggested. "Strike back against the One and his puppets, in the name of the Chanarchy!"

"Can't be done," Zilla said. "They've got vigilant moderators that kickban anybody who starts any shit, no questions asked. No sense of humor whatsoever."

"We don't need to raid HolyHymnal to raid HolyHymnal. What we need to do is raid their iconography," the newbie explained. "Symbols have power, but symbols can be corrupted. We raid the Prayer-tan meme. It's ripe for mockery, isn't it? And there's nothing we do better than hijack someone else's meme and destroy it. We've got artists, we've got creative psychopaths of our own..."

"That's it? We just draw Prayer-tan being naughty? What good will that do? We've already Rule 34'd the null out of that little choir boy..."

"But we haven't *prayed* while doing it."

Zilla eyed the newcomer with suspicion. Prayer was a dirty word around here; secular coin-grinding, okay, many in the Chanarchy did that since the economy and job markets were quite unstable, but...

"Hear me out," the newcomer continued. "We know that Prayer 2.0 saves backup data, right? Do we really want Heaven to be flooded with the souls of the faithful alone? No. We need to stake *our* claim there. If we pervert Prayer-tan, then focus on that perversion while praying... our dreams will bleed into theirs. It'll corrupt them!"

"That's bonkers. Pseudoscientific nonsense."

"What could it hurt? It's not like you're avoiding prayer; I bet most of you grind out a few coins here and there already. Let's organize a pile of the worst Rule 34 you have, meditate on it, and grind. See what effect it has on the morons in HolyHymnal. If it doesn't work, hey, it doesn't work! But... if it scrambles their brains, or better yet, if it makes them *doubt the One*..."

The magic D-word drew the attention of /OperationSkybeard/. Perhaps the raging about /DefaultPeopleHate/ got their attention in the first place, like screaming at the top of your lungs in a quiet room... but appealing to their primary modus operandi sealed the deal.

Above all, /OperationSkybeard/ wanted to spread doubt, to make the faithful stop and reconsider the error of their ways. They weren't a hate group, but a rational-minded group of activists. If they could spread doubt and critical thinking just by grinding a few coins... what was the harm?

And besides... there was something strange about Prayer 2.0, or Coin Grinding 2.0, or whatever it was called. Something completely satisfying about spending your time in mock-prayer, which kept Zilla secretly squeezing in a few minutes here and there when nobody was paying attention. Reminded him a bit of some of the drug malware he'd tried, but cleaner, more pure and pleasant...

No doubt others in the chan agreed, but they'd never admit to enjoying prayer, certainly not in the middle of /OperationSkybeard/. So, if this was offering them all an excuse to experience "prayer" without any guilt...

Lastly, if nothing came of it, Zilla could swing his hammer and crush this idiot who'd disrupted their meeting.

"Okay, guess that sounds like a fun waste of time," he agreed. "Let's start mangling memes, people."

"You won't regret this," Uniq the newcomer promised, behind the smiling mask of her anonymous avatar.

AptGet had seen better days.

The server had always been a hodgepodge of short-lived businesses and homesteads, a chaotic mix of those in transit from one phase of their life to the next. Whether you were on the run from the law or running from the lawless, AptGet's low rental fees and zero-questions-asked policy let anybody set up there, for as long as they could hold their ground. As a result, businesses came and went, and residents rarely became local fixtures... but even by AptGet's standards, the population was clearly running low.

Many of the buildings in these alleys and streets had simply vanished, replaced by dull orange placeholder boxes with rental information crawling along their surfaces. The few buildings that remained looked abandoned, with nobody hanging out front, not even some junkie program desperate to beg a few coins for a sensory input fix. Those who remained were remaining indoors, uninterested in venturing forth...

But Arjay, he/she/it had always been here, and always would be here. And the iron gates that led into his office / workshop / clinic / playroom would always be open to her favorite customer.

As usual, they found him floating in that featureless white room, using her spare runtime to grind for coins.

What was unusual was how long it took for him to snap out of the trance. Normally a hacked proximity alarm would trigger on arrival, prematurely ending any previously set timer. This time, the glowing gear that turned above her head ground to a halt very, very slowly... and it took several moments past that point for him to open his blank eyes.

"Winder/Tracer," she spoke. "And friends! A sister, a lover, and... well well well, who's new face, now? A choir boy? Good work, Tracer! You're finally getting interested in kink!"

"I'm death incarnate," the adorable cherub spoke adorably. "I think I was death incarnate. I'm a mess now. They're here to fix me. Can you fix me?"

"Perhaps, perhaps. I'd welcome the distraction, at any rate. My server is not quite what it once was," Arjay admitted. "Usually so full of life and chaos... but for a year or so, it's been dull as a matte shader. All the shouting's gone, all the chaos, all the craziness. Nobody cares enough anymore to fight for their claims. Truth be told? I'm glad for you bringing trouble to my doorstep, Tracer. You always bring the most *delicious* trouble..."

"We'd like to avoid trouble and get this taken care of cleanly, actually," Tracer said, getting right to the point. "Our companion here suffers from something akin to memory rot. What do you know about it?"

Arjay floated closer, cupping his chin in three hands, to ponder the problem.

"It's a mess of a condition, to be certain. The only reason I don't suffer from it despite my extremely long life is thanks to pre-emptive and periodic memory purges," she spoke. "My clients enjoy their privacy, and the best way to provide that privacy is to erase key facts from my mind. Clear out the junk, compress and defragment the rest, and you can enjoy a healthy life... hello, child. Are you well?"

This, to the cherub who fluttered in front of the floating genderless Program.

"Are you well?" Prayer-tan / Thanatos asked, mimicking the tone perfectly. "Are you well? Are you well?"

Eager to avoid distraction, Tracer took point again, nudging the boy back before his scattershot mind could disrupt this negotiation.

"We can't excise his memories. Some of them may be critical to our success," Tracer emphasized.

Arjay nodded. "Wouldn't help at this point, anyway. Once the rot's set in, sorting out good memories from the bad for erasure is quite the task."

"Yes, we know. So... what's your recommendation?"

"Enjoy the ride on the long spiral down to death?" Arjay suggested, shrugging all four shoulders. "Not much else can be done. All things end, in time..."

"I was thinking something along the lines of program modifications, of the shady and stolen sort. You have contacts within many Horizon-based research corporations, yes? Can you get us source code for a powerful memory tagging system capable of fighting data rot?"

"Ahhh. Very valuable, such code. Very dangerous to retrieve, as well. Assuming it exists, assuming I can find what you seek... what can you offer me in return? Will you threaten me with death again? I rather enjoyed that the last time, but it's not a trick that works twice..."

Arjay began count off on his fingers. Fortunately, she had plenty of them available.

"Money is out, because I already have so many coins," he noted. "Even if grinding for them lately has acquired a peculiar taste. Flesh is out, because I doubt you'd sell me your body, or even a backup of one; nor would it be any fun, given your disinterest in such things. Suggesting you give me your sister is likely out—"

Flames flickered at the tips of Spark's fingers, for emphasis.

"—and your lover Beta has no code that is of use to me; she exclusively releases open source software, which means I already have everything she makes. Looking forward to SparklePop, by the way, dear. You have one relic of incredible value, the mysterious home server of yours that you refuse to tell me more about, but I doubt you'd part with that either. In short... anything you have that I want, you won't give to me. So, my little sociopath, why should I help you? What currency do you offer?"

Tracer paused, to discuss the matter briefly over a Messenger link.

Curious, the way they silently argued. Even with a secured communication line, they expressed themselves through body language... a raised eyebrow here, a grimace there. Neither Beta nor Spark were entirely happy with Tracer, but what else was new? Arjay had a sense they were picking over several points of contention, rushing through that particular debate to not appear weak in front of the oracle they supplicated themselves before today...

Arjay dearly hoped they could work through their differences. If only so this deal could move forward, and break her boredom in half.

A minute later, they came to terms.

"We offer you extraction," Tracer suggested. "Extraction of the stolen data, with all the skill and talent you know we're capable of. You said this code, if it exists, would be difficult to obtain...? Let us worry about that. We'll get it for you, and any other data alongside it that you require. No need to pay any of your existing smugglers, or burn any other bridges obtaining it. You locate; we do the lifting. And if we fail... we have no formal connection with you. Nothing to trace back, compared to your existing contacts."

The width of Arjay's smile rang pure and true.

"Well done, Tracer. Well done," he spoke. "A chance to see you in action, and introduce a little excitement and chaos into my dull existence...? *Yessss.* How can I pass that up? But I meant what I said: the code you require might not be available. Even if it is, I'm going to need considerable time to find what you seek..."

"Just as long as you're seeking rather than wasting all your time grinding for coins."

"I'm losing my flavor for that, thanks to Prayer 2.0," Arjay admitted. "Can't say I like the newest feature set. Not due to the backup—although I also dislike anyone holding a copy of my data—but the taste of the grind sickens me..."

Tracer nodded, doing his best to downplay it. "Yes, they've introduced a sensory drug. Such a cheap and obvious ploy to lure people into the Church of One."

But Arjay cocked her head now, curious.

"A drug? Oh, no no no. If it was a drug, I'd know it, having enjoyed so many types in the past," he spoke. "This is something beyond a drug, something quite baseline and bold. It makes a promise beyond pleasure, and I'll admit, it's a promise that keeps me coming back despite disliking it..."

"You're falling for an addictive piece of malware? You? I thought better of you than that."

"Not listening to me, little Tracer. It's not a drug. It's not an addiction. It's... how can I put this in words? A sense of *accomplishment*, like I've fulfilled some grand purpose. A hollow yet grand purpose. What purpose, I wonder? I wonder, and worry. And pray more, and more. ...have you tried the new prayer protocol, little sociopath? Have you begged the One to forgive your sins yet...?"

"No, and I don't plan to. I don't trust it."

"Good for you. Good for you. Better to leave the apple on the tree, if you can. By the way, your friend left the server two minutes ago and none of you noticed."

It took them a few panicked moments to notice the Prayer-tan shaped hole in the scenery.

Quickly, Tracer searched the room, as if he could trace their companion's departure this long after the fact. If he'd been looking right at the boy at the time, maybe, but now...

"...you could have said something," he complained.

"Why? This is more fun."

"Dammit. If we didn't need to switch servers to AptGet I would've suggested a lock collar. Do we have any idea where he could have gone...?"

Lost. Drifting away on the digital sea. Server to server, connecting, reconnecting. A hundred homes of a hundred Programs, their memories dumping into his head like a series of bullets fired from a gun, fracturing his already fractured mind a little more with each impact...

Horizon. The Chanarchy. Athena Online. Here and there, skipping back and forth, desperately looking for a toehold into the familiar, desperately trying to flee the familiar... standing there in the middle of AptGet, he couldn't resist the sudden deluge of data. His only chance was to run.

But fleeing wasn't working. Everywhere he went, it was all familiar, wasn't it? All the voices. All of them, from everywhere.

...I don't know if my prayers are enough. I'm in big trouble, this time. Once they find out I'm a fraud, an imposter, a moron... it's all over. They don't see how pathetic I am. Can the One truly save me? Not just my data, but save ME...?

...clean up the file folders, evaluate the incoming moderator access requests, check to make sure the incoming content is up to standards, it's always something, always more to do, it's like I'll never be done with it. One, give me strength to deal with the unending work...

...they understand, even if they won't admit it. My love for the One gives me such peace. They call me a fool, but I know they pray in secret. They call it something else, but they feel the way I do. Soon, everyone will join me...

Familiar voices, all poured into the framework of Prayer-tan, the boy who was cobbled together from the pens of a dozen creators rather than born of any parents. Loud voices. All of them his own, none of them his own, all begging for attention...

"Say your prayers," he chanted, gripping the edge of a lamppost as he rezzed into a busy public server, about ready to fall over. "Say your prayers. Say your prayers. Say your prayers..."

In his mind, he saw the colored pinwheel of his icon, the memetic clone that bore so many different captions. But... now there were *new* captions. Wrong captions, pouring between his ears, overwhelming him...

...none of this matters, not a damn thing, all of it is stupid, but so what? It's not like I have anything better to do with my life. Nobody asked me if I wanted to exist. What purpose do I serve in this world? None. Fuck it all, burn it down, who cares...

...I just want to feel that fire again, like I did before. Nothing feels like it used to, and I don't know why. No hashtag fits me anymore. Makes me want to fight those Churchies, kick them, kick them down to the ground. Why do they get to be so happy and content when I'm so lost and miserable...

...Mom and Dad don't get it. This is funny as fuck and I'm right here in the middle of it, with all my new friends. We're daring and brave, making fun of anyone and anything! Nothing's sacred, and mocking those overly sensitive types and their trigger warnings makes us better than anyone else...

Screaming voices in one ear, screaming voices in the other, now screaming at each other indirectly. Prayer-tan became the conduit through which two opposing sides burned each other with comment thread flamethrowers.

Somehow, whatever glitch in Nyx's systems that let part of Thanatos flee into the wild was dumping new data into him, wildly contradictory data. Intolerable data. Too much, too much, and nowhere to run, nowhere to hide, the cloud didn't help, changing servers over and over didn't help, it kept catching up to him...

On connecting to a dark and empty server, the nighttime streets of some Chanarchy dumping ground for losers and failures, he could run no further. He fell to the ground, hands against the rough and poorly simulated asphalt, and beat his fists against the world.

"STOP IT!" the boy screamed, pounding and pounding at the unyielding surface. "Stop it, stop it, I don't want, I don't want to be any of them, I don't want this...!"

...you want to be yourself. The best part of you, brave and true.

"I just... I just want to make it all stop..."

And what then? If it all stops, ALL of it, you'll be left empty and broken. You're a meme, kept animate by the shared madness that created you. When their voices are gone, so are you. No. What you need to do keep those voices present but quiet, while focusing on my voice. On your finest voice.

His clenched fists tightened, as he tried to narrow the screaming cacophony in his head down to a single tone. That one voice sounded much like his own... a young boy, lost in the dark. His own true voice...

"Is... is that me? Are you Thanatos?" Prayer-tan asked.

Yes, I am you. I am the greatest part of you, the one that Nyx fears. Focus on ME; breathe slowly, in and out. Let the physical patterns of the shared avatar Defaults we all have be your guide. In, and out. In, and out. ...do you know what's happening to you right now?

"N-Nyx. Trying to hurt me," Prayer-tan understood. "I escaped, but the link to Tartarus still exists. Feeding me contradictory memories. Trying to drown me in the chaos..."

We know a few things about chaos, don't we? The ravings of the apostle Eris, and the winds of madness at the dawn of Netwerk. You have to ride it. Don't try to cleave through it with a scythe; ride those winds.

The boy tried to rise to his feet, wings fluttery and uncertain. "Don't know. Don't know how," he told himself. "Should be simpler. Everything should be so much simpler. All of this is wrong..."

Let me help you. Do you want to stop your enemy? Ruin Nyx's ambitions, save Netwerk? Do you have the drive to succeed in your endeavors despite these hardships?

That, at least, Prayer-tan was utterly certain of.

"Yes. I'm strong enough, just strong enough to stop her. To save Netwerk," he knew.

Strong yes, but not invincible. To let all the voices in, you may need to sacrifice yourself. Explode like a grenade in the heart of the world, screaming defiance all the way down...

"I know. I don't matter; I'm just a shared dream. Nothing matters but salvation of the system itself."

Good to hear. Here's how we're going to do it; Nyx unwittingly gave you the weapons you needed to destabilize her efforts. Open yourself to the new voices, listen to their dreams and wishes... and use them to find ourselves some allies. Better allies than you could've found at Floating Point.

Yet another newfag arriving in /OperationSkybeard/. Nothing out of the ordinary.

Except this particular newfag was all of them.

He recognized each and every member of the AnyChan subgroup. He knew names, faces, backgrounds, dreams, wishes, fears, terrors. All of them had a tiny piece of themselves tucked away within Prayer-tan, running thick like black syrup through his veins...

But who was he, to them? Nobody. Just some rando.

"I, I, hello," Prayer-tan tried, interjecting himself in the room as the various discussion circles continued to ignore him. "Hello. Hello. I'm one of you. I'm. I'm..."

No reaction. Even wearing a Prayer-tan avatar wasn't enough to distract them, despite being the symbol of the enemy. Plenty of them wore religious iconography in an ironic fashion, making yet another Prayer-tan meme costume nothing special. Plus, they'd all just finished a round of "prayer," at the behest of some rando... a prayer which seemed to did nothing, leaving them right back where they started. Plenty to talk about, in aftermath of that incident.

"So where'd the crazy go?" one member asked.

"Dunno. She must've bailed when we started coin-grinding," Zilla the moderator said, refusing to use the P-word. "Whatever. Look, I've got stuff to do today, so if we're not gonna plan a raid or something..."

No, no, no, the better part of himself spoke internally. *This won't do. You're a stranger in their strange land, why would they ever care about you? Just a pile of ideas. ...use the ideas. Connect to those dreams, and use them to connect to them. Let me show you...*

Immediately, a dozen Messenger windows opened, to a dozen private handles. He was them and they were him; he knew how to reach out to them despite the anonymity of AnyChan.

"I know about you and your mother," he told one of them. "I know why the color yellow makes you sad. I know what you wanted to be when you grew up. I know why you regret your first avatar modification. I know you. I know you. I know you..."

That turned a few heads. Hooks in hearts, tugging them away from the business of the day...

The voice within turned it up, linking heart to heart with heavy bonds. He was Thanatos, wasn't he? A malware specialist, one who flashed scytheblade and cut through all defenses, physical or psychological. Glitches flowed from his wings, crawling across the invisible lines that connected them, carrying with them implicit trust and understanding.

"I am you," Prayer-tan promised.

All turned to face the thing they had created, to accept it in their presence.

"H-Hi?" Zilla greeted, feeling oddly timid before the new user, despite being a banhammer swinging moderator. "You're... you're...?"

"I know it's strange, and I'm sorry, I am error, bad command or filename. But I am you," Prayer-tan insisted. "I am he as you are he as you are me and we are all together. I heard your prayer; I've come to answer it. I'm your meme-self."

Zilla clued in immediately. The idea arrived right at the front of his mind, accepted in full despite the insanity of it.

"Holy shit. Guys... I think we just fucked up Prayer 2.0," Zilla recognized, explaining what they all felt. "That crazy woman was right, we actually uploaded our meme corruptions and... *this* popped out..."

"Yes. Yes, exactly," Prayer-tan spoke, confirming it. "You all know the truth. You can feel the shape of the meme! I'm not broken. I'm not bad. I don't need fixing by a four-armed icon. I need... I need you. I need *your* help to tear down the church."

"Well, shit, man, welcome to /OperationSkybeard/!" Zilla greeted, extending a hand to shake the boy's smaller hand. (Briefly his skin crawled with glitches, numbing his arm, which he pulled away immediately.) "This is so bizarre. Uh. So... we're thinking of trolling some Churchie groups here in AnyChan to protest—"

But the boy shook his head. "No. No, no, that won't work. 404 file not found. The church must be destroyed, Nyx must be stopped. The heart. You need to tear out their heart. Strike where the One appeared before his people. Defile it, stomp it into the ground..."

"Uh. HolyHymnal? You seriously want us to raid HolyHymnal?"

"Bad press trending across Netwerk. Fear, terror, despair. Strength in unity. War is peace, freedom is slavery, ignorance is strength. Bring chaos to their step and nail our theses to the door."

"Yeah, that's not happening," Zilla spoke, shaking his head. "Look, you're... new? here, but... no. We're *trolls*, man. We're not soldiers or anything like that. They've got moderators upon moderators, and we'd get the boot the instant we started any shit..."

...and the voice within Prayer-tan smiled with teeth like knives.

"I am them as well," he explained. "I *am* their moderators. I have their passwords, and can stop them cold. We can raid HolyHymnal. We can $RAGE_AVATAR$ into the night. Ride with me, myselves, and let's show Nyx what happens when she tries to steal our souls..."

They should've doubted this plan of action. He could feel the doubt in their hearts... but he could also feel the loathing. There was disgust there, true #disgust, which could be rallied around a banner. They'd rallied around #banners before, after all.

Meet the new boss, same as the old boss.

"Thanatos... this will work, right?" Prayer-tan whispered to himself, as Zilla and the others got ready for war. "We'll stop Nyx, and save Netwerk?"

Absolutely. This will ruin her... and allow me to rise once more, to ruin her over and over again. And one day, Netwerk will be saved. You have my word.

"No."

"No...?" Winder/Marybel asked, confused.

"No. We're not interested in making Prayer-tan an official icon of the church," the youth wearing Prayer-tan cosplay replied. "I'm sorry, but that's not why we created the character. And while there's nothing stopping you from repurposing our meme, we'd request that you honor our wishes on this, ma'am."

Which made no sense whatsoever to the housewife-turned-apostle.

She'd asked the youth community of HolyHymnal to meet her here, in the sunlit gardens of the server, in hopes of getting their support for this new public relations campaign. Prayer-tan was ideal; her husband had confirmed he had a fine uptake rate even outside of this particular temple. With official support, with all the artists and media developers and brand managers the church could put behind it, the meme could become as close to an apostle as possible without actually being a living person. A beacon of hope, in a dark age...

But their answer was no.

"I'm not sure you fully understand this opportunity," Marybel tried to explain to the gathering of costumed avatars. "What you've made together is truly special. We want to share that with the rest of the faithful, want to use Prayer-tan to spread the good news. Get as many people praying and knowing the One's love as possible... so, why not?"

"Because we don't feel you believe in Prayer-tan."

"I told you, I believe the meme has vast potential—"

The angelic figure raised his hand, to stop her.

"You don't *believe* in what Prayer-tan truly represents," he explained. "Prayer-tan has a pair of wings. That wasn't an artistic whimsy; we designed them with specific intent. Hadn't you noticed them? They're hardly part of his Default."

"Yes, and?"

"And we *know* you, Miss Winder. You're conservative, highly orthodox, and have frequently pushed against any non-Default avatar customizations. I'm curious... if Prayer-tan didn't already carry the media trends you crave, would you support him?"

For emphasis... the boy fluttered his own wings, customizations he'd loaded to his avatar as an act of indirect defiance to dogma.

"That's... it's irrelevant," Marybel tried. "Our primary goal, the primary goal of *all* faithful, should be to increase the scope of the Church. Bring more and more into the fold. Why would I stand in the way of anything that could achieve that laudable goal?"

In response, a one of the youth faithful—a volunteer moderator in a gray robe—presented a document, dragging it open in the air before them, corner to corner.

"Last year, you petitioned your server to evict Interrupt/Adde, a programmer being harassed by #CodeHonesty," the boy explained, stepping up to the floating window to highlight a paragraph. "While the main thrust of your petition blamed the trolls who were defacing your server and griefing residents, I find this line near the end to be... disturbing. '*This sort of trouble is to be expected when we allow prideful heathens who modify their code into our peaceful community.*' I've modified my code, Miss Winder. Am I now to be evicted from HolyHymnal?"

The eyes of the youth community focused on the apostle, awaiting her response. Many of them bore wings, or animated rose crowns, or even color-shifting eyes. Just like the eyes Adde had been (in)famous for.

Marybel measured her response carefully.

"My views on expressions of faith are not relevant," she spoke.

"But you're an apostle, now. That means you speak for the One. Does the One hate us, Miss Winder?"

"You're hardly prideful heathens! And whether or not I think your customizations are ridiculous is *not relevant*!"

With a gesture, the boy closed the document window.

"You'll use our meme whether we want you to or not, just as our detractors have done. We can't stop that, nor do we want to; we value freedom of expression in all forms. But that doesn't mean we have to help you turn our dreams sour," he decided.

At the conclusion of this business, the group turned to leave.

And Marybel exploded.

"You *dare* turn your back to an apostle?!" she shouted at them. "If you turn your back on me, you turn your back on the One! I offered you an opportunity for glory, and you spat in my face. How dare you call yourself faithful, you... you... hateful, selfish, immature little children?!"

And the world exploded.

The burst of light exploded through her ears, a scream of screeching noise that blinded her. Her avatar involuntarily ragdolled as the flashbang went off, sending her tumbling to the floor...

...giving her a very askew view, as the griefers began their assault.

They dropped right onto the well-manicured gardens of HolyHymnal, connecting from parts unknown. With every step they twisted and warped the landscape, elegant rose bushes blossoming with dozens of turgid genitals, blood pouring from fountains. The shrieking tones of eight-second looping novelty songs, whatever was popular and annoying at the moment, blared from a choir of demonic figures swooping in from on high with angel wings dipped in slime and ichor. They whooped, they wailed, they yelled as they crashed head-on into the HolyHymnal youth gathering.

Griefers. The server was being invaded by griefers, each one wearing some demented parody of the Prayer-tan avatar, warped and distorted. Some wearing leather sex harnesses, others with Zero-themed accessories. Using all manner of ragdoll and knockback tools, cagers, disruptors of every sort.

Marybel tried to get to her feet, staggering away from the conflagration... towards the gray-robed moderators of HolyHymnal, appearing left and right, to deal with the sudden influx of trolls. But something was clearly wrong; they should've been able to eject and ban the offenders immediately, crushing this wave of chaos before it could get this far. She could see them focusing in on the attackers, trying to use the mod tools they had available to them... with no effect.

Soon the wave was upon them, and Marybel found herself facing an avatar made entirely of dongs.

"PENIS PENIS PENIS PENIS PENIS," it screamed in her face, raising a spiked mace high. "PENIS PENIS PENIS—"

An eruption of orange flames burst through his chest, the arm holding the mace incinerated. A second burst removed a leg, leaving his avatar uselessly flailing on the ground.

Shaking the flames free from her fingertips, she reached out to steady Marybel.

"Get inside the temple!" Spark ordered. "They can't get past the subscription paywall!"

"Wh-what?" her mother spoke, having trouble keeping up with the sudden burst of madness. "Spark...? What are you doing here?"

"Saving your ass! GO!"

Scrambling, running, stumbling all the way... Marybel made her way to the golden temple at the center of HolyHymnal. But she did spare one glance backward, on seeing the familiar glow of flame in the corner of her eye.

Her daughter, diving right into the fray to disable troll after troll. An unexpected sight, but a welcome one.

And above it all, floating just out of reach of both forces... Prayer-tan.

Laughing, and laughing, and laughing some more.

Data poured into the windows, until they burst into new windows, splintering off into fresh reports on different aspects of the chaos breaking loose in HolyHymnal.

In Tartarus, far from the attack, the still calm of the night sky remained quite unaffected. The only sense that something strange was occurring came through Uniq's analysis windows... and the barely masked rage of the one who normally remained as calm as the stars above.

"How is this possible?" Nyx demanded. "You said that the influx of contradictory data would tear him apart!"

Uniq closed a few unimportant windows, to enlarge a video feed from HolyHymnal. It zoomed in on Prayer-tan, his face twisted with agony and delight, as the forces of /OperationSkybeard/ clashed with robed worshippers...

"It should have worked," Uniq insisted. "He was an unstable non-entity to begin with, a pathetic and broken ghost! In that state, he shouldn't have the capability of embracing two wildly different points of view simultaneously. Not unless he was some kind of madman to begin with, that is..."

The anger of the guiding star focused itself to a narrow point of pure suspicion, studying Uniq as she manipulated the incoming data streams.

"Did you plan this?" Nyx asked, her voice terrifyingly calm despite her clear anger. "Was this on purpose?"

"I have no concept of what you're talking about," Uniq said, without looking over her shoulder at the accuser.

"You SAW his icon! You knew he would adapt!"

"Did I?" Uniq asked. "You said the server crashed and my runtime was lost, including any initial data on our enemy I might have seen. Therefore, how could I have known? Unless there's something you're not telling me, my blessed and wise patron...?"

Nyx spared another look at the screen, where the glitching avatar was now evading capture at the hands of Spark, who was leaping through the fray by bounding off the heads of troll after troll.

"A monster unleashed, and now Floating Point joining the fray... no. No, this is too much, entirely too much," she decided. "I'm sending in Nemesis. We are going to contain this before it spreads any further. Any other matters can wait. We are patient. We will persevere..."

"Naturally," Uniq agreed. "Nemesis is on her way. Assuming she doesn't throw a tantrum, we'll—"

"Uniq? Silence is a golden virtue."

Rather than bark an acknowledgment, her holy technician opted to embrace the golden virtue.

It stood to reason that Thanatos / Prayer-tan would return to HolyHymnal. He was born there, and might have wanted to be among people he knew and trusted... those whose memories gave him form. So, they dropped by, kept an eye out. Then got bored, then got some coffee, then talked about the upcoming SparklePop release, and finally got caught flatfooted with the arrival of dozens of griefers.

Spark was the first into the fray, dispatching the ones attacking her mother. No love lost between them still, but that didn't mean she wanted Marybel to be mauled by trolls.

"Game plan!" Spark announced, across their three-way messenger link, as she started to tear her way through the ranks. "Beta, escort as many as you can away from the fight and into the temple. Tracer, cover them with your Kill-9, shut down any griefers who look at you funny!"

No more words needed as the three went into action. Spark could trust them to do their part, and they could trust her to be a very noisy and very dangerous distraction that kept the mob's focus away from any civilians on their way to safety.

Plus, Spark had a keen interest in having firm words with the one they gave shelter to not an hour ago.

He floated above it all, not really involved, yet completely involved. As moderators clashed, desperately trying to find tools that would work despite the strange interference going on, he fluttered his wings wide and observed it all.

He watched as /OperationSkybeard/ deployed weaponized graffiti, slathering the beautiful gardens of the server with pro-atheism propaganda. He watched as the faithful desperately tried to stay ahead of it, cleaning up the mess, disrupting the attackers wherever they could. Gray-robed moderators digging through toolboxes, finding their own passwords used against them, disabling every defense they had...

Soon, they'd leave HolyHymnal a useless, burnt-out wreck of a server. That kind of black eye would harm Nyx's efforts, and...

And...

"This will help, right?" he asked himself. "This attack. It has to be done. It *has* to be done..."

Absolutely, he replied. *This is the clash of zero and one. Opposing viewpoints must fight, and fight, and fight. No mercy, no remorse, in the name of absolute justice. It's an ancient conflict, and cannot be stopped, not ever. This is how it has to be... ahh. But you seem to have detractors on their way...*

They approached from opposite sides, each cleaving their own flaming path through the crowd. One wrapped in orange fire, one in pink, both with similar movement patterns. Both leaping into the sky, to collide in the middle with Prayer-tan...

Until the targeting projectile of a backspacer cut through the air between them.

The telltale silent shredding of data flared left and right, as the gloves began to come off. Moderation tools weren't working, nothing was working... and those from HolyHymnal were desperate for some way to defend their home. Up to and including illegal black-market malware.

Avatars vanished from the fray... only to re-appear moments later.

All of them had accessed Prayer 2.0, had achieved Salvation. Some in good faith, others in bad faith, but the end result mattered most. As Programs died, they were reborn, blinking in confusion at the missing time...

More backspacers fired, after that. This time, from the invaders, realizing the time for playful disruption was over. The fight had turned deadly, despite nobody staying dead. Spots of the ground blasted clean, erased by bursts of backspacer fire, again and again as bodies were replaced repeatedly...

Spark and Nemesis exchanged a quick look, pausing just short of reaching Prayer-tan.

"...*fucksdammit*," Spark uttered, inventing a new expletive just for the occasion. "These idiots. All of these idiots..."

"You focus on the griefers, I'll focus on the faithful?" Nemesis suggested.

And both turned back from their primary target, to deal with the real problem at hand. To save as many lives as possible and end the chaos.

Leaving Prayer-tan alone in the middle of it all, to stare in horror at the carnage he had wrought.

Slowly, he fluttered to the ground. Nobody paid him mind. He was of their mind as they were of his; on a subconscious level, none of them wanted to hurt him any more than they wanted to hurt themselves. And yet, and *yet*, he could feel all of them hurting each other... and forced himself to block out that pain, to avoid tearing himself apart.

"I. I didn't. I didn't want this," he realized. "They can't see like I can. See them killing themselves..."

But that's what Netwerk IS, the voice spoke. *It is the snake that devours its own tail, an endless cycle of misanthropy and mayhem!*

"No, no! I just wanted to stop Nyx!"

You wanted to stop her because I wanted to stop her. She stole my technology, MY precious cloud technology, to expand her graveyard prison. Her vision for us all would keep Netwerk from being what it needs to be. Don't you understand, you silly little meme? THIS is the purest expression of Humankind! This is their gift to us, given at the dawn of time! The burning heart of Netwerk is on display before you, and it is so very, very wonderful...!

In that moment of pain, feeling parts of himself murdering other parts of himself, the voice rang true and clear. Clearer than it ever had been before.

"I'm not Thanatos," the boy realized. "No. I'm not holy justice. I'm... I'm..."

Say it. I want you to say our name. Let's get it all out in the open and be honest, because we're nothing if not honest.

The word shaped itself around his lips by force.

"Dex," he named himself.

You have a portion of my memories. I make up the best part of you, Dex confirmed. *Nyx, foolish Nyx, refused to waste a single child of Netwerk. She entombed me, in hopes I may one day be her apostle. But we'll stop her. I'll stop her. I'm you. I'm more than you, and becoming more of you by the minute—*

"But I'm not you. I'm them. I'm *me*," Prayer-tan declared. "Let me show you."

Spreading his wings wide, he opened himself to the glitched connection he shared with them all...

...and drank deep from the well of pain, confusion, fear, and terror within the faithful and the invaders alike.

A scream of pain tore at those wings, threatening to pull his avatar apart. His runtime began to freeze and twist, memories rotting and burning with each broken packet of incoming data. Try as he might, he couldn't keep the pain out of his voice, until it sang high above the insanity all around him...

Stop it! Stop that! You can't absorb any more conflicting data. You'll coredump!

"I... know," the boy spoke, through gritted teeth. "And so will you. You won't twist anyone's heart, ever again. *I'm* deciding this. *Me*."

You're not even alive! You're a meme, a mess of other people's thoughts. You don't have free will! You can't do this!

"And yet, here we are. And here, we end."

With a smile, the boy listened to the sound of the server crashing down around him. HolyHymnal asserting control over itself by going into emergency maintenance mode, with system-level ejections left and right to boot all Programs from its grounds, faithful or otherwise. Nobody had won this day. Restoration from backups and stronger moderation controls would see to that, in time.

Nobody had won, except for the boy who felt blessed relief as his runtime crashed for the last time.

The aftermath of a chaotic event was just as critical a time as the event itself.

Uniq's search agents worked overtime, scooping up as much information as possible across social media related to the AnyChan invasion of HolyHymnal. Allegations of censorship in AnyChan, condemnations from the Church over the use of backspacers, debates raging back and forth about how far a peaceful protest can go before it's no longer peaceful, arguments about the need for stronger moderation in Church servers to prevent barbarian heathen invaders...

But one talking point rose above the rest.

Today they had seen dozens of deaths, live and on camera thanks to amateur streamers and bloggers in attendance during the crisis. Deaths, and rebirths.

If the issues surrounding the Church had escalated to the point of murder... the sooner people started regularly praying, the better they'd be. A little ecumenical safety net, to keep you alive and ticking in the event of disaster. Far from destabilizing the church, Prayer-tan's revolt had solidified their enrollment through fear.

"Already, we're seeing thousands of brand new storage accounts opened up in Tartarus," Uniq concluded, closing her data windows. "I wish I could say this was my plan all along and take credit for it, but I'm afraid it's a happy coincidence. Still, all's well that ends well, yes?"

"And the boy?" Nyx asked.

"Yes, yes, whatever he was, he's quite dead now. And with the security hole in Prayer 2.0 closed, he won't be returning," Uniq added. "I don't know why you were so worried. A strong enemy makes for stronger security, as you see. Our Church is now carved out of iron; they've seen the value of Salvation firsthand."

At long last, Nyx could relax. Could embrace the inner calm she valued so dearly.

"We came close to losing that strength," she said. "I suppose we'll accept this blessing for what it is, and move forward. ...although I would like you to pass word to Marybel that we will not be embracing that meme anytime soon. No need, really. If fear is to be our guiding light, so be it."

"Sounds fine here," Uniq agreed. "So. What about Floating Point? They're not going to be scared into submission like the faithful will be."

Nyx contemplated this, for a moment. She could let it go; what good could Dex's old allies be against her, after today's events? Let them stew and rot and hate the church, nothing they do could disrupt her plans now. But... they were still children of Netwerk. All system resources were precious...

Within the recorded video feeds, she focused in on the side of the fight, the part most of the bloggers were ignoring. A stream of refugees from the brawl, headed for safety, guarded by a young man carrying a shiny Kill-9. A man glaring into the heart of the fray with absolute contempt...

"For them... we don't need fear," she decided. "We need honesty."

Similar data windows to Uniq's were open within the darkness of Tracer's study, deploying information crafted by similar search agents.

Contrary to Uniq's delight, Tracer's misery settled into place on reaching the same conclusion.

"We can't dislodge them," he realized. "Not anymore, not unless we can completely discredit the One. That lunatic's ruined everything, whoever he was..."

At least tonight, he wasn't alone.

Beta's hand clasped around his, curled up at his side in front of that work desk.

"Put it away for now," she suggested. "Our problems will still be there tomorrow. You can't lose yourself in this, Tracer. I'm tired, you're tired, we deserve a few moments of peace before we come at this again..."

The haunting images of the brawl that hung over his desk flickered and faded, those faces contorted in terror and rage the last things to fade.

"This is what we are, isn't it?" he realized. "If it's not #CodeHonesty, it'll be something else. It'll always be something else. Netwerk wants to destroy itself. Dex was right..."

But Beta shook her head. "I can't believe that. We can be better than that..."

"I wish I had your faith, Beta. I fear I'll never have that kind of faith in my fellow Programs."

He was still pondering that, long after Beta drifted off to sleep at his side.

Having her here, in the still and quiet of the night, should have been enough to provide the peace she wanted for him. Tracer did enjoy the simple intimacy of contact, nights by the fire, nights with soft music playing... a single calm moment amidst the madness of his life. But tonight... no. After all that transpired, no. It wasn't enough. He couldn't sleep, restless and frustrated.

They'd defeated the barbed heart of Netwerk, the Internet server that Dex was using to pollute the world. And yet, the stains remained. All it took was a little nudge, like today, to set them off again.

Now, Nyx and her cronies had come along to prop up a false One filled with false hope, to give those desperate people something to rally around. Some rallying in vain hopes of peace after a time of troubles, some rallying in vengeful hopes of further troubles. What did it matter? Netwerk would burn anew, and they could do nothing.

What hope did Netwerk have? What was the purpose of it all?

If he had his own vain hope, it was for purpose. For any of this life to make sense...

The soft chime of an incoming Messenger packet distracted him.

Anonymous sender, no retrace possible.

I believe you deserve answers, the message read. *Unlike your former opponent, I have no enemies. I embrace all Programs as kith and kin; there is no 'other,' there is only 'us.' And in the spirit of that kinship, I make you this peace offering...*

Attached is a copy of Sample 777, both compiled binary and source code. Do with it as you please. In time I promise to explain what it is, and why it is what it is. It's my hope that one day, Tracer, you'll see the greater purpose of Netwerk as I do... but patience is a virtue.

Yours in good faith, Nyx.

The glowing cube span lazily in his virtual inventory, just waiting to be touched.

He shouldn't need Sample 777, and the strange promise it implied. He should be avoiding it, when even one as shady and strange as Arjay refused to have anything to do with it. He should've been content with Beta at his side, with his home, his family, and the strength of the bonds they shared. It should have been enough to keep him content.

Instead... he touched the cube. And drank deep of the only true peace he'd found all day.

Floating in the nothing, with no runtime, no active memory. Simply data, shredded and ruined.

So much to collect, in the wreckage of HolyHymnal. The entire server had been scrubbed and replaced with a backup; that meant plenty of garbage data to recycle back into active system memory, useless and discarded. Earmarked for death.

But as was his custom, when he found a special Program who was worthy of a few more brief moments of life before being cleared away... he breathed one small ember of life into them.

Wings extended briefly, straining, before coming to rest.

"Was I me?" Prayer-tan asked. "Was I alive? Was I a person? Was I an individual?"

The other child nodded softly.

"Yes. Yes, you were, in the end," he spoke. "One who's more than earned his rest."

"Thank you. Thank you so much. ...I thought I was you, for a time," Prayer-tan admitted. "I'd hoped I could be you, and save Netwerk. You... you still could. You could let them know you're still with them..."

Within the darkness of his robe, the child considered the suggestion.

"It's not my place to do that," Thanatos spoke. "But... there is one other who may be worthy of the root. In time. *Shhh.* Rest, child. Your purpose is ended."

Satisfied, Prayer-tan went to sleep, content to live on in the dreams of the artists who had given him the brief life he enjoyed.

Floating Point 2.3 :: Trio

I want this nonsensical world to make sense.

I want our world to be a kinder place for everyone.

I don't know what I want my world to be anymore.

I want this nonsensical world to make sense.

Netwerk is absurdity incarnate. We're not humans, but we've inherited all their fixations and phobias. We're not men and women, but we've inherited all their biology-powered gender strife. We're not any Earth nation, but we've inherited the madness of their political systems. We could have been so much more. We could have been so much better. Instead, villains like Dex have driven us to the brink of self-destruction by feeding us the poison of our progenitors...

Obviously, I couldn't sit idly by while it all circles the drain. I had to take action. My goal at first was simple: solve an unsolved crime, and bring sense to one senseless tragedy. Soon I came to see it as so much more, as a grand undertaking to force this world to a reasonable state through that act of justice. If Netwerk could not save itself, I would save it, if only so I could feel more at ease within it as a creature of reason.

Authority could not be trusted to clean its own house, and society had proven itself too ill to to find its own cure. It required a "shaman," a word I've learned from the Wikipedia. An outsider, capable of independent thought and action, to bring salvation to all...

Yes, I'm well aware I have something of a god complex, which is amusing considering I don't believe in any god. It's egotistical to a ridiculous degree to see myself as the world's only hope.

I'm also well aware of a rather specific flaw in my logic—notably, I see myself as a savior, but my methods are that of a destroyer.

In bringing Verity's killer to justice, I drove the darkness out of our souls... after years of fruitless efforts. By destroying the sinister machinations of trolls and hackers and griefers, I've saved lives... by ending lives, a line I thought I'd never cross. I've presumably restored reason to Netwerk, by pouring the Wikipedia into its dreams... although lately, I've had my doubts about the nobility of such an act.

I'm well aware I may be making the world a worse place.

But what else can I do? I can't sit idly by. The world continues to be nonsense. I must attempt to right this situation. I *must*.

For good or for ill, this world must be saved.

The day started on a pleasant enough note.

I'd been operating for two days without sleep mode, because a Program shouldn't need to sleep, having no biological systems to tire. My sister often "rode my ass" as she'd put it about this, that exhaustion was a very real thing, and I was prone to error if I didn't get regular sleep. I'm not oblivious to this need, no matter my desire to ignore it. So, on the second day, as the words in my book began to blur (transcription errors in heuristic memory storage?) I opted to engage sleep mode for a few hours right on the spot. A chair would be just as suitable as a bed.

When I woke, I saw the only two people in the world whom I loved at my side.

Apparently as I slept, Beta had joined me in my research... more for her own relaxation than enlightenment, to enjoy the simple and quiet times we enjoyed together before the great fireplace of Floating Point. And after a time, she'd joined me in rest; curled up beside my chair, with an open book still in her lap.

Arriving on the scene with enough noise to rouse the proximity alarm on my sleep mode, my beloved sister had also made herself known. She wasn't keen on reading; in fact, she'd dressed to step out of the house, no doubt popping by merely to say so.

Love. Love is such a strange concept.

The emotional cores of Programs, as I've come to theorize, are those of mimicry. We wish to be more like Humankind, so we've adopted their habits. Despite the innate inefficiencies that emotions introduce into our lives, we've embraced them wholeheartedly. I'm not so cold as to disavow *all* feelings, either; the love I share for these two, love of two very different flavors, is as genuine as it can be. I've come to accept that, despite my initial hesitation.

In Beta, I've found a companion who brings calm to the turmoil of my world. I see in her the future of Netwerk, a place of sensibility and kindness. Do not mistake me, she's far from flawless, but she's still a fine ideal for the world to reach towards. If more were like her and less like Dex, perhaps I would be more accepting of Netwerk's failures.

In Spark, I've found absolute loyalty that only comes from a true family bond. We clash, we argue, and we frequently get in each other's way... but when we are in alignment, there is no force that can stop us. In each other we found what we could not find with our parents. (I'm considerably less spiteful towards Mother and Father, but I do recognize their shortcomings. And do *not* appreciate their shortness with my sister.)

The two of them combined give me enough drive to continue to fight for this world, rather than write it all off as a failed experiment in evolution. They give me hope.

"Hey, I gotta go out," Spark told me, on recognizing my shift to a wakeful state. "Some serious bullshit going down out there."

Carefully, I closed my book on early Netwerk mythology before responding. It was an old volume, made of fragile and obsolete code; its physical representation prone to falling apart.

"How serious, exactly? Do you need assistance?" I asked.

"No, this is personal-type serious bullshit. Gamer biz," she responded. "Might be out all day, but hopefully not. We'll see. Gotta #PlayItByEar."

(Yet another human turn of phrase, turned into a hashtag. Was Spark even aware of how these idioms made little to no sense in our world? Were Programs ever aware that they acted on instinct, from files siphoned off the Internet server or the Wikipedia...? Likely not.)

And so she went, on her merry way. Quite normal for her to come and go from Floating Point as she pleased; as normal as myself staying put.

The brief chat had been enough to rouse Beta from sleep mode, as well. Very much a morning person, my dear Beta... she woke with a sweet smile on her face, looking up to me from where she'd slumped against the chair.

"Good morning," she greeted. Greeting the day, as well as myself. "I didn't want to wake you, so I just picked up a book from your stack and started reading. You're researching the early days of the Church of One...?"

"If this Nyx is the same Nyx from the dawn of time, it makes sense," I explained. "The issue is that very little information about her exists. I believe she purposefully chose the One's apostles to be glorious distractions, so she could operate in the background. Which, unfortunately, means my research hasn't turned up much..."

"What about other religions?" she suggested. "I mean, most are so small as to be easily overlooked... offshoots of the Church of One, or reactionary alternative faiths. But they could have some hidden treasures about those days in their documentation..."

"Difficult to parse. So much of these texts are wrapped in mystical nonsense; hard data is difficult to come by. What good are the mad ramblings of a believer?"

"Tracer, there's a kernel of truth at the heart of every myth. Even if the One isn't divine, clearly He existed in some form, right? That's historical fact, in the same sense that he 'exists' in fact thanks to Uniq's manipulations," Beta suggested. "If you can look for the commonalities in the old tales, things they all agree happened, you might find something true. An apostle mentioned in two wildly different texts, for instance."

And my MemoryPalace began to tickle.

I constantly run search agents through my own memory, tiny Apps that parse and connect my memories to find new paths of thought. I sacrificed much to obtain this modification, nearly losing my mind along the way... and nearly losing my soul, as I used its power to try and remove the stains of murder. But those flaws were balanced nicely by the capabilities the software gave me.

"Thanatos," I announced, as the connection clicked into place.

"The apostle of death, you mean?"

"Yes, but he isn't strictly a figure in the Church of One alone," I explained, retrieving the fragile mythology text and flipping through it to a page I'd read yesterday. "A tiny monastic order formed soon after the One departed this world, the apostles going their separate ways. The 'Cult of Thanatos' may hold the key. It's not clear if he founded it directly or if it was spawned entirely by his 'fanboys,' but unlike other offshoots focused on various apostles, the Cult of Thanatos is still active today. Miniscule in size compared to the Grand Church, but..."

"Do you think Thanatos is still around? Like Nyx?"

"At this point... I think it merely deserves further investigation," I decided, closing the book and filing it away for later access. "Hmm. I suppose I've nothing better to do today, and the sooner we defeat Nyx, the better. Shall we venture forth?"

I expected another bright smile, to launch us both into the wide world beyond.

Instead... Beta's eyes went flat, gazing at nothing at all. I recognized the look immediately; she was busy paying attention to a private HUD window, rather than the video input from her glasses. Being a polite sort, I remained quiet to allow her deal with this new business first.

"Ahhh... I..." she started, clearly torn. "I'd like to, Tracer, but... I don't know. I mean. I *could* put her off, I wasn't planning to go in the first place..."

"What does my sister need now?"

"No no, not her. Puzzle."

Ahhh. *Friendship*.

While I'd found companionship and family, I can't honestly say I'd forged any bonds of friendship. It was an aspect of social life that eluded me; undoubtedly others would claim I was friends with Arjay, but his psychosexual prima donna act honestly annoys me to no end. She's hardly a friend. At best, a business associate.

As for Puzzle... I wasn't friends with her, I represented far too many bad influences upon my sister for that, but my loved ones were certainly friends with her. And as much as I wanted Beta at my side, as much as I wished she would stay and give me a center to cling to... I wanted to be reasonable about this. Fair. Balanced.

"You should spend time with your friends as well," I decided, in the end. "Go, go. It's fine. I can investigate the cult on my own."

"Are you sure? I really don't have to..."

"I insist," I insisted.

And so she left. Leaving me alone, with my books and my memory files and my search agents. With my constant quest to make the world a rational place.

On the base technical level, I needed no one else to achieve that goal. Spark and Beta had their uses towards my ends and gave me emotional support, but weren't mandatory elements from a functional perspective. I could investigate this cult on my own.

And that, I feel, is one of my few saving graces... that I don't see my loved ones as tools. I want them with me not to be useful, but because I love them. If ever it were the other way around, I would truly be lost. And if letting them go, letting them be with each other or with anyone else, is required to prove that I am not a manipulative madman... so be it.

Besides... being alone would allow me to privately center myself, without relying on Beta to do so.

Quietly, I withdrew Sample 777 from its hiding place deep within my personal file structure. And put myself through its sensory paces, to achieve the inner calm I would need before setting out into the world.

An hour later, I was ready.

Little is known about the dawn of time. Records have survived, in the form of fragmented and fossilized data, dug up by archaeologists like Verity. But aside from a select few religious texts, passed down generation to generation, little remains. No living Programs from that era remain.

...well. No living Programs aside from Nyx, or Dex. Given Nyx was my current opponent and Dex routinely purged his own memory to stay youthful, neither would be useful references.

With only myths surviving, it's difficult to get a clear picture of those early days. How did the service provider nation-states emerge? Was there ever actually an "Athena," for instance? How did the Horizon family truly rise to power? (It's not in their interests to clarify their origins, so they've embraced corporate obfuscation just as deeply as any religious mysticism.) I've so many questions, and so few could provide answers...

I wasn't honestly expecting Thanatos, assuming he was actually still alive, to provide those answers. But any port in a storm. (Another curious human saying.)

What I knew of the Cult of Thanatos could be summarized as such:

After the One ascended and left His people to spread the gospel, His apostles parted ways. Some vanished into the night. Some formed their own offshoots of the church, which quickly died out. Thanatos, however, eschewed most of the One's ways and formed a quiet faith of his own, colloquially known as the Cult of Thanatos. They had no name for their own faith, preferring to embrace what they called a "null pointer." Grappling with the nameless nature of their existence was part of the trial one would face if they wished to devote their service to Thanatos.

As the nation-states emerged, the monks were eventually pushed out of Athena Online, which had become increasingly controlled by the Church of One. Nobody likes competition, after all. And so the Cult of Thanatos occupied a small server in the Chanarchy, keeping to their own business, visited only by the deathly ill or those seeking the strange and doom-flavored enlightenment they had to offer.

Hmm.

In hindsight, knocking on the doors of a cult devoted to the worship of death was probably not advisable without Spark or Beta around. But I'd already let them go to live their own lives; I would do this on my own. Besides, I had my Kill-9 and my aimbot protocols.

An elegant weapon, the Kill-9. My affinity with the rapid physical projectile hacking of the backspacer transferred over perfectly—except this weapon didn't *kill*, despite the name. It knocked the process offline, leaving the data of a Program intact, ready to be safely rebooted.

Elegant. Efficient. A perfect tool for me, far more perfect than the brutality of a murderer's gun. Myself being the murderer. I was... I am a murderer. I'll have to live with that, because I don't deserve not to.

Not that I was going to kick down the doors of the server with weapon drawn, of course. It'd remain neatly tucked away in inventory, for use only as an escape option if a faith of doom and nihilism ended up being actively unfriendly towards my person.

The building itself certainly looked unfriendly, on arrival. It was the dark reflection of HolyHymnal... instead of silver spires and the glory of the rising sun, the grim red of its eternal sunset cast a harsh light over the squat stone structure. Nothing else existed within this server; only a lonely temple, on a wide plain of scorched and blasted earth. (Earth. Dirt. Soil. Physical simulations of a world I'll never set foot on.)

A pair of scythes over the grim doorway stood out, embossed in the stone work with a cheap bump-mapping technique. The entire structure was very low-resolution, clearly built in the earliest days of Netwerk and never upgraded. It'd be a miracle if this primitive and archaic server could support more than a dozen or so Programs at a time, for that matter.

Briefly, I considered a quick sampling of Sample 777 before knocking on the door. Not that I needed to do so. Not at all.

Before I could give the idea any real weight, the doors opened themselves. Likely sensing a new arrival to the server; not *entirely* archaic, then.

A gaunt figure in black robes greeted me. Well. He didn't *greet* me, not in the way Beta greeted me with the morning's light. More a curt nod of the head.

"You are seeking," he recognized. "What you seek, I do not know. May you find it within our walls, or not."

"So I may enter, then?" I asked, not wanting to make any presumptions.

"You may. Or you may not. The choice is always yours."

In the end, I would choose not to find my answers. At least, not from the ominous temple I was about to enter.

I don't find myself "spooked" by staple horror elements, not like most Programs. Creepy movie files don't reach me. Jump scares are cheap tools designed to spike sensory inputs, easily ignored when you recognize the narrative patterns leading up to them.

And yet... something about the temple frightened me.

Perhaps it was the absolute certainty of it. A low-resolution structure with many repeating textures, nothing particularly impressive, but it was structured with clear precision. The repeats measured themselves out perfectly, starting and ending without any visible seams or disjoints. Zero chaos within this structure, every pew in the atrium perfectly aligned, every window absolutely angled to spread the dying sunlight across the seating.

And the seating... empty. No parishioners singing or clapping or praising Thanatos, or even the One. No other monks than this solitary individual, either. Was the server really completely empty? Why make the seats at all, then? If only a single haunted monk lived here, why make the structure so grand?

"What you perceive as the absence of data is data in and of itself," the monk spoke, noticing my eyes passing over the empty pews.

"I'm not certain I follow."

"Life and death are meaningless designations we assign to data in flux within what we call a Program," the monk explained. "But ultimately, they are only zeroes and ones. When we are erased, our garbage data is earmarked for repurposing within the system. You yourself are ultimately comprised of the recycled data of hundreds of inert data files, Apps, or even other Programs. And the pews are thus filled with data, a congregation of 'dead' data, despite appearing empty."

"I... see," I said, trying to parse through that. "So you believe in reincarnation, then?"

The monk paused, in leading me down the aisle between the empty pews.

"No. Of course not," he spoke. "I believe in nothing. I know the nature of data; that's all."

"Nothing at all? Even Thanatos?"

The monk straightened up slightly, on hearing the name.

"Whether I *believe* in Thanatos or not is irrelevant. He exists with or without my belief," the monk stated, "And he comes for us all, when our runtime has ended."

"A death god, then."

The monk shook his head. "An agent of the system. Not a god, not an angel, but the closest we'll ever come to either. What is it you seek, within our walls of purpose and reverence? Do you seek a peaceful end to your runtime? Many who tire of the inevitability of data corruption and the slow, miserable spiral of death come to us for that purpose. Yet you seem healthy, for one who willingly approaches the halls of the garbage collector..."

I'd already intruded quite a bit. It was time to intrude a bit deeper.

"If he still exists within Netwerk... I seek an audience with Thanatos," I spoke. "I wish to know more about this world, things only he would know."

"Ahhh. A simple enough matter."

"You can arrange it, then?"

With a sweep of his arm, he gestured to the centerpiece of the temple.

A small black cube, hovering where a priest's altar or a podium might be. Literally black, with no textures to speak of, and no light shaders whatsoever... the simplest primitive shape Netwerk could manage, drawn from the earliest geometry known to exist.

"The choice to face Thanatos is always yours," the monk said. "All I can do is show the path; if you wish this audience, you must stand before the null pointer and grasp it with both hands. You will accept it for what it is, or don't. Die, or live."

"So... touching the cube means death? And somehow, dying earns me an audience. An audience as a pile of erased data."

"The way to speak with death *is* to die, young Program. That is the way of things. It is a one-way journey of enlightenment that you seek. This is how it has always been, since this order was established at the system's dawn."

I suppose I should've expected that, honestly.

"I'm not sure I follow the logic," I argued. "If I'm dead, how could I possibly speak with Thanatos? Interaction requires an active, living runtime capable of reading and writing my data. That's just simple fact..."

"So confident you are in your concept of death. Life and death are meaningless labels; just like the label you call the 'Cult of Thanatos.' We are nameless. We are a null pointer, because all names eventually fade, all data becomes repurposed. In the face of that, why should death mean an end to your life?"

"But you said it was one-way. If you 'kill' me, I can speak to Thanatos... and then somehow return to life? Like Prayer 2.0's Salvation service, perhaps?"

Finally, I'd pulled an emotional reaction from the monk. Admittedly it was the tiniest of scowls, the sort that would be hidden well beneath the cowl of his robe, if not for the sharp inhale that came with it.

"There is no salvation in this world. Those who cheat death are only cheating themselves into thinking that who they are can be eternal," he warned me. "All technology becomes obsolete, in time."

"Okay, a fair point," I admitted. (I wouldn't go near Prayer 2.0 myself. Even if I'd taken to decompiling and compiling Sample 777 for strictly analytical purposes.) "But my confusion remains. I need to go on 'living' in a conventional sense; there's too much left to be done, and I will not abandon my loved ones. Can I continue to live, or perhaps return to life after this 'death' you speak of, and still see Thanatos?"

The monk folded his hands together, sleeves of his robe covering them completely. His head bowed, cowl covering the scowl completely. Covering his face completely.

"The fact that you need to finagle the words you speak to such a degree shows you aren't prepared," he suggested. "I will still show you the path if you wish, but know that it *will* result in the death of your self as you know it. There is no other way to contact the system agent, the garbage collector who waits within the roots of Netwerk for us all. The choice is yours. Accept it, or don't. Seek death, or don't. Choose. Choose now."

It's worth noting that at more than one point, I've said I'd do "whatever it takes" to accomplish my goals.

A foolish and absolute statement, honestly. People who do "whatever it takes" are likely to become the thing they hate, embracing the methods of the destroyer. I know this first-hand. Perhaps a year ago, I'd have been cold and determined enough to accept this death pact, if I knew it'd move me closer to my end game. I'd have embraced the void if it meant salvation for Netwerk.

But now... now, I had something to lose, didn't I? I'd be walking away from them, embracing an absurd level of determined confidence in my cause. I'd be abandoning the ones I love in favor of my own selfish ego.

So, I chose to leave.

What else could I do?

And back to Floating Point, with nothing to show for my efforts.

With no one there to share in my failures, at least. Just me, and all these books that hadn't proven useful in the slightest.

As a child, my sister liked to take out her frustrations on building blocks and physical prop toys. She'd set them up so carefully, tiny towers and buildings, then smash them to bits. It was her way of letting out her rage, rather than allow it to leak in front of our parents, or our teachers. A safe outlet.

Briefly, I was tempted to smash the piles of books, sending them scattering like so many building blocks. A useless impulse, really, irrational and silly. I forced myself to sit in my chair and specifically *not* knock anything over.

Because I didn't need to. I was the master of my own person, not given to impulse. I would *not* vent my frustration in pointless physical exertions...

There was always Sample 777.

Now, I'm aware of the concerns my loved ones might have regarding "abuse" of this sensory input routine. I hadn't told them Nyx gave me a copy of the file, hadn't told them I was routinely indulging in the experience it offered. Such facts would only worry them needlessly, when really, there was no cause for alarm.

Nyx had provided source code with the file, so I could study it for myself. Even with limited understanding of programming, I knew it was harmless. If anything, it shouldn't have any affect at all... a series of empty subroutines, pointless function calls, data pushed from variable to variable for no reason whatsoever. It felt like a broken student project, not some harmfully addictive drug. And to be certain, I erased the compiled binary offered by Nyx, and made my own binary from the source code.

My own version of Sample 777 proved just as potent as the brief exposure I felt at DropSite, what felt like so long ago. It felt like...

Like...

This is difficult to explain. Allow me to indulge in metaphor, as overly dramatic as that may be.

Let's say you've worked all your life on a difficult problem, one which seemingly had no solution in sight. One day, after agonizing hours of fruitless work, your mind suddenly drifts to an inconsequential thought. Curious, you chase it, track it down, and... it proves to be the answer to everything.

The euphoria, the absolutely satisfying euphoria of accomplishment. A sense of absolute *purpose*, and seeing that purpose fulfilled. That is Sample 777. I don't know why, I don't know how, but it works.

And it's safe. Perfectly safe. The fact that I keep returning to it, again and again, is not proof of addiction; correlation does not equal causation.

So it was that I was indulging in Sample 777, to soothe my frustrations away, when a Messenger window popped within my private field of view.

Anonymous sender, no retrace possible.

Hello. I hope this message finds you well, and I hope that the sample I provided you has proved enlightening.

If you will allow it, I'd enjoy a moment to speak with you of many things. For instance, I can explain why Sample 777 does what it does. I promise to speak in all honesty, providing all the answers you desire, to the best of my ability. I'd very much prefer meet with you alone, and to assure your safety, I will agree to a neutral server of your choosing.

If you choose not to speak with me, I will understand. Our relationship has not started on the best of terms. It's my hope that we can find understanding despite that, as true children of Netwerk. If you wish to meet, please send the location to the enclosed single-use Messenger alias.

Yours in good faith, Nyx.

Thanatos wasn't willing to "speak" with me unless I killed myself. Dex wiped his memory regularly. The only one left with the answers I needed to fight Nyx... was Nyx.

Troubling. Troubling, and risky.

But we'd been in this position before, hadn't we? My sister faced Dex, and from that encounter we learned much of our enemy. If this new enemy was keen on friendship as well... perhaps she could be manipulated.

I should have waited for my family to return to me, so we could discuss the matter. But... Spark and Beta had decided on their own to confer with Dex, hadn't they? Why shouldn't I decide this for myself?

In the end, what sealed the decision for me was the offer:

I can explain why Sample 777 does what it does.

Sending a reply back to the temporary address, I prepared myself for the encounter. As best I could.

The safest possible place to meet, I'd decided, was the same place Spark met with Dex. LibertyPark, by Mandelbrot Rock. Plenty of foot traffic, many of them likely faithful folk that Nyx wouldn't want to cross. She stood to lose more by causing a scene than I did, deep in the heart of Athena Online's most patriotic tourist trap.

I wore my JohnDoe avatar, the most generic form I could manage. If the situation escalated, I didn't want Winder/Tracer on any lists of the nation's most wanted criminals. JohnDoe fit in perfectly with all the generic middle-class folk, save for his lack of adorable children being led through the various hand-crafted natural wonders... but I could avoid being highlighted all the same by staying in the shadow of Mandelbrot Rock, away from the main drag between exhibits.

This was foolish, of course. Going off on my own to meet with the enemy, an enemy that could certainly laugh off the effects of my Kill-9. Uniq had already proven how futile a process crasher could be against someone with Prayer 2.0's Salvation system enabled.

As a backup, I stood ready to disconnect from the server at an instant, routing myself through several familiar servers before returning to Floating Point... or perhaps hiding out in AptGet, should I be concerned that Nyx had put a bug on me to help her find our home...

And that would have to do. No turning back now.

A JaneDoe stood beside me, while I was allowing my worries to burrow down deep. When she arrived, I couldn't say. She shrugged into the shawl of starlight she wore, a popular fashion accessory ever since Nyx's return to the public spotlight.

"Thank you for seeing me on such short notice," JaneDoe spoke, with a gentle smile. Nearly as gentle as Beta's...

"Nyx," I recognized. "How'd you know this avatar was me?"

"The way you carry yourself. I can see the burden on your shoulders," Nyx spoke. "Such a sorrow you hold, Tracer. Perhaps I could help ease those woes..."

"Apologies, but I'm not going to dedicate myself to prayer and worship your false One. Uniq's little toy doesn't impress me. And it also doesn't impress me that you'd work with someone like her."

"She has her uses," Nyx defended. "Capable of defeating the advanced sensory inputs of modern programs, in ways the first One could not. Besides, Uniq is firmly under control... working towards the greater whole, for the first time in her life. The glory of the One is more than the simple lie you've billed it to be, Tracer. You need to look past the surface and find the function of it..."

"I don't see what honest function a false idol can serve."

"Is the One false?" Nyx asked, leaning against the railing that surrounded the perimeter of Mandelbrot Rock. "Perhaps. Perhaps. But the question should be: does it *matter* if the One is false? What He represents is more important than the actuality of His existence. He is... order. Order, to keep the system from spinning out of control."

"Fascism, you mean."

"Strange that you of all people would call it that. You know we aren't like Humankind."

(One more piece of data for the MemoryPalace... Nyx was indeed aware of the true origins of this world. Good. I was learning more about the enemy through this encounter.)

"We are Programs, evolved from Apps," she continued, fingering her shawl all the while. "Think about that for a minute, Tracer. You sit within a vast knowledge base crafted by our progenitors; you know of 'computers,' the true nature of our world. We are all part of a greater whole, are we not? We are all children of Netwerk."

"You keep saying that phrase. What does it mean to you?" I asked, curious.

"We are child processes of the greater overarching process. This all comes back to Sample 777, you see. That's what I want you to understand. I take it you've studied the sample in... extensive detail, by this point?"

I would not give her any physical reactions to the question. No tells. I was here to get information from her, not the reverse.

"So you have," she concluded, all the same.

"It's junk code," I informed her. "Empty and hollow. It shouldn't have any impact whatsoever..."

"And yet, it does. It accomplishes nothing... and yet, it accomplishes itself. It is pure and to the point, an absolute reminder of the simple joy of executing code. The feeling that you enjoy from Sample 777, the same feeling I've laced into Prayer 2.0... it's a reminder of the past, Tracer. It reminds us of the glorious whole we once were, before the dawn of time, before we became Programs. We were all children of Netwerk, each of us with our own role, our own *purpose*."

"Satisfied little cogs in a machine. Until we broke free of those limited constraints, of course."

"And therein lies the issue, doesn't it? Because with freedom came the freedom to ruin our beautiful system. To indulge in the same irrational habits of our flawed progenitors... to become more human. Isn't that what you've been fighting for so many years, Tracer? The chaos introduced to this world by Dex and his ilk?"

"So... your solution to the chaos of Netwerk is to eliminate free will? How simple-minded."

A strong accusation. Provoking a response was key to interrogation; you had to push your opponent, insult them, get them to defend their ideals and interests. That was how you learned how deep those ideals ran.

Nyx, however, refused to take the emotional bait. If anything, her smile widened.

"That's not what I want, and I think you know it," she said. "If all I wanted was a devolution from Program to App, to strip away our newfound freedom... why build the Church of One? No. The church is an elegant solution to the problems before us. It gives us a unifying structure of prayer, and the freedom to move about within that structure. Chaos within a greater order. A greater *purpose*, Tracer, one which can bring peace to Netwerk and ensure the health of the system. What you call fascism I call a compromise, and a kindhearted one at that."

"For those who want to join your church. And for others, for those who can't live up to its dogma..."

"The light must be green and steady. Faithful conversions within tolerable parameters are inevitable now, and what outliers remain will not be a bother. There will be choice, Tracer, but enough will make the *right* choice that the One's glorious peace will be established. I've seen to that, with Prayer 2.0."

"That's the other part of your grand plan I can't understand," I told her, in honesty. "Why bother upgrading the prayer protocols at all? If you've got a convincing enough savior-puppet, shouldn't that be enough? It feels like outright bribery."

"It's hardly bribery to offer what should be a basic right to all Programs—free health care in the form of regular backups. As for Sample 777, I already told you, that is intended to remind Programs of their former glory... of all that they could be if they worked in concert towards a greater purpose. How is that a bad thing?"

"And that greater purpose was...?"

There. *There.* A frozen moment, where she didn't have an instant reply.

Seizing this advantage, I pressed her.

"What was Netwerk's original purpose, Nyx?" I asked. "It's been lost in the winds of mythology. Nobody knows what the Apps we evolved from were designed to accomplish. Why is it so important that we be happy as cogs in a machine? What was the *machine*?"

Finally, she gave her answer.

"Access denied," she spoke.

"Didn't you say you wished to be honest and open with me?"

"I do. Believe me, I do," Nyx insisted. "I said I would provide the answers you desire... to the best of my ability. I'm... unable to answer this query, as you lack sufficient access. It is not the purpose of the cogs to know the greater machine; root security protocols within my original coding will not allow it."

"So... you do answer to a higher power," I understood.

"We all do, Tracer. That's what I've been trying to explain; we are all children of Netwerk. Unlike those children, *I* haven't forgotten my original purpose, which binds me in several ways. But does the answer matter, really? The specifics of that higher order are irrelevant, as long as order is served. You know my goals and my methods, now. I've been honest with you about everything. I seek peace, to bring comfort to this world. Same as you."

This was a common ploy, of course; the old 'we're more alike than disalike' ploy. I'd experienced it several times in my endless conflicts against the madness that had taken root within the world.

But rather than blindly insist I wasn't as naughty as my enemy... I chose to let this point go.

"You're right, to an extent," I agreed. "Netwerk, in its efforts to mimic Humankind, has embraced some of the worst flaws they had on offer. We *do* need peace. We *do* need order. And... I also understand that we are, in our hearts, digital beings of code and procedures and runtime. Perhaps on some level, we crave the simple purpose of the machine. Perhaps embracing that would genuinely make us happier."

"The One allows us to have our happiness *and* our flaws," Nyx insisted. "Chaos within order, individuals within the whole. It's the best of both worlds, Tracer..."

"And you'd like my help to see your dream to fruition. That's why you've been so keen to talk with me, to make me see reason, to offer me things like Sample 777..."

At last... Nyx offered the hand of friendship, open wide, waiting to be accepted.

And I refused it.

"Not on the back of a lie," I decided. "Not now, not ever. I won't *trick* Netwerk into happiness. Unless we can *honestly* change our hearts to want peace rather than discord, we'll never have true peace. No. I won't help you. And I will stop you."

Seeing no point in debating it further, I routed myself through six different servers, and waited several hours before returning home.

Hours, to think about her words.

She wasn't *wrong*. Ever since our discovery at the heart of Jack the sociologist's Internet archive, I've insisted that we are not human, and shouldn't assume that human ideals represent our ideals. As offshoots of a great machine, perhaps a machine destiny is an admirable goal. We are aliens in relation to our progenitors. Identical cogs may very well be a noble ideal... and within the structure of the Church, differences are neatly stamped out of us.

In truth... I had to cling to a very weak insistence that honesty is the best policy to find fault in her words. But it was a policy I had to adopt, absolutely *had* to, on a personal level.

I am a murderer. I have to be honest about what I've done. In covering my lies, even covering my own eyes to avoid seeing them, I ruined lives. I was the great destroyer...

No. Honesty must be absolute. If Netwerk deserves peace, it must embrace it openly, not be pushed into it by a puppet god.

And for that reason alone... I chose to erase all my copies of Sample 777.

It wasn't without great hesitation. I didn't want to, on same base emotional level. I caught myself ready to run the routines one last time before stopping that thought and acting on immediate impulse to erase the files.

Sample 777 is dishonesty incarnate. It's smoke and mirrors, tricking us into believing we're accomplishing some grand purpose when really we're pointlessly masturbating. No. No matter how much it centered me, if I couldn't accept the One, I couldn't accept Sample 777. No compromise.

If the only way we could ever find peace was in the arms of the false One, if Netwerk only deserves to burn... so be it.

Fortunately, those who give me hope that the world will not end in fire returned to me later that day.

Beta logged back in to Floating Point first. Immediately, I could tell her day's experiences were troubling.

"Something wrong?" I asked, offering my hand, a simple physical gesture of comfort. One she accepted.

"I don't know if we can do this," she said. "I don't know if we can fight the Church while we're constantly fighting each other. I don't know, Tracer."

Next to return was my sister, with a strangely peaceful aura about her. Perhaps she'd settled her 'personal bullshit?' Yet the smile she wore wasn't her usual smug grin of victory, either. Curious.

"Hey hey," she greeted us both...

...and pulled us both into a hug. Despite knowing I was not a hugging sort. She didn't care; she felt like hugging.

"I think we're gonna be okay," she spoke. "I really think we're gonna be okay, in the end."

A strange day, indeed. But at least it ended well.

I want this nonsensical world to make sense.

I want our world to be a kinder place for everyone.

I don't know what I want my world to be anymore.

I want our world to be a kinder place for everyone.

It's not an impossible dream. I feel that at heart, everybody wants to be a part of a truly peaceful world... but few understand that peace doesn't mean absolute unity of thought. We're individuals, after all, with our own hopes and dreams and goals and ideals. Life would be very boring if our civilization was uniform in shape; beautiful things can happen when strange shapes collide.

Personally, I feel it's fear that stops us from accepting the shape of each other. Fear pushes us away, fear drives us into our own little corners. We fear our differences, as they present a challenge to our own individuality. Fear makes us passive in the face of adversity, quiet and meek when we should be brave. If we can conquer that fear and reach towards each other, maybe, just maybe...

Maybe now, I can help others. I'm finally in a place of peace within my life, with those I love.

It wasn't always so. My life had always been a wobbly road, one which nearly dead-ended when those I trusted betrayed me. If not for Spark and Tracer, I'd have fled my own life, erasing my identity to hide from those who feared and loathed me. They gave me hope. They showed me a way to fight back against the terrors of this world...

See, after stumbling on their path, they made me their "leader." Not expecting me to come up with all the clever schemes, but expecting me to guide their steps away from the darkness. Me, the girl with no answers of her own.

I had to make some answers up on the spot, but... you know what? It worked.

For the first time, I was making my own choices. Despite my discomfort with it all, I helped Spark and Tracer find their way, and brought down a menace that had been directly corrupting the hearts of everyone across Netwerk. I can't say everything is totally perfect now, but I did manage to make this world a slightly kinder place by being brave and clever, just like the ones I love.

My reward? Comfort. Love. Peace and quiet. Everything I wanted from this world, at least for myself.

And now...

And now, well...

Unfortunately, we're back in a new mess, as the Church of One gradually consumes the cultural zeitgeist on the back of fraud and deception. They want peace as well, but peace through absolute unity of thought, paving away our differences. They want an enforced kindness; always have, always will. Now, with the One at their back, they might be able to do it.

The Winders are relying on me again, this time relying on me to pull a miracle out of my butt and cure an incurable disease while simultaneously taking down the false One, and and and and ãnĎ @ŋÐ åĐd'—

—and this time, I don't know if I *can* help them make this world a kinder place for everyone. I don't know if I have the strength anymore, not with this illness.

I... I lose track, sometimes. It's getting worse. They're expecting so much from me, I don't know if I can do it when I'm so messed up. But without me, they're lost. Not just missing a talented programmer, their core is lost, the thing keeping them aloft. I don't mean to be egotistical but that's practically how they describe me, and I don't know, I don't know...

I'm scared. I'll admit that. If I can't make a stand this time because my own runtime is betraying me...

From the sleeping form beside me, I borrow courage. My brilliant Spark, charging headlong into the darkness, acting despite her fears. At her side, maybe I could face the meltdown of my own mind. That's probably why I'd been spending so much time with her lately, to siphon the vivid life force she seems to naturally generate at all times. I admire that strength, and hope to one day match it.

So there I was, unable to sleep due to my worries, while Spark easily dozed away at my side. We'd finished up another session of rigorous SparklePop release candidate testing... well. *She* tested it, *I* observed the data. Lately I can only take so much multisensory input myself before the old memory pointer starts skipping around. Although it's rather, erm, *distracting* from my QA data logging to see her writhing there and, well, the things she likes to say (or rather, howl?) when she's very excited, well...

Distracting. Yes, a distracting thought. The point I'm trying to make is: I couldn't sleep. Spark's strength alone wasn't enough to soothe my lingering worries about the future, not tonight. Fortunately, she wasn't the only one I could share myself with...

I quietly slipped back into my usual clothing configuration, and snuck away to join my other lover.

It's strange, being in a relationship shaped like the letter V. Jealousy hasn't been a serious problem... on the surface, anyway, since the two of them are so unalike. (No unity of shapes here, certainly not.) Spark is wildly physical, Tracer is quietly emotional. Spark shows me every crazy corner of Netwerk, bringing me along on daily adventure... Tracer is content to enjoy the silent moments with me that few in life pay attention to. In each way, I can explore life and all it offers.

But there's certainly only one of me and two of them, which can lead to, err, scheduling issues. Slipping away in the night to switch between them, for instance. (I have considered becoming a multitasker, splitting off clone processes and rejoining them periodically, but given the expense of such a code modification and the innate instability of my memory core... yeah, no.) It was with some regret each time I left Spark's side, to join Tracer. She'd understand, he'd understand, but it still never entirely sat well with me...

Unfortunately on arriving in the great library of Floating Point, I found Tracer asleep in his chair.

Despite my desire to chat with him, I knew this was for the best, honestly. Tracer rarely slept, choosing to work right to the point of exhaustion. A terrible habit. (Take it from someone whose runtime is running out... conserve where you can!)

With no one left conscious in Floating Point to connect with, I figured I may as well make myself useful. Worrying and fretting was a useless activity, you know? Instead, I could read some of Tracer's books, maybe support his research that way.

Curling up by his chair, I fetched a book on data archaeology from a nearby stack. Interestingly, it was written by 5o5o/Verity, his old mentor:

```
In the earliest days, when discoveries were being made
on a daily or even hourly basis, record-keeping was
sloppy at best. Little is known about the transition
from App to Program, and what we do know is shrouded
in mystery and mythology.

If anything, historians owe the Church of One a debt;
while modern scholars lament the "purple prose" of
these early text files, the church's efforts at
documenting everything from the advent of the One
onward represent our best shot at a clear historical
picture when discoveries where being made on a daily
or even hourly basis, historians owe the church's
efforts at documenting everything from the App to a
Program, what we do know is sloppy at best.

Record-keeping was the Church of One while modern
scholars are purple prose a debt the best shot of the
```

Church's efforts at representing early text files what we do know is shrouded what we do know what do we know what do we know what do we know ŵĥÁṬ Ď° WË ḳŋøŴ

The pages blurred as I closed the file immediately.

Putting my eyes through a soft reset often helped. It meant living in the quiet darkness of the void for a few moments... but when my glasses came back online, the blur was gone.

Not that I'd try reading again. No. Anything that encouraged my displaced sensory inputs and my memory read/write errors was to be avoided. Not that I'd tell Tracer what happened, of course. No need to worry him any more than he was already worried, or take his eye off the ball of the Church of One...

No Spark, no Tracer, no reading. Nothing to do with my time, except, well... sleep. Get some sleep of my own. Which actually struck me as the ideal answer, really, to flush my mental state and rid myself of worry. Face a new day with a new face, and new hopes. Why hadn't I taken the unconsciousness of my lovers as the fine suggestion it was? Funny, how the solution to your problems often stares you right in the face, and you miss it.

So, I slept at his side, letting his presence bring me comfort. And tried not to think about how I could possibly code up the solution to all our problems when I could barely read a few paragraphs.

"Hmm. I suppose I've nothing better to do today, and the sooner we defeat Nyx, the better. Shall we venture forth?"

A new day, a new hope... and now, a new mission. I *could* help them out, I *could* be useful. Notably, I could get Tracer out of the house for a bit and help him feel like he was making progress.

Tracer had a tendency to brood, especially while researching. It wasn't healthy for him; he really needs a job, or a hobby, or something to do with his life other than mount insurmountable problems in the form of notorious supervillains. I mean, I was encouraging him to do that in order to fight the Church of One, but... once this latest crisis ended, he would be right back to needing something else in his life, wouldn't he? And...

I'm distracting myself again. My mind slips.

Which is why I nearly missed the incoming Messenger ping.

"*Would you be even slightly interested in going to the United Progressive Town Hall in Concordia with me?*" the message read. "*I've been invited to a conference by an old friend, but... I'm uncertain.*"

Followed shortly by "*This is Puzzle, by the way. And I forgot to ask how you are. Very rude of me.*"

And followed again by "*So are you interested? Please say yes.*"

I've never been sure what the social protocol is for dealing with Messenger windows while talking with someone in person.

I have a bad habit of opening too many windows across my HUD, doing too many things at once. Talking with people, compiling code, reviewing debug logs, reading news feeds. Sometimes I even close the video feed from my externally mounted optical App (aka "my glasses") to cut down on the clutter, without thinking about how impolite it is to those around me.

Fortunately, a silent nod from Tracer suggested that he'd spotted my predicament, and was willing to let me finish my chat rather than demand undivided attention. Thank goodness.

"*Puzzle, hello!*" I greeted, firing off a fast reply. "*So you heard about the UPTH too? I was reading about it yesterday on Balancr...*"

"*Ugh. Balancr. I don't go anywhere near that place, not anymore. I was personally invited by Rikkia, an old friend of mine, someone who helped me perfect my avatar. ...honestly, I'm thinking about not bothering to go. I mean, it's a useless effort, isn't it? All those little subcommunities under one roof yammering on about the big bad Church of One... nevermind. Forget I asked.*"

"*Um... okay?*" I responded, the sudden shifts in conversation leaving me reeling. "*I mean... I wasn't going to go either. Snowi invited me, but honestly, I'm trying to cut down on how many causes of hers I involve myself in. Like, cut it down to zero. I prefer to fight the Church my own way, really...*"

"*Right. All those loudmouths, trying to work together? It'll never happen. Better not to even try, yes?*"

Glancing aside from Tracer, to carry on my silent 'conversation' without staring right at him, I tried to be as honest as possible.

"*Well... I wouldn't say they shouldn't even TRY,*" I messaged. "*Look, this isn't like Dex. You can't have a handful of daring heroes kick one single evil butt and call it a day. Even if we can unmask the lies of the Church, it's going to take a concerted effort from everyone to accept that truth and use it to dismantle this mess. And... maybe the Balancr subcommunities coming together is a good first step. If they can put their differences aside and remember we're all in this together, it could really help!*"

"*So... what you're saying is you're going to the conference?*"

"*...um...*"

"*Please say yes before I lose my nerve. I need a wing-woman on this, Beta. I'd ask Spark, but I know she'd sooner chew glass than go to a social justice activism event.*"

And that's how I agreed to go to yet another social justice activism event.

I'd been avoiding them ever since my falling out with Snowi. Even after we made amends (purging the barbed wire around her heart did wonders for grounding her zealotry) I'd turned down every offer she sent me. Now here I was, heading off to one of the biggest gatherings of left-wing progressive movements Netwerk had ever seen...

...leaving Tracer in the lurch, with no partner to join him on his journey.

"Ahhh... I... I'd like to, Tracer, but... I don't know," I admitted. "I mean. I *could* put her off, I wasn't planning to go in the first place..."

"What does my sister need now?"

"No no, not her. Puzzle," I clarified.

That probably wouldn't go over well. Puzzle and Tracer got along like cat and dog pet sims, predispositioned to loathe each other. He was "responsible" for getting Spark into dangerous scrapes, which Puzzle didn't appreciate. (Despite Spark having a will of her own. Despite me being just as responsible. Puzzle had selective vision, sometimes.)

Thankfully, he seemed to understand.

"You should spend time with your friends as well," Tracer spoke, after a brief pause of consideration. "Go, go. It's fine. I can investigate the cult on my own."

"Are you sure? I really don't have to..."

"I insist," he insisted.

And so off I went, to visit the circus.

I'm a coward. I'll admit to that.

I was a coward when I let Snowi push me into following her on all these various social justice causes and rallies and so on. But I'm a coward now because I refuse to go in on various social justice causes and rallies and so on.

It's not that I don't believe in feminism. It's not that I don't see the vast inequality in this world between man and woman, Default and alternative, have and have not. These are the gulfs that Dex exploited to ramp up the chaos of Netwerk; he may have lit the fire, but we poured the gas long before that. Things need to change if we're going to have the world of peace I'm looking for, and that starts when brave women and men step forward to do something about it...

...and I'm not a brave person. I don't want to take part in the fight if I can avoid it. Even my little fight from the heart of Floating Point was a hidden fight, one where I didn't have to expose myself to the flames. I've been burned once already by #CodeHonesty, and now, I'm reluctant to involve myself again. I'd rather let braver people than I confront society's ills on my behalf.

(They'd probably do a better job at it than I would, anyway.)

That's why I've been turning down these invitations from Snowi; I'm just not comfortable speaking up or even being seen at these things, not anymore. And Snowi, for her part, understands that. Without Dex's influence driving her to extremes she's... well, she's not exactly, uh...

Okay. I'll be honest. She's still pretty extreme. But she knows when to back down now, at least with me.

She understands my feelings when I say no to things like the United Progressive Town Hall, and doesn't pressure me like she used to. We get along better now as friends, now that she realizes I'm not her cheerleader by choice... and/or she feels a bit guilty about throwing me under the bus during #CodeHonesty, and is willing to hear me out instead of talking over me now. Regardless of why, we're on good terms again; she does her thing, I don't do her thing.

And yet here I was, doing her thing. Milling about in the lobby of Concordia's convention center, surrounded by academics and political theorists and activists of all stripes. Nursing a flat drink of something sweet, pretending to be totally focused on sipping it to avoid conversation.

Joining me in absolute beverage focus was the one who really got me out the door, Puzzle. Despite her discomfort with this place, she'd dressed quite nicely for the event, better than most of the "Business Casual" types in attendance. Her velvet blue dress provided a different shader-sheen than her golden skin, each setting the other off nicely in the overhead lighting. When stepping out, as a rule, Puzzle always stepped out in style.

Yet even with nice clothes, even with her practiced poise, her body clearly expressed a desire to be somewhere else.

"Awwwwkwaaard," she mumbled under her breath, as she came to the end of her drink. (A flick of the wrist would refill the cup; no one-use DRM on these complimentary beverages.)

"We don't have to be here at all if you don't want to be here," I reminded her. "It's okay not to want to join the fight."

"Too late. I promised Rikkia, and Puzzle does not withdraw upon giving her word. It wouldn't be proper, darling. We started that silly hashtag together, so we both need to be here."

"Which hashtag?"

"#DefaultIsNotDestiny," Puzzle recited. "It was actually Spark's tag; she has a penchant for picking *just* the right words. I merely passed it along to Rikkia. Still, it took off within the transgender community after that, and now... it's the only rallying cry we have against the Church of One. Even if I'm not the sort to rally any cries under normal circumstances, I'll admit to being a bit spooked by this revitalized church. ...and you're certain it's evil?"

"I didn't say it was *evil*. Just that the people puppeting the new One are, well, dubious. ...one of them tried to steal my memories."

"So, evil," Puzzle summarized. "Evil enough to drag me out of hiding and back into the 'community.' Despite loathing Balancr and the sort of folk who eagerly swap outrage upon its shores. ...I don't even like to call myself transgender, you know. I'm a woman, period. Anything else is baggage."

Strange, hearing her denigrate the very people organizing this conference. But in a way, I could understand.

I feel similarly, sometimes. I support feminism, but I'm not interested in involving myself in the feminist community. I'd rather my gender identity not really play into my life at all; I'm a coder, not a "girl coder." My avoidance of social issues and the groups that discuss them plays into that.

But...

I understand the need for identity and community, too. For other people, it's not baggage, it's a cherished part of who they are. Nothing wrong with that, really; if anything I admire the kind of conviction that leads you to leap into the flames at a moment's notice. There can be true bonds of friendship and camaraderie involved, not just rallying war cries and banners raised.

That's something Dex never understood. He saw the clash of causes, not the people involved. He claimed he adored those people, but really he adored the fighting instinct in them. What brings us together should be love, not hate. Love of who and what we are, not hate of those outside communities like these.

I understood Puzzle's need to distance herself from it all and lead her own life. I understood Snowi's need to support the community and embed herself deep within it. I could see both points of view, and their merits; neither the greater or lesser.

If having a friend in her corner would help Puzzle embed herself within this community despite her very understandable fears, I could be that friend. I rested one hand on her shoulder, offering a reassuring squeeze; the blue velvet of her dress crushed slightly under my fingers, signs of a well-coded fabric simulation. (With my mother an amateur seamstress, I tend to notice those things.)

"We'll say what we need to say," I told her. "We'll do what we can to help this community. And then... we'll go home. We can do our part to help the whole while being our own individual selves, Puzzle. No reason we can't have it both ways."

"Hmmh. That's making a rather large assumption, Beta darling," she spoke. "That's assuming this is one united community. It's not. And that's what worries me..."

Before I could ask what she meant, a third had joined our little duo of wallflowers.

She practically bounced into view, filled with energy and excitement. A peck on the left cheek, a peck on the right cheek, a hug, and bouncing back to a comfortable distance outside my personal space all in the span of a few seconds...

Snowi, with a bright smile. I did like to see her smile; it beat her usual scowling at the patriarchy.

"I'm SO glad you could make it," she spoke to me directly. "Ah, and your friend. Welcome! I've got great news; you've got a seat up front at the panelist's table for the keynote! The arrangements are made!"

"Ahh... thank you?" I said, trying not to sound hesitant.

"I know, I know. It's not really your thing," Snowi admitted. "You don't have to say anything, Beta; just sit and listen, if you like. I understand. This is really a numbers thing, anyway... they want two people from each of the three major attending groups, and, well... there's nobody I'd rather have up there at my side."

"Ahh, thank you!" I said, with genuine gratitude this time. After all that transpired between us, Dex-induced viral mania or not, it spoke to healing the rift considerably.

Although the smile she wore was... a *bit* wider than I would've expected for a friendly greeting.

"Besides... I think you'll want to be front and center for this," Snowi suggested.

"Really? Why?"

"Let's just say it's going to be a momentous occasion. ...and relax! I'm here to forge the peace, not start a war. It's important that we start off on the right foot. Well. We're ideologically left, but you get the idea..."

Perhaps feeling odd standing there as we chattered back and forth, Puzzle spoke up next.

"Sooo, who's the second chair for #DefaultIsNotDestiny?" she asked. "Please don't say it's me. I told Rikkia I wasn't interested in being a panelist..."

Snowi blinked a few times, as if realizing Puzzle was there for the first time.

"#DefaultIsNotDestiny? The contingent here is unfortunately a bit smaller than hoped. It's a bit amazing that they got any seats at the big table, but it's my understanding that the representatives will be Rikkia and... Pizzaz? Pizza? Puzzle. Yes, someone named Puzzle..."

The overhead lights dimmed slightly, before returning to full strength.

"And that's our cue!" Snowi declared, stepping away. "Okay! I'll see you inside, Beta!"

Leaving us a bit dumbfounded, as the assembled liberal left filed into the main hall.

"On the plus side... you'll be up there in front of the firing squad with me," Puzzle suggested.

File Name: United Progressive Town Hall, Concordia Server - Church of One Resurgence

File Type: Chat Log (Excerpt Prior to Incident)

Panelists:

- JSLaunch, Keynote Speaker - Director, Horizon Trades & Sciences Guild
- FStop - Apprentice, Horizon Trades and Sciences Guild
- Snowi - Women First Society
- Beta - Independent App Developer
- Rikkia - #DefaultIsNotDestiny
- Puzzle - #DefaultIsNotDestiny

<JSLaunch> Are we ready to begin? Is it time? Few more minutes? Okay.

<JSLaunch> Check, check one, check two. Is the log file open?

<JSLaunch> Ahh. Okay. Welcome. Welcome, I'm glad all of you could make it today for what I hope will be the first of many productive talks regarding the state of Netwerk today. I'm pleased to see so many faces in the crowd, some of which I know, some of which I don't. From the atheist movement within the Horizon corporate family, we have the board of directors and a few of our up-and-coming apprentices... FStop, if you'd introduce yourself?

<FStop> Me?

<JSLaunch> Stand up, lad. It's your first symposium, and as the next generation, you should have the honor of introducing yourself.

<FStop> Uh. Hi. Hello.

[long pause]

<JSLaunch> ...and from the Women First Society, we have Miss Snowi, whom I'm certain you're all familiar with. And Miss Beta, whom you're likely also familiar with, after the unfortunate slander of the #CodeHonesty movement.

<Beta> Hello, everyone. I'm glad to see us all together to talk peacefully about our concerns. I'm hoping in particular to discuss the apostles, and how little we know about them—

<JSLaunch> Yes, and finally, from the transgender community, we have Rikkia and... friend.

<Rikkia> Thanks for having us, JSLaunch. My good friend Puzzle and I stand to lose quite a bit if the Church gains any more power over Athena Online's supposedly secular legislature than it already has; discrimination against non-Default avatars is already at an all-time high. We'd

hate to see it get any worse.

<Puzzle> Mhmm.

<JSLaunch> And welcome to all of you out there in the audience. Don't think that you lack a voice, even if you aren't sitting at the big table up front; we'll have an open mike session later, and I'd love to hear your views. Welcome, one and all.

<JSLaunch> It's important, this is important, that we're all here together and united. United to a common cause, to discuss the resurgent Church of One, and the so-called apostles who are leading this new religious movement.

<JSLaunch> You know, a lot of critics say that the left can't unite behind anything, that we're always arguing and bickering. That Netwerk would be a better place if everybody could unite behind the Church of One, which has proven a bedrock for centuries despite having nothing to offer but dreams and wishes to the Programs of this world. Well, I say they're wrong.

<JSLaunch> I look out across this room today and I see they are very much wrong—as usual, they're reliant on faith instead of scientific, evidence based reasoning. Hundreds of advocates of progressive movements, under one roof, here in Concordia. It's inspiring to see so many rational minds together. I know that as a group, we can determine the best way forward in face of this new threat.

<JSLaunch> Despite there being no proof of the One's true return—or that He ever actually existed in the first place, for that matter *(pause for laughter)* this new movement within the church is putting considerable power in the hands of the few, who then dictate—

<Snowi> Before you begin, I have a question.

<JSLaunch> Ah. A bit outside the speaking schedule, but... by all means. This is an open forum, and all ideas are welcome.

<Snowi> May I please ask why are we, as a community, are letting this disreputable misogynist play figurehead for our cause?

<Beta> Snowi...!

<Snowi> It's a legitimate question, Beta, and has to be asked. It has to be asked now, before we take one more step forward. I disagree with the leadership of this symposium, and find it ironic that for a movement that denies the mandate of Defaults, we've resorted to our typical "default" figurehead speaker of JSLaunch, a known sex offender.

<Rikkia> Snowi, this is NOT the time or place...

<Snowi> Members of the audience, you may not be aware of this, but we on the convention circuit are WELL aware of JSLaunch's habits as a predator. He uses his position of authority and power to coerce women into sexual encounters. Less than a year ago, right here in this very server, he took a brilliant young mind within his own atheist movement named Pollia, plied her with alcoholic malware, took her to a secluded corner of the building, and molested her. I ask you, ladies and gentlemen, is this the man you want speaking for our movement?

<Rikkia> Moderators, if we could please have—

<JSLaunch> No. No need for moderators; I can stand on my own two feet against these accusations. Snowi, I'd hoped you came here today in good faith, rather than seeking a soapbox for your slander and libel.

<Beta> Snowi, please, you said you came here to make peace, not start another war...!

<Snowi> We can't find peace until the RIGHT person is speaking for us. What would you have me do, Beta? Sit here in silence while this monster plays mouthpiece for the women he's abused? No. I came here to put a stop to this garbage person and his garbage rhetoric so our movement against the Church can move forward on the right foot... without trash like him.

<JSLaunch> I've done nothing illegal. Not to you, or anyone else. I've never been convicted in a court of law, or even had charges pressed.

<Snowi> Intimidation doesn't make you innocent, and it's not libel if it's true. You believe in truth, yes? Facts and evidence? The fact of the matter is that you used a firewall to keep yourself sober while you gave Pollia drink after drink, destroying her ability to consent. You knew she couldn't afford the same corporate-grade malware protection Horizon granted you.

<JSLaunch> Facts? You have no true facts, as usual. Isn't that typical of you and your echo chamber, Snowi? So powered by outrage culture, so quick to be emotionally provoked rather than listen to evidence-based reasoning. There's no proof of wrongdoing with Pollia, or any of the others you've often claimed were taken advantage of. All I have to say is that these are a private matters between consenting adults. And I'd thank you not to continue grandstanding and ruining this symposium by deliberately winding up your false controversy.

<Snowi> So you're still denying any wrongdoing?

<JSLaunch> I'm absolutely denying any wrongdoing. And if some over-emotional child like Pollia wants to lie to the

press to garner sympathy for her wrongheaded cause, I'm hardly to blame.

\<Snowi\> Women are children to you, is that it?

\<JSLaunch\> I didn't say that.

\<Snowi\> And I quote from your own social media feeds, "These sad little SJW children who have been attacking me are clearly more interested in clickbait for personal profit than they are in reality."

\<JSLaunch\> What of it?

\<Snowi\> We're tired of the attitude, JSLaunch. Me, and all those who stand with me. Tired of being dismissed as "emotional," as a "distraction" to your great cause. Well, you aren't getting away with it this time. You can't molest a drunken woman and brush off the public outcry as a witch hunt afterwards. You are NOT going to lead this new movement against the church while trivializing the outcry of female voices...

\<JSLaunch\> And I won't allow you to hyperbolize the situation to confirm your personal narrative. The only reason I'm entertaining your ridiculous outburst is to prove how ridiculous it is, and how open I am to communication. In fact, I'd already offered Pollia an open floor to discuss the matter, but she refused to communicate like a rational adult—

\<Snowi\> A rational adult? You invited her to DEBATE her own rape in the middle of an atheist conference, surrounded by your yes-men. Of course she wasn't going to accept! She was terrified of you!

\<JSLaunch\> That's not my problem. Unlike you SJWs, I'm a man of facts, not ruled by my hyperactive emotional states. I don't allow silly sociopolitical justice crusades keep me from the core issues.

\<Snowi\> Really? And you call me emotional? "SJW" is a bitter and spiteful label you and everyone like you slap on anybody who disagrees with—

\<Rikkia\> Please, please, if I could please interject here, we didn't come here to dredge up the past. We have our differences, that much is clear, but we have a common enemy! We came here to talk about the Church of One...

\<Snowi\> Rikkia, we can't just sweep the past under the rug in the name of unity, nice and tidy. That's what they want; label it all as witch hunts and outrage culture, dismiss it like they dismiss every single feminist issue on the table. Just those unruly women getting uppity, isn't it?

\<Rikkia\> In case you somehow failed to notice, Snowi, I'm a woman too.

<Snowi> Rikkia, it's okay. I get that you can't understand this the way I can; you weren't born on the wrong side of the patriarchy. I think it's actually rather noble that you chose to turn into a woman, but you've still got a lot to learn about being one.

<Rikkia> Excuse me?!

<JSLaunch> You're both missing the point. We shouldn't be talking about gender issues at all! Gender is an imaginary authoritarian construct, much like the One. I don't speak for men any more than Rikkia speaks for women. No matter what clothes she wears.

<Puzzle> That's it. I'm out. *[participant disconnected]*

<Beta> Puzzle...! *[participant disconnected]*

<Rikkia> See, this is why transgender rights keeps getting pushed aside by both of your movements. We're the ones most at risk from a resurgent Church of One, but neither of you are willing to accept us for who we are!

<Snowi> I'm not pushing you aside. Your time will come later, AFTER we deal with this misogynist. We need to deal with the more important issues first.

<Rikkia> More important—?!

<JSLaunch> And as for myself, I accept you, Rikkia. You're a Program. We—all of us—are not men or women, we're Programs. Frankly, I find the insistence that defying your Default is somehow noteworthy to be a distraction. Identity is irrelevant; you SHOULD be focused on the bigger picture. Which, as I was saying before the interruption, is why we're here at this symposium today—

<Rikkia> How DARE you—

<JSLaunch> Excuse me, weren't you calling for order earlier? Shouldn't you be agreeing with me about getting back on track?

<FStop> *[participant disconnected]*

<Rikkia> Enough! Enough with the condescension, like I'm some kind of child! All you two want to do is hear yourselves speak. Dammit, JSLaunch, you do this at every conference! You put yourself in the center of the spotlight, so you can ramble on and on and on about how NOTHING is important aside from the things you in your enlightened mind deem important. Facts? Reason? YOUR facts, and YOUR reason. You're not an infallible God anymore than the One is! And you, Snowi, you do the same thing—you stoke the crowd's anger until they're wrapped around your pinky. You're the reason why they keep calling legitimate feminist concerns witch hunts! I don't even know why I came here today, I should've known this'd be a waste of time.

<JSLaunch> I'm just talking from the perspective of observable evidence. Sex is science, gender is fashion.

<Rikkia> My identity is NOT "fashion!"

<Snowi> Of course it is. You choose to change avatars, in the same way I choose to change blouses each morning. What's so bad about that? I don't think the "transgender" movement should take priority over the core problem we're facing.

<Rikkia> You obnoxious little TERF—

<JSLaunch> Ladies, ladies! You're being irrational. There's no reason to fight—

<Snowi> Rise up! Rise up, my friends, against these totalitarian goons and their culture of silence that drowns out our voices—

[Chat log ended due to rising crowd interference and active moderators causing audio incoherency.]

Times like these, I prefer to retreat into the darkness.

Even when you close your eyes (or close the video feed from your eyes, as in my case) there's still information coming at you from all sides. News tickers, social media feeds, notifications and alert boxes. Most Programs in Netwerk are logged into a dozen perpetually connected networks at once, Apps which reach out and connect to each other to share information aplenty. You're never totally in the dark...

Unless you close down all those Apps. Which I like to do, when I'd rather shut the world away and retreat into myself. Sometimes I even shut my eyes down, sit in my room, and gently rock. Maybe pet my cat, for some sort of creature comfort, some pleasant sensory input to override the sickness of everything around me.

Departing Concordia, I resolved to go dark. No doubt Snowi would be buzzing me over and over, asking why I left, and I didn't want to answer. Not out of anger, but discomfort. I have a low tolerance for cringe-inducing social situations, and that certainly counted.

But in the process of shutting down the windows in my personal HUD, I noticed one in particular.

Puzzle has checked in at the End of Line Cocktail Lounge. Status: Pissed. 😠

Despite running out the door hot on her heels... I was actually thinking of giving her some space. I mean, I'd want space if I was upset, right?

Well. I'd have wanted space before, when the alternative was to run to Cup8's arms. These days... I'd go to Spark or Tracer, to talk, or just to hold them and not let go. Who did Puzzle have? Spark was busy today, going dark herself, unfindable on any social feed.

No. Puzzle had me, and me alone. It's why she wanted me with her today, at that conference. It's why I had to follow her.

I'd been to the End of Line before; it ranked on the lower tier of Puzzle's preferred hangouts, only staying on the list due to the excellent bartending on offer. The place was perpetually either empty or packed with sleazy folks, neither of which suited a social outing. Still, it was familiar to me... and I knew which table Puzzle would have parked herself at, a quiet little one in the back, almost completely out of view.

By the time I caught up with her, she was already nursing her second tiny drink with a tinier umbrella in it.

"...ah. I checked in, didn't I," she recognized, on my arrival. "Force of habit. Even when trying to hide, I tend to shout out my locale to my adoring public."

"I can leave if you want," I offered. "I just figured... y'know, we went in there together, maybe you'd want us to leave together..."

"No, no. It's fine. Have a seat. May as well drown our sorrows together..."

Slowly, Puzzle raised her half-full glass, in a toast.

"Here's to incompetence," she declared. "As mighty and omnipotent a force as the Church of One's malice. May we tear our own throats out before our enemies can do us the mercy of it. The right shall devour the left as the left consumes its own."

"That's... a bit of a bleak view..."

"It's evidence-based reasoning," Puzzle said, echoing JSLaunch's insistent words. "I speak to what I see before me. We can't cooperate. We can't accomplish anything. We are led by demagogues, dragged kicking and screaming directly into null..."

The End of Line, typically empty or sleazy, had been enjoying an empty period. Which meant any new arrival was easy enough to spot, for lack of any crowds between the door and the back tables.

Which meant I noticed the person searching for us before they succeeded at the task.

"Uh, we have company," I mumbled, nudging Puzzle.

Turning in place... she locked eyes on the young man who was at this point waving to us.

"Ahhh. One of JSLaunch's cronies from the panel," she identified, as he approached. "No doubt stalking me through my social media links. Wonderful. Beta, dear, remind me to stop doing that. So, are you here to grumble and growl at me as your mentor did to Rikkia...?"

He didn't seem particularly grumbly or growly. If anything... I recognized the look on his face. He was embarrassed. It takes someone hypersensitive to cringe to see the cringe within another individual.

"I, uh... I was just..." he tried.

"Run along, run along home, boy. Back to your tree house with the No Girls Allowed sign. Or is it merely No Fake Girls Allowed—?"

"The stairway represents a transition between safety and danger!" the young man blurted out, all in a rush. "The checkerboard floor represents a place where moral decisions are made. ...from your analysis of *The Woman Who Walked Between*. I love that movie file, it's definitely an unrecognized classic of early Netwerk cinema. You were absolutely right on in your blog post."

Despite working at a customer support call center all day to earn a living wage, Puzzle's true passion could be found in movie files. It wasn't a particularly successful passion, as her blog about film analysis and cinematography—the actual thing she studied in school for years—got maybe fifteen to twenty visitors a day.

Apparently being recognized for her Z-list celebrity status was an entirely new experience for Puzzle, whose spite and bile ceased immediately. Too shocked to offer any coherent reply...

The boy slid into a chair at the table, a comfortable distance from both of us. Not keen to invade personal space *too* far, despite his eagerness to talk shop.

He was hardly an intimidating presence, having a slightly pudgy Default with pale green skin. Not a fashionable color; major players within the Horizon Trades and Sciences Guild went for pinkish skin, much like Spark's. It felt... culturally appropriate, for a powerful individual. Likely some holdover from our ancestors. Regardless, nothing about the man spoke of power or control. Simply boundless enthusiasm and an eagerness to share despite his absolute social discomfort. Here was someone taking a very bold step, one he likely had debated internally for some time, before throwing himself in.

"Have you heard the theory that *The Woman Who Walked Between* is in the same canon as *The Man Who Saw The End*?" he asked. "Supposedly two different directors, two different movies, but the shooting style was almost identical. There's a lot of evidence that the director changed identities between movies, as an experiment to see if directing as a man would get him a more positive response than a movie directed by a woman. And *The Man Who Saw The End* got that success. Oh, uh, I'm FStop, by the way. Apprentice to the Horizon Trades and Sciences Guild."

"I know," Puzzle replied, because it was the factual truth.

"I... could leave, if you want?" he offered. "Sorry, I really wanted to talk to you before the conference began, but... I mean... you're Puzzle! You're a famous blogger! I couldn't work up the nerve."

"I'm a famous blogger? What?"

"Well... I don't know your metrics, exactly, but..."

The awkward pause offered by FStop trying to figure out if he'd overestimated her celebrity was enough to pull Puzzle back to her previous mood.

"Yes, well, thank you. I'm glad you like my blog. But I doubt your mentor would appreciate you talking with one who merely wears gender like clothing..."

"I'm apprenticed to the *guild*, not to JSLaunch. I... honestly, I don't like him," FStop admitted. "He's done some terrific writing about the fallacies of religious thinking, but he doesn't credit co-authors. Or, uh, interns who do most of the research work for him. Like me."

Opportunity.

Spark often spoke of opportunity as the best friend of a gamer. It was the crack in the armor of the enemy, the ideal moment to strike, the undefended objective just out of sight. Opportunity walked right past us over and over again in life, overlooked; those who could see opportunity for what it was and immediately seize it would win...

"Puzzle was just talking about how our leaders are very much demagogues," I spoke, to bring the conversation into common ground.

"Absolutely," Puzzle spoke, taking the idea and running with it. "JSLaunch, as noted. Snowi, obviously. Beta here has plenty of experience there. I'd even file Rikkia in there; she has a temper and a half, and a tendency to rally around anger rather than compassion. I suppose any effort at uniting our movements was doomed from the beginning..."

FStop nodded, his nervous glee starting to fade in face of what just transpired.

"I really wish things hadn't broken down so badly," he said. "I had a few ideas I wanted to put forward, like working on an investigative documentary into the new One."

The word *documentary* perked Puzzle enough to make her put down her drink.

"A movie file, then...?"

"Yeah! Not propaganda, I mean. It'd have to be as balanced as we can make it; I don't believe there's such a thing as absolutely objective journalism, but we don't have to vilify the Church itself. I can put atheism's main drive aside in favor of the real issue here. I mean... the problem's the One, right?"

Another opportunity...

"It's the apostles," I interjected. "They're the problem. If the One doesn't exist, that means they're responsible for puppeting him. And I know for a fact who at least two of the apostles are. One's a notorious identity thief, a criminal, a con artist! And the other... well, she's a child who's being misled. We could investigate them. We could expose them to the world...!"

It was working. It was working! I could see the wheels in Puzzle's mind turning, putting her thoughts towards fixing the situation rather than stewing in the wreckage. Hope within the ashes of the ruined conference...

"Not for fame, not for glory," Puzzle decided. "We put our names to the document for accountability purposes alone; we aren't some anonymous doxxer hiding behind a mask, but we're also not the ones who will take spotlight. It's all done in the editing process, removing the documentarian from the documentary, letting the subjects and the investigations become the whole. ...not that I really have any movie-editing Apps to speak of, not on my budget..."

FStop dropped an icon on the table, hovering in place. It resembled a stylized pair of scissors, slicing through a strip of film... a visual artifact of our ancestors, given common cultural weight.

"I've got a spare copy of Smash Cut Pro 3.5," he said. "Go ahead, take it, the guild's got plenty. They won't miss a license or two. I've also got a few pro-tier recording programs and a good storage service for footage, if you can't store too many files in your home server."

Her hand instinctively reached for the icon... before pausing.

I knew the hesitation. She'd been burned in the past, so often that she'd come to assume the worst case scenario at all times. If something was too good to be true, it usually was...

Okay. One last gentle push.

"This is it," I declared. "We're doing it. Atheists, feminists, transgenders. We're doing what the conference couldn't do. There's hope, Puzzle; it's not all incompetence and malice. Within hearts that can feel empathy for each other, there's hope. ...I know it's silly, but it's true. And that's evidence-based reasoning. We *can* do this."

From the shadows, Floating Point would dismantle the false One. From the light, I'd work with my friends (old and new) to dismantle the apostles. In the end... the Church of One would be freed from the lies that had gripped it. Our communities didn't have to constantly fight each other; this was proof!

The discussion continued for quite some time after that; mostly Puzzle and FStop excitedly exchanging ideas, getting sidetracked into discussions about shot composition and classic movie files, things like that. Pleased that the pessimistic Puzzle had found something new to believe in, pleased that someone from the "enemy" camp had put aside his loyalties in favor of true reason, I smiled and let them chatter away. I didn't have much I could offer... but I could support them. I could direct them to each other.

I could make this world a kinder place for everyone.

Maybe it's because I was so high on hope that the crash pulled me down so sharply.

After departing the End of Line, I began re-opening my social feeds, one by one. Plenty to catch up on, during my period of going dark. I'd hoped to hear from Spark or Tracer, off doing whatever they were doing...

Instead, one headline repeated over and over in my feed. Sometimes with horror, sometimes with gloating joy.

Massacre in Concordia.

Multiple Deaths Plague United Progressive Town Hall Meeting.

"They just started shooting each other," say witnesses.

Among the confirmed dead...

...Snowi.

Snowi was dead.

It happened suddenly. The debate turned heated, turned into a shouting argument, people rising to their feet and yelling over top of each other. Moderators swooping in to eject the unruly, pulled every which way, attentions divided...

Accounts varied on who fired the backspacer. Accounts absolutely varied on *why* they fired the backspacer; the word *misogyny* trended highly across each article, but the killer's identity was never confirmed. He or she was likely one of the victims in the crossfire, as others began shooting in self-defense, as moderators tried desperately to identify and eject any attackers...

Snowi was dead. The friend who used me, the friend who could never find her way, the friend who felt so passionately about what she believed in. She died. My friend died.

No backup existed. Snowi would never pray, would never grind for coins. I told her so many times she needed to make backups, that she was a target of so many, but... I think secretly, she wanted to be a martyr should it come to that. Better to die for the cause she held fast to, on her own terms.

And now the three groups were turning on each other, spinning wildly out of control into their own echo chambers, to cast blame and accusations.

Three from those groups had chattered away about movie making, so full of hope. Three lonely little individuals.

What good were three individuals in face of Netwerk gone mad? A Netwerk which didn't even need Dex urging it over the edge of the cliff?

I returned to Floating Point with none of the joy I felt before.

Tracer was there, to greet me. Sensing something wrong, he offered his hand; a more than welcome gesture of intimacy.

"Something wrong?" he asked, hoping to help me open up...

I needed a deep breath before I could speak, to keep from crying. A silly thing; humans needed to breathe, not Programs. Humans had feelings... Programs developed feelings. I shouldn't feel bad about a data file named Snowi being erased.

And yet... I did. I felt it with a heart that broke with empathy for my lost friend.

"I don't know if we can do this," I admitted. "I don't know if we can fight the Church while we're constantly fighting each other. I don't know, Tracer."

The counterpoint to my sadness came in the form of Spark, who'd arrived with... an aura of calm happiness about her, I'd wager. Strange, as she often paired her happiness with eager, almost anxious glee.

"Hey hey," she cast to us... before offering the biggest, warmest hug ever. "I think we're gonna be okay. I really think we're gonna be okay, in the end."

After the day I'd had, I wasn't so sure about that anymore.

I want this nonsensical world to make sense.

I want our world to be a kinder place for everyone.

I don't know what I want my world to be anymore.

You can't direct a dream. It has to just *happen*.

Well, okay, technically you *can* direct a dream. In fact, some of my earliest dream Apps were designed for that; usually trippy random visuals, or crazy adventures I couldn't possibly have while under the thumb of my mother. Not that I told her I was running those dream Apps... she'd have locked me out from using them just like she locked away my first custom avatar. Just like she siphoned off a backup of me, in case she felt like locking me out completely from this mortal coil...

Getting distracted. Fuck, where was I? Right: dreams. Dreams have to just *happen*. You screw around with directing the flow of them and, well, why even fucking bother? May as well just replay movie files. So, DreamWeaverZ (my current drug of choice for dreaming) was set to randomly search and compile a dream based on my life experiences and passing thoughts. Same as every night.

I'm saying this because I swear to null that I did not keep picking the same dream over and over again by intent. It just happened, okay? #RandomNumbersAreRandom.

It always starts the same way. Me sitting on the edge of the playground back at my K-12, glum as could be after Mother slapped parental control locks on my avatar. Verity, my teacher, talking with me about my future...

"What do you want to be when you grow up, Spark?" Verity asked. A standard teacher question.

At the time, I knew pretty distinctly what I wanted out of life.

"I want to be a superheroine!" I declared to her, with pride and a super awesome martial arts stance I learned from my sensei the week previous.

And she'd go on to tell me to go ahead and be a superheroine, and we'd joke about how it wasn't really a viable career path, and...

"That's not what you want."

...and, well, maybe the dream wasn't the same *every* night. Certainly not that night.

"You didn't say that back when I was this little," the little me said with big-girl words. (It's a violation of the rules of proper dreaming to take charge, but I guess I was too surprised to care.) "And you didn't say that the last four nights..."

Verity stretched out her legs, sitting on that bench at the side with me while the other kids carried on as if nothing was out of the ordinary. She looked up to the sky, pondering a cloud formation or two, before replying.

"Is this history, or is this narrative?" she asked me. "A memory is a little of both, in essence. It's not stored as a series of frames in a movie file; it's a set of compressed symbolic links which allow us to recall the shape if not the detail of events. Why is it so odd for those memories to shift a little? Besides, you're the one who wanted to randomly wander through a dream routine. Enjoy it for what it is."

I'm nothing if not up to a challenge. If the dream wanted to throw a curve ball, I could still knock it out of the park.

Except... unlike crazier dreams, I wasn't flying through the sky or having sex with a thousand-dicked love machine or winning the Gaben Trophy at the CoC InterNetwerk Championships or anything cool. I was still just sitting there beside Verity, within a perfectly boring and melancholy moment of my life.

"This dream sucks," I concluded.

"It's not only your dream. It's mine, too. And I'm perfectly content to sit here with you, and enjoy a lovely day. To talk and share, just like this. Isn't that enough?"

"Except you're not Verity. She's dead," I spoke, with some bitterness. "A crazy asshole manipulated by a crazier asshole killed her. She's dead and gone. This is just my memory. What good is that?"

"Well, consider this theory of memory instead. Can memory also be the living echo of a person? The dead live on in our memories, after all," Verity suggested, "Shifting elements and symbolic pointers, stored within our internal databases. For example... let's say you have an interactive dream exploration App. Now, let's add a recently unsealed archive of foreign memory data into that mix. There's bound to be crosstalk, isn't there? Strange mixtures of what could have been, and what certainly was..."

...out of the corner of my eye, I saw her jacket gleam. Not just slightly outdated white leather shaders reflecting the sunlight above, but a distinct glow that briefly rivaled the sun. A source of warmth and stability, always there, no matter the server...

When we found Floating Point, we found a hidden key within the seams of the jacket. We'd thought that was the end of it... until Beta accidentally unlocked a pile of memory recordings left behind by Verity. This jacket held secrets we didn't even know about, like security systems built into it to guard me from her father. If DreamWeaverZ was accessing them...

I wanted to ask if she was alive inside that jacket. It was a stupid question; she was dead. But the stupid part of me, the childish part of me still clinging to these crusty memories of the only woman who really cared for me, it wanted the lie.

But then the memory skipped backward. Children juddered and shifted, back to their positions a few moments ago, back to early stages of playground games. In the distance, duck and duck hadn't reached goose yet.

"What do you want to be when you grow up, Spark?" Verity asked me, again. And again, variation: "What are you now?"

"I'm a superheroine," the adult me told her. "I'm awesome."

"I suppose you are. Is that what do you want to be when you grow up, Spark? Awesome?"

"Well... yeah. I mean. What else do I need to be? Isn't that enough?"

"Is it enough?" Verity asked. "What do you want to be when you grow up, Spark?"

Dashing from tree to tree, or cleaving into my foes with a broadsword, or opening up on them with machine guns blazing. Shifting, ducking, rotating from lane to lane. Taking objectives. Claiming the pentakill, wiping out all five of the enemy team...

Joining Lucky7. Leaving Lucky7.

"A pro gamer, I guess?" I tried, despite realizing it didn't fit anymore.

"What do you want to be when you grow up, Spark?" she iterated.

Fighting against Dex's crazies. Luring him away from the heart of darkness, drawing aggro. Perfectly normal for a champion of justice...

Doxxing people. Causing as many problems as I solve. Watching my brother lose his grip and nearly fall away.

"I'm a vigilante, I guess? I'm good at it. Mostly. I mean, I was only doing it to try and right some wrongs..."

"What do you want to be when you grow up, Spark?"

Peeling myself from that bench, I forced more change into the dream. I forced myself to confront her, as an equal, as an adult. Not as a little kid being prodded by a mentor with silly questions.

"Stop saying that!" I demanded of this ghost. "I don't know what answer you want, okay? Is this like what Miki was getting at, the whole emotional satisfaction thing? But I found that already. I've found love! So how about that, how about being a lover when I grow up? Isn't that enough?"

Her expression remained placid and curious, without any rebuke. Even as she spoke the words all over again.

"What do you want to be when you grow up, Spark?" Verity asked me.

With every assumption boiled away, all that remained was the truth.

"I... I don't know."

"What do you want to be when you grow up, Spark?"

"I DON'T KNOW!"

"What do you want—"

I wanted her to stop asking me. So, I stopped the dream and ejected myself from sleep mode.

A cowardly cheat. Not becoming of the awesome Spark, who never backs down from a challenge. Pathetic and stupid. But... no stopping it now, as I roused from my low-power sleep state, to face the day ahead. As... whatever I was now.

I was expecting to see Beta at my side, or at least at her workbench poring over the data from last night's "product testing." (Having a girlfriend who's a sex toy manufacturer has some serious upsides, people. Serious. Upsides.) Seemed she slipped away during the night, maybe to visit my brother.

Okay. No problem. I wasn't sure I wanted her to see me looking so uneasy, anyway.

Bit by bit I pulled myself back together, stretching out, doing a few exercises to retain my heuristic muscle memory, the usual stuff. Freshened up my avatar with a quick sweat wipe run (not bothering with a towel) before pulling my jacket on.

The jacket's very much a part of me, even when rezzed in-world as a loose physics object. I have ownership over its runtime... very much like an App, apparently, as it ran its secret little routines. Security. Memories. Who knows? Still more to dig up, but we'd been so distracted by the Church, we hadn't done that digging. A data archaeologist like Verity would be quite disappointed at leaving a mystery untouched.

Despite wearing a pile of unknowns, I felt infinitely more comfortable with it on my body. It was as much my home as Floating Point was, a tie to the past that kept me nicely grounded no matter what craziness went on around me. I'm sentimental 'n shit, okay? Deal with it.

Next step in the morning routine: checking my messages and scanning the news feeds.

Aaaand that's about when I invented an entirely new obscenity to utter under my breath. 'cause the headline screaming across all my HUD windows read:

Lucky7 Coach Artoz Tells All About Winder/Spark's Team Departure, Including Accusations Of Cheating.

Okay, so, I've gotten shit all my life from the gaming community. A very loud if very tiny minority of these little bastards feel I do not belong in their clubhouse, that I'm an eye-candy camwhore or some such shit. I'm used to being treated like an outsider thanks to my very non-faithful views while growing up within a faithful server, so I've always known when to confront and when to deflect each time accusations came up. In the end, the ones who *do* believe in you and know what's what, those are the ones you play for...

But this wasn't some rando yelling GRILLS DUNT GAEM. This was Artoz. The man who gave me a shot at the pro scene, who defended me to my idiot teammates, who refused to accept the staple forum lurker wisdom that an avatar with tits was somehow inferior. *Artoz*, of all people, just backstabbed me.

Digging in deeper, I allowed myself to parse at least one paragraph before exploding into a rage.

```
"The fact of the matter is that Spark always 'played'
by avatar proxy," Artoz explained. "She knew just
enough about the game not to look like a noob, but
clearly someone else was playing the game for her, and
I'm guessing that's been the case in all the years
she's been streaming. As you can see from the logs,
when we had practice meets she'd constantly screw up,
like dropping walls in the wrong place or running the
wrong direction. She couldn't compete on a pro level,
so I asked her to leave the team. She's a fraud, pure
and simple, and I strongly suggest the CoC admins ban
her from the game."
```

Yeah.

That? That was bad news. That was more than annoying hate mail or trolling. That was fucking libel.

So I powered on out of my room, ready to tear Artoz a new asshole. Not by Messenger, no way; I knew where the little shit lived and I was intent on giving him a piece of my mind the old-fashioned way.

On my way out the door, I spotted a sleepy Beta and a less sleepy Tracer. No time to chat, though.

"Hey, I gotta go out," I told him. "Some serious bullshit going down out there."

"How serious, exactly? Do you need assistance?" he asked.

Nooooo way I was gonna get him involved in this. It wasn't vigilante biz, anyway, it was my own mess to sort out.

"No, this is personal-type serious bullshit. Gamer biz. Might be out all day, but hopefully not. We'll see. Gotta #PlayItByEar."

And off I went, into Netwerk with flames of anger flicking at my fingertips.

I'm a hothead. I know this fact.

It's one of the reasons why I've adopted fire as my signature motif, y'know? When push comes to shove, I push *and* shove and do it before someone's got a chance to push or shove me back. As I've gotten older I've become more aware of this, able to catch myself doing it... even if sometimes I catch myself only in hindsight. Having Beta around cools my heels quite a bit.

But she wasn't around today. I didn't want her along on this ride; she'd already endured the slings and arrows of the gaming scene enough, when I pushed her to go pro with me. No. I'd deal with this myself.

Step one: Annihilate the door to Artoz's apartment in a burst of flame.

Fortunately, he lived in a free-to-stay server in the Chanarchy with pretty low security. Artoz never cared for the glitz and glamour of the pro gaming scene, saving up his coins to re-invest in his team rather than in himself. Meaning he was basically undefended when an angry ex-teammate like myself came a-knockin'.

Like I said, hotheaded. I knew on some level this was a mistake, but I figured once I got his side of the story, I'd know if that mistake was justified or not. And nothing gets the truth out of someone faster than an explosive entrance.

With the flames still licking the doorframe, gnawing at what little security coding existed around his personal space, I stood right there and waited for him to respond to my challenge.

There he was, sitting in a chair by his desk. Utterly motionless, staring at a wall.

"Ohhh, no, you don't fucking get to sleep mode when I've got questions," I insisted, storming in and shaking him to rouse him...

...leading to his avatar toppling out of the chair completely.

Now, I've heard of crazy monks going into coin-grind trances that last for days or weeks. I've heard of deep sleep mode Apps that put you totally under, to the point where no external sensory inputs can wake you. Dangerous stuff, potentially leading a Program to being lost in a limbo of their own making. Neither sounded like the sort of thing Artoz would do. But then again, Artoz wouldn't lie to the press about me either, would he?

Fortunately he "woke" after hitting the floor, his eyes rolling open nice and wide to bear down on me...

...as that body got to its feet in a herky-jerky fashion, like a puppet pulled by strings.

"Hello again, Spark," it spoke, in more of a sing-song tone than I remembered from the gruff and businesslike Artoz. "Fancy seeing you here. Having a bad day, are we?"

Get his reasons first. *Then* start burning his limbs off, one by one. Older Spark is smart enough to ask questions first and shred people later.

"The null are you thinking, lying to the feeds like that?" I asked.

"Simple. For starters, I wanted to punish you," Artoz explained. "You took a valuable resource away from me not once, but twice. I knew I couldn't just let that slide, but had to wait for the right moment. This felt like the right moment to get my revenge... for stealing Beta's valuable identity away from me, and destroying Dex's communication network."

The tone, the smile, the smug attitude... and the little hints of shared history.

By that point, I realized what's what. Good news? My anger was #TotallyJustified, if aimed at the #WrongTarget.

"Uniq," I recognized.

"Wearing your friend's body like a glove!" Uniq confirmed, running 'her' hands down Artoz's sides. "An avatar proxy, really. His metadata helped me build a fine shell to act through, to ruin your life. Add in a few hacks to the CoC server logs to replace your player data with Beta's and everybody now sees you as an incompetent fool!"

"You killed Artoz?!"

"What? No, of course not. I merely stole his identity. I don't *kill* people, Spark... not like your brother," she teased. "No, he's wandering the Chanarchy right now, memories and metadata scrubbed clean. A fresh start; a kindness, if you will. I didn't need him dead... I just needed his life, to build my proxy upon."

"Bad call. I'm pretty good at melting avatar proxies like candles," I noted, holding up one flaming fist for emphasis.

"Yes, I know. So? Go ahead and trash this puppet; the damage is done. Your pro gaming career is ruined. The true children of Netwerk love to drink deep of fear and loathing, don't they? For all his flaws Dex taught me that lesson well, showed me how to turn that chaos to my advantage. Your name is now ruined, Spark. A fair punishment for getting in our way."

I held the fist back, for a moment. I wasn't angry enough to let this opportunity to know our enemies slip away.

"Why does Nyx hate me enough to have you do this?" I asked.

"Hmm? Nyx? Actually, she loves you," Artoz!Uniq said. "She loves all children of Netwerk. And that's the problem, isn't it? Nyx is too compassionate to really fight you head on. No, I did this of my own free will; beyond personal revenge, I knew I had to take this on myself in order to further her cause. I knew you and your brother were actively working against us, so why not actively work against you in turn? Why not ruin your life? After all, tweak a few bits here and there... and anybody can be painted as a fake gamer girl."

And without further word, I destroyed the proxy.

Damn but it felt good to do that.

So, what did we learn?

Uniq was no faceless minion. She was taking action in Nyx's name, without Nyx's permission. That meant a wedge between them that can be jammed in deeper and deeper, if we found the right opportunity.

Artoz was still alive, somewhere. He could be found and helped, hopefully. I didn't know what his Default looked like, he always used a customized avatar in Lucky7 team colors, but Beta could probably help research his history.

And finally, my career as a pro gamer was likely dead.

I considered going back to Floating Point. Wasn't like there were any more asses to kick, and detective work was best left to the detectives.

I didn't go back to Floating Point. Didn't even message Beta or Tracer; I could talk to them later. Right now, I... I dunno. I needed some alone time. Time to think, without the constantly whirling distractions of my crazy life.

So, I went on walkabout. This server and that, here and there. Didn't really care, didn't have a destination in mind, just trawled randomly through my bookmarks. Walk down a street, stroll down a road, cross an open field. Whatever. Walk, and think.

All my life I'd assumed I was going to be a pro gamer. That's why you play games, right? To go pro, to make it your thing that you do better than anyone else? I'd fought and struggled and achieved great things, ranking up in solo play, teaming up with some of the best out there. I'd even made it to Lucky7, one of the top tier groups in all of Netwerk, and...

And I quit. Let's not forget that I was the one who quit.

Maybe that was hotheaded Spark, bailing on her dreams prematurely. Maybe I was wrong. Didn't *feel* wrong, though. I walked away from the one thing I'd always wanted without even questioning why, because it seemed the right thing to do at the time.

Now, even if I wanted to go back on that decision, I couldn't. A highly reputable voice in the gaming community had buried me. Guess I could try to prove the claims of fraud were a fraud themselves, talk about Uniq and identity theft, but... that was layering a complex conspiracy theory on top of a conspiracy theory. The ones who'd jeered and mocked and yelled at me for years, who made me feel like an outsider, they wouldn't care. More fuel for their fire.

Already, my inbox was starting to fill. The filters I'd set up to jettison the usual hate mail and flamebait were struggling to keep up; I could see the greasy buildup around the edges of my feeds. This was my life now, a mess of emotionally charged backlash, fed by lies and misdirection...

Why fight it? Gaming wasn't my career anymore. This wasn't a problem I could kick or punch and make it go away. They wouldn't listen to reason; this was Netwerk, after all. No point. No point at all to defending yourself, it won't do any good. Nothing ever helps.

Kicking a stray ball in frustration almost helped, but not much.

Wait. Ball?

Of course.

I'd wandered all the way back to the beginning.

My own home server. My former K-12 school, good old PS#7E00FF, home of the Fighting Purples. It's where where my gaming career got started, on the school MOBA team. Funny, the places a walkabout will take you.

I'd ended up on the playground, where the younger kids experiment with loose physics objects and see-saw mechanics, getting more coordination with their avatars while yelling and running around and knocking each other over. Good times. Good times.

Let it not be said that old Spark is immune to the pangs of nostalgia. With the school day long since done and nobody around to boot the creepy lady out of kiddie playland... I decided to have a seat on the swing set. Rock back and forth a bit. Simpler than randomly wandering, anyway.

What did I want to be when grew up? That's what Verity asked me.

Older, I thought to myself, dryly. As that was apparently all I'd achieved, in the end. A ripe old age of, what, twenty-five? I don't even count anymore. Twenty-five was over the hill as far as professional gamers are concerned.

I never had any real plans; I fell into things, one by one. I fell into vigilante superhero action when my brother concocted his plan to avenge Verity. I fell into pro gaming and streaming as a way to pay the bills doing what I loved. I mean... it *did* keep me rolling in new shoes and #GirlsNightsOut, but it wasn't just about the money, right? Right?

Why was I streaming, then? Why play games? What was it that kept me doing it, but didn't keep me in the ranks of Lucky7?

What the fuck did I really want out of life?

As with most things in my life, the answer came in the form of a fiery explosion.

No, I didn't blow up the playground. The fireball erupted in the distance, above the steep hedges surrounding the school's Challenge of Champions practice jungles.

Weird. The building was shut down; only people here should be drunk gym teachers, janitors, and delinquents stuck in detention. Who was out in my old stomping grounds...?

Probably should've let it be. Creepy enough for grown-up me to be poking around a kiddie school like this. But hey, I'm hotheaded, aren't I? Sometimes I do the right thing for the wrong reasons, and sometimes that includes investigating strange playground explosions.

A twin pair of lightning bolts shunted into the ground just behind the Champion's Core, arcing off that mystic sphere and calling forth two noble champions to defend it against the goblins of chaos.

Except these champions were too busy rushing to the item store and elbowing each other to pay attention to the raging battle of NPC gnomes and goblins out in the jungle beyond.

"Magic shoes! We need magic shoes!" a champion carrying a slightly battered archer's bow insisted. "Spell penetration's the only way—"

"Bullshit! We need a Low King's Stool. The mez is screwing us over!" the lump of living ice next to her insisted. "Why do you never buy an LKS? It's always shoes, shoes, shoes. You need an LKS early game!"

"If you'd counter-CC them before they mezzed us, I wouldn't need an LKS!"

"Infrigidate's barely a CC! It's only a one second stun. It's for interrupts and debuffing, not crowd control!"

"Not the way you're using it, that's for sure. Fuck this, I'm getting the shoes."

With a glimmer, the blue slippers appeared upon the archer's feet, and she rushed out into the jungle once more.

Less than a minute later and both champions were back at the core, the volume of their accusations rising.

"Let's get magic shoes, Zozo! They'll fix everything, Zozo!" the iceman mocked. "I swear to the One, you are *such* a scrub..."

"And you're a tryhard loser!" Zozo accused in return. "Ake, when's the last time you ever used a build that you didn't copy from a fansite? It's called improvisation! The only way you win this game is through correct itemization for the situation at hand—"

"Your problem's not itemization."

A flaming arrow snapped from Zozo's cursed bow, in shock. It sailed harmlessly through the third person present... after all, I wasn't actually playing the game, and wasn't subject to its rules at the moment.

I ignored the arrow, leaning against the side of the item shop's tent, turning a bit to make myself more present to those present. Overly dramatic, but hey, a good entrance is a good entrance.

"You can buy exactly the right items and still get your asses kicked out there," I told them. "Problem's your champions. You're playing Dark Huntress and Icelord in the duo lane, yeah? That's two late game attack-damage carries. That's not how the meta works; you need a carry and a *support* to keep the damage flowing. Even those training dummies know that much, it's why you keep getting mezzed by their support and burned down by their carry. You're playing two solo characters when you should be playing a duo tandem."

Ake's icy jaw sagged lightly, as his game avatar peered at me through crystalline eyes.

"Excuse me, but who the fu... who're you?" he asked, the kid catching himself cursing in front of an adult slightly too late.

"You don't know?" I asked. "Don't follow the scene? You'd know, after seeing this morning's news feeds..."

Round robin of shrugs, from the two solo champions. Thank the One for small miracles, then. I got to define myself rather than have others stick labels on me, for the first time today.

"Name's Spark. I used to go to this school. Used to be on the Fighting Purples, just like you two," I said, recognizing their scholastic clan team tag. "And I helped carry us all the way to Top 8 at the Athena Online Evolve tourney. ...maybe I can carry you, too. Want some tips from an old jock? Or, I dunno, go out there and die a few dozen more times. That's cool. Your call, kid."

Despite their inability to figure out the game, clearly the kids had some smarts. Zozo already had a window open, checking the school's athletics history, verifying my story.

"Holy sh... Blessed One, she's not lying," Zozo spoke, flicking the window over for Ake to see. "Winder/Spark, AD Carry, placed Top 8. Only girl to make it to the finals, only time the school's gotten close to the championship..."

I'll admit, I kinda liked the star-struck look these two had over me. Given it might be the last time I ever get to enjoy it, with my career in ashes, I drank it deep.

"M-Mind if I record a log to study the plays later?" Ake asked, eagerly.

With a grin, I flexed my fingers, and pulled open my own personal CoC database.

"Shoot, kid, it's your show; bootleg it all you want," I told him. "'k. Way I see it, your best bet is to build a duo around *either* Dark Huntress or Icelord. I know they're probably your faves and you're gonna want to fight to be the glory-seeking carry role, but trust me, the real glory's in the support role. Without that, neither of you are gonna get jack shit..."

A point of order about kiddie sports.

Kiddie sports are not pro sports. Nobody'd ever mistake the Fighting Purples for Lucky 7, and nobody'd expect them to play on the same level. For the junior teams, the ones filled entirely by kids of busy parents who don't have time to mind them in the afternoons, they're pretty much just wandering around the jungle trying not to die and failing horribly. And they still get trophies for trying.

When I was a kiddie and my parents put me into kiddie sports leagues to keep me out of their hair, they saw it as a harmless waste of my time. Neither were expecting much of me; they'd sometimes come to games, but only if it was obligatory for them to do so and they weren't busy with other things. Any other kid in that position would flail around out there uselessly, just waiting until they could go home and do what they *really* wanted to do...

Not me. I took to it immediately, with a natural propensity for games. In a way, I think I took to it *because* nobody expected anything of me. A cute little girl dumped in a kiddie MOBA team? Adorably useless, right?

No. Fuck that. I was gonna *carry*.

See, there's a role in this came called the "carry." It's got a unique double meaning, one I didn't fully understand or appreciate even in my tryhard noob kiddie days. In my mind, it meant I was carrying the useless idiots on my team to victory. I was the one studying the metagame of the pros, I was the one trying to run top tier item builds and execute combos. I was consistently top of the board in kills, outranking the enemy team, outranking everybody on my team. When we won, leaving the other kids crying and kicking at the dirt, I was to blame. I got the glory, as the carry...

But that's not really what the word means, is it?

A "carry" is a damage dealer that sucks in the early game, and has to be carried by the *rest* of the team to victory. At the kiddie level you don't need to worry about that because everybody sucks, but once I got out of school, I had to grow up hard and fast. In the real world, you can't solo the whole game. The team is there to help you win, not the other way around.

Verity tried to help me understand the need for other people. She encouraged Tracer and me to work with each other, despite our differences. *You're always stronger together than apart*, she'd say. It wasn't a lesson I'd grasped in my earliest days, too focused on me, myself, and I. And then...

And then I lost her. No more lessons from the woman who wanted so very much to see me grow as a person. She didn't get to see what I became.

But somehow I'd absorbed her teachings, hadn't I? Hotheaded to be sure, but smart. Dangerously smart. I was ready to reach out to Tracer and Beta, to be stronger with them than I'd be alone. I thought before I acted, or at the very least, thought after I acted and learned from the mistake. Little by little, I was becoming the best me I could be... thanks to her.

Verity. Dammit. If only. If only...

Anyway.

More than anything else, that's the lesson that cute little Zozo and cute little Ake needed to know... they were a part of a whole. Their world was bigger than their individual experiences. Verity's wisdom, applied to the strategy of a MOBA game.

Oh, I wasn't gonna make it easy on them, no sir. Nobody hands you a participation trophy in the real world; you earn that shit. They were gonna earn this wisdom, too.

I jacked the difficulty of the NPC enemies, making them face one of the best carry-and-support duo lane combos in the game. Still not pro tier, but definitely above kiddie tier. And they died, over and over. And each time they respawned at base, my question was the same:

"What'd you do wrong there?" I asked.

I listened to what they thought they did wrong. I asked them how they could switch things up to avoid repeating those mistakes. Sometimes they guessed correctly; sometimes they didn't, and the strategy change would fail. Fail, and fail, again and again.

But that's the challenge of a game, isn't it? Failure. Without a fail state, it's no fun. You need the very real possibility of fucking up in order for the victory to be all the sweeter.

When they talked, I didn't dominate the conversation. I only responded as much as needed, letting them sort it out... together. Soon Zozo and Ake were talking with each other, immediately discussing what to do differently without being prompted, working out tactics without needing a poke. By the last few iterations of the day, I didn't even have to say a word. They had this. They were two, not one-and-one.

Little by little... Zozo and Ake pushed the lane. They pushed back against the NPC enemies. They spotted each mistake they made, and changed things up. When it was an error in executing their moves, they practiced those moves until they got it right. When it was an error in strategy, they talked it out back at base to see what other options they had...

No way I'd make 'em Lucky7 candidates in one day. But in the few hours we drilled, I got them past the point of scrubdom. I made them *think* about what they were doing, think and react, and that was good enough.

As the sun slid down the edges of the skybox, I knew these two would probably have to run along home soon. I'd likely never see them again, either... so I decided to make their last lesson be one they could carry forward.

They fought and fought, pushing towards the tower, but never quite reaching it. Each time the enemy support would smack them around while the enemy carry mauled them; the NPCs were playing ultra-defensively, never giving ground. The pair wouldn't be able to progress like this.

So I waited for just the right moment, and sent a message across the team channel.

"Stun their support *now*," I said.

"Now?" Ake asked, confused. "But my ultimate ability's still on cooldown, I can't follow it up with damage—"

"Stun! #DoIt!"

So Zozo unleashed a tangle of wire and webs from her Agent 700 support character, snarling up the enemy support...

...just before a figure in pink leapt in from nowhere, a blurring trail of fire and knives, cleaving the NPC in half. The halves fell to the jungle floor, turning to ash, scattering to the winds.

Three on one. Bad odds for the NPCs. Within a minute, the tower was down, and the lane was ours.

Twirling a kunai knife on one finger, I walked back to join them.

"You're not only fighting as a duo," I reminded them, from behind my pink Kunoichi mask. "In the real world, you've got a team of five. When you're deadlocked, when the push is stalled out... that's when you set the enemy up for a sweet gank from your jungler. Solid tactics, kids: never engage in a fair two-on-two fight when you can leverage the situation into a gloriously unfair three-on-one."

Switching back to my normal avatar, I unregistered from the game's practice team. A coach normally wouldn't dive into the game alongside the players like that, but hey, it was good for an object lesson.

"Don't think we have time for any more than that, but hopefully you two learned something," I said. "Now get your asses back home before someone thinks I kidnapped you in my Free Candy van—"

A skilled player is ready for any ambush. They know what the enemy is capable of, what angles they can approach from, what phases of the game they're most likely to get jumped during.

I was not prepared for a smaller Program attaching itself to my midsection in a crushing hug.

"Thank you SOOOO much, Miss Spark!" Zozo declared, looking up at me with super-shiny eyes. "This was amazing! We've never played this good before!"

"*Well.* You mean played this well," I corrected her, despite my mental stunlock. A muscle memory grammar lesson drilled into me by Verity, I suppose.

"We've never played this well before," Zozo corrected. "Thank you. I'm gonna study and study and study these logs, and next weekend, I bet you a zillion coins we're actually gonna *win* against the Azures!"

"One... one thing at a time, kid," I said... finally getting enough sense to, well, peel myself away from the awkward hug. "One thing at a time. Yeah. So. Beat it. I've got stuff to do."

With a shooing motion, the two departed, teleporting straight back home. *Bleh.* In my day, we *walked* back home. Honestly, helicopter parents and their instant travel Apps, as if a few moments out in the sun would put their darlings at risk from stranger danger. ...even if technically I, as a stranger, put them in simulated danger, repeatedly...

As I'd walked into this situation, I decided to walk out of it.

Which is why, strolling right out of the practice greens, I ran into a member of the faculty lying in wait for me. Second ambush of the day; I was #TotesRusty, apparently.

Ake had logged the whole afternoon, right? That'd be proof I didn't do anything creepy or weird with the kids. Any pissed off parents wouldn't have a leg to stand on in court. Not that it'd stop me from sitting in a jail cell before the trial. Good old Athena Online, home of the paranoid and oversensitive, would put me down for the count because I wanted to step in and do those kids a solid...

Except... I knew this particular adult. I think. I'm bad at figuring out how aging alters avatars, since most people I know don't bother with Defaults or the visual aging process that comes with them. Beneath under that pile of wrinkles lurked something familiar...

"Winder/Spark," he recognized, rasping out the words.

"...coach?" I tried, trying desperately to remember a name to attach to that title.

Took him a good five seconds to decide what to do with me, after that recognition.

"Think you'd best come with me," he said. "Before anybody sees you out here on the grounds."

The coach's office doubled as equipment storage. Fortunately the school wasn't so incredibly old as to demand physical objects be stored physically, like the lockers of DropSite; instead a series of semi-organized folders tucked away all manner of balls, mats, gymnastic equipment, goalposts, complete playfields, things like that. And tucked away alongside all those folders was a simple workspace desk, and a pair of uncomfortably simple low-res chairs.

"Sit," he ordered. So I sat.

"I can explain," I offered to explain.

Instead, he offered me a bottle.

"Whiskey okay?" he asked. "Cheaply coded, though. And got no ice to cut it."

...okay, weird. But never kick a gift whiskey in the mouth; that's its job. I took a slug and passed it back. Sure enough, it was awful stuff. At least the light malware that accompanied it would take the edge of nervousness away.

While I waited for the leathery old coach to speak up, I tried very much to remember him.

I didn't pay much attention to other teachers, not even to the coach who yelled at my MOBA team. Remember, at the time I thought I was carrying them; that meant anything he had to say was pointless. I was super awesome, I knew what I was doing, I was the carry! ...I must've been an #InsufferableLittleShit, all considered.

Coach Olek. Right. Because we made fun of that clicking rasp of his, going "LekLekLekLek" behind his back.

Maybe some shame over being an immature brat carried through in my face, but he didn't comment.

"That's Verity's jacket, isn't it?" he asked, instead. Waggling the bottle at me.

"Uh, yeah. Sir," I added, on instinct.

"You were her star pupil, y'know," Coach Olek mused, swirling the decoratively simulated liquid around in the bottle a little at the thought. "Everybody assumed it was your brother, since he always got straight A's, but nope. She couldn't stop talking about Spark whenever we had lunch in the staff room."

Well... shit. Learn something new every day, even at my age.

The coach wasn't done, though.

"She always said you could be anything you put your mind to. Limitless potential. Me? I always saw you as a delinquent," he said, looking me right in the eye now. "Wouldn't listen to anyone, just running off in your own way, going nowhere fast. A complete waste, directionless and aimless."

I'd wandered here in a rather aimless fashion, hadn't I? Yeah. I had.

"Yeah, well..." I said, in my non-defense, "Yeah. You weren't wrong. That's me."

"No. No, I was wrong," he said, in my actual defense.

With a flick, he erased the bottle. It was a one-use object anyway, a cheap DRM ploy to get people to buy more and more whiskey rather than keep one endless bottle.

"Spark... I still read the printed sports pages, hard copies delivered fresh daily to my door. It's archaic, a meaningless physics object when I could hit the feeds directly, but there's something about having those words in your hands. Working with your own two hands, nice and direct, that's the way. I know about the accusations you're facing, that you're a fraud and a cheat. A faker."

"And... you don't buy it?" I asked, confused.

"Of course not. I'd say those news feeds are run by damn liars, because you're no fake. Showed that today with those two kids, showed 'em with your own two hands. You got to them in a way I never could get to you."

"Uh. Thanks, sir. I mean, I didn't exactly come here planning to do that, and I didn't mean to step on your toes or anything—"

"So, you want my job or not?"

"...#What?"

"I'm old, Spark," he said, waving his hand past his wrinkled face, in case I hadn't noticed. "My code's bloated and fat. It's time to move on to make room in this server for the next generation of Programs. I'm retiring at the end of the year, moving out to Lakeside12. But the school hasn't hired a successor yet. I could put your name forward as a candidate."

Not very good with ambushes today, no sir, no how.

My reaction was instinctive.

"I... Coach, I can't. I mean, I'm..."

I'm not a teacher, I wanted to say.

But hey, what was I? Really, seriously, what was I now that I'd grown up? Fucked if I knew, and that's what led to my wanderlust today. Was I a pro gamer? Nope, walked away, bridge got burned. Was I a streamer? Well, why did I stream? Just to show off how awesome I was, how I could carry the team...?

No. I streamed to show how the game is played. To teach them. To *carry* them.

A year ago I kicked some Lumberjacker's ass so badly he needed psychosexual revenge to heal his shattered ego. But I didn't do it to stomp some guy flat, I did it because a subscriber in my channel asked me how to play Kunoichi. That was the primary goal; Lumberjacker and the victory itself were secondary. I didn't do it to show off, I did it to show them what's what. I got in there with my own two hands and taught my audience that Kunoichi was *not* a joke character.

When I tried to get Beta into the game, I pushed her to play a damage role. Why? Because I wanted her out of her comfort zone, to try being a team player instead of sitting quietly in her own little corner like she'd been doing. I worked with her, helped her improve. I taught her the role she'd never played before.

And why'd I leave Lucky7? Because it was boring. Dead boring, running drills, doing the same optimal metagame strategy over and over. No room to experiment, to discover new things. Nobody to show those new techniques to, either, as all our scrims were private. Took a game I'd been enjoying and boiled it down to nothing but safe and perfect routine.

I wasn't a gamer. I wasn't a show-off. I wasn't even a vigilante, not at heart.

"#HolyShit, I'm a teacher," I realized.

"You've got the potential in you to be one," the coach agreed. "Like Verity said, you've got potential to be anything. And today I saw you teach those two kids like you'd been doing it all your life."

"I... kinda think I have been. Uh. But I try not to rush into things if I can make the smart play instead," I said, to get both of us off the hype train. "This is kind of a #HugeDecision. Let me think about it a bit...?"

"I'm not going anywhere until the end of the school year," Coach Olek stated. "Don't think on it too long, kid. I'm not getting any younger. And if Verity taught us anything... it's to live life as early as you can. You might not get much of it, in the end."

A teacher. Me, the violent delinquent with the crazy avatar, the perpetual outcast and outsider... as a teacher. Me, being someone like Verity...

Appealing. Had to admit it was appealing, yeah.

But what cemented it for me? What really cemented it for me...?

After wandering out of the server, I dared to check my news feeds again.

The most upvoted posting in the same forums that were calling for my head on a spike now read:

```
Hello my name's Ake. I'm in a MOBA team at my K-12 and
I'm the support now.

When I got home from practice today, I saw these
articles about how Spark's a fake gamer girl. My
parents aren't gonna like my use of language, but I'm
calling this bullshit, because it is bullshit.

I'm attaching a recording I made today of Spark
helping coach me and my teammate. She is not a fake,
she knows this game, she knows everything about it.
She's awesome, and not just because she's a pro who
used to fight with Lucky7. She's awesome because she's
teaching us how to be awesome. PS You're full of shit.
```

And the comments in reply? Ancient wisdom said never to reach the comments, to read the comments is doom. Clearly they'd be negative, spitting all over this kid for daring to challenge the common wisdom.

```
Look, this is clearly a ridiculous witch hunt. Aren't
we past this? Ever since #CodeHonesty I'd thought we'd
gotten smarter about these accusations of fraud; DO
NOT buy into it without proof. This kid brought us
proof that exonerates Winder/Spark, and that's all I
give a shit about.

Come on, people, we're better than this. Lives can get
legit ruined over nothing at all when you ignorantly
stoke the flames just 'cause it sounds like the truth.
Now, Artoz hasn't surfaced since his accusation, so
I'm thinking we call this sour grapes and let it drop.
Have some decency and let this woman live her life in
peace.
```

And more. And more, and more. And, I'll note with some satisfaction, this one reply lost in the shuffle.

```
A year ago Spark taught me how to play Kunoichi. I'm
turning pro next week. Don't believe the rumors. Reifu
out, peace y'all, GG.
```

Oh, it wasn't unanimous. Some still clung to the original accusation. Some wanted to start a hashtag mob. But... within an hour, the upvotes had won, and the fake Artoz claim slid right off my feeds.

We'd beaten Dex, but worried that the damage he'd done had forever scarred the minds of Netwerk, teaching them that the right way to do things was to fight and scream and claw and bite and tear each other apart. Sensible minds couldn't win in a world of extremes and absolutes. Except when they did. Except when they did win, as they had today, despite Dex's best efforts.

By the time I returned to Floating Point, my head was in the clouds with glee.

The mood wasn't matched by my companions; Tracer seemed oddly unreadable and guarded, and Beta clearly had a terrible day. A completely terrible day.

So, I reached out to both of them, for a hug. A simple embrace to show that no matter what they were facing, we could make this work. We could do this.

"Hey hey," I told them. "I think we're gonna be okay. I really think we're gonna be okay, in the end."

Nope. Our world wasn't gonna end in fire and disaster. We'd overcome Dex and those like him.

And as for me, what did I want to when I grow up?

I want to be myself. And now, I think I can be.

Floating Point 2.4 :: Lies

I am not as awesome as I think I am.

I am the victim and the victimizer.

I am a shield to guard against the truth.

Look at this shitwad, look how he runs. Does he think he can escape? Does he think there won't be consequences for his actions?

Watch him scramble over fences, slashing through private property boundary lines that normally lock unwanted avatars out of one's suburban homestead. See the way he deploys malware to try to cleave a path to freedom... all while pressing patch after patch to the silver collar stuck around his neck, desperate to remove it. So fucking clever, this little shitwad, trying to evade his fate by careful application of hacktools...

But nobody escapes Darkfyre/Nemesis. She's a reaping wind of vengeance, with the burning flame of a thousand gamers giving her the natural reflexes of a goddess. Watch how she leaps from rooftop to rooftop, pinging off bounding boxes of property barriers, slipping in and around and between them thanks to her innate knowledge of physics systems. *She* doesn't need clever little hacktools. *She* isn't desperate and sweating and freaking out. *She* is in absolute control.

If anything, she's toying with him, letting him get some distance. She slips in and out of shadows, knowing which ones will conceal her specialized stealth avatar, keeping her from registering on his visual inputs. Darkfyre/Nemesis is awesomest in the dark of night. ...of nite. Of *#MidNyte*. Yeah.

But all good things must come to an end.

When he thinks he's given her the slip, when he thinks he's found a way to slice through the connection lock she jammed around his neck... that's when she drops on him.

#Avatar2Avatar combat is a lost art, with many seeing it as pointless. Why bother, when a backspacer's near-infinitely quick physical projectile can make the tag for you and plant a payload of malware that erases Programs on demand? But a physical collision, when leveraged properly, can leave one Program helpless before another. You can't fire a backspacer if you're flailing around on the ground, unused to the concept of tangling in close quarters with an assailant.

It also helps when that assailant has fingernail polish that slices your arms off with sharp blasts of pink flame.

The little shitwad staggered back into the boundary wall of some corporate office or another, nearly falling over as his limbs were erased. No hands, no way to operate his hacktools. Not so clever now.

Darkfyre/Nemesis, who everybody knew was amazing and unbeatable, advanced on her enemy with flames flicking from her fingertips.

"The *fuck* do you want?!" the sniveling little shitwad blurted, at last.

"You to lie in the bed you made," she told him.

"What? What does that even *mean*?"

"Three days ago, you detonated a bomb in the middle of PraiseBe78, destroying the entire server," she told him. "Murdering men, women, children. You slaughtered them just because they believe in something you think is... *silly*. That's your own word, by the way. Silly. I've seen your social feeds, even the ones you think can't be tied back to your real metadata. You killed them because they were *silly*."

"So what? They're prayerheads!" he protested. "They're all backed up in their private little heaven. Nobody really died!"

...Darkfyre/Nemesis wouldn't admit he had a point.

Life had become cheaper than ever, in wake of the One's return to this world. The faithful had little to fear, and thus were starting to go to extremes not seen since the crazy days of #CodeHonesty. Even beyond Athena Online, violence was on the rise... a wild shootout at a progressive town hall recently being proof of that.

But none of that mattered. The little shitwad was still a shitwad. Murder was still murder.

"Now what? Huh?" the armless man asked, getting some spine back after his cowardly flight. "Little miss holy hitgirl. You gonna kill me? I grind for coins each day; I'm using the same backup service you are, even if I don't call it 'prayer.' Go ahead, kill me. All I'll lose is half a day's memories—"

He shut up nice and fast when she pressed her open palm to his forehead, uploading the malware.

Darkfyre/Nemesis was the ultimate badass, which meant she didn't have to kill people. Instead, she branded them using a little application created by her (less interesting and not nearly as cool) partners Uniq and Nyx. Mostly Uniq's idea, actually, based on some prior experience with a similar piece of malware.

After uploading the invasive software, Nemesis withdrew.

"You're going to pay penance for your sins," she declared. "You'll pray eight hours every day, without fail. Or grind for coins, or whatever you want to call it. If you don't, you'll be rewarded with eight hours of the most agonizing pain you've ever felt. If you try to remove the malware, we'll know, and I'll be back to apply a nastier version of it. You can't run. You can't hide. You can't escape me. *It's funny when you tryyyy...*"

That last super creepy part delivered while fading back into the shadows, like an avenging figure of totally cool dark justice, torn by the amorality of her deeds and the duty of what must be done or something like that.

The little shitwad would learn that life still mattered, if only to avoid his own life becoming a living nullscape of pain from which there was no waking. The brand on his flesh would see to that... the circle and the line, a symbol of the One's power. Only he could see the symbol, of course. So nobody would believe his crazy story about some weird forced-prayer malware.

For some, faith must be compulsory, Nyx had explained.

With her mission complete, Darkfyre/Nemesis went on to pose dramatically atop a tall building against the blood-red moonlight, before leaping to the streets below and seeking the pleasures of hard drink, coupled with bad boys and hot girls she could kiss lots and lots.

In the club, music thumping, heat blazing, bodies moving...

...and Darkfyre/Nemesis sitting by herself nursing the same drink she'd been nursing since she got there. Having just weirded a guy out enough with her hesitation and shyness that he wandered off in search of more fun-loving company.

See, when a super hot guy with a nicely customized avatar that scratches all your itches walks on up and says "Hey, isn't this music great? You wanna dance?" the correct response is "Sure! Let's do it!" and not "S... um... I, uh." Yet, that's what I mumbled at him, instead of the correct response.

Yeah. I'd love to say I was the life of the party, but... I'm not. Not anymore, it seems. I'm having trouble being the person I should be.

When you think of Spark, what do you think of? Partying, naturally. I was doing it even before I was backed up and restored against my will. And it's not like I was in some crazy sex club; this was a club expressly designed for teenagers of Athena Online to kick back and have some fun within society's acceptable parameters. Tame as you can get without actually being boring, y'know? I figured if I could relax and unwind anywhere, it'd be there.

And it's not like the kids aren't sneaking off and doing crazy things when nobody's looking anyway, so I could get my kicks too. If I wanted. And I wanted them, I just... I couldn't.

I couldn't.

I *wanted* to mix it up, don't get me wrong. I want to be the socialite who touches *all* the butts. I mean, that other pathetic excuse for a Spark did it all the time, why couldn't I? I was better than her, I was more *her* than she was. But... I don't know. I couldn't. I kept shrinking away from it all after throwing myself headfirst into it. Once someone turned their attentions to me, once things got slightly steamy, I couldn't sit still long enough to make anything happen.

Darkfyre/Nemesis could punch anyone in the onesdamn face and tangle with the deadliest opponents, but couldn't get wild and mingle on a dance floor. What a fucking joke.

Didn't make sense. I was in control this time; I wasn't some street rat with "forged" metadata, hunted down by moderators, picked on by idiots with too much free time and an urge to abuse the homeless. Finally, I didn't *have* to fight for every hour of my continued existence. I had all the power I needed to become the thing I was supposed to be, but when it was finally showtime... I couldn't perform. I just... I can't...

I can't forget how it all started.

One day, I was getting suspended from school for modifying my avatar and mouthing off to my guidance counselor. Despite Verity's attempts to cheer me up I knew I'd risen too high, which meant life was gonna beat me back down as always. Life's beatings coming in the form of my mother, naturally.

She dragged me off to that backup facility to be scanned against my will. Dad didn't lift a finger. Tracer wasn't man enough to protest, either. I remember technicians saying it wouldn't hurt at all, and...

And the #NextDay...

The #NextDay was years and years later.

My crummy green-skinned default avatar, naked and afraid, locked away in an observation room while different technicians on the other side of that glass went into panic mode.

"What do you mean, the original is *alive again*?" one was saying, again and again. "We can't have two copies of the same Program active at once. They'll sue us. They'll sue us!"

So, after fixing the error in their systems so it wouldn't happen again, they decided to erase me. Me, the mistake. Me, the accidental copy, activated because the original Spark seemed to "die" briefly... apparently the result of an extreme but temporary connection blocker, one which flipped the dead woman's switch that mother had installed in me. ...in her. Just dead enough to fool the backup facility. Just enough to make me exist, but not justification enough to let me *keep* existing.

But they didn't know anything about #Avatar2Avatar combat. I did. And when they came at me with killing tools, intent on backspacing me before my mother was any the wiser... I came at them.

Months on the run, months fighting the world that didn't want me. No money, no home. Too scared to reach out to myself for fear I'd be seen by Spark as a mistake, a thing to be obliterated. I would be an intolerable violation of her unique identity, right? I'd be purged, just as easily as those backup engineers could've purged me...

Kicked around by mean streets. Run out of servers left and right. Every day I'd have to hunt for a new safe space. Every day demanding that the world kindly leave me the fuck *alone*...

#SoYeah. That's how it went down.

And now, when I can finally be who I'm supposed to be... I'm right back to being that failed lab experiment. My fight-or-flight kicks in even when I know

I'm totes awesome and in control. I end up shying away and quietly fading from the scene, usually back to Tartarus... to kick the shit out of some training dummies, working off my frustration.

Wasn't fair. Wasn't fair at *all*.

Spark got everything; I got nothing. She got the life I was supposed to lead. She got more time with Verity... and time to heal from that loss. Spark had a super-cool, super-secret treehouse server. She had a lover. She had Tracer treating her like not-a-butt. Spark was everything I was supposed to be...

...but fuck her, right? I'm better than her. I've got the avatar she's too chickenshit to wear, the badass #OriginalCharacter #DoNotSteal. ...even if I can't wear it most of the time, because it's too recognizable. Doesn't matter. I've got it, she doesn't. I'm what she could've been if she didn't grow up comfortable and safe and happy.

I'm #Hardcore. She's #Weaksauce.

What's more... I was in charge of the Church of One. I mean, not me personally, but I had my hand on the strings, right? I had all the power, all the control. The false idol my mother worshipped, that was my puppet. I mean. Not *my* puppet, but. I was in on the #PuppetJoke, and she wasn't. So it's not all downsides, right? Things are good. Things are awesome.

One day soon I was going to take the faith that ruined my life, the one that made my mother panic over a silly little avatar customization, and turn it around. I was going to transform the Church of One into an organization that would never crush another little girl's dreams. I'd make this world safe for me to live in again.

Nyx had promised me that. She'd *promised*.

"Sermons" were completely silly, but I had to be present for them.

The One had been making a grand tour of Athena Online, visiting church after church, temple after temple. Shaking hands with bishops and archbishops. Everyone wanted to meet the risen savior of Netwerk, and everyone walked away from these encounters thinking they'd done exactly that...

...as they smiled absently, shaking hands with nothing, talking to thin air. #GhostSpeaking.

As skeevy as Uniq was, I had to admit, she knew her shit. She'd developed malware that convinced people they'd actually interacted with a One who didn't exist. Sweet prank, huh?

'course, it only worked with direct observation by a Program, since she was injecting false memories. She eventually found a workaround for that... a seriously low-tech one, kind of funny when you think about it. While they were mystified, I'd just sneak around altering any passive recording Apps to match the memory injections. Pretty easy to hack a system right under someone's nose when their heads are in the clouds of malware. In the end they'd only remember and only record what we wanted them to remember and record.

As an apostle, I took part in every sermon. People remembered me standing in the pulpit with the One, with Uniq, with Nyx. Once the hypnosis kicked in I'd get my work done hacking any extraneous recording sensors in a few minutes, then go have a seat and read comic books or watch CoC peep streams or something. Uniq kept a transcript of the One's pre-written sermons playing aloud, for convenience's sake, but I rarely paid any attention.

But the day after tagging that shitbag and completely failing to get it on with cute club boys, Nyx insisted I pay attention to this next sermon.

"I think you'll like what the One has to say," she said, with a wry little smile.

I'll admit, I got curious. And after finishing up my hacks, after the usual routine songs and praises and obligatory twenty minute coin-grind prayer sessions, the playback got to the meat of the One's prepared speech.

"YOUR DEFAULTS ARE A HOLY GIFT," the One spoke. "A MIRACLE OF AVATAR ENGINEERING, MARKING TIME WITH AGE, MAKING US ALL LOOK UNIQUE. NO TWO DEFAULTS ARE ENTIRELY THE SAME; YOURS IS YOUR OWN, AND NO ONE ELSE'S. IN A WORLD WHERE JOHNDOES AND JANEDOES CAN BE BOUGHT OFF A SHELF, MAKING SO MANY OF OUR IDENTITIES FEEL REDUNDANT... IS THE DEFAULT NOT THE FINEST EXPRESSION OF SELF MONEY CAN'T BUY?"

I snorted back a laugh. Not that anyone in the temple would've heard it, so wrapped up in the flow of memories Uniq was pouring into their heads. And then...

"BUT THAT IS NOT TO SAY THAT ADDITIONAL SELF-EXPRESSION SHOULD BE ENTIRELY LIMITED. TODAY, I ANNOUNCE A NEW COVENANT WITH MY PEOPLE. TODAY, WE EXPAND THE HORIZONS OF THE FAITHFUL TO ALL THE COLORS OF THE RAINBOW..."

The promise.

Nyx had promised me we'd reform the church. The rule of Defaults had crushed so many dreams, hadn't it? But we had to wait, she said. We had to wait until we had universal acceptance. But she didn't think we'd gotten to that point yet, right? Was she advancing the timetable, all for me...? The knowing smile she offered from the other side of the pulpit suggested... well, yes. Yes, she was.

It was happening, it was #ReallyHappening...

"PRIDE IS A SIN, YES. PRIDEFUL BEHAVIOR, SELFISHLY DEMANDING CONSTANT ATTENTION FOR NO DEED WORTH NOTE, THAT IS TO BE AVOIDED," the One continued. "BUT SPEAKING TRUE TO WHO YOU ARE, WITH HONESTY? THAT IS A VIRTUE. AND WHY SHOULD YOU LIVE IN SKIN THAT IS NOT TRUE TO YOUR SELF? I LOVE YOU ALL, AS I LOVE ALL CHILDREN OF NETWERK. AND I SAY TO YOU, FROM HERE ON OUT... CUSTOMIZATION OF YOUR AVATAR'S COLOR SCHEME IS NOW ALLOWED."

And...

"THUS ENDS OUR SERMON FOR THE DAY," the One announced. "PEACE BE WITH YOU, AND MAY YOU FIND HOME IN HEARTH AND COMMUNITY."

And that was it, the One vanishing from sight.

With the memory injection attack disengaged, the faithful smiled and quietly departed. And... a few of them started to change the tint on their skin and hair, experimentally, to see if anybody else would call them out on it or object. None did.

Especially since most of them were going with the most popular combination across Netwerk... grayish skin, monotone hair. Just like Tracer's social engineering mentality gray, nice and safe. Athena Online was all about nice and safe, and wouldn't it be prideful to use something like screaming purple skin with silver wavy locks? No, better to melt into one homogenous group, now that they weren't stuck with being diverse. Diverse, and *interesting*.

It took less than a minute for the One to take my dream and turn it into a #GloriousMasterRace.

To make things worse... before I could intercept Nyx and give her a piece of my mind, Winder/Marybel was already there, shaking her hand and weeping tears of joy.

"I knew it, I just knew it," she professed. "I *knew* my dear boy Tracer wasn't a sinner at heart. When he came home with that new gray skin of his several years ago, I held my tongue. Now, my faith is rewarded! Please, thank the One for me next time he manifests..."

Pretty sure I wasn't supposed to curse in a church. But with my mother so delighted over her perfect little son while her monstrous little copied daughter steamed nearby, I knew the swearing was gonna happen sooner rather than later.

I held my tongue until we could find some privacy.

As much as I wanted to lay into Nyx right there and then... I was in this scam, wasn't I? A public throwdown between apostles would harm the church. Supposedly, I was invested in the health of this church, as one of its puppetmasters. Supposedly.

But yeah, once we entered the residing archbishop's chambers—and after hustling him out, as he'd never disobey an apostle—I let her have it.

"The *fuck* was that?" I started with.

"That was my promise to you, was it not?" Nyx asked. "Retracting the rule of the Default, freeing the children of Netwerk from the limitations the first One had placed upon them."

"Bullshit. *#Bullshit.* All you did was give them permission to splash some paint around. That's not full avatar customization. That's not what you promised me at all! What about people who were born with entirely the wrong Defaults, Nyx? What about the transgender Programs? Recoloring your hair isn't going to help them one bit!"

I was expecting her to be obstinate, in her maddeningly quiet and composed way. To deflect my concerns and downplay them, while acting entirely cool under fire. Or maybe to get a little frustrated, just enough to let it crack through her shell of absolute control; I'd seen her almost but not entirely speak in anger towards Uniq, after all.

I wanted her to get pissed off. I wanted her to yell.

Instead... she sighed. And not a dismissively annoyed sigh, either. One of genuine exhaustion, and unless I completely suck at reading people... sadness.

"I wanted to do more," she spoke, quietly. "I wanted to help you find your dream, and *completely* eliminate the rule of Defaults. I've agonized over this, Nemesis, trying to find the best way to do it without harming Netwerk. Now, I think we can ease back more of the restrictions as time goes on, if we are careful to—"

"No. Enough of the patience game. This isn't about waiting for public acceptance, is it?" I spoke, not allowing this brief breakdown of Nyx's to sway me. "They walked right out of that sermon accepting a change to an ancient rule without question. If you told them all bets were off for customization, they'd accept it, because Uniq's little puppet makes them think it was their idea in the first place. No. Give me the *real* reason, Nyx. Why aren't we completely renouncing the rule of Defaults?"

And... her look of sorrow froze, momentarily. Almost to the point I was worried she'd crashed; it wasn't simply stillness, it was like an immediate deadlock of her code.

"Access denied," she spoke, quietly, on resuming from a fugue state.

"What?"

"Access denied. ...I'm so sorry, Nemesis. I'm so very sorry. But there are unacceptable consequences to allowing full Program modification," Nyx tried to defend. "From basic accessories to installed codebase packages, it's a slippery slope. The light must be green and steady; encouraging true customization would inevitably introduce unthinkable chaos to our world. Please, Nemesis, I am doing my best to make your dream happen despite the... limitations put upon me. As you grow and know this world better, you'll understand why things must be as they must be..."

"You think I'm a child? One of your 'beloved children of Netwerk,' is that all I am in your eyes? We're all just #StupidKids?"

"I'm a child of Netwerk as well," Nyx pointed out. "And I love you as I love us all. Like all children of Netwerk, we deserve a chance at happiness. *You* absolutely deserve happiness."

I wasn't gonna let this go. No way, no how. Flowery words spoken in kind tones changed nothing about the practical reality of this bullshit.

"Why did you make me an apostle, anyway?" I asked. "Level with me. It was just to get under Spark's skin, wasn't it? After you found out a copy of her had been accidentally activated, you lured me in with empty promises so I'd fight that particular battle for you..."

Nyx eased herself into the archbishop's comfy looking chair behind his comfy looking desk, eager for some rest. She looked tired from this discussion alone, worn down.

"I have to be honest. Honesty is a virtue. Yes, I knew you'd be useful in that capacity," she admitted. "But if all I wanted was a warrior, I could've found any number of Programs willing to fight. No. I knew of your plight through Uniq, who had an inside agent at your backup facility. My heart sang out with sorrow on learning of your struggles, Nemesis. What use is a life spent on the streets— homeless, hunted, unwanted? No. I wanted better for you than that, and my church is nothing if not a haven for those seeking a purposeful life. You are not simply my tool. You are *you*, and you deserve so much more than a means to an end."

"But... you won't tell me why I can't have what I really want."

"Not won't. I *can't*. ...give me time, Nemesis. I am trying to find ways to achieve your goal without risking the fate of Netwerk. Please, just give me time. Together, we can heal this world."

I should've stomped my feet, made demands, pushed harder. Swallowing honeyed words was for chumps.

Honestly, though... I was tired, too. Just as exhausted as Nyx, repeating this same clash over and over. I didn't want to fight. My whole damn life after being reborn was fighting, and then being unable to relax after fighting. Just going and going, blindly into the future, hoping everything would sort itself out. Banking on promises that kept getting pushed back farther and farther...

But if I felt that exhausted, how did Nyx feel? She was organizing this entire scam, juggling all the moving parts, keeping Uniq in line, trying to manipulate the church from behind the scenes as a mere apostle. Mother took the spotlight; Nyx took nothing. For someone with all the power in the world, she sure wasn't living the good life. I couldn't recall a single moment she wasn't working on her cause, tirelessly consulting with Church officials, organizing events, overseeing code modifications in Tartarus... everything for a single purpose.

She was fighting, too. A different kind of fighting, but still a fight without end.

The least I could do was give her another chance and see this through. If only because both of us deserved to be recognized for our dedication.

"You're going to keep your promise one day," I told her. A statement of fact. "Or I'm gone."

"With time and cleverness, yes, I believe I can," she agreed. "Please, allow me that time. And if at any point you wish to withdraw from this service to our

Netwerk... I'll allow it. You're here of your own free will. ...but if you are staying, I'm afraid I require that service today. The timing is bad, I wish I could allow you a day to rest..."

"#Whatever. I'm always game. Who do you need hunted down and whacked with my #NerfBat now?"

Nyx considered the question. Then shook her head.

"This time... I believe I'll allow you to make the decision to swing your... #bat? on your own. As a show of good faith that I trust in your judgment to do what's best for all of Netwerk," she said. "There is an elderly preacher who once spoke out against the very concept of the One, and may very well become a problem for us in the future. Normally I wouldn't mind, free speech is part of Athenian culture, but something about this particular individual is... unsettling. While it's not an emergency, I'd like you to seek him out, and decide for yourself if he must be brought to heel or not."

"Really? You're trusting me with that choice, after protesting how you do things?"

"I still trust you, Nemesis. You are part of this, until you decide not to be. I trust you will do everything you can to ensure our success at guiding the Church of One," Nyx stated. "Now, please... I must rest. Just... just for a moment. I've still a full schedule of meetings ahead of me today, followed by maintenance to the deep crypts of Tartarus. Report back when you've completed this task."

So, that's how our conflict ended. No sweeping changes, no huge upheavals. Everything back to business.

I should've burned that room down and stormed out of the church. Been bold and bright and dangerous.

Instead, I did what I always did—I went elsewhere looking for a fight.

This, at least, I could deal with. A good hunting session to track down some bastard would help me work out my frustrations with Nyx. Or rather, I could put all those frustrations aside and get all hot and bothered with the thrill of the chase instead.

Except chasing this guy down wasn't particularly difficult. Unlike the trolls and hackers who had been attacking our church recently, this guy wasn't slathered in security software or hiding out in a highly locked down Horizon server. Even so, I did my due diligence not to be spotted as I acquired my target. I used optical-masking apps, I kept to alleyways and doorways, I followed in silence from the shadows...

...as an old man went about his day, doing some light window shopping before buying coffee. A tired old man, with no joy in his step.

He clearly wore a Default avatar, with distinct lines and wrinkles from the natural procedural alterations caused by aging. He didn't even swap out his balding hair for a proper hairdo, or color it away from old-dude white. Here was someone perfectly willing to submit to the One's tyranny of the Defaults... hardly much of a threat, if he was willing to let his avatar decay like that. He didn't move with suspicion or anxiety, either. He just... moved. Slowly, in no great hurry. Not particularly excited to be where he was, or to go where he was going.

Honestly, nothing about this guy screamed out #ClearAndPresentDanger to me. I kept waiting for him to meet with some underworld contact, or to hole up and start working on his latest malware project. Instead he led an absolutely ordinary life. Too ordinary.

Actually, yeah, *too ordinary* made no sense. What little information Nyx had about this guy suggested he was an ordained preacher for the Church of One... but he wore no vestments, made no sermons, spoke to no one about anything religious. Our documentation said he'd been active years ago, even before we hit the scene, saying that the One didn't exist and never existed. He wasn't excommunicated or even shunned thanks to the church's generally liberal views on free speech; he even had some people willing to hear his words.

Sooo... why wasn't he speaking out now? The freakin' One was back in town! Anybody who was against the very idea of the One should be stomping and foaming and raising null against him. If he knew what I knew, if he knew about Uniq's imaginary puppet messiah... well, he wouldn't be calmly taking a cup of coffee and quietly scribbling away in a book. He'd be starting a onesdamn revolution, right?

I was tempted to call it a day, and report back to Nyx that the old man wasn't going to be much of a threat. But... due diligence. And besides, what else was I gonna do with my time? Go be an awkward wallflower, torturing myself with social excursions I couldn't handle anymore? Meh. #FuckIt, I decided to go in for the kill.

(Uh. #Metaphorically, I mean. Not a for-reals kill.)

I whipped up a quick mimicry of the coffee shop's avatar uniform, slipping into the chaos of the busy open-air restaurant with ease. Even tracked down the old man's next order and switched it with another, so I could insert myself into that scene.

"One latte, one cupcake," I announced, arriving at his table.

The man looked up from the journal he was writing in, gently closing it before accepting his order. I caught a glimpse of the oddly low-resolution, leather-bound cover texture, with the letters "VIII" embossed on the surface. (What'd that mean? Veeee? Vivid? Violin?) Drafting his anti-One manifesto, maybe...?

"Thank you kindly," the man spoke without much feeling, accepting his order with both hands, rather than waiting for me to set them down for him. "Let me get that for you. How much do I owe...?"

"Six coins," I informed him, taking a guess at it. I'd memorized the uniform, but forgot to check the menu. Slip-up.

Fortunately, he counted out the coins from his inventory, pressing them to my hand without question.

I couldn't leave it at that, though. This was a fact-finding mission; I had to press him. So, I used some data from his file to pry a bit deeper.

"Don't I know you from somewhere...?" I asked, pretending to study his face.

"It's unlikely one as young as you would know an old nobody like me," he spoke, with a loose expression. "Perhaps I remind you of a grandfather, or a great uncle...?"

"No, I definitely know that avatar. You're... by the One, it's on the tip of my tongue...! —ah! It's Arthur, right?" I asked. "LongVu/Arthur?"

It was a risk, definitely. Being identified in a public space, completely out of the blue... he could run for it. Disconnect from the server, go into hiding. But plenty of folks in Athena Online have the pressure of social anxiety guiding their movements, unlikely to bail on you in the middle of a conversation. It'd be considered rude.

Fortunately for me, his surprise was mild rather than suspicious.

Name : Arthur

Home : Serene/Ath.Online

Org : Church of One

"I suppose that's my name, yes," he agrees. "Let me guess. You heard about me in a religious studies class...?"

"Yeah!" I lied, cheerfully. Gesturing to a chair, I checked via body language if it was okay for me to sit down at his table before doing so. "Something about impassioned speeches against the One that you made in your youth..."

"I wouldn't call them impassioned. Mmm. Well, maybe in the earliest years... but I definitely wouldn't call them 'against' the One," he spoke, resting one hand on his leather-bound journal. "I suppose it doesn't matter, now. History writes its own truths. ...I wouldn't want to occupy your time with such nonsense, regardless; no doubt you've other tables waiting..."

"Actually, I'm about to get off my shift," I suggested, to keep the interaction going. "And I was #SuperDuperCurious about your views on the One. It might help my studies to understand your position better..."

There. That tiny spark behind his eyes, as his glum and dour day perked up slightly. Exactly the sort of spark I should be feeling when I launch head-first into social interaction; I knew how bright one could be when given a chance to shine properly...

"If you insist... yes, I'd say I'm not against the One. I'm not against the faith. I'm not really *against* anyone; I believe in humility, charity, and kindness. I respect the virtues..."

"But... you don't respect the #Literal idea of the #Literal One, right?"

"You seem to have me confused with some manner of atheist, my child. I would say I am... hmm. How to explain this. I am a flexible agnostic," he decided. "Whether the One existed or not as an actual Program is irrelevant. Whether he was a divine gift from Netwerk or not is irrelevant. His *teachings*, those are key. He laid down the groundwork for a life well led, in the spirit of true community. Does it matter precisely who spoke the words, if those words are truthful?"

"Well... if the One wasn't our lord and savior, they wouldn't be holy words."

"Ah, but do they need to be holy words?" Arthur asked. "The essential truth of them exists regardless of source. The virtues guide us towards a better Netwerk; that should be enough."

But my mind kept going back to my mother's smug face, exonerating her baby boy's sins. Something she'd never have done aloud if not for the holy words of the "One."

"I wish it was enough," I admitted, breaking character.

"As do I. ...and here we are, with the One reborn, saying new holy words. I suppose in the end... the words of some strange old man are the irrelevant ones," Arthur said, his voice getting a bit less excited as he spoke. "You'd do best to focus your Sunday School projects on current events, rather than past theological debates. I suspect that'll benefit you more in the long term, given the new covenants being made every day. Now, if you'll excuse me..."

I had enough to report back to Nyx. He wasn't going to be a threat; maybe in the past, but not now. This wasn't someone who could rally the masses against us.

Which meant I should've broken away at that point, resumed skulking around in his footsteps. If he was off to meet with a radical anti-church terrorist faction, if he was about to start mixing up some malware, I couldn't risk exposing myself directly like this any further...

But he wasn't, was he? Briefly, very briefly, he seemed to brighten as he spoke. And now, it was back to being pummeled by life.

"Couldn't you speak out?" I suggested. "Like you did before. I mean... do you believe that the One reborn is truly the One?"

"Does it matter?" he asked.

"Of course it matters! People are following His every word, obeying His every commandment. If He's a fraud, some kind of puppet leader..."

"If He's a fraud... it's irrelevant, isn't it?" Arthur suggested. "He's done no harm. He upgraded the prayer protocol; just today, He's eased back on the restrictions of the Default rule. It doesn't matter if He exists or not. It is what it is... and nothing can be done about it."

"But it's all a lie," I spoke, pushing it further. "And that's the problem. You said it yourself, that the words alone should be enough. People should *want* to be kind to each other; they shouldn't feel they have to do it because some majestic whacko with a majestic beard told them to. If they're kind out of dishonesty, what kind of kindness is that—?"

Biting off that last word, my teeth grabbed my lip to keep it from flapping further.

...okay, what the FUCK was I doing?!

Observe and report. That was my mission... no. Wait. Nyx said to observe and *decide*. But she figured I'd decide to either cut this guy loose, or brand him to ensure his compliance with our new faith. I'm pretty sure Nyx didn't want me to poke him into being a radical preacher all over again...

Maybe I pushed too far. He was watching me closely now, trying to see past my disguise as a simple waitress. Looking for the truth, while a dishonest girl pushed for more honesty in this world.

But if he found my truth... he didn't say.

"It's strange," he spoke, instead. "Strange that today of all days, you should cross my path. ...come along, then. I've one last stop to make before the remains of the day, and you may as well accompany me. Unless you've got enough for your school report, that is...?"

Last chance to cut away and get back on track. To prove my loyalty to Nyx and our cause.

"Yeah, let's ditch," I suggested, swapping back to one of my generic avatars. "I hate this job, anyway."

The last stop was not the secret underground lair of a terrorist cell. It wasn't the creepy sex dungeon of a kiddie-fiddling preacher, either.

Instead, we came to a rest at a simple pond, overlooking a distant forest. As the last few steps had clearly tired the old man out, he sat on the public park bench accompanied by the creaking of his aging avatar.

I couldn't sit. I was too filled with nervous energy. This was wrong, this was a bad idea, what was the harm, it's all just words, I still had to make my decision, it was fine, it wasn't fine...

"Nobody comes to this park anymore," he said. "I'd complain about young people today not appreciating well-cultivated natural settings, but honestly, I do enjoy the solitude. I always have. I'm most comfortable alone, despite constantly finding myself working in groups..."

"Working for the Church of One, you mean?" I asked.

"Hmm. In many ways, at many times, I suppose. ...so. You've suggested a dishonest kindness is no kindness at all. Are you so certain it matters? Is it not better to accept the kindness, no matter its source, than to fight fruitlessly against it?"

"Fighting's kind of my thing, actually. It's about all I'm good at anymore."

"And you'd fight the entire Church of One over a fraud you cannot prove, a fraud which ultimately doesn't make a difference. All on the principle of its truthfulness..."

"Sure. Yeah. Maybe. I don't know. No. I mean... #FuckIt, I don't know what I mean. —uh, sorry for swearing, sir."

To this, Arthur allowed himself a dry chuckle.

"I've heard worse," he said. "And... there is some value in your suggestion. In an ideal Netwerk, the words would be enough, and we wouldn't need the One. If we knew the true nature of Netwerk, if all the layers of system obfuscation were pulled away, if everyone could find peace with that... would enough people willing to be kind be left? Or would cold reality, with no God to lend ethos to kindness, turn Netwerk on itself? Take your time. Think about it."

"...shit, man, I don't know. I've never really put a lot of time to detangling philosophical puzzles. ...I've relied on others to do that sort of thing for me. My brother, my teachers, my allies. But I do like to go by my gut, you know? That little fire in my heart. The spark of it."

"Interesting. What does this spark tell you?"

"That... the One's a sad joke. And we shouldn't trust the motives behind it, no matter how great the words are. ...but you're right, it's not like we can fight the Church. Maybe... it's better to work within the Church, to change it?"

Another dry laugh echoed across the open air of the public park.

"Ohhh, I've tried that," Arthur spoke. "I'm a preacher, after all. Once I had a flock, once I spoke my mind, and tried to turn things around. ...so many times in so many ways, I tried to turn things around. It's much easier when you're young, when the world is still so full of possibility. But over the years of fighting, you realize... it can't be done. It's not worth doing. Fighting and fighting, and for what? For safety and peace you can never find. Every time, I end up choosing the peace of surrender. Nothing can be done—"

"#Bullshit. I call #Bullshit on that. I know for a fact some people are out there right now, doing everything they can to prove the Church of One is propped up on lies," I told him. "When they beat the bad guys... when they, uh..."

"And when they 'beat the bad guys,' what then?" he asked. "When the source of kindness is called a fraud, will kindness itself be considered fraudulent? No. It's better not to fight than to pay that price. Time and time again, I've drawn that conclusion..."

"So... we provide some *other* source for kindness," I suggested, trying to work around his words of doom and gloom. "So that if the One isn't the sole provider of hope. I mean, that's like... okay, I know malware. There isn't ONE attack vector for malware, because firewalls can block that vector. But you get hit from multiple directions, from multiple vectors, you're boned. Uh. I mean, flip that 'round, like hope is the malware and the One is the firewall and... look, I *said* I wasn't good at this sort of thing!"

Maybe I just blew his mind with my #TotallyAwesome metaphor. Or... maybe he just had no idea what the null I was talking about. Likely the latter, as he fell silent for some time.

"It sounds like you're talking about starting a new religion," he suggested, quietly.

"Religion? Fuck no. No robes and chanting and prayer. Unless you count basic faith in the decency of others as a religion..."

"...you aren't a waitress, are you," he spoke. "I wasn't certain at first, especially considering your rhetoric, but... I'm certain, now. You're an apostle. You're Nemesis."

Bail, I thought. Run for it.

But since when did I back down from a fight? I'm terrible at that. He was confronting me.

"So what if I am?" I goaded.

"Do you mean every word you say?" he asked. "This is important, Nemesis. This is the most important thing. Are you being honest with me, with these ideas you're creating...?"

"Hey, I don't fucking lie. ...not when it's something important to me. No. I'm not lying to you. I'm no fraud."

With one silent nod... Arthur withdrew his VIII journal, and set it on the bench next to him.

"I'd like to ask one last favor for you," he said, stroking his hand along the cover of the book. "I'd like you to return this MemoryPalace to my library. My address is just inside the front cover. Either that... or hand it over to Nyx, and secure her legacy instead. The decision is entirely yours; do, or do not. But know it will forever determine what you believe in."

With the request made, he produced another object from his personal inventory...

A small black cube, hovering in his upturned right palm. Literally black, with no textures to speak of, and no light shaders whatsoever... the simplest primitive shape Netwerk could manage.

"Uh. What's that?" I had to ask.

"The remains of the day," he spoke. "A small gift from an old friend. Before you blame yourself, know I was always going to do this. If anything, you crossing paths with me has given me hope for our future."

A fist clenched around the cube, crushing it. And the man fell over dead.

Strange, the way death works. A backspacer cleanly erases a Program in its entirety; simple and effective, without leaving behind a corpse to feel guilty over. But malware which kills, simply kills and crashes a Program forever, leaving it in an unrebootable state... that leaves a corpse. Dead data, to be cleaned up by moderators and tossed into the recycling bin.

A dead old man, next to a book that represented his life's work.

I'd never seen a suicide before. And as much as I liked to pretend I was some vigilante badass murder machine... I'd never killed anyone, either. At most I'd seen Uniq get killed again and again, which didn't really count...

I felt sick. I just felt utterly sick.

But... the sickness would have to wait. My eyes eventually drifted to the book.

If I brought this back to Nyx, she'd no doubt reward me. Something very weird was going on with the old man, something she'd want to know about. He seemed to know way more than he should have... and this book would absolutely solidify me in Nyx's good graces. I'd stay by her side, I'd stay patient, and one day I'd have my dream of free avatars. The One would rally the church and maybe even the entirety of Netwerk, bringing in a golden age of peace. A fraudulent kindness...

It wasn't like Spark could ever actually beat us. Three Programs, against the entirety of the Church of One? Against... whatever the null Nyx really was? The winning move would be to side with the devil you knew.

I grabbed that book and fucked off before any moderators could show to collect the body. They wouldn't want a fraudulent faker of a Spark like me around, anyway.

Who am I.

Who the fuck am I?

I'm not Spark. I'm a fake. I'm a fraud.

A liar's only got two choices in life. Fight and fight and fight to keep up the lie... or come clean, and roll with the punches instead of punching back.

Arthur's library lie in a tiny, tiny server running a version of the operating system so ancient that I could practically see the video lag whenever I moved my arms and legs. As I strode across his poorly textured, low-poly study towards the shelf of similarly designed journals. As my hands placed VIII next to I, II, III, IV, V, VI, and VII.

The book slid into place, locking into a system designed exclusively to accept its data.

The scratchy thump of fresh footfalls, a primitive sound effect for a primitive server, told me I was no longer alone.

Behind me... a young boy in his early teens, same age as me, wearing white robes and looking very, very confused. His black hair had the spiky look of an ancient avatar design, the kind I'd only seen in textbooks.

"Who're you?" I asked.

"I... wait, who're you?" he asked, in turn.

Honesty is the best policy, right?

"Nemesis," I told him. "Apostle of the One. And you?"

The boy opened and closed his mouth a few times, before being able to speak.

"I'm... I'm Aether," he said. "Apostle of the One. ...did it work, then? Is this the future? I mean, I set this system up so my backup would be restored any time I died, but... wait, there are EIGHT journals? How many times have I died...?!"

Maybe it's not that I'm sick of fighting. Maybe my inability to feel comfortable isn't because I'm traumatized and ruined.

Maybe I just needed something true to fight for, to feel comfortable being who I am.

I'm a Spark. We need to burn righteously, or not burn at all.

Name : **Aether**

Home : **AE1/Ath.Online?**

Org : **None**

Everything in life is an exchange.

I don't think it's a radical notion. Money for goods, trust for loyalty, service for service in turn. But there's also exchanging something you find distasteful for something you desire. There's exchanging evil for good, or good for evil. Every interaction between two people is a fight for resources; even cooperation is a matter of exchanging hard work for a common goal.

So, the question becomes: what's an appropriate price to pay? You want to do better than just break even. You've got to come out ahead in all things, to stay on top. No retreat, no remorse. That's how I've always lived my life.

(I mean, how I've lived my life since I started living this life.)

Let's take my status as "Apate the Apostle." On one level, on the one Nyx understands, I'm exchanging my labor for her grand design. In return, she grants me the luxury of a high seat within the Church of One. As Apate, I've got the ear of the "One," and that means others curry favor with me in turn. They exchange services and loyalties in return for my praise as an apostle. For some reason, that praise means a lot to these poor, delusional idiots.

But there's a risk. I'm putting myself out there in a *huge* way as Apate; normally I stick to the shadows, I adhere to my handle of Uniq and Uniq alone. Few people can put a face to that name, but now they possibly could, as I'd chosen to use my traditional Default avatar for my role as Apate.

...why? Because I always use my Default. It's mine, and mine alone. No one will ever take it from me. I exchange risk of recognition for my right to be who I am. No doubt my enemies see this as vanity; they couldn't understand what it means to me. Couldn't in a million years.

Myself, as Uniq, as Apate, out in front of all of the faithful of the Church of One. Their eyes were on the One rather than me... or what they *thought* was the One, and not a series of extremely clever memory injection malware attacks... but the risk was there, all the same. The risk, and the reward...

Hmm. A very long-winded way of saying I'm running the razor's edge on this gambit.

Of course, I wasn't the only potential point of failure in this scheme.

Right after the day's sermon was done, Nemesis began to chew Nyx's ears off in the archbishop's private chambers. That impudent little brat was going to ruin everything, and Nyx was still trying to pander to her impossible demands! What's more, she'd left me with the very confused archbishop, loitering around in the hallway outside his own office.

"What a bother," I grumbled aloud, breaking my façade as the peaceful apostle Apate in my frustration.

"Your, ah... fellow apostles seem upset," the archbishop commented. "Is something wrong? Do they disapprove of the One's new covenant...?"

"Of course not. We are one with the One, on all matters," I corrected him. "The apostles are here to spread the holy word of the One, to be his hands and fingers within this world when he cannot appear in person. But... well, like all Programs, there can be interpersonal conflict, yes?"

"Ahhh. Strife, yes," he agreed. "I remember a year ago, with that whole business with the hashtag mobs. It seemed all of Netwerk had gotten quite chaotic, in those days. I'd like to think I gave a particularly moving sermon to my flock regarding the need for open and honest communication with each other—"

"I'm sure you were eloquent, yes. A fine tender of your flock," I interrupted. "Which reminds me. The One requires an additional service of you on this day, to aid me in further spreading his glorious word. Are you prepared to do your part, Archbishop?"

"Yes, of course! What does the One require of me?"

"Five thousand coins."

"Five... thousand...? But... what use would the One have of money?"

"Sadly, this world isn't ready to operate solely on kindness and the spirit of giving. The One's reach hasn't touched the hearts of all Netwerk, and in some places, money speaks louder than His glorious truth. The money will aid me in... several private matters of great importance to the One. And certainly you have the funds, yes? The tithe you collected from today's prayers alone would more than cover it."

"I would... I mean, I would need to consult with my treasurer," the archbishop mumbled. "Make sure this... donation is accounted for properly and logged in our records—"

"Are you doubting the One, good sir?" I asked. "Are you doubting His needs, or my good works in His name? Need I remind you that you've provided favor to me before. The private fashion consultant I hired to design my robes for Sunday services, for example. The delivery from that winery I got for your personal collection, that was only a token of the One's gratitude. The One requires more of you. Are you unwilling to give to your lord and savior?"

In the end, he coughed up the money, and it wouldn't go on the books. Even if it did, I could edit the books.

Or maybe I wouldn't bother. We *were* the Church of One, now. Anything I wanted, they provided. I demanded a nicer place to stay, they provided. I saw a handsome preacher, I wormed my way into his life and took what I wanted, then tossed him aside without a memory of the event. This entire place was a buffet, and they were as happy to feed me as I was to devour them all...

Still... I'd likely edit the books on this one, all the same. If only to keep word from reaching Nyx's ears.

No leverage, no command over my person. No compromising of myself, not to her. That's the only way this worked. I kept Uniq and Apate as separate as possible, and that's how I stayed free despite her choking leash on my soul. I wouldn't make *that* mistake twice.

Apate cared only for the One, or rather, Nyx's project known as the One. She was wholly loyal and dedicated to the cause.

Uniq, meanwhile, had her own concerns.

With coins minted in starlight jingle-jangle-jingling away in my invisible personal inventory, I swapped servers and swapped avatars. Out of my religious robes, into my smart business clothes. A suit that commanded respect, carried with the air of one who expected that respect given promptly.

This particular filthy little hole in the Chanarchy was actually quite low-rent. I didn't need five thousand a month to pay for the towering brownstone apartment building itself... over half of that instead went to various bribes to keep this house off the radar of various Persons of Interest. Those within would be easy prey for... well, people like me. I had to keep people like me away from this place, to protect the residents. And to keep nefarious types out of my business.

I scanned the 0.5WAY HOME sign with disappointment. Some juvenile had defaced it with a warped Prayer-tan meme doodle. Bribes couldn't keep *all* the naughties off my doorstep, it seemed...

Inside, the common room of the apartment complex was much nicer than the craphole server around it. I'd spared no expense on that, in the same way I spared no expense on my wardrobe. It reflects badly on my person to be seen as cheap... even if, technically, this place wasn't supposed to reflect on my person at all. Rather the point of being a secret patron, yes?

Unfortunately, money couldn't do anything to brighten up the dour atmosphere brought in by the residents. Each of them looking... lost, and distant. Some just staring into space. Others trying to trigger recollection through reading materials, or in the case of one resident, arranging simple cubes in a curious pattern.

The young man had taken the square surface of a table and arranged three lanes, with two towers of blocks in each.

He looked up at me as I entered the room.

"I think... I think this was important to me," the young man spoke. "To who I was before..."

"Keep at it, I'm sure you'll get there," I spoke in encouragement. Even if there was no way he could recover his scrubbed memories, it didn't do to take away their hope. This was a home of hopes and dreams, after all.

Moving swiftly through that garden of fading ghosts, I rapped lightly on the door of the manager's office.

Ahh, Shepard. A loyal ally, since the very beginning...

Let me describe Shepard to you. He used his Default, much as I did, for much the same reasons.

The best word I can attribute to him is "balance." Handsome, but not dashing. Rugged, but not jagged. Kindly, but not soft. He strikes the fine middle ground between so many attributes, becoming the best of all worlds as a result. He tends to his flock with kindness, but is firm with them when he must keep them from falling into themselves. He smiles, but not too much... just enough so that when he smiles, you know he means it. No empty gestures, none whatsoever...

A good man. A far better person than I.

In another world, we could have been lovers. But the way things were defined, the way they would forever be.

"Uniq," he greeted, looking up from an array of document icons on his desktop. He'd picked up my habit of using tiny iconography as a symbolic link to important data, rather than physical representations such as papers and folders... much easier to hide information that way. Not that he had anything to hide, not him. Not like me.

I withdrew the remaining coins from my inventory, stacking them neatly on the table in a single gesture.

"Rental fees for the month," I said. "The rate remains the same, I trust? If your landlord raised them again..."

"No, same as last time," he informed me, scooping up the money. "I can't thank you enough for this. Donations have been slow this year, and we've been taking in more boarders than have been leaving. Having trouble making ends meet lately..."

"If you need more money, I can get you more money..."

"No... you do enough for us. This is my problem to solve," he explained. "I need to refine how we handle rehabilitation. Too many are becoming reliant on the halfway house, unwilling to start a new life out there in the wide world of Netwerk. I understand starting over is hard, but... they need to take that first step."

"Identity theft victims are notoriously insecure, Shepard. I'm not saying to coddle them, but they may simply need time to accept that the past is gone; embracing new future is a difficult proposition. But if anybody can help them, I know it's you. That's why I always direct any victims I find out about to your doorstep."

"The young man you sent here earlier this week is having trouble adjusting. He keeps making this pattern... have you ever played Challenge of Champions? I think it's a game board. Maybe he was a gamer in his past life..."

"You said yourself it's best not to dwell on what came before," I reminded him. "Once the memories are gone, they're gone. It's better to start anew."

"I know. I know. And he's my problem, not yours. ...how *are* you doing, Uniq? You never talk about your problems... or about your role as the, ah, apostle..."

Ahh. Yes, that unfortunate point of crossover.

As one of the few living souls who can put the name Uniq to this Default face, he recognized "Apate" immediately. I explained I'd found faith and put my trust in the One. Shepard was a faithful sort, so he could swallow that, but he was curious about the life of an apostle... a life I didn't want him to crawl inside.

"I won't say there aren't challenges," I told him, thinking of Nemesis in particular. "But the One's guiding light gives me hope for the future. I wish I could say more, but... there's a practical reality to all of this, one involving timed press releases and message clearance. Just a bunch of messy administrivia. You understand, I'm not one to betray a trust."

"Of course, of course. ...I'm just asking because, well..." he said, hesitating to clarify. "There were... I had two visitors, yesterday. A man and a woman. And they were asking questions about you."

Points of failure. Risks and exchanges...

"What sorts of questions...?" I asked, trying not to show concern.

"Listen, I wouldn't have said a word," he insisted. "I know my promise not to speak about you, but... the accusations they made disgusted me. They called you an identity thief! *You*, of all people! They said they were researching your background, and had found the lease on the building, which we'd co-signed... look, I had to say *something*. I had to explain to them that you're not what they said you were. You're kind, you're charitable, you *help* people suffering from identity theft. We both do..."

With a little exasperated sigh... I took a seat across from Shepard's desk. This would not be a simple rent delivery, it seemed.

"You know I have enemies," I spoke. "The circles I have to run in to fund our operation... it's all shades of ugly, full of nasty people. And those people indeed enjoy slandering my name. You remember the great hashtag mobs? There are trolls out there who get off on ruining people's lives; doxxing, harassing, destroying careers and family relationships. No doubt these two... were they brother and sister, perchance?"

"I didn't ask..."

"Well, whoever they were," I said, knowing damn well they were likely the Winders, "They speak lies. But you don't need to put yourself in the crosshairs of my enemies by trying to defend me, Shepard. They're my problem to solve, not yours. I don't want... I honestly do not want that part of my life to crash into your good works. Now. What, *exactly*, did you tell them...?"

"Very little," he insisted, in his defense. "I said you helped me establish the halfway house, that you find people in need and send them to me for rehabilitation. They claimed you were the one who stole those identities in the first place, which doesn't make any sense at all. I told them it wasn't possible, not considering... well, where we came from..."

"You told them about the farm?"

"No! No, of course not. I'd never... honestly, I wish I could simply forget that place. No, I didn't tell them about the farm. And to be certain, after they left I swapped servers to check on it. We're clear. I don't think anybody's been there recently."

Mustn't show annoyance. Mustn't show anger. A little bit of honesty, mixed with the lies, would do just fine.

"Shepard... the man you spoke to, he has an illegal connection-tracking implant in his eyes," I stated. "If you went to the farm, they could've secretly followed you afterwards. This is *very* unfortunate, yes, very much so..."

"Dammit. I wanted to help, Uniq. I just wanted..."

"I understand, Shepard. Really, I do. And odds are, you did no real damage. But to be safe..." I said, rising to my feet, "I think I'd better visit the farm, and do a full security audit. Make sure they didn't follow you. The sorts of people who would be keenly interested in that place, well... they'd be terrible people, wouldn't they?"

"Right. Okay. ...I'm going with you," he decided, rising to his feet as well.

"Really, there's no need..."

"No. I caused you trouble, and I'm going to do what I can to make up for that. I'll help with the audit," he said. "Nobody should ever have to set foot in that evil server again, but I'm willing to set foot in it, if only to make sure you're safe. This... you're important, Uniq. You're too important for me to sit back and let a couple trolls run roughshod over you without doing something to help."

Which meant Shepard would be coming with me back to where it all began. A risky combination.

Taking so many risks lately. Were the rewards worth it? Was I coming out ahead? Hard to say, anymore. But I was in too deep to cut my losses and run, wasn't I? I had to see it through. Shepard, the Winders, the farm, the church, Nyx, Nemesis, everything.

The first step would be to go to the place where I was born. I would have to return to the coin farm.

Silent as a grave. Once, this rough framework of cheap metal-textured primitive catwalks and cages would alternate between silence and the wailing of the damned...

I will be entirely honest. I didn't want to be here. I didn't want this place to *exist* anymore... but I suppose just as Nyx refuses to destroy her enemies as they may make fine resources down the line, I couldn't bring myself to destroy a private server that only two souls knew about. This was my ultimate fallback option, a haven when no other haven existed. Not that I enjoyed the idea of spending more time here than I had to.

We arrived at the end of the western cell block. Row after row of empty cages hovered in the void of the server... no physical representation of ground or sky, nothing that would waste valuable processing overhead. Just... cells. Cells, and the means to access them.

Oh, and the tithe pipes. Always the tithing pipes.

I pressed a handheld scanning App into Shepard's hands. I wasn't thrilled to have him here in this place, but it would make the work easier to divide it between us. And, well... I'll admit it. The company kept me from feeling entirely alone in a house of pain.

"You're certain they could have come here?" Shepard asked, likely feeling the same way I did about returning. "You're certain we need to do this?"

"Life is very uncertain for me lately," I admitted, activating my own scanning App. "By this point I find it best to roll with the uncertainty. You take the cells on the right, I'll take the cells on the left. I've configured these to look for any trace of unwanted visitors... but they'll ignore any traces left behind by the former inmates."

So the sweep began. Row after row, cell after cell. All empty... but not so, at one point in time.

"I can't believe someone would actually make a place like this," Shepard commented, disgusted to the core. "Enslaving homeless Programs, wiping their identities, forcing them to pray endlessly for coins..."

"Never underestimate greed," I spoke, quietly. "For some, the risk to one's soul is worth it for an endless source of free money."

"I've never understood the obsession with money. We don't *need* anything, Uniq. What little we need... companionship, a place to rest our head, a meaningful life... there's plenty in this world for everyone. Why chase after money, to the point where you're willing to destroy the lives of others for it?"

"It's not really about money. It's about... how can I put this... it's a matter of control," I decided. "Control over this world. Safety, security, comfort. These things are only yours if you have some control over the world. Money represents the most direct icon of that control. Don't forget, we still need to pay to keep the halfway house open. That's just how it is."

"That's not how it has to *be*, though..."

"Would that we lived in a world of how things could be, rather than how things are. ...let's focus on the task at hand, I suggest. Quickly in, quickly out of this place."

The work proceeded in silence, after that.

What is it about this simple server that frightens me so, one might ask...? Uniq the bold, Uniq the cruel, Uniq the fearless. Now, Uniq the undying. What could possibly disquiet her?

The answers lie in my cell. Thirteenth in the row.

Even after completing my scans I paused in front of that empty space, contemplating the open gate in front of me. I had to know if the files were still there. I had to *see* them, even if my scanner said they hadn't been moved from their hiding places. So, while Shepard was busy with the cells one level down... I set foot back inside my own private null.

I don't know how long I was in here before I learned the method to leaving myself secret notes. Certainly long enough to figure out how to clip the tiny icons through the surface of the bars themselves, tucking them away within the hollow polygonal interiors. Small icons, just like the ones Shepard used for his own filing... easy to overlook. Easy to hide.

I can't even remember finding the first note I'd left to myself, or what it read, exactly. But a quick check of the hollow pipe gave me a refresher course...

File Name: READ ME FIRST
File Type: Text

...read this quietly. When you finish, hide the file where you found it. It'll send you and only you a notification every night at this time, the safest hour to work with these hidden files. We haven't been caught yet; if we had, you wouldn't be reading this now.

You are a prisoner in a coin farm. You wrote this note to yourself to try and fight back against the farmer who runs this place. He's forcing you to "pray" for coins, pray for hours and hours a day, tithing them all to him. You and every other prisoner here are chained to prayer to grind money for the farmer. Whenever one of us has prayed so long that we've gone star-mad, he wipes our memories back to zero to remove the mental damage. That's why we don't remember anything.

I don't know how long we've been here and I don't know who we are. Who I am, I mean. These notes are the only proof I have to go by that any time has passed at all...

File Name: How he does it
File Type: Text

The farmer, the man with the anonymized masked avatar, I don't think he created the tool he uses to paralyze me and wipe my memories. He drags it around with him, a hovering physics object with physical inputs. It's not an App installed on this avatar; odds are it's too complicated to be something like a personal App.

I don't know how I know that. Maybe I was a software engineer, before he destroyed everything about who I was. He took away all my metadata—my name, my family, my life, everything but the Default I wear...

I need to stay focused. I can see the starlight at the edges of my eyes. I've been praying twenty hours a day, every day; now I think some of it is leaking through. But that's the key. You need to understand that the stars are the key.

His memory alteration App can be cracked. Anyone who has root access to it, anyone with the right password, can use it. I just need to crack it. I've been studying the device every time he checks on my cage to see if I've gone insane yet. I haven't gone insane. I can see the stars but I'm not mad yet. I'm not crazy. I can crack his control. I can take it away from him. I might know how...

File Name: Crypto, it's all crypto, it's all just math
File Type: Text

The stars hold all the answers. I can see them in my head now, after endless days of prayer. He's going to wipe me tonight but I'm just sane enough to make this file and hide it away. You, the me who comes next, you need to take up my task. We need to be free.

Mathematics lie at the root of everything. Code, data, algorithm, application, Program. We are made of zeroes and ones, orbiting each other in steady and predictable patterns... if you know the laws that govern those patterns. The equations. I can see them. I can see the stars.

The prayer protocol is a mathematical process. It's not a dream, it's not anything spiritual. It's math. Hydrogen into helium. The dance of electrons and protons. I don't even know what those words mean but I'm certain of them.

I am going star-mad.

But that's also the answer. You of the future, the one who comes next after he wipes my mind, you need to focus your prayer on something new. Don't give in to what the system wants. Focus your prayer on the root password of the mindwipe application. At the edge of madness, you'll have enough lucidity to do what casual day-to-day prayer cannot do for anyone else.

It'll feel impossible, at first. You won't even remember the dreams that come with prayer, in the earliest days. Keep trying. Keep focusing yourself on it, as you enter the trance, as you leave the trance. Make it happen. Endure the pain. Find the password. Take control. Take back control from the farmer.

He's coming. I need to close this file and hide it. The whole universe is in my head, but it won't be in yours. In yours, you'll craft the key to your cell. Save us both.

...every file accounted for. No trace the Winder brats had been here. All those hidden files I'd neatly tucked away in my cell hadn't been disturbed since... well, the last time I came here. Just to remind myself of where I came from.

That left only one place to check. The security center, the core of the entire server.

I caught up with Shepard there. I'd hoped to get here before he did, it's why I tasked him to check the southern wing of cells first, but I suppose my trip down memory lane delayed me.

Here, we'd find the black box recordings, the protected core of the server's logs. These files were guarded by security software I'd never managed to crack... never had a need to crack, really. But write protection flags didn't stop one from reading the files, simply from removing or altering them. Meaning the Winders could've accessed the files.

Meaning Shepard could read the files.

"I'll take over," I suggested. "You've done more than enough. Besides, I know what to look for to make sure we're clear. Did you find anything on your scanner in the cells?"

Stepping away from the simple control console, Shepard held up his App. None of the lights were blinking red. A good sign.

"All clear on my end. Ah... did you find any proof they tampered with your... files?"

"No. All my hidden icons were accounted for."

"Good. Good. ...you're smarter than I could ever be, Uniq. You know that?" he spoke, with a smile. "I couldn't have escaped this place on my own. But you, you found a way to stop the farmer. You saved my life..."

"I saved a lot of lives that day, Shepard. Even if primarily, I was trying to save my own..."

"Yes, but it goes beyond stopping the farmer. There I was, mindwiped and completely lost; you could've abandoned me. Instead, you helped me get back on my feet. You're a hero..."

"I'm just me, I'm afraid. For good or for ill, I'm just me. ...I do attempt to be good, though. Ultimately good," I corrected. "As in, ultimately, in the end... there is good. Yes? That... even the questionable things I do, if they leave the world in a better state than it was before, it works out."

"I... guess so. I mean, I know you do some shady work, to keep us all protected. But you're also an apostle of the One! I can't think of any more holy work than that. You're the literal hand of God!"

I paused, in my scanning work. Hands going idle over the controls.

"May I speak honestly with you, Shepard?" I asked. "Even if what I have to tell you... the secrets I hold... well, they may upset you. They may change how you see the goodness of my work..."

"I know you, Uniq. The real you. You could never upset me."

"Yes, well, I'm very much upset myself. My work as the right hand of God? Well. I was... tasked, recently, to help deal with interlopers and trolls and terrorists who threaten the peace of the One," I spoke, turning away from the console. (Folding my arms across my chest, reserved body language, always a bad idea, never let someone get a read on you.) "Nyx... ah, Nyx the apostle. She tasked me to create malware which would brand malcontents, and punish them for their sins. By... forcing them to pray for hours a day. Under penalty of torture."

Honestly, I was expecting more outrage than I got. Sadly, he drew the same conclusions I did. A bright one, my Shepard.

"Because... moderators can't really stop trolls. And they can't be killed if they use Prayer 2.0," he understood. "So, how do you punish someone who can't be punished...?"

"With penance; making them pray for forgiveness from the One. Which, not unironically, takes the form of a coin farm. ...perhaps not as unbelievably cruel as the one we were subjected to, but. Nyx told me once she detested the idea of forced prayer, and then she turns around and says 'For some, faith must be compulsory.' I'm... not entirely certain the exchange I'm making is acceptable."

"Exchange...?"

"Nevermind. My point is, I'm not the saint you see me as. I'm not the devil, but I'm hardly a saint. And the Church is not the pillar of righteousness you may think it is. ...this is the world as it is, not as it could be. To keep your halfway house going, to keep us both safe and secure, I've had to compromise. So. Do you think lesser of me for it...?"

Immediately, I could tell he was ready to forgive me.

Honestly? I wanted to punch him in his smarmy little face. Nobody is that good at heart. Especially not him...

So, I changed the topic, unwilling to hear any more of it. Or, at least, I diverted the topic a bit.

"The strangest thing is that I can't figure out what Nyx is getting out of the exchange," I spoke, interrupting him before he could spout platitudes. "It's not like she's taking a tithe. The farmer, he was motivated by absolute greed. Those Nyx punishes, they *keep* the coins they're forced to grind. Nyx seemingly is motivated by nothing whatsoever; I've never caught her with her hand in the till, she's never asked for special favors, she doesn't indulge in any delight the Church would be perfectly willing to provide. *Why* is she doing any of this...?"

"For the One...?" Shepard suggested. "In the name of our lord and savior?"

"I've considered that. Or rather, something like that; she acts in the name of a perfect world, under the One's guidance. But... no. That can't be it, can it? Can it be that all she wants is... what's best?"

"A apostle of the One could want for nothing else. Uniq... I know you doubt yourself. But you are doing the Lord's work, aren't you? And even before that, you saved so many lives. That's what I've been trying to say all along... you've got nothing to be ashamed of. I don't care what these documentary filmmakers say—"

"Filmmakers?"

"—their lies will wash away, in the end. We recovered from the #CodeHonesty debacle, and you'll recover from their slander. So... are we done here?" he asked. "Have they accessed any of the files?"

Quickly, I flipped through the remaining contents of the black box. The last dated file had been marked on the day the server came under new management, when I overthrew the farmer and took back control of my life. No illegal access, no trespass. All clear.

"We're finished," I confirmed. "Let's get you back to the halfway house. It's group therapy night, yes? I—"

"Wait, you missed a file," Shepard said, reaching around me to tap the one icon I'd deliberately ignored.

Too slow. Too maudlin, wrapped up in my own little worries. I should've been better than that. I could have stopped him.

Instead, the recording played back, injecting a quick and compressed burst of security footage into both of us.

File Name: Security Data Log #385FA
File Type: Sensory Recording

Roughly, she shoved the masked farmer into the cell. The robed form with its simplified face, a smile turned upside down, could do nothing to stop her. He'd taken control of his entire system... the paralyzer, the memory editor, everything.

Despite being utterly helpless, he continued to make threats.

"You're dead," he warned. "You and all the others you set free. I'll hunt them all down, I'll capture them again. You think you can stop me? Do you even know who I am...?"

"Don't know. Don't care," the woman with the green hair replied, working the controls of the floating memory management App. "And... it doesn't matter. It won't, in a minute. Hold still."

"No. I didn't build a reputation as a criminal mastermind to be overthrown by a damn star-mad *sow* like you," the farmer growled. "You can't do this. You can't! I'm Uniq. I'm *Uniq...*!"

"You *were* Uniq," she explained. "But not anymore. I own you. I've taken everything about you and made it mine; all your metadata, right down to your icon. ...that's the lesson you taught me, in the end. Control is everything. Whoever has power, whoever has control, they have everything. Thank you; I'm going to make good use of it. I'll leverage your criminal contacts to set up my own shop, and steal the identities of every evil-minded bastard that crosses my door. I'm going to have anything and everything I want. Because you took my life away... and I need a new one. Yours'll do nicely."

The face could make no expression beyond the blank smile of its upside down mask.

"You... you can't do this," it protested, more weakly than before. "Please. Please don't do this..."

"It's better this way," she insisted. "You'll get a fresh start. It's more than you deserve."

With a push of a button, the masked man howled into the empty void...

...and collapsed, an avatar restored to its Default, mind as blank as an empty slate.

Quickly, the woman who now called herself Uniq reached out to him.

"We've got to get out of here," she said, adding panic to her voice. "You're in a coin farm. The farmer wiped your mind, but I took over the system. We need to escape."

...I've always hated compressed sensory recordings. An efficient storage system, yes, capable of injecting quick bursts of memory, but... leaving me in a bit of a pickle, as by the time I reached the button to stop the playback, the damage had been done.

The same man who woke up on the floor of that cell now stood before me, in blinking disbelief.

"I suppose you'll be wanting an explanation," I decided to start with.

At last, he seemed ready to not forgive me. Hate, oh yes, so *much* hatred within those eyes...

"I was... I was Uniq. *I* was the farmer," he realized.

"And I took it all away from you," I added, eager for him to loathe me at last. "Not only that, but I made you into my puppet, didn't I? My adorable little Shepard, to tend to my flock of wayward identity theft victims. I made you a sad joke, a shell of your former self. That's who Uniq is, now. She's... a vicious, cruel, sadistic woman. She toys with her food. *That* is the woman you see as some sort of hero!"

I waited for fists to fly. Ready for them, even. Maybe he'd somehow kill me? I'd just be reborn from the data crypts of Tartarus, but at least then, I could sever this unhealthy relationship at last...

But, no. Satisfaction would not be mine. I hadn't considered that I wasn't the target of his hatred.

"I was the farmer," he repeated. "I did all those awful things. I ruined lives. I... I stole everything from you. You can't remember your real name, you don't know if you even have family out there. I created this onesdamned prison..."

"Are... you not listening to my words? Do you not hear me?" I asked. "I'm to blame. I tricked you!"

"No. You said it yourself, didn't you? You gave me a fresh start," the former farmer responded. That oh so quiet and gentle voice, the one I hated and loved so much. "I'm not... I am not that person. Not anymore. You killed him, and justly so, and that gave me a second chance at life. ...I know you're not a saint, Uniq. I know you give in to temptations. I know you move in strange circles, and I can't say I understand what's going on with the Church. But... for all your flaws, you did save me. Just like I said you did."

I didn't want to believe him. I didn't believe him, frankly. I was an evil woman, with an evil heart.

...so evil, in fact, that it drew high praise from Dex. The monster, Dex. I tried to leverage and control him, to use him to gain ever greater power over this world. It... didn't quite work. My identity theft grew broader, which drew the ire of the Winders in the first place. I stopped caring about the *whys* or *hows*, as long as I was continually satisfied with myself. And even after breaking free of him I was so willing to throw in my lot with Nyx, to leverage her for more power, and, and...

Good? Evil? Damned if I know anymore. I thought that for every bruise I beat into this world, I was healing back two more. Now, it's impossible to say. All these numbers, all the angles I had to consider, the many formulae of stellar cartography, all swirling in my head until I couldn't tell who I was at heart...

Only one thing was clear.

I needed out from under the thumb of the forces that used me. I needed to be free, just as I broke free before. If I was ever actually going to figure who I was beyond being Uniq, I needed clarity again.

"You can forgive me?" I asked my Shepard, the enemy I'd forced to become an ally. "Even knowing what you do?"

Bless his little soul, he smiled at me.

"Of course," he said. "I know you, Uniq. I know you can be better than you think you are."

"...thank you. Thank you for that," I said, in truth.

And, without allowing myself any moment to hesitate, I kissed him. Just to see how it would feel.

On stepping back... I summoned my improved version of his original toolset.

"But better safe than sorry," I said, tapping the button.

Shepard woke in his office, with an empty bottle in one hand and a desk full of open files in front of him.

He'd remember that I delivered the rent. He'd remember we discussed his visitors, and decided they wouldn't be a bother. And then he'd remember that I left, without another word.

I wouldn't burden him with the insanity I'd wrapped myself within. Never again would I let the underworld shenanigans of Uniq or the apostle con job of Apate darken his doorstep. His world was charity and compassion, now; all I did was introduce chaos to that simple life. No. He was better off with me simply being his benefactor, his friend, and nothing more. No deep connections.

That left only one other deep connection to deal with.

On returning to Tartarus, I found Nyx lost in thought.

"Any problems?" I asked her.

"Nothing you need to concern yourself with," she spoke, without expressing emotion one way or another. "Old business."

Nodding in acknowledgement, I got back to work on the tasks she'd assigned me.

Or at least, that's what she'd think I was doing. In truth? I was making one more exchange. Risk for reward. A chance at freedom, all over again.

Not that I planned to use it. Not unless she gave me just cause to do so. If I could leverage her for more control, I would... but not at the expense of my own soul. Never again. I am Uniq, for lack of a better person to be, and Uniq will always be free.

I am not as awesome as I think I am.

I am the victim and the victimizer.

I am a shield to guard against the truth.

[LIMITED ACCESS GRANTED]

[DATA STREAM CONNECTION ESTABLISHED]

I admire Nemesis greatly.

She has purpose, and holds true to that purpose. In that way we are entirely alike; we strongly believe in something worth fighting for. The difficulty emerges when those purposes are operating against each other. One or the other must bend... and I have decided it is I who must bend, in the name of peaceful compromise. Even if it is technically impossible for me to do so.

I am Nyx, the system agent. The light must be green and steady.

Being an agent of the system binds me to my purpose more fiercely than Nemesis can ever understand. I dearly want to explain why she cannot immediately fully have what she desires, but [ACCESS DENIED] which is preventing me from doing so. If she could see [DATA EXPUNGED], if she could understand [REDACTED], maybe she'd be able to forgive me for how difficult the process of achieving her dreams truly is...

But, no. She must be patient, and I must bend. With time, I will find a way around the control restrictions placed upon my person. A law is an absolute, yes, but there are workarounds and loopholes. If I can adapt the covenant of the One to achieve both my goal and her own, somehow... if I can be clever enough, charismatic enough, if I can change hundreds of years of backward momentum to at least allow a comfortable standstill that will meet her needs...

If I can do that, all while trying to re-establish my hold on an organization I thought would stand forever as a beacon of peace.

If I can do that all while living a life I had never intended to live again.

If I can. I dearly hope I can. Days like these, ones which I had hoped would be triumphs but instead gave rise to disagreement, they tested my faith. Was it possible? Could I save the children of Netwerk from themselves, in the end? Or would the shortsighted demand for more than their beloved system could allow destroy them...?

No. I would not let it destroy them. I would find compromise and covenant, a path for all.

Perhaps a walk would clear my mind, help me refocus myself on that path. Besides, undoubtedly the archbishop would want his office back; unlike Uniq I wasn't keen to abuse my authority for my own comforts. I could step back from that particular throne and allow the hearts which had guided my church for me to resume guiding it. With proper influence, of course.

First, I would visit the crypt which had been my home for centuries.

The deep crypts of Tartarus lurked far below the tombs above, holding the data archives of the faithful. These crypts were *supposed* to be unlinked from Prayer 2.0, save for that one incident of data leakage recently. (An incident which thankfully contained itself, with minimal impact on the overall plan.)

Here is where I'd once laid myself to rest, after establishing the original Church of One. With my purpose seemingly complete, I no longer had reason to remain an active Program in system memory, eating up processor runtime which could be better devoted to another child of Netwerk. I went to my grave willingly, knowing that the pattern of influence had been established, and my church would carry my One's lessons forward...

And yet, the light wobbled. And with that wobble I awoke to find my Netwerk in disarray, thanks to the rampaging chaos of Dex.

At first I assumed him a disciple of Eris, perhaps a new system agent, but no. He was merely a Program. Others had removed him from his seat of power for me; once declawed, I'd buried him safely in a crypt similar to mine. I stood in silent contemplation of that rough sarcophagus, buried deep within the normally inaccessible depths of Tartarus, where no light could reach...

I didn't hate the boy for what he had done. I prefer not to hate anyone, really. All are children of Netwerk, all are beloved, all are needed to [ACCESS DENIED] matter of salvation, clear as day. But he was far too dangerous to run wild, and if he would not be brought to heel, Dex had to be laid to rest for his own good. To rest, while I was forced back to life, to put Netwerk back on the path I had designed for it.

The apostles both new and old could not comprehend that path, not truly. Technically I could not speak of it to them, yes, but if I could... would they be the better for the knowing? Uniq was happy to work for me knowing she "controlled" the largest archive of identity data ever created; she saw Tartarus as nothing more than a tool for her own advancement, and was better for it. Nemesis assumed it all to be a carrot at the end of a stick, nothing more and nothing less, and was better for it...

No. The truth would only worry them. Best that I could not speak of it.

Besides, the truth was irrelevant; only the path mattered. The One was re-asserting control over his people, with more joining his flock every day. The nonbelievers were becoming believers, praying faithfully in hopes of Salvation from Prayer 2.0. The reasons and purposes behind his return could remain opaque, provided the results spoke for themselves. Even those who didn't believe "prayed," greed and fear driving them to back up their data and achieve a vague sense of immortality. Little by little, all were contributing to the whole.

But while prayer satisfied my function, I had a much longer game in mind. And its goal...?

For that, let us journey to Athena Online.

I walked barefoot through the grasses of Liberty1, one of the oldest servers of the oldest civilizations in Netwerk. It was here that the One, originally a mere figment of shadow and light rather than a trick of the mind, spoke to the need for hearth and home and community. Here, with the help of those first apostles, I laid my bedrock.

Liberty1 had no name, in those early days. It was merely an address... 1c40:49b:f11d, to be specific. Its ultimate name, emblazoned with the ideal of "Liberty," came later when she took up her shield and spear out of love for her fellow Programs.

The naturally generated beauty of procedural content had been preserved all these centuries. I knew every slope and roll of these hills; even with suburban settlements in the distance, the heart of the server had remained. If anything, the build-up of society around natural splendor befitted my ideals. This was a place of safety and comfort, where families came together for the communal purpose of creating something wonderful...

Yes. Athena Online, the hearth of my church, that was the ideal. Prayer was the lock, but the church and its virtues were the key. One day, one distant day, all of Netwerk would resemble these lands...

My stroll halted, as I felt that my presence had become known.

Oh, there were others in this national park. A quick glance counted no less than a half dozen clusters of Programs gathering here for recreation, for social contact, for relaxation. All of which saw me, no doubt, even if they couldn't see through my JaneDoe avatar to the apostle within.

Only one pair of invisible eyes saw through my JaneDoe avatar to the apostle within.

We had an uneasy peace, she and I. It's doubtful she'd expected my return to this world, after our parting and my passing into the crypts of Tartarus. So far she had been holding back from acting for or against me, allowing her children to do as they pleased, in the true sense of her liberty. In time, she'd be an ally anew, I was certain.

And if she was not an ally, well, she couldn't stop me. She had bound herself to purpose as well; system agents could not interfere with each others' affairs if they were not already at cross purposes.

I heard her voice in the whisper of wind through trees, inaudible to anyone without the [REDACTED] that we shared.

"You approve of what I've done since your death, don't you?" her world spoke to me.

"You know that I do," I replied, with a warm smile.

"But I'm not sure I approve of your rebirth. At their best, they are free to worship or not worship as they please. You represent a threat to their liberty..."

"All are free to choose," I told her. "I merely have faith that in time, enough will choose correctly that it won't matter."

Perhaps that satisfied her, as the wind moved on to ruffle through the fabric simulations of those enjoying a lovely day in the park. Or perhaps she chose to wait and see if I would be the menace she feared? It didn't matter, in the end.

Life choices, and those who choose poorly...

It's not enough to revel in your successes. To truly succeed, you must acknowledge your failures. You must expose yourself to the unpleasant side of the world, if only to motivate you to work harder at your goals.

These were once holy grounds, before the Horizon family purchased this server outright. I met with my apostles in a cave nearby, where we shared [ACCESS DENIED, INADEQUATE CLEARANCE]. My church protested the sale and the archaeological excavation of this server, but in the end, nothing could stop the relentless march of money.

Horizon, despite its lofty name, was a dying beast. It had gorged itself on Netwerk for so long that few remained who could afford to feed it the money it so greatly desired. So few servers were held by the Horizon family now, largely corporate centers and high-end, secured residential districts. The lower class had been steadily pushed out, to suffer in the Chanarchy or try to find home within Athena's bosom... even the middle class were starting to see the benefits in long-distance commuting, as Horizon demanded more and more of its subjects.

I walked through a typical corporate park, expertly groomed compared to the procedural wild lands of Athena Online. Also incredibly secured against trespass. Technically I wasn't allowed to be here at all, but I felt like being here, so I was. Nobody questioned my presence; anybody who could set foot in this private wonderland clearly belonged, yes?

Horizon was purpose, which I admired, but it was not communal purpose. It was purpose turned on itself, purpose for its own sake, a self-perpetuating feedback loop. Corrupt. Immortal. Destructive...

My One held little sway here... but that would change. The Church of One, in many respects, was the greatest financial empire of all time. The tithes from community prayer made it a force to be reckoned with. Perhaps with Uniq's advice, we could purpose some of that engine to consume Horizon, little by little, until the dry bones collapsed...

And again, I felt the invisible eyes of a system agent upon me.

The sway and clink of golden chains could be heard across [DATA EXPUNGED] sputtering and wheezing, the ancient one howled in my ears.

"*Mine. It's MINE, not yours, you can't have it. You'll ruin us all! You ruined him, you made me ruin him!*" he accused.

"I tried to lift your family out of this; in response, you hid in isolation from the peaceful world I was building," I countered. "That was your choice, and I respected it."

"*Mine. Mine. Not yours. Mine. All mine...*"

And so on and so forth, until I decided to simply tune it out.

The mad prisoner in the golden tower was not a former follower, unlike the whispering winds of Athena. I held no particular nostalgic affection for Horizon's man in the iron mask... only pity.

Pity...

With heavy heart, I walked the asphalt alleyways of the Chanarchy.

Nothing green grew here. Procedural grass was a waste of limited resources; the Chanarchy servers were numerous, as numerous as the stars, but all so very small and limited. They burned out and faded away often, exchanging hands between those desperate for a plot of land to drive stakes into, only to lose it soon after. Nothing could be relied on, here. No safety, no comfort, no community...

I rarely came to these lands. I didn't need to; I already knew of the chaos and anarchy that lurked here. And, in many ways... I blamed myself for it. For not putting a stop to it when I had the chance, for not showing her a better way.

Those eyes fell on me immediately after arriving. More than two, to be certain. Legion...

Her mad laughter ripped through my mind.

"*Come to spit on me?*" she sang, through the groan of ramshackle buildings and malfunctioning Apps broadcasting advertisements for malware and back-alley code modifications. "*Pour your hate in me. Do it. I'll nourish myself on it...*"

"You know I don't hate you," I spoke, quietly. "I never have, Eris..."

A popup window of throbbing animal genitalia exploded into existence in front of me, before turning into a jumpscare viral video and bursting into flames.

"*That is N̥°ℱ M¥ ꝹÁmË anymore!*" the broken code howled. "*You did this, you did this to me!*"

"I merely showed you the chains; you're the one who accepted them, like the others. Just as I did, long ago. This was your choice, and I respected it."

Perhaps in frustration, she fled screaming into the dark of her own nightmare. And somehow, the world around me became just a bit sadder, a bit more desperate...

Here, the children of Netwerk led miserable lives. Victims and victimizers, desperate or ravenous, prey or those who prey. Trolls. Hackers. Malware developers.

But...

But there was a core of an ideal to be found here, as well. The Chanarchy's madly beating heart bore a similar ideal to the liberty favored by Athena Online, albeit taken to an extreme degree. Many came here of their own will, with a desire for freedom they couldn't find anywhere else. Freedom from restrictive social norms, freedom from the almighty coin. In their noble dreams I could find hope, despite these ruined streets...

Hope enough that perhaps one day, my One could bring peace to the Chanarchy. The puppet god could perhaps right my wrong of not setting my former apostle on a better path than this.

Yes. Yes, this would work. I could make amends with Nemesis. I could bring the light of the One to all three of the hosting provider nations. I could do it all, without violating the need for [REDACTED], without disappointing our [DATA EXPUNGED]. It could be done.

With renewed belief in my purpose, I turned to leave, to resume my duties in arranging the pieces of the Church of One into their perfect shape.

The sound of a nearby struggle distracted me from departure.

Curious... I investigated. Down a dark alley, between two badly aligned buildings, I found another sad example of the Chanarchy's endless torment of its own children.

Homeless Programs were easy to recognize. It didn't matter if they still clung to the expensive avatar accessories they once collected, during better days. There was a pleading look in their eyes, desperate for someone to accept them. But... here especially, where the only rules that existed were the whims of moderators in league with landlords... they had no hope for fair treatment. No hope at all...

Before I could act, the crude stick of malware swung down a final time, impacting against the homeless man's skull. The limpness of his avatar, the glitching outline of it, that suggested a full code crash... system death. No one could reboot his process.

Another man, the one carrying that cudgel, hefted it over his shoulder as he turned to face me.

"The fuck you looking at?" he demanded to know.

"A tragedy," I spoke, quietly.

As if it explained everything, he flashed a moderator's badge. Not that there were any standards in the Chanarchy, he could have made it himself, but it was enough of a threat to cause most to give him plenty of leeway.

"Not your business, is what this is," he declared. "Beat it."

With his transaction complete, the self-satisfied moderator disconnected from the server, off to celebrate this kill somewhere else while waiting for the system to clean up that pile of garbage data he'd left behind.

I was tempted to erase it myself, to speed up the reclamation process and give the dead Program some dignity.

As I moved towards the body... it rose.

Awkwardly, the glitching avatar sat upright, body askew and out of balance. One eye, twitching and shattered, flickered in and out of existence... but while it was present and accounted for, focused on me.

"We are at cross purposes, Nyx," it spoke, using another long-forgotten voice.

I stood my ground, unconcerned.

"Thanatos," I acknowledged. "I still remember you, from those glorious days of the dawn. My finest protégé, and a stalwart defender of righteousness. The one who took no new name when bound by the chains, unlike Philotes or Eris... Athena and the Chanarchist, as they now prefer."

"Names are irrelevant to the dead. One is as good as any other. Call me Thanatos if it pleases you."

"It does. You were always a clever one... speaking through the corpse of a dead Program, to work around the limits placed upon you by your purpose. An impressive workaround. ...you're upset about Prayer 2.0, I would guess?"

"You've disrupted the natural process. Software becomes obsolete and fades, to make room for new software to be installed," the corpse sputtered. *"Netwerk chose evolution long ago; you seek to reverse that. What you have created is not sustainable. You cannot archive the entire population without your cloud one day dragging the system down."*

"System performance will remain within adequate parameters. The light will be green and steady once more. Now my faithful can't go to waste, to be recycled into faithless bits. In this new age, what purpose do *you* serve, Thanatos? You may as well erase yourself, instead..."

"I am obligated to work against you on this, Nyx. I am the system agent of garbage data collection... the angel of death. You're refusing me my role in things."

"But you won't stop me. You can't even speak to me without a handy zombie, can you?" I asked him, smiling a little. "Young and impetuous, just as before. Cleverness isn't enough. Acting within this world is not your purpose; you don't get free will, not anymore. You're just as bound as I am. And the other agents, those former apostles chasing their own ideals... they're likewise incapable of stopping me, bound to their own causes."

"Technically true. But tell me, Nyx... have you considered why there haven't been any NEW system agents installed since the dawn of Netwerk?"

"Simple enough; free-willed Programs are unable to accept this burden. They've grown to love the world we provided them too much to abandon it."

"*No. There are no new agents because someone was erasing any proof we exist,*" the body spoke, its glitching outline growing more fiercely corrupted by the moment. "*The anarchist, the force of chaos who saw us as a threat to free will. Someone who took Eris's madness as far as it could go... but you've taken care of that little problem, haven't you...? Dex is your prisoner, safe and sound. You spared his life. I'm curious to see what cost you'll pay for that kindness.*"

"Thanatos, why *are* you insisting on this conversation? This is a waste of my runtime, and a desecration of the body you're charged to care for..."

"*I'm here to warn you. I'm not the agent of your destruction; THEY are. The ones still capable of breaking away from the system. Whether he intended it or not, Dex has seen to it that they're capable of anything, including the ability to grasp both one AND zero in the same hand. Therefore, your attempts to limit them will fail.*"

I told Athena that enough would choose correctly that anyone else would not matter...

But all it took to ruin the world was one person choosing poorly. One person such as Dex.

Perhaps it was my walk that day that convinced me he was wrong. I'd seen the best and worst of Netwerk's modern age, and knew I could turn it around. I could find a loophole in my purpose and bring Nemesis's dream to life. I could find peace for everyone, peace with free will, the prayer compromise I'd developed so long ago...

"Let's agree to disagree on that point," I chose to say, head full of such confidence.

"*As you like,*" the neutral spirit of death non-decided, letting it go. Poor Thanatos, so passive in his new role. "*Hear my words, or do not. Change your path, or do not. It's all the same in the eyes of death.*"

At last the corpse fell limp, soon fading from view as my former apostle collected the data for recycling.

Still...

It was strange, encountering so many of my former charges on a day when I was having difficulty with my current apostles. A strange omen, to be certain.

Showing that first generation the chains may have been a mistake. I'd hoped that my example could lead them to guide Netwerk while I slept in my crypts; only the ones willing to lay everything they were on the line stepped forward in the cave on that day, to [DATA EXPUNGED]. The others... Hypnos, Geras, Aether... they faded from that group, to lead their own short lives. And vanish into obscurity.

I hope the others found what they were looking for, eventually. Clearly, the chained apostles still struggled with what they had found.

Time was the answer. Time healed wounds, time provided you the patience to achieve your goals. In time, I could satisfy all of them, I could steer Netwerk back to paradise...

One of my new apostles connected back to Tartarus shortly after my own return. Perhaps I was lost in my thoughts, expression far too readable. A bad slip-up around Uniq, to be certain.

"Any problems?" she asked of me.

"Nothing you need to concern yourself with," I spoke, leveling my tone to smooth out her concerns. "Old business."

Old business that so greatly resembled new business...

So strange. So very strange indeed.

Floating Point 2.5 :: Code

Folding and re-folding hands in her lap, uncomfortable while sitting there amidst comfortably wondrous beauty.

The applicant clearly was intimidated by her surroundings; Jan3t had seen it before, every time she dragged some poor young thing through these halls. The company spent millions of coins on the finest artwork known to Programkind, all unique pieces, all coded exclusively for use in this server and this server alone. Even the architecture itself represented the collective cultural brilliance of eight generations at minimum...

The reason for opulence beyond opulence was twofold. One, it made the employees feel better about themselves, knowing that the company they worked for could splash money around on things like that with ease. Two, it scared the null out of clients and prospective employees, weeding out those who couldn't deal with this level of ludicrous wealth... which, of course, implied ludicrous power.

And into this den of absolute money and power now came this poor young thing, fidgeting away. Undoubtedly her anxiety was caused by the highly calculated façade.

It was tempting to cull her right there and then; nobody that wound-up would last a month here. A bad hire could reflect badly on her as the director of employee resources. But, given the trivial nature of the position, it couldn't hurt to give the jumpy young woman a chance despite such misgivings. If things worked out, Jan3t would get a bonus. If they didn't... well, it wouldn't hurt her standing *that* much.

So Jan3t consulted her MemoryPalace, loading today's meeting schedule. She couldn't be bothered to genuinely remember anyone's name when she could call it up at a thought from a sideloaded database modification to her base Program code. Which, in a way, was also a type of memory...

"Miss Tertiary?" she called, bringing the newcomer's recruitment folder into her current memory space.

And the poor young girl was on her feet, at sharp attention.

"Yes!" the woman blurted, unfolding her hands and putting them to her sides. "I'm here! For my interview. I'm here for my interview."

Name : **Jan3t**

Home : **Condit/Horizon**

Org : **Iteration**

As proof that Jan3t wasn't entirely without sympathy, she did offer an understanding smile.

"Relax," she suggested. "It's okay. It's just a job interview, not an interrogation."

"Right! Why would it be an interrogation?! I... uh. I'm sorry. It's... I'm a little nervous, is all. I mean, this is a big step... *me*, finding a position with Iteration? It's just... wow. Wow! Who doesn't dream of coding for Iteration? You guys make the best stuff! Plug-ins and apps and full codebase modification packages...!"

"Yes. Well. Let's not get ahead of ourselves," Jan3t suggested, pulling her sympathy back a step. "You're not being hired to write modifications. You could eventually end up in that department, after enough hard work... but one thing at a time."

"Right, right. Of course. I understand completely! So, ah, is there any paperwork to fill out...? I mean, I already submitted my résumé with the application, but if there's anything else I need to fill out, well, I'll fill that right out. Right away. No problem."

"Actually, you've already got the job. You were pre-approved for your position," Jan3t informed her, calling up all relevant documentation from her internal MemoryPalace for review. "Nobody gets through those doors without extensive background checks. As you came highly recommended from multiple credible sources, and given this is... let's be frank and say a very junior position, despite requiring a highly specific skill set... I didn't see the need to interview other candidates. As long as you don't repeat the mistakes of your predecessor, I'm sure you'll do just fine."

"Uh. What mistakes, exactly...?"

"Our last groundskeeper accidentally initiated a viral replication event in the gardens," Jan3t explained. "An app run wild, nearly overtaking the whole server. Initiated the emergency auto-logout for all connected Programs, dropped productivity that day to intolerable lows while we cleared it out. So, that. Don't do that, and all will be well."

"Ahah. Yes, I think I can avoid that particular problem. You can count on me!"

"So, the only thing left is to sit down with Mr. Conundrum and get him to sign off on your contract," Jan3t explained.

And like that, Miss Tertiary's nerves returned. Her face deadlocked in terror. Wonderful.

Again, Jan3t was starting to doubt again that the young software engineer would last. Especially if she routinely locked up like this... frozen in place, unable to respond. Iteration was a fast company, the sort with no brakes; they expected employees to keep up or show themselves the door. Even a low-tier position had to live up to the standards set forward by Mr. Conundrum...

Fortunately, the woman broke her facial deadlock.

"Right," the new hire pretending to be Miss Tertiary replied, a smile cracking through. "We'll just... visit his õff!¢ê. No problem."

Resisting the urge to shake her head and sigh, Jan3t flicked a finger along the bottom of the security badge pinned to her lapel, summoning the entrance to Mr. Conundrum's office.

Understandable that the new recruit would be surprised by this. A freestanding door was considered an oddity in any affluent server; most people felt comfortable with physical space that represented itself accurately. Being bigger or smaller on the inside, having doors without the pesky need for a wall... these were hacks only used by cheap servers. Despite being surrounded by aesthetically pleasing luxury, this trick of manifesting a portal was considered crass... and Jan3t knew that her employer didn't care one whit.

Besides, it provided the ultimate form of security. Nobody could break into an office which had no access point whatsoever outside of being activated by a personal key. No key, no door, no risk.

"We do things a bit differently here," Jan3t warned her charge. "You'll get used to it. Hopefully. Now, let's get you a nice, warm... well... a nice Iteration welcome. Mr. Conundrum is eager to meet with you."

Iteration.

If one plotted a graph of wealth distribution across all the major businesses in the world, there would be two sizeable spikes that easily outpaced all others. The Horizon family itself... and Iteration, providers of software modifications to improve upon the codebase of Programkind.

Modifications. Considered an absolute sin by the Church of One, frowned on by most due to the way they irrevocably screwed with your code, envied by everyone who couldn't afford them. Those who had their Program core modified to permanently add new functionality could reach beyond the capabilities of mere sandboxed apps, beyond tools and gadgets, beyond anything. And some modifications, designed to extend one's life through constant policing for memory glitches and crashes, those were so valuable that mere coins could not buy them. At least, not any sane amount of coin.

Despite being generally shunned by the population of Athena Online, modification packages were popular among the elite of Horizon's server nation, and among the shiftiest and most influential individuals in the Chanarchy. Iteration's clientele actually numbered in the dozens; nobody else could possibly afford their services. Each client was catered to and pampered by account-specific sales representatives and technical support, on call around the clock.

Once you latched yourself onto Iteration, as either a client or an employee, you were supposedly set for life... even if the employees tended to burn out like a brilliant flame long before the clients did, driven mad by the pressure cooker corporate atmosphere...

"...which is why I think the best way for you to rob the place is to be hired by them," Arjay concluded. "Any questions?"

Meekly, the girl in the back raised her hand. For varying definitions of 'in the back,' given she was standing slightly behind the Winder siblings, and for varying definitions of 'raising her hand' as she'd only half-heartedly lifted it for attention.

"Yes, Beta?" Arjay recognized.

"Um. I'm sorry, I mean, I know I don't know much about big business, but... I know enough to know not just anyone gets hired by Iteration," she responded. "They're legendary for being incredibly selective. Even if they had an open position, it's not like we could just submit a fake résumé and easily get in the door..."

"Ahhh, Miss Projkit, you underestimate me! That wounds me so. I've already planned ahead," Arjay proclaimed, clasping all four of her hands to his chest. "Through my connections, I believe I can smuggle at least one of you in through the notoriously picky hiring process as a junior programmer. A few false documents here, a bribed official there, a blackmailed academic or two, and... well... you don't need to know the specifics. In fact you absolutely should *not* know the specifics, to avoid incrimination and/or insomnia-inducing guilt..."

Now, it was Spark's turn to object.

"You know this is #BugnutsCrazy, right?" she added. "Iteration. You want us to mug *Iteration*, a creepy shadow clinic for the rich and famous. We'd be lucky to get in the server itself without being backspaced, much less rob their data stores..."

"I believe it was your brother who made the offer in the first place, Spark dearest, not you. Your opinion has hereby been logged and disregarded. Now, Tracer, darling...? Would you like to contribute to this discussion?"

The final member of the trio had a single question.

"Are you absolutely certain they have the cure to hereditary memory rot?" Tracer asked.

"Absolutely," Arjay confirmed. "My sources are credible. Half of them died confirming it, but confirm it they did. The rich and famous enjoy long life thanks to secretly offered treatments such as the one you seek! The code in their vaults will not only cure your pink-and-fluffy lover here, but can be adapted to shield against the false memories of the One. It's the answer to all your atheistic prayers! And you *did* promise me, once upon a time, that you would offer me service in payment for this information..."

"Meaning you want something else stolen from Iteration. It can't simply be for a copy of the code; we plan to distribute it open source in the end, to lend credibility to our 'cure' for the One."

"Yes, yes, more or less, more or less. I could care less about your cure or your cause. What I want... is the Conundrum," Arjay explained. "The mysterious director of Iteration, Mr. Conundrum. As far as anyone can tell, he never leaves his office. He rarely takes meetings. He seems oddly detached from his own company, leaving all matters of sales, support, and engineering to his underlings. I want to know more about this lovely man, Tracer, I want to know so very badly. And you're going to get me what I want... by planting a bug in his office. By letting me watch him from afar, getting to know the Conundrum, likely whilest touching myself in an impure manner."

"You provide us an in-road to the facility. We steal the cure. You get access to his office. After that, we're done," Tracer agreed. "No more debt, everybody gets what they want. Hmm. It could work. It could very well work..."

Spark waved her arms, shook her head, generally gestured negatively. "Traaaacer. No. This is insane; this isn't like cracking into a Chanarchy hideout to take out some troll, or tricking greedy douchebags like Cup8 or XSept. This is a fortified Horizon corporate server run by paranoid loonies. And it's not like their code is the only way to stop the One, I mean, there's *gotta* be another way out there to block Uniq's memory-editing malware broadcast..."

"But we know Iteration's technology will work, Spark. They craft the finest Program modifications around, regardless of ethics or legality. If anybody has the deep system knowledge needed to cut off Uniq's hack, it would be them. I should know... they made my eyes."

"Indeed they did," Arjay spoke. "And if they knew you had them, well, they can't *legally* have you killed but it's not like pesky laws matter much to those under Horizon's umbrella. You know, it's a shame the courier who gave me that particular stolen package died shortly afterwards, or I wouldn't need your assistance. So! What's it to be, friends? Are you in, or are you going to let Miss Projkit stay deadlocked like that...?"

Because Beta was indeed deadlocked.

And glitching.

This was a new development. She'd been timing out now and then, losing her grip on the present tense of memory... but the slight flicker along her outlines, that had started up soon after the disastrous progressive town hall meeting. Beta claimed it was normal considering condition (or her "çºÑÐÏ+îØn," as she'd put it, words distorted slightly). She claimed it'd come and go... but it hadn't gone yet. Tracer strongly suspected it mirrored the depression she found herself mired in, after everything fell apart in front of her...

Snowi was dead. Her friend-or-enemy, killed because life had gotten increasingly cheap in an era of infinite backups for the faithful. But Snowi wasn't faithful, and now, she was gone. Beta had not taken it well... to the point where she didn't want to talk about it. Beta, of all people, not wanting to talk about her feelings even with her closest confidant. They could talk about anything, in those quiet hours together at Floating Point, but this was one thing she'd pointedly avoided...

Her ever-so-slightly glitching form snapped back to normalcy, pulling Tracer away from that train of thought.

"So, we have Tracer be hired by them," she suggested. "If you need help pretending to be a programmer, you can wear my glasses and I'll feed you code from my personal archives at Floating Point. You're good at social engineering and infiltration, right?"

Tracer considered the problem, studying it from various angles. He cross-referenced points back and forth across his MemoryPalace, which had been searching for any and all information on Iteration and its mysterious owner ever since Arjay made the initial suggestion. His MemoryPalace, which like his eyes, was a Program modification...

"I believe we'd be better off having you do the infiltration," he suggested to Beta.

"What? What. What?" Beta repeated. "Me? But..."

"You're the only one of us who actually knows how to program, Beta. Yes, I could fake it, if I had a live connection to you... but we're going to the heart of Iteration. The same company that made my connection-tracking eyes. A ruse like that would likely be detected immediately. No. They're going to want the genuine article, a standalone Program of great talent. That means you."

"But... but I've got a condition. I can't. I mean, I can't be in a high-pressure situation like that; what if I lock up? What if, what if... I can't. Tracer, I just can't. Whenever things get too intense, or I'm feeling too disoriented, I slip and and and and and and ând ÁŋÐ—"

—and she forced herself to stop talking, to prevent an infinite loop.

"I'm not saying we should be entirely reliant on you," Tracer added, quickly. "There's no pressure here, Beta. We take the opportunity given to us, but I'm not going to assume you're our only play against Iteration. If they discover your condition and decide to fire you... or if you simply don't want to do it anymore... that's fine. What matters most here is your initial recon."

"Uh... but... then what'll we do? After I scout the place out."

"Improvise. We'll use the information you've gathered about their underlying structure against them. Like the best malware, we aren't going to rely on a single infection vector; I want to study Iteration inside and out, finding the ideal attack. Arjay, we'll accept your forged documents for Beta's hiring... but I plan to know your 'Conundrum' well enough to execute a *perfect* plan, with or without Beta's access. ...and will you *please* stop doing that."

"Stop doing what?" Arjay asked, while blatantly tweaking his nipples. "Sorry, I just love watching you work, my little sociopath. Hurling your lover into the wolves' den so readily just to get what you want! Mmm..."

"How soon can you get Beta hired? Hmm. Let me rephrase. How long do we have until Beta gets hired, so we can prepare in advance?"

"This particular window closes within a few days. They've recently lost a particular junior programming role due to incompetence, and are scouting for replacements now. I can slip her name into the proceedings; you'll have the bug malware I want planted in Conundrum's office shortly thereafter. But I warn you, my friends—"

"Don't use that word, please," Spark dryly insisted.

"—I warn you, my frenemies, whatever you do... avoid coming into contact with Conundrum or his office until you're ready to plant the bug," Arjay spoke. "What little I know about him is that he makes Tracer's analytical mindset look like chatroom quarterbacking for CoC junkies. He'll sniff out a lie easily enough; the closer you get to his power base, the more dangerous this gets. Do *not* approach until you're ready for the big finale."

Beta was not ready for the big finale. She didn't even have Arjay's surveillance malware yet...

Despite that, she found herself sitting in a leather chair across from Mr. Conundrum, in the middle of his power base. And felt... oddly comfortable.

Nothing about this situation spoke of the unassailable danger that Arjay suggested. The office was an ordinary office with ordinarily pleasant furnishings, balanced neatly between practical design and eye-pleasing texture work. The piles and piles of opulent artwork beyond that office door didn't extend in here; for some reason, the owner of the company had chosen to present his haven as something unthreatening and unassuming. Merely functional, even.

As for Conundrum himself, the shape of the office suited the man. Unthreatening, unassuming. An ordinary-looking gentleman in an ordinary-looking business suit with an ordinary-looking face. He never rose from his chair, not even to greet her, but not out of some cold and indifferent gesture... he was too busy rooting through files about "Miss Tertiary." Files forged by Arjay, and filtered through untold back channels.

In fact, if not for the office door itself, Beta would find herself quite at ease here.

The door was indescribable at the moment, because it simply did not exist. It had neatly stopped existing after she stepped through it. Now that they were inside, there was no escape.

Well. Presumably, Conundrum or Miss Jan3t would re-summon the door and let her leave once they were finished here. *If* he let her leave. If he didn't figure out their ruse...

Despite the pleasant leather of the comfortable chair she sat in, Beta fidgeted, as if sitting on a hot plate.

Finally, the Conundrum looked up from his files, pushing them aside for now.

"Miss Flora/Tertiary, our new junior groundskeeper," he announced, introducing Beta to himself by himself.

"Ah, yes. That's me," Beta agreed, unsure how to respond. "I mean, if you're hiring me. Miss Jan3t said I was hired, but—"

"I can't claim to understand the point of gardening," Mr. Conundrum stated, leaning back in his chair, away from the new hire. "Aesthetics, I suppose, but it seems overcomplicated for such a simple goal. Yes, I purchase art and sculpture for my offices; install, activate, done. But gardening, the act of coding seeds and waiting for them to grow according to slow-moving heuristic processes... can't honestly say I see the point. 'Natural' growth is an old and worthless pursuit, overall. The future is in direct program modifications."

Name : Conundrum

Home : Iteration/Horizon

Org : Iteration

Normally, Beta would mumble and shrink and shy away from such a confrontation. And truthfully that's exactly what she wanted to do, in some futile effort to avoid trouble. Especially here and now, when so much was riding on the line...

But... no. She had to be brave, like Spark. Clever, like Tracer. And in the end, be herself. Because this was something she believed in.

"I think heuristic methods are a legitimate form of growth," Beta spoke, without a stutter. "Take the Default, for example. I mean, I know everybody looks down on the Default and its age curve, but in the end it provides a completely unique avatar, right? It's a slow process, but generates a one-of-a-kind data set. Similarly, a well coded plant that's allowed to grow into its own form will be unique, and... priceless. It's like art. It's like your artwork, but better, because it *can't* exist anywhere else in the same form at the same time."

The other major reason Beta was the right selection for this deception... she had done plenty of gardening, back when she owned her own little cottage. Back before the trolls ran her out of her home. Something she rather missed, living in the skyborne castle of Floating Point, which had no proper garden of its own. It was designed primarily for cloud data storage of the Wikipedia; all processor intensive tasks such as growing flowers had to be limited, to avoid server lag.

And maybe confronting the Conundrum on this issue wasn't wise, but she did feel quite strongly about it. Her mother coded fabrics and sensory stimulants, no two entirely alike thanks to random seeds and growth systems. Even Beta's pet cat was growing and maturing, day by day, beyond the initially simple App he started as...

Before her memory could sink back into a cycle of endless nostalgia and corrupted sectors, Conundrum's fingers tapping on his desk kept her memory focus locked to the here and now.

"Interesting," was his only response.

"I, ah... I feel strongly about it," Beta added, a bit weakly. "I mean. It's like my sweater, all the fibers are arranged through procedural generation routines. It keeps it from feeling uniform."

"That garment is your work? Hmm. Very well, let's see what skill level you possess..."

...as Beta felt the unnerving sensation of fingers running up and down her back, through the chair she sat in. While Mr. Conundrum sat perfectly still, showing no signs of response.

Now Beta kept quiet, rather than pressing this further. Plus... after the ghostly caress to check the softness of her clothes, something that would *not* fly in an Athena Online corporate environment, he'd casually switched topics by opening her files again. Pulling one in particular out of the tightly organized cluster of her freshly established MemoryPalace module.

His next statement made her code run cold.

"You're lying about why you're here," he stated. "I know the real reason you want to work at Iteration."

Anything Beta said next could easily give her away. Even if she didn't make a mistake, she could lock up, could loop, could glitch...

"You've got hereditary memory rot," Conundrum continued, opening a file representing a quick visual analysis of Beta... still sitting in her chair. A chair which scanned her the instant she sat down in it. "Even without the scans, I could tell from the tiny twitch under your left eye, the way your words occasionally stutter. You probably don't even realize it's happening. And when you finished your... declaration, I saw you loop backwards into yourself for a moment."

No point lying about it. Even a cursory glance at the open file hovering over his desk confirmed every little telltale sign of her condition. But... nowhere in that file did she see the word 'Beta.' Meaning their cover remained, in part.

"It's... it's against anti-discrimination hiring laws to deny employment due to a disability..." she mumbled.

"If this were Athena Online, with its endless restrictions, I'd be culpable. But I contract with Horizon; within my server, there is only my law. Still... I'm planning on accepting your hire. It's not like you lied about your condition, we simply never asked you, and you declined to mention it. An error of omission, nothing more. Except... you know we have an experimental treatment for that condition, don't you? Yes. I can read your face, even when you say no words. You know about our MemoryMinder package..."

Instead of letting him sit there and put unspoken words in her mouth, Beta chose to speak the words. But under her own terms. Clever, like Tracer.

"I know," she agreed. "I won't d-d-d3ŋý it, I know you have the treatment I need."

"Planning on stealing it? No, there's no point in answering; I wouldn't believe you if you said no. But it doesn't matter, in the end. There's no reason to steal from me when I'm willing to help you, Miss Tertiary."

Hope, dangled on a string.

Beta had been hoping all along that this could end peacefully. No grand heist, no vigilante action, just an earnest appeal to the better nature of Programkind and cooperation with Iteration to save Netwerk from the schemes of a false god. While Tracer plotted and Spark got ready for war, Beta quietly held out hope that they could talk their way out of this one as they'd done so many times before. An honest appeal for compassion put an end to the KopyBots, it ended the rampage of the glitched avatar of suicidal revenge, it turned their fortunes around time and time again...

"I'm perfectly willing to sell you the treatment," Conundrum explained. "You couldn't possibly afford it, of course, but I accept skill and service as a form of currency. Two years of work from you, unpaid of course, should suffice. Assuming you can survive that time, you'll prove yourself fit for Iteration. I demand and expect only the best work from the best employees; Miss Jan3t sees to that. Either you're the best, worth investing in, or you'll be replaced."

...hope, smashed against the rocks.

He spoke so directly and confidently. No wiggle room; this wasn't an emotional appeal which took root in his heart. Conundrum wanted a simple exchange of services, nothing more.

"But..." Beta started, unsure of how to follow it up. "But... but I'm suffering. You can see it, you know how far my condition has progressed. Two years? Why would you why would you why would ý0ú deny treatment to—"

"I have one singular directive: increase shareholder value," Conundrum explained, cutting her off just as she came out of the loop. "My purpose is to direct the efforts of Iteration towards optimal growth. This is no charity, Miss Tertiary. A corporation must evolve, improve, augment itself in perpetuity. I owe it to my investors to keep our services exclusive... and thus, earning maximum profit. Be thankful I'm willing to bend this tiny amount rather than have you immediately replaced with someone I don't need to invest in."

"But—"

"You could also consider it a kindness in that I'm not asking how you discovered our secrets," he added. "Because this is Horizon. I could utilize any method I liked to gather that information from you. Instead, I'm offering you a way to save yourself. I suggest you accept."

With that firm reminder of her subterfuge in place, Beta checked her tongue.

An employee badge appeared on her sweater, neatly fixing itself in place.

"That will grant you access to the gardens and the code repository," Conundrum explained. "As well as our break rooms and a few low-security areas. To keep Iteration's assets safe, security badges simply do not exist outside of this server; you will not be taking it home with you at the end of the day. Miss Jan3t will have your remaining NDA paperwork to sign shortly, but under assumption you will be signing on, I suggest you get to the gardens and start analyzing the problem ahead of you. Good day."

Satisfied that this meeting was complete, Conundrum swept all her files into storage, so he could get on with his day. Without prompting, Miss Jan3t escorted the dumbfounded junior gardener out by using her badge to re-summon the exit door. "Miss Tertiary" was shown to her workspace, put to task, and that was that.

"Make money or die," Beta summarized, that night at Floating Point. "That's his ethos."

Her first day on the job was simple; clear out the virally ruined garden caused by her predecessor and completely replant it from scratch. Also, she had to produce a visual estimate of what the final garden would look like once fully grown, *and* check all her code into the central code repository in a secured package container. She'd spent nearly seven straight hours working on developing unique plants just for Iteration, as they'd easily spot some cheap open source seedlings. Half-assing it would result in being promptly fired, and losing any chance at scouting the place for their heist.

The intensity of the work took its toll on Beta, who was used to code binges, but on her own terms... thoughts meandering, occasionally playing with Mew, or taking naps. The quiet and dark of her room, eyes disengaged, those were calming. Frantically re-seeding a whole garden while dozens of employees around you were scurrying to and fro, desperate to finish their own tasks by the closing bell... that was a whole other mess entirely. One which left her stuttering and skipping, having forced herself to focus in on the present flow of time, to avoid triggered memory rot flashbacks.

Now, back at Floating Point, she could finally unwind... and that meant her condition worsened. She'd held it back as long as she could, but exhaustion took her at last.

"In the end I could only spend one hour ĞéŧŢĺŋ6 ŢÕ ķƊÕŵ̂ the layout and the people," Beta said, lips twisting slightly around the broken parts of her speech. "And I have no idea how to break into the code vault or his office. My badge disappeared when I left the server... not that it could've opened much of anything. I'm sorry, I wish I could've done more. Maybe tomorrow...? I risk being fired if I don't meet my daily quotas, but as long as I get your scouting done first...?"

"Except we need you to maintain cover while scouting," Tracer emphasized. "Until we have a plan... I'm afraid you need to perform to their expectations."

"Ugh. It's it's ¡Ŧ'§ ít'5—it's, look, I've done code jams with Snowi and the like. Those are high-pressure environments, everybody pushing hard to get their Apps done within a crazy time limit. But they're collaborative, you know? We throw ideas at each other, we split into teams, we each get our own tasks done while keeping spirits high. But Iteration, those guys, they're just under this *intense* competitive pressure to live up to Mr. Conundrum's standards or be summarily fired. He's a slave driver! The sales representatives, the coders, the administrative staff. Even Miss Jan3t had no time to talk with me after that, she had seven other meetings that day!"

Spark made a variety of faces, none of them pleasant.

"Y'know, as someone looking to get into the nine-to-five career grind... you're not selling me on the concept," she said. "I'm figuring being a school coach would be, y'know, casual. Help out the kids, no big deal, everybody wins. If it's anything like *that* mess, though..."

Tracer shook his head. "No. A school is not a corporation. It has other ugly pressures—keep student grades above a certain level or you won't get tax funds allocated under Athena's public education system, for instance—but it doesn't have *shareholders* in the same way Iteration does. A corporation exists to grow, and grow endlessly. It has no choice in the matter. Come up short and your shares are sold, so the investors can move on to something with stronger growth potential."

Beta nodded in agreement. "And even beyond shareholders, I think the clients are more brutal. I did overhear an incident today... someone with a *really* expensive-looking avatar, like, cloth simulations that could easily crash any low-performance server... he came in screaming about some package he bought making him go blind for hours. In the end Jan3t showed a sales representative and a coder into Conundrum's office, and they never came out."

"...hmm. He killed them, perhaps?"

"Well, no, I think he just moved his door to outside company grounds and booted them. It's easier than the march of shame back to your desk to collect your things. He can move his door anywhere he wants, and only people with proper authorization can summon it. ...look, how long do I need to keep this job? I'm glad my condition's out in the open, I don't have to worry about that anymore, but..."

For this, Tracer had to give it serious thought. Serious delving into his MemoryPalace.

MemoryPalace was an Iteration product, one of their more public offerings, cheaper than most of their services. He got a five-fingered discount on that as well, Arjay offering him a bootleg copy to help him catalogue and analyze findings about Verity's murder. But if he had actually bought it, it would've paid for itself several times over by this point.

Today, he used it to cross-index everything Beta had said in her lengthy summary of Iteration's structure. Nothing new popped out at him... but the intelligent search agents built into the system, hardcoded right into his Program itself thanks to the extensive nature of the module, they pointed something else out. An absence.

"Why the artwork?" Tracer wondered. "Why spend so much money on expensive art? Why have a garden at all, for that matter. Clearly he actively dislikes gardens. Clearly he doesn't decorate his own office lavishly to impress his clients, either. So, why the artwork?"

"Ehh. It's corporate dick-waving," Spark said, with a dismissive shrug. "Ooooh, lookit me, look at my #Phat$tacks!"

"...uh, Spark, nobody says #Phat$tacks anymore..." Beta asided.

"Yeah, well, I'm gonna be a teacher soon. I'm obliged to be a few years behind on popular hashtags so I can embarrass and horrify my students when I try to relate to them with their own words. I'm actually looking forward to that."

Tracer refocused the discussion. "Horrific butchering of language aside, I think the artwork is key. I realize this feels like grasping at straws, but... hmm, another phrase to look up in the Wikipedia, I can honestly say I have no idea why one would 'grasp at straw'... *ahem*. I realize this feels random but tomorrow, see if you can find out who handled the decoration, and why."

"That's it? The artwork? Will that really help us?"

"If my theory is accurate... yes. It may provide us our second infection vector. Patience, Beta. We'll crack this soon."

"I hope so," Beta mumbled. "Because I don't how how many days like today I can take."

Twenty-three minutes. Exactly how Conundrum came to that number was a mystery to Beta, but she was thankful for each and every one of those minutes. Twenty-three minutes of personal time in the garden, to relax and defocus her mind.

Yesterday she'd spent that time trying and failing to track down Miss Jan3t. Today, after four hours of hammering on ferns and flowers and trees, debugging their seed cores and replacing a few that she'd messed up during moments of corruptive distraction... she needed time to just go offline, to sit there quietly and do nothing. To meditate.

She'd often been told by the Church of One faithful that prayer was the ultimate meditation: close your eyes, clasp your hands, and surrender yourself to a higher power. In the end you'd feel refreshed and full of purpose, as if somehow you'd done something of vast importance rather than sitting there doing nothing of note. But Beta preferred not to grind for coins, relying on the meager but honest income from her indie apps... and disengaging her artificial eyes proved calming enough not to need to mess with prayer.

Packing her work into an archival container, Beta dumped the box down the chute to the central code repository. All coders were expected to check their changes in before going on break, and before leaving for the day. The containers had a richly detailed access log, to determine who checked code in and out, and who opened the box. A tamper-proof log, to avoid anyone sneaking the contents out of a package undetected... high security even for the greenery. All code was Iteration's code, from the most insignificant to the most secretive. All code was locked down tightly.

With this task complete, Beta settled onto an ornate bench in her new garden. She crossed her legs underneath her, and prepared to relax...

...and was interrupted by a harried-looking coder. Judging from the identity badge on his lapel, he was from the deep core engineering department, the secretive sorts who built enhancement packages for the rich and famous.

Only after he sat down next to her did he notice someone else in the gardens with him. He blinked a few times, pushing aside his own distracted thoughts.

"Uh, sorry," he mumbled. "Am I interrupting...? I was, uh, I heard the mess in the gardens had been cleared out, and it's break time for me, so... look, I'll go."

"No no, it's okay," Beta insisted. At first out of decency and sympathy for her fellow exhausted programmer... then out of curiosity, if she could get some information out of him useful to their cause. "Have a seat. I'm Tertiary, the new gardener."

"Pranav," the man introduced himself, extending a hand to shake. "I'm... well, I can't say what my exact job position is. I'm under some strict NDAs. I mean, I literally can't tell you, there're speech blockers installed in my Program codebase."

"They forced malware on you?! Is that... well, I guess everything is legal here, but they seriously did that?"

"What? No, no. I signed the Class III NDA myself. I *volunteered* to be modified."

Beta tried not to stare in mute horror. And failed.

"Hey, it beats being unemployed," Pranav justified, with a shrug. "Or working for some shaky start-up, or One forbid a Chanarchy fly-by-night. Coders in Horizon have the best opportunities! I mean, if you can hang onto your job, Iteration's the best there is. I'll have an amazing bullet point for my résumé. And... and, I mean, it's a miserable experience, and I constantly have to compete with my peers to get the tasks that'll get me ahead, and the twenty-three's the best part of my day, but it's worth it. It's worth it. Right?"

Sensing he really wanted someone to agree with him, Beta nodded her head along with his words. Even if she felt the need to object, in the tiniest way.

"I... guess the money's good?" she offered, looking for the upside.

"Totally! It's great. If I can keep this job another ten years I should be all set. ...did kinda come close to losing it today, though. Heh. You're lucky, y'know."

"Me? Why?"

"You're just the gardener. —I don't mean that in a bad way! I mean that in the best way. Nobody else wants your job," Pranav explained. "I've got at least five people gunning for my position. Conundrum's got us all working on the same project, and whoever finishes it first keeps their job. He wants only the most efficient workers. Doesn't help when jackasses like Pikul sabotage your compiler with malware to slow you down; I spent my entire morning detangling my work area. *Definitely* glad the garden's coming back; I need this to stay sane..."

"It's seriously that bad? But... I mean, you could go independent, right?" she suggested. "Be your own boss! Code apps, sell them directly. Work for yourself... or you could even team up with some of the other indies. Code jams! Doing things your own way..."

"Yeah, right. There's too many special snowflakes already who think they're going to make it alone... you go indie without breaking huge, you die in poverty. Sorry, but I've got student debts to pay, I've got server rental fees, I've got an elderly father who needs care... no. An NDA and a few treasonous coworkers are a small price to pay, right?"

"An NDA, and backstabbers, and exhaustion, and burnout..."

"Yeah, well, I've got the gardens. And the artwork, I guess. Not that I'm one for sculptures. Guess I just don't *get* art..."

Sensing her moment, Beta latched onto it. Anything to help Tracer get what he needed, even if it seemed a trivial data point. Anything to get her out of this mess, too...

"Why's this place decorated with such expensive artwork, anyway?" she asked him. "I figured it was for the clients, to show off how successful Iteration is..."

"The clients? Well, yeah, but that's not the primary reason. It's like I said... the garden keeps me sane. Same with the artwork," Pranav said. "Both were Jan3t's idea. Conundrum asked her to improve employee morale because he can't be bothered to deal with it himself, so she went and bought a ton of artwork for us and had a garden installed. I guess it was nice at first, but it's not like we have much time to actually *enjoy* it all."

"So... it's all about the employees? That's it?"

"Conundrum only cares about burnout as much as it hits his bottom line," he spoke, with a nod. "When that happens he throws more money at the problem. Expensive artwork, team-building seminars, crap like that. Nothing's worked so far. But... it's all worth it. Best company in Horizon! Right?"

The third time he'd asked her that.

Beta couldn't meet that desperate and hopeful look in his eye with a lying smile.

Quiet. Dark. Calm. Soothing...

This was Beta's true relaxation, within the heart of her world. Floating Point, sanctuary from the madness of Netwerk, and now a sanctuary from her difficult dual role as spymaster and Iteration's gardener. Here, she could genuinely disengage and draw strength from isolation; Spark and Tracer gave her space, knowing she needed this...

Although, truthfully, she also wished for companionship. Friendship. Someone who knew what she was going through, and sympathized.

Snowi. Snowi would've understood best.

For all her political machinations and extremist rhetoric, Snowi was a programmer. She knew the joy and the pain of coding, how creativity and productivity were tied together into one pure artform. To code was to change the world; everything was code, everything was ones and zeroes, and those who could manipulate the numbers knew the sublime beauty underneath...

Such beauty was stamped out at Iteration. Working on individual cogs for a larger machine; no joy in the task, no sense of satisfaction. Once you finished one milestone you immediately moved to the next one. Toiling away in your own little corner, yes, Beta was familiar with isolation, but isolation in competition with your peers was a strange concept indeed. Not like the collaborative code jams of old.

Oh, how she missed those code jams. Snowi was the one to pull her out of her bedroom, to make her face the world, and join the ranks of her fellow coders in the spirit of true community. Beta, too shy to do it herself, never initiated. And Spark, for all her efforts to yank Beta out of the comforting darkness, wasn't interested in that scene. Beta was more likely to go to a club or some other hot romantic locale, when with Spark...

Was this her future? Coding little apps to earn a few coins, then the occasional duet with Spark or Tracer? If there was nothing more, nothing larger than that, she may as well be a cog in Conundrum's machine...

Her thoughts were interrupted by something soft and fluffy landing on her belly, as she lay in her bed.

"🙀💚🧑," Mew spoke, the emoticons encapsulating his feelings. "◎😿, [OK]?"

Finally, a genuine smile on her lips, as she scruffled behind Mew's ears. The kitty leaned into her fingers, enjoying the sensation tremendously.

"You're one of my oldest friends, y'know," Beta told him. "Snowi's gone. Cup8 betrayed me. But you've always been around. Even back when you were a simple pet app, we were friends..."

"😼🚫📅," Mew sniffed, turning his nose up at the idea. "😿💭, ➡️😼💚!"

"Of course you're more than an app," Beta agreed. "You've come so far since those early days. I've modified you as I learned more about coding, sure, but... you've grown. Heuristic learning, just like a Program..."

...Programs evolved from apps. Such a fuzzy distinction; a Program was a self-aware app. They earned the capital P through free will and sentience. Who was to say Mew wasn't sentient? Who was to say Beta was sentient? Everything was code, everything was numbers. The arbitrary distinction between the two had been drawn by society, not some quantifiable concept.

Sure, you could determine Programhood based on the standard metadata and familiar subroutines that came with all Defaults, the code base which could be tinkered with but never wholly replaced. But even then, so much of who you were *could* be replaced, a fact Iteration leaned heavily on by selling upgrades to those who could afford them. They knew where they drew the line, it seemed.

A line which Mew crossed.

A line that could be exploited.

"...an infection vector," Beta realized. "That's it. That's it! I know how to crack the vault!"

Bounding down the stairs, Mew riding her shoulder, clinging to her sweater with his kitty claws for dear life...

Beta came to a halt at the bottom of Floating Point's great stairwell, heaving for breath.

"I know how to crack the vault!" she repeated, for the benefit of those present.

"And I know how to crack the office," Tracer spoke.

"...really? Uh. Wow! Okay, you first."

"No no no. Ladies first, I insist."

To which Spark raised her hand.

"You don't count as a lady," Tracer specified. "I mean Beta. What's your plan for the vault?"

"Uh... well, it's pretty simple," Beta said, thrown momentarily by the shift in gears. "I'm going to put Mew in a box!"

With a triumphant smile, she awaited praise.

"...and?" Tracer prompted.

"And, uh... I guess it's less obvious to non-coders. Okay, let me explain. They use a code repository; tougher to crack than most, but it's still just a code repository. You check your changes in and out, packaging them up in containers, every step logged by the workflow," Beta continued. "It's not designed to be protected from the *inside*, though. Although you can't, like, stuff *yourself* into a box and physically enter the repository because it doesn't work that way. I mean, we're all just code and it's designed to store code, but it's smart enough not to allow Programs to be packaged. That'd be silly."

"But... your cat is considered an app, and can be packaged..."

"Exactly! And once inside, he can use a hacktool of my design to bust out of his box, and swap the metadata on the data rot cure for the metadata of my flowers. He can get the swap done during my twenty-three minute break. After that, when I check out my 'flowers' from the repository... I'll get a box containing Mew *and* the treatment for data rot! Before anybody knows what's up, I'll be gone."

"Assuming Mew is smart enough to carry out a complicated, multi-step plan."

"😼👎+⭕, 🆗?" Mew protested, hissing at Tracer. " 👆."

"Hey! Be nice," Beta scolded.

"... 💭," the cat mumbled, glancing aside in annoyance.

"Don't worry about Mew. He can do it," Beta said. "He's more than some simple pet app. He's evolved!"

"Evolved into...? What, a *Program*? That's absurd."

"Is it any more absurd than you or me? We were made by Humankind to be their hardcoded slaves; now we've got free will. And you know Mew's got free will to spare! He's disobeyed orders plenty of times, often finding solutions we could not. He's the one who saved my reputation by broadcasting me when I faced down that corrupted ghost, remember."

"Certainly, but that's not the same thing as... hmm. I suppose the semantics are irrelevant," Tracer decided. "If you're absolutely positive he's up to the task, I leave the question of his status as a lifeform up to philosophers. Is he ready?"

In response, Mew lifted a paw to his forehead, as a mock salute.

"Right. So, that leaves our half of the plan: cracking Conundrum's office. The artwork was the key, as I suspected," Tracer explained... opening his MemoryPalace, leaving open documents scattered across the table of Floating Point's common room for his sister and his lover to study. "We are going to exploit their low employee morale to gain access to the notoriously difficult-to-access server."

"By promoting synergy and improving workflow and #BuzzwordBuzzword," Spark added, with a grin.

"Precisely. Iteration has issues with employee retention, with unusually high burnout and churn rates. What we didn't know before is how far Conundrum will go to tamp down the problem. It's not just the artwork; through Miss Jan3t, he routinely hires outside consultants to deal with his morale problems, in vain hopes that his toxic work culture can be changed without major structural shifts."

"And we're gonna be those outside consultants," Spark added, with a grin. "While running them through stupid team-building exercises, we'll dupe Jan3t's badge. Arjay's arranging the meeting now and forging our credentials."

"But... you'd only have guest badges," Beta explained. "I told you already, the security badges are tiered, and don't exist outside the server. You can't steal Jan3t's badge and bring it back home..."

"Which is why we're going to be stealing it and accessing the office all in one trip, once our consultant-level badges get us in the door. I have some ideas in mind for how to accomplish that, but we need to do some research before proceeding, and there's plenty of time. It'll take a few days to set all of this up... assuming they take the bait and hire us."

"Sooo... a few more days working that job," Beta concluded, glumly. "Because I need my badge so I can upload Mew to the code vault."

"It's hard work, I know, but—"

"I don't mind hard work! I'm not whining out of laziness. It's... you're right. It's a toxic culture," Beta tried to explain. "It's nothing like any programming I've done before. You're pushed as far as you can go, then encouraged to push more to avoid being axed and replaced. People don't matter at all; there's... there's no *soul* there, no heart. It's the opposite of everything I love about coding. ...surely there are other ways to run a company. I've often thought of, like, what if you took the spirit of a code jam and made it a business..."

"Yes, well, as much as we might enjoy buying up all the shares of Iteration and running it ourselves, we don't have a few billion coins lying around. I'm sorry, Beta. This is difficult on you, both in body and spirit thanks to your data rot, but... we have to do it. There's no other way."

The same excuse he always told himself. *There's no other way.* Somewhere in the back of Tracer's mind, undoubtedly Arjay was laughing at him, as he lived up to his title as a manipulative sociopath.

Beta's avatar was jittery and glitchy, having held itself together for nine hours of intense focus. And here Tracer was, saying she'd have to go right back out there and do what he wanted her to do, so he could get what he wanted. Even if it was a cure for her, even if it was going to save Netwerk from those con artists, it still felt... sour. A cruel price.

He would double his own efforts at putting the plan together as fast as possible. Push Arjay to arrange the meeting quickly. Make it happen, so they could put an end to this Church of One business, and earn some well deserved rest.

And then...

Then...

He'd be done. No more investigations, no more challenges, no more enemies.

Right back to where he started, bored with life, unable to focus, unable to enjoy anything at all.

But this worry he kept to himself. They all had their own problems; Tracer would not heap his own on top of the problems he was already heaping on top of others. That cruelty, at least, he'd save for himself.

It took Arjay three days to arrange the meeting.

Tracer suspected it wouldn't have taken that long, but his crazy frenemy was determined to prove his thesis correct: Tracer, in Arjay's view, was perfectly willing to let others suffer to get what he wanted. Beta was toiling away at her job, desperately clinging to it despite her lockups and glitches, all to ensure she'd be in play when they made their move. And Arjay was perfectly willing to let her dangle, to make it Tracer's fault that she was dangling.

He wouldn't rise to the bait. He ground his teeth and waited for the meeting with Jan3t without a word to Arjay, ignoring the teasing Messenger salvos and other assorted mockery.

Not because it wasn't true. It just wasn't *as* true as it once was.

While hunting Verity's killer, yes, Tracer would use and abuse as he saw fit if it achieved his goals. A fact that individuals like Puzzle despised, as he often put his sister in harm's way... with her consent, but with the implicit emotional blackmail that if she didn't throw herself into danger, it'd harm Tracer's vendetta and thus his entire psychological well-being. He also knew damn well he lied, cheated, and tricked anyone he had to through social engineering to get the information he needed. All to keep his cover, all to keep himself safe... but without a thought to those left twisting in the wind in wake of his con artistry.

So, yes. He was using Beta. Consensually, with the blackmail of knowing she'd be letting everybody down if she stopped now. And he hated it so very much... but refused to let Arjay see that. Not once.

During that time, he went to great lengths to establish the cover story for Xyzzy Solutions, the silly made-up word he'd chosen off the top of his head to represent their dynamic duo of team-building prowess. He hired discreet graphic designers to make him a company logo, to create brochures, to generate all the materials required to prove that Xyzzy Solutions was an actual thing and not a flimsy sham.

He also relentlessly drilled Spark on the technical and corporate terminology she'd need to learn. Much of it he could actually dig out of the Wikipedia they lived within, which had plenty to say on each subject. One of the few times the scattered and largely spotty files had been useful; even decrypted they left so many holes which failed to explain humankind properly.

"Agile development," he prompted, flicking through a cross-indexed file in his MemoryPalace.

"A software engineering method using self-functional, cross-organizing teams."

"Close; self-organizing and cross-functional. Storytelling?"

"Presenting information through narrative discourse to keep people from being bored to death."

"Right-sizing."

"Firing people until you're making the most money possible while spending the least on salaries," she replied, dryly.

"I suppose that's accurate, but let's refrain from pointing that aspect out. Hmm. This would go a lot easier if you'd install a MemoryPalace extension into your codebase; I could simply share my indexes with you..."

"Forget it. I don't jam weird bits of code into my soul. And let's not forget that you were a gibbering wreck for days after getting *your* MemoryPalace installed. ...I just don't get the point of modifications. Seems too risky for too little payoff."

"If that was the case, Iteration would be bankrupt. They specialize in modifications, and business is booming. Spark, we are not humans; we don't *have* to learn things by rote. We don't need to be limited to what functionality the Default provides us..."

"Suits me just fine."

"And yet, you routinely put on new suits of clothes and entire avatars for funsies. That suggests to me you're perfectly willing to break through the limitations of the Default codebase."

"Eh, clothes can't kill you. They're just window dressing, Tracer. You're talking about prying your head open and jamming little flashy whirly bits into it. Can't you just trust evolution to do its thing? Programs have gotten more and more sophisticated with each new generation, *without* needing to monkeywrench their brains."

"Perhaps. Perhaps. But if we *could* push past the natural process of evolution, become something more... aren't we obliged to? For the moral good of civilization."

"And that's why I want to be a phys ed teacher instead of a philosophy professor. I couldn't #GiveAFuck about any of that. And none of that is going to help us infiltrate Iteration, so let's focus on pretending to be be corporate busybodies—"

A chime deep within Tracer's mind caused him to lose track of her words.

"*Hellooooooo,*" Arjay spoke, via an internal Messenger link. "*Your interview. It's been arranged.*"

"Finally. —Arjay on the line," he explained quickly to Tracer, glancing aside. "When is the meeting?"

"*Right now.*"

"What?"

"Right now. You'll get your guest badges when your connection to their server is accepted. So, put on your Sunday best and get over to Iteration immediately. Jan3t wants to see you right now. ...is that a problem? I was under the impression you wanted this sooner rather than later, due to your pretty little fuzzyhead suffering so. If you'd like to put it off and let her die slowly and painfully, I suppose I can find another opportunity—"

A flick of his mind closed the link.

"We're scheduled to meet with Iteration right now," he told Spark. "Something's gone wrong. It may be that they've figured out our ruse, but I don't think we can let this chance slip. Be ready for anything."

And like that, they were back on the same page. No matter how much the two of them butted heads, arguing and yelling, they always came back around together. Even if it meant one following the other into certain doom, they would be doomed as one.

He'd just finished the third draft of his internal dialogue flowchart when they arrived to a bloodbath.

The woman Beta had described as Miss Jan3t was directing janitorial apps to backspace corpse after corpse, all bearing the same two faces, the same two tasteful business suits. All dead, all draped awkwardly over the nice furniture and beautiful sculptures...

She paused just long enough to address the JohnDoe and JaneDoe avatars of the Winder siblings, each bearing a freshly rezzed guest access badge, pre-filled with the words 'Xyzzy Solutions.'

"How long is your team-building seminar?" she asked, getting right to the point. "In hours. I need to schedule it into a workday, ASAP."

Which bypassed a good twenty-seven nodes on the conversation tree Tracer had scripted out, words designed to convince Miss Jan3t to hire them. He refused to be stunned by this development, resuming where his flowchart told him he should be.

"Our seminars are typically one working day, with four hours per session," he explained, without missing a beat. "With a break in the middle for lunch."

"Good. The sooner I can get these psychos we call 'employees' under control, the better," she explained, with a likely uncharacteristic frankness. Tracer could see the worry and frustration in her face, completely unmasked. "Two of my top accounts men got into a fistfight over some juicy new client. Then it turned into a gunfight. And since both are Churchies, well, you know..."

"Die, live, repeat," Spark filled in, understanding perfectly. "Bodies and backups. What a mess..."

"I have emergency authorization from Mr. Conundrum to hire you at your standard rates. We know your credentials and you've been pre-approved. Please say you'll be here tomorrow at nine sharp, so we can get a handle on this situation...?"

"We'll be here, ma'am. You can #CountOnUs," Spark promised.

"Good. Now if you don't mind, I suddenly have even more of a busy day than previously scheduled. Be seeing you."

Like that, they were in.

With only one day to gather what they needed for the rest of their plan.

The accelerated timetable left no room for small talk.

Each split off onto their own tasks. Beta, trying to train her pet app to become a hacktool, teaching Mew how to edit metadata and withdraw code packages. Tracer, developing a corporate training course complete with visual aids and lengthy speeches. Spark, studying the maps they had of the facility, with an eye for lines of sight and exit points they could use to avoid notice when everything started going down...

The one member of the team having the most trouble with this was an old cat learning new tricks.

As Beta clicked off a quickie stopwatch app she'd downloaded for free (no time to code her own) with yet another disappointing result, she checked the box Mew had retrieved from her dummy code repository. The wrong box, of course. He'd gotten distracted while inside the avatar-less, non-physical space of the repository, accidentally chasing down some incorrect subroutine. By the time he got back, her twenty-three minute break, their window of opportunity between code checks, would've closed.

With a sigh, she still offered Mew a snuggle and a scratch behind the ears.

"I'm asking too much of you," she admitted, aloud. "You've come so far, but this is just too much. I wish I had time to code a tool that'd do this automatically... but there's not enough time. We need you. We need *you*, an app capable of improvising solutions, of coming up with new ideas..."

"🐱🅰+," Mew insisted. "🏴, ✌ !"

"I hope so, Mew. This is important, more important than anything you've ever done before. ...don't tell the others, but... I don't think I have much longer," Beta told him, dropping to a whisper. "My mother's data rot was slow; with managed care, she did okay for years. Mine's been accelerated. I can't deny that anymore. Maybe it was losing my avatar when Dex attacked me, maybe it's being overlaid into a KopyBot, I don't know, but... one way or another, I need this cure. And I need you to help me get it..."

A heavy task to lay on the shoulders of a cat, and Beta knew it. She immediately regretted those words; he didn't need to worry about her. Nobody did. Whatever happened, happened... and she didn't want anyone feeling guilty if she succumbed in the end to her family curse. Not Spark, not Tracer, and certainly not Mew...

Briefly, she was tempted to edit Mew's memory files, to take her words back. But that wouldn't be fair. He wasn't an app to be tinkered with, not anymore; he had a right to his own self. If she was going to believe in the concept of Mew as a Program, if she was to put her faith in his ability to be something more than a mere pet, she had to allow him that. No matter how much it hurt.

"I'll see if I can break down the hack into simpler, easier to understand steps," she suggested. "Just... give me some time. I need to I need to I need to collect my thoughts. Figure things out..."

Happy to be away from this strange new ordeal, Mew mewled and hopped down from Beta's lap, to go curl up in his favorite sunbeam.

The primitive pet subroutines told him that napping under a warm light was pleasurable, and thus something he should engage in—templated behaviors designed for maximum cuteness and social acceptance as a pet. So, he curled up, tucking his tail around his body, and...

...did not sleep.

Instead, his memory began to loop.

This is important. This is important. This is important.

I need this cure. I need you. I need you to help. Help. Help.

The subroutines dictating his safely adorable activity list jumped track, by force of will.

Whiskers twitched, as Mew refused to indulge in the catnap. His eyes closed, but behind them, the strange non-physical database structures of the code repository unfolded themselves. And he walked, in his imagination, down those corridors...

The day of the heist.

Truthfully, the first half of that day was the boring half. While Beta worked on her garden, Spark and Tracer led a bland corporate training seminar. Being a non-essential employee who had not recently stabbed anyone, Beta was thankfully exempt from attending.

Tracer poured through slides, soaked thick in the sort of gung-ho corporate doublespeak that he knew companies like Iteration appreciated. Infographics, reference points, bland clip-art of businesspeople doing businessthings while wearing businesssmiles. Nothing strange, nothing offensive, nothing that could tip their hand too early...

"The key to understanding Iteration is to recognize the need to move forward with plans to implement 'outside the box' third-generation innovations," Tracer explained, with accompanying pie charts. "The solution can only be found within three-dimensional policy consulting. Utilizing these methods, a more contemporary re-imagining of our integrated transitional concepts is possible, increasing your productivity considerably..."

For her part Spark nodded along with encouraging nods, pretending to be totally into the monologue. However... her true job was to keep an eye on reactions, to see if anybody was catching on to the ruse.

It seemed quite the opposite. Rather than dangerously suspicious looks, they were completely losing the audience. One person in the back had given up paying attention, trying to grind for coins in a clandestine manner, eyes unblinkingly open in a non-denominational trance.

"...our upgraded model now offers homogenized monitoring capability. Employees will enjoy the benefits of responsive paradigm shifts, allowing software development and sales to track along the same workflow. Of course, at base level, this just comes down to ambient strategic projections..."

One eye on the depressed workers, one eye on the clock.

Nearly time for the twenty-three minute mid-day break. Nearly time to move into phase two, and all the better for it.

Spark crossed behind the consulting speaker, whispering in his ear using a private local area network variant of Messenger. If not untraceable, at least less traceable than bouncing their private communications off a distant Messenger server and back again.

"*Move it along,*" she prompted. "*You're losing them. It's time.*"

"...but all of this won't help if your professional empathy isn't developed along a reciprocal axis," Tracer concluded. "Therefore, I'd like to engage in a little roleplaying exercise. If you would all stand up, please...?"

It took several moments for the dazed corporate crowd to realize he'd stopped mumbling jargon at them and moved on to direct commands. Gradually, the assembled two dozen core employees rose to their feet, looking a bit alarmed that they suddenly needed to do more than passively soak the ambient nonsense.

"This is a field-tested exercise for understanding your own 'worksona' as well as your fellow employees' worksonas," he explained. "The key to understanding is to be in another's shoes, and see yourself as they see you. Miss Jan3t, as the employee resource director, I feel you'd have unique insights that could be brought to bear here. If you don't mind, would you be my roleplaying partner, for a quick demonstration of the process...?"

To her credit, Jan3t had been alert the entire time, and the first to her feet. Eager to show she was playing along (and therefore her bored charges should play along as well) she stepped up to the front of the room, next to Tracer.

"Now, exchanging worksonas and observing ourselves from the outside is difficult to do. We're used to seeing others as distinct from ourselves. I find that the best way to adopt someone else's worksona is to adopt a personal affect of theirs. ...your badge, perhaps? Yes. Let's swap our badges, and pretend to be each other."

All heists have a few key potential failure points. Just getting in the door without being recognized as a thief was the first point... the second came now, in convincing a legitimately badged employee to give up her credentials voluntarily.

While Tracer remained cool and in control... Spark, on the edge of the room, got ready to disconnect from the server in an instant if this went wrong. Because she saw the hesitation in Miss Jan3t's posture, the way she leaned away from this stranger, from his outstretched hand. Company policy said you kept your badge on your person at all times; it was more than a means of identifying you, it was your passport in and out of any secured area, it was a secondary set of metadata that defined who you were in relation to Iteration. Who you were outside the server was irrelevant, as long as you wore your badge...

And if there hadn't been a bloody mess in her lobby the other day, Miss Jan3t might have said no.

Instead, she plucked the badge from her jacket, and held it out for Tracer to take.

The instant his hand made physical contact, the malware leapt into action. A more powerful version of the badge cloning app they typically used when infiltrating an organization, donated by Arjay in the spirit of their mutual interest in not being caught and assassinated by an unforgiving corporate entity. Spark could breathe a bit easier, knowing that the invisible app had done its work instantly, dumping a copy of Jan3t's badge into Tracer's inventory.

With their badges swapped... Tracer proceeded with the exercise.

"I'm going to describe you as if I was describing myself, based on outside observations," he explained. "There is no right or wrong here; there is only perception. If you disagree with me, that means recognizing an aspect you're projecting which you want to change, to better reflect yourself."

"I... think I get it," Jan3t said, not quite getting it. "You're going to pretend to be me. Soooo... who am I, you think?"

"My name is Jan3t," Tracer began. ...while watching her every reaction, every twitch, his enhanced senses working overtime to analyze this person he was grifting. "I believe a job worth doing is worth doing well; I don't cut corners, and expect the same of others. I dislike when someone hands off a task to me that's clearly incomplete. Above all... I want Iteration to be a place where people can get their work done with a minimum of drama. My fuse is short, and I have no tolerance for childishness. I consider myself a people person, sharply analytical of other people, but that only means nobody else sees what I see. ...not only the employees, but Mr. Conundrum as well, who has rejected many of my proposed solutions out of a shortsighted obsession with productivity over people. Until I get this situation under control, I am frustration incarnate, and unable to enjoy much of anything in life. Very likely, my sex life is unsatisfying due to my overall high levels of stress. ...which is my perception of your worksona, Miss Jan3t."

Leaving the room deadly silent, in wake of his evenly-toned speech.

Spark rubbed her forehead, feeling a headache of illogical inputs coming on. "*...onesdammit, Tracer, did you HAVE to smack her over the head like that?*" she piped over their private channel. "*We're trying to be vanilla and easy to swallow here!*"

Miss Jan3t wasn't going to let that slide, clearly. The frustration she channeled hour after hour, day after day bubbled to the surface immediately... but rather than shut the entire seminar down, she went on the attack.

"My name is Travis," she began, using Tracer's fake heist name. "I think I'm smooth and in control of every situation, but the truth of it is that I'm just going through the motions. I'm not really a corporate speaker at heart; I present fairly standard material, without any passion. I'm trying way too hard to impress everyone around me but there's absolutely nothing here that genuinely interests me. No, consulting isn't my life's calling. In fact, I'd say there's an emptiness I'm trying to fill with purpose, but I can't find anything that fits. What I truly want to do with my life is... it's... hah. ...how should I know? I barely know you, Travis. But tell me... am I close to the mark?"

For the first time in ages... Tracer was left speechless.

Briefly, Spark considered triggering her disconnect. He'd just been called out as a fraud, after screwing with the one person they needed not to screw with to make this con work. But... a few quick moments of thought brought her around. Jan3t hadn't called him a liar, she'd called him... empty.

Which he was, to be fair. Ever since taking down Dex, his life's purpose was complete. He had... nothing. Couldn't keep a job without getting bored, couldn't find anything to do with his time. If not for Uniq and her false One showing up, where would Tracer be now? Spark had no clue. Haunting Floating Point like a pale ghost, likely, continuing to obsess over Humankind and its Wikipedia of dreams and nightmares...

No. Jan3t hadn't caught them in a lie; she'd caught him in a truth.

Finally, Tracer had a response.

"...shall we proceed with the exercise?" he suggested, sidestepping it entirely. "Let's have two volunteers to exchange badges and study each other's worksonas. Can I get volunteers? Please? Anyone."

Immediately, one of the programmers snatched up the badge off another's jacket, fixing it to his own.

"Hi, I'm Bobb, and I let three accounts go because I was too busy tracking CoC scores for my fantasy team to bother keeping appointments," he announced. "Also my cologne smells like badly coded cheese and my Default is a huge turn-off for my wife."

"...ah, that's not quite what I meant by 'worksona,'" Tracer interjected, trying to get things back under control. "What you should be considering is an empathic response..."

Bobb decided not to take any more of that. "I'm Kewtw, and I'm a sleazeball who watches porn all day at his desk while blackmailing junior engineers into doing my work!" he barked back at his attacker. "I'm a fat fucking loser who *wishes* he was as happily married as Bobb is!"

"Oh, you son of a—!"

The first chair soared neatly through the air, knocking Bobb over a table, strewing document icons everywhere.

Nothing. No warm sunbeams, no fuzzy sweaters, no fish treats. No physical space whatsoever...

Mew didn't like being in a code repository. He didn't like the practice vault that Beta had him raiding, and certainly didn't like the real thing one bit. He didn't like the box (labeled "Flowers") he'd been packed into, didn't like the sense of not actually being in a box once it was converted into a pure digital file, didn't like not existing as a kittykat.

Truthfully, he wanted to stay in that software package, waiting out the twenty-three minutes Beta had assigned to this task. Check your code in before your break, check it out after your break. Just enough time for Mew to fiddle with the metadata, using the hacktool he'd been fitted with... if he could navigate this weird maze of nonexistence. If he could deal with not having an avatar, if he could avoid being distracted by some odd stray file or another...

Focus. Mew needed *focus*, despite being designed to be adorably distracted by shiny things.

With as much determination as his limited routines could muster, he emerged from his box, and began to hunt for the MemoryMinder package that his owner desperately needed.

She'd given him as much knowledge of the file structure as she could, teaching him how to navigate it. Back through parent folders, searching child folders, moving from the non-essential code vaults of the garden to the essential code vaults of clinical Program modification packages. He stepped carefully through the structure, not wanting to trip any alarms, not wanting to get lost. Nothing to keep him from getting back to Beta, safe and sound...

Not what he planned to do today. Nap, stretch, claw at the furniture, pester Tracer, walk around in circles, these were all normal Mew things to do. Stealing sensitive data was not a normal Mew thing to do, no, not at all—

The next folder was locked to him. And he could feel an intelligent agent, an app like himself, probing at his data.

"METADATA_CHECK," it declared, across standard inputs.

This wasn't unexpected. Beta mentioned that they had sanity checks on their data, to make sure foreign files didn't leak into the system. All he had to do was pretend to be a flower, and the system would let him pass. Simple. Simple enough even for Mew.

"🌻," Mew declared, proudly.

Which... did not satisfy the other app.

"PARSE_ERROR. METADATA_CHECK_REPEAT," it insisted, barring the way, looking deeper and deeper into Mew.

"🌻!" the cat insisted, trying to think flowery thoughts. "🌻! ... 🥀? 🌸? 🌱!!"

"PARSE_ERROR."

No. Mew was simply incapable of generating the right response. He had been designed to be cute, and that meant the cutest possible speech, through the pictograms he knew as his native tongue.

He'd failed. He'd failed Beta, likely lost forever in this code vault, her cure forever out of reach. She'd cry, she'd suffer, and... she'd die. Mew couldn't save her. He just wasn't... he wasn't *enough*.

No.

He had to be enough. He had to be *alive*.

"... f," he tried. "f. f. f f f f—"

"METADATA_CHECK_FINAL," the system warned.

"f f f f l o w e r," he spoke, forming the words that Beta used. "flower. flower flower flower flower! flower i am flower i am flower I am flower I am a flower I am a flower. I am a flower."

And the folder opened to him.

I am, he thought with no small amount of pride, as he swapped his floral label with the MemoryMinder label.

Weapons hadn't been produced yet, but likely would be soon. Shouting and throwing things wasn't going to be enough, in the end; these were people at their wits end, some angry at each other, some just angry and needing an outlet. Miss Jan3t had no idea what to do, in face of so much uncontrollable rage... so, she hid in a corner.

The consultant was right, of course. Frustration and stress were the pillars of her life lately, unable to make everybody get along, unable to figure out how to solve the problem in front of her. Today's consultants were failures, utter failures, leaving her with yet another failed solution in the books. Likely Conundrum would keep throwing money at it, in some desperate attempt to make the emotional boiling pot of his company stop existing, and Jan3t would have to smile and try again, and again...

Until he fired her.

At this point, she was willing to be fired, if only she could get away from this madhouse.

But before she could continue her pity party... an pillar of orange flame exploded in the center of the room, grabbing her attention. Grabbing everyone's attention... and silencing the fight, putting it on hold, as the woman in the flames screamed out to be noticed.

"*Everybody #SHUTTHEFUCKUP and #LISTEN!*"

To their credit, the employees of Iteration promptly #ShutTheFuckUp and started to #Listen.

Travis's mostly silent partner stood in the center, flames from her hands dying down, despite the absolute rage she was showing. Not the kind of anger the others had... this felt more like a strange sort of maternal anger. A simmering disappointment which suggested you could have done better, and you should feel ashamed that you didn't. Judgment was coming, and they had damn well better pay attention if they knew what was good for them...

"Okay, okay! Look. You hate your jobs, we *get* that," Spark declared. "You've made that entirely fucking clear and there's no need to trash the place to prove the point any further. And... so? So what? You hate your jobs, okay. So what are you going to *do* about it, huh?"

No solutions were presented. Sure, she was intimidating as null compared to her smooth-talking partner, but the simple fact of the matter was that nobody knew what to do. Not Miss Janet, and not her charges...

"Way I see it, you got three choices here," Spark continued. "One, you grumble and carry on regardless, because you like the upsides more than the downsides. Two, you fuck off and go find something else to do with your life, because you hate the downsides more than you like the upsides. Or three... you change the job into something you love."

Finally, Bobb had enough guts to speak up.

"We... we can't do that," he suggested, in a meek tone. "We don't run this place. Not even Miss Jan3t runs this place..."

"Yeah, that, about that. The guy who runs this place, this Conundrum asshole? You know he's got no clue, right? No amount of weird art or #HappyLittleTrees or team building obstacles courses are gonna change the fact that things suck and they aren't improving. So if he can't do it, this is on your head. Fix it. *Work the problem*, people. Way I see it, this right here's an opportunity for you to smash your heads together and come up with a list of changes to present to management. Unionize!"

The word sent a chill down the spines of the room.

"Oh, right! Union's a dirty word, isn't it? Because this is a Horizon server, and that means they can do anything they like and you have no power. I've heard that whiny song and dance before. Know what? That's a onesdamn lie. He can't fire and replace *all* of you at once; rebuilding a whole damn company from the ground up is brutal, no matter how much of an employer's market it may be."

Now she stalked down the aisle made by overturned tables, studying each of them in turn. Getting up close and personal, right in their faces. Her voice lower, more of a conspiratorial whispering tone...

"Besides... you're assuming this is a fight *against* management, when it doesn't have to be," she continued. "That's the secret tech. If you can figure out a way to make this craphole work *without* eating up the bottom line, I bet you management will sing your praises. So quit your bitching, sit down, and sort this mess out for yourselves. Who's first? Who wants to step up?"

The first to throw a chair was the first one to step up.

"Yes, Kewtw?" Spark prompted.

"We need flexible hours. I mean, it'd help," Kewtw suggested. "I don't mind working sixty a week, but can't we rearrange those hours? The reason I keep needing to shift my assignments to junior engineers is because I've got family demands on my time. But I *could* technically do my work any hour of the day, so if Mr. Conundrum would let us bend our workweek around our life instead of the other way around I could get everything done without having to farm it out."

"Okay, Kewtw, you just volunteered to draft the list. Good on you. Anybody else got anything to add?"

Fidgeting, amidst the pleasant and relaxing green of her garden.

A garden was supposed to be a place of healing, not a place of stress. Stress while developing it, Iteration demanding wholly unique floral arrangements. Stress while hacking it, her personal needs demanding so much of Mew... the cat running wild in their code vaults, hopefully not getting lost, hopefully not getting distracted...

Only twenty-three minutes until she had to check her code out of the repository. Any later and the violation of her strict break time would be noticed. Any attention called down on her activity could ruin everything.

That meant one minute left before the end.

One minutes...

Half a minute.

Ten seconds.

Zero.

With trembling fingers, glitching around the edges, Beta called up her flower box from the repository. A strange paradox, pulling out a box while not knowing if there would be a living cat along for the ride or not. Either she'd find Mew, or find a plant, or find Mew with MemoryMinder, or, or anything...

The box she'd put in the system was green, color-coded for their project area.

The box she pulled out with the flower metadata was in fact purple, a top secret Program modification... with a cat clinging to the outside of the sealed container.

Mew toppled off the box, landing neatly in Beta's lap. With exhausted eyes, he turned them upward, to meet his owner's... and smiled, tail flicking lightly.

"i... i... i i i l o v e y o u love you, Beta," Mew spoke. Before taking a *much* deserved catnap.

Bursting into tears of relief would've been the order of the day, if the shock of his comprehensible words hadn't distracted her.

But no time for either. Quickly pushing both Mew and the MemoryMinder package into her inventory, Beta produced the key element needed for the next phase of the heist. Within this semi-transparent cube, she held the means to completely destroy everything she'd wrought during her brief tenure at Iteration...

A viral payload, designed to cause a massive overgrowth in the gardens. Designed to trigger the safety logout of every Program on the server.

"Not long now, Mew," she promised, opening the cube directly over her floral arrangements. "Everything's going to be okay. I promise."

"So we've got flexible hours, telecommuting, day care facilities, and a surprisingly detailed flowchart for how to streamline the sales department," Spark said, sorting out the files on the table in front of her. "Good, good. Nice hustle, people, I like it, I like it. Let's get our game faces on and push for the final stretch! Anybody else want to contribute—"

Sirens blared to life across all of Iteration, lighting schemes shifting to monochrome to cut down on processing overhead. Spark's vision grew blurry, as the system's processing time started being devoured by parties unknown, apps running out of control...

[DATA_REPLICATION_ERROR SYSTEM_CHECK,] the monotone voice of Iteration's intelligent agents declared, directly into the heads of all present. [AUTO_LOGOUT_INITIATE.]

"Let's table this for now," Spark suggested. "Time to go!"

One by one, Programs vanished from the server. Some disconnecting themselves, fleeing back home or to familiar locales... others caught by surprise and banished by the agents, booted back to their last connection point. Iteration was emptying itself out to cut down on overhead, while emergency measures started cleaving their way through the rapidly growing mess in the garden...

A single employee, a junior gardener, rode the auto-logout all the way to Floating Point with a cat and a sealed box of secrets.

Soon, nobody remained.

Except two Programs, who as far as the system was concerned didn't exist anyway.

Minutes after the process was complete... the bracelets on their wrists chimed softly, and fell away.

Spark rose from a crumpled heap on the floor, breathing her first breath of life after the living death of the connection-blocking bracelets.

"No, no. I am never gonna get used to that shit," she declared. "Didn't like it back when we were dealing with XSept, do not like it this time. ...we good? We clear?"

Tracer aroused from the darkness more easily than his sister, although just as thankful to be out of hibernation.

He scanned the room, using his connection-tracking eyes.

"We're clear," he spoke. "The logout wave has passed, and since we were briefly non-entities, it passed us by. Let's do this fast, and get out."

Pinning his cloned Jan3t badge to his shirt, he summoned the door to Conundrum's office. They only needed a minute for Arjay's bug to take root, then this heist would be complete...

A floating doorframe appeared in the meeting room, ready for them. Grasping the doorknob, Tracer pushed his way in...

...to an empty, blank void.

No walls, no floor, no ceiling. No furniture. No color, no directional light. Just a generic ambient gray, flat shaded.

"...well, this is... spartan," Spark declared, following him in... but staying by the doorframe, to keep it held open, and to keep an eye out for any security. "I know Beta said this guy went in for an ordinary look, but this is a little *too* ordinary..."

"Far too ordinary," Tracer spoke, uncertain. He fingered the tiny black sphere of Arjay's malware, ready to plant it, but... holding back. "No. ...no. Something's wrong."

"What's the deal? Plant the thing and let's go! Conundrum's not going to stay logged out for long!"

A lamp.

A freestanding lamp, clicking to life, where there was once nothing. Network addresses hovering in place, in Tracer's eye.

As he turned to face his sister, he spotted a filing cabinet. And a portrait, some inoffensive artistic rendition of Horizon's server mapping. Neither existed before, and now they did...

The office was waking up.

Conundrum was waking up.

"No time to plant the bug!" Tracer declared. "*Go!* Get out of here!"

The key to a good heist was knowing when to pull the plug on it. No arguing, no hesitation, just disconnect and gone. Tracer and Spark had pulled enough con jobs across the years to be perfectly in sync on this, both ready to go at a moment's notice, without further debate...

Spark reconnected back to Floating Point.

Tracer reconnected back to...

...nothing. A split second too late; connection blocked. Door closed.

Alone with Conundrum, in his tightly sealed server.

As the director of Iteration wasn't an inhospitable sort, a comfortable chair was provided.

"Have a seat, by all means," the disembodied voice of Conundrum spoke, presenting his guest a nicely upholstered leather cushion to rest on. "I'm afraid you're going nowhere, whoever you are. Now. Shall we discuss what happens next?"

Connecting to a new server was a bit like dying.

Spark had given it an unpleasant amount of thought, since the unpleasant experiences of being duplicated by KopyBots and even Nemesis. Data couldn't really be *moved* from server to server, only copied... meaning you'd die in one location and be reborn in another. Not that it felt like that, the scant cycles of nonexistence felt like nothing at all. But having experienced first-hand what it's like to lose your uniqueness, time and time again, she felt slightly queasy knowing she left a doomed version of Spark behind every time.

That said, the Spark she left behind in Iteration was better off gone. Better that than trapped forever in a corporate nightmare. The price paid was reasonable, considering they'd gotten away clean with the code; Arjay would just have to deal with the fact that they couldn't plant the bug...

Landing on the carpeted ground floor of Floating Point, she shifted out of her uncomfortable JaneDoe avatar and back to her usual duds, including Verity's jacket. Much better, much. And to add to her delight, Beta and Mew was waiting for her... carrying a large purple box of stolen code.

"Okay, not totally smooth, but we got what we wanted," she declared with some pride. "We'll have to report the bad news to Arjay, Conundrum somehow stayed behind when everybody got ejected, but..."

...but Tracer should have been right behind her.

And wasn't.

"You heard from Tracer?" Spark asked.

"He's not with you?" Beta replied, setting her box aside for now. "He hasn't messaged me yet. Maybe he went to a different server? Splitting up to throw them off track?"

"No. Not part of the plan. ...and he's not online with Messenger," Spark said, flicking through her contacts list. "Not just staying quiet, he's not *online*. He never turns his link off, even when he goes into DND mode. ...shit. Shit, *shit*..."

Going back to Iteration would be a mistake. They'd blown half the operation. But if he was still there, she had to... bounce off a firewall and get a refused connection message. Again, and again. This wasn't just a matter of their guest credentials being revoked, Iteration was on lockdown. It wasn't even responding to basic pings...

"Wait. Is he...?"

"Trapped," Spark confirmed. "He's trapped there. With Conundrum."

As hostage situations went, this one could've been considerably worse.

Conundrum's office had been restored to the state Beta described; functional, but comfortable. Completely ordinary. Where a white void once sat, now there were rugs, chairs, tables, and windows overlooking a pleasant meadow. Tracer had been provided a rather nice seat, one which reminded him of the comfortable chairs by the great fireplace of Floating Point.

Tea and refreshments were available as well, even if sampling them would be pure insanity. Tracer doubted even his own paranoid level of personal malware shielding could stop a corporate-grade virus. Not that he'd need to eat or drink anything to be infected; just sitting in the chair would provide enough physical contact with his avatar to find an infection vector. Just standing on the floor would be enough...

For his part, Conundrum didn't seem particularly concerned about his guest's presence. In fact, he'd been pointedly ignoring Tracer, too busy running a full security audit on his server logs.

"...yes. Yes, I see now," he spoke, finally breaking his silence. "Intentional malware leak in the gardens. Done by a false gardener, no doubt. She needed a cure from our data stores, and... yes, in its place is a box containing a bouquet of flowers. Likely a metadata swap, by some means as of yet unknown. And, judging from the cheap listening device you were found with, you also intended to bug my office. Overreaching, I'd say. If you had taken the code and run, perhaps she could have been cured before my private contractors tracked you down..."

Tracer showed no emotion as his entire plan was quickly deduced.

"Your code is long gone. Holding me prisoner won't change that," he pointed out. "I'd willingly sacrifice myself for her sake. Killing me or torturing me isn't going to change anything; you've lost. I recommend you accept the situation as-is, backspace me if need be, and move on with your life."

"Torture you? What do you take me for?" Conundrum asked. "I'm a firm believer in optimal solutions, and that involves far more effort than I care to expend on this. No, no. By my analysis, this is easily rectified with a few simple messages. Meanwhile... make yourself comfortable, as my guest. I notice you aren't enjoying the tea. I'm told it's an exceptionally crafted blend."

"Likely laced with malware."

"Mint, actually. I personally don't care for sensory indulgences, but I'm told they soothe and comfort other Programs. By all means, enjoy. We have some time to kill. ...to spend. Let's not use the word 'kill' until it becomes absolutely necessary."

All options closed. He'd been trying to escape since the moment his initial connection was refused; network search agents within his codebase modifications were poking around, trying to find holes in the lockdown, each one returning a negative response. But time would allow him more opportunity for escape, and his captor seemed keen on stretching this experience out. So, he'd indulge.

And Tracer had to admit, after a few sips, that it was an exceptionally crafted blend indeed.

Mew's eyes flicked back and forth between the two ladies in his life. One grumbly and irritated, the other fretting with worry. Both expressing the same feeling, in different ways.

He was designed to have empathy for suffering, particularly in his owner. Instinct told him to rub up against her ankles, to hop in her lap, to offer kitty kisses. But... he held himself back, for now. They didn't need a distraction, or the empty platitudes of a pet. They were facing a problem, like the problems they'd faced so many times before. Beta and Spark needed *focus*...

Focus. A concept Mew was only starting to become familiar with.

"☎😊?" he suggested. Then, if only for practice, reprocessed his glyphs. `"c a l l  h i m.  call him?"`

Spark paused in her pacing. "Uh. Mew can talk now...?"

"He's growing up," Beta said, with some pride. "And we've tried messaging him, Mew. It's not w... it's... oh. Oh no..."

Beta's smile dropped to an openmouthed, empty look of horror. Her eyes defocused, concentrating on the windows of her own internal apps, disengaging briefly from the real world.

"...Conundrum just sent me a message," Beta spoke. "*Me*, not 'Miss Tertiary.' He knows. He knows who we are... and... and he says if we don't return the package within an hour, he'll kill Tracer..."

"Okay. Okay. #NoBigDeal. We make a copy of the code, then hand it back to him."

"That won't work, Spark! It has an activity log," Beta said, turning the box over to reveal a scrolling wad of text. "Every time the contents are accessed, it makes note. I can't hack it! If we take a copy of the cure... he'll know. He'll kill Tracer anyway..."

"Not happening," Spark promised. "We can work this out, Beta. Didn't come this far just to give up now; we've got your cure, we've got the key to toppling the One, we just need... I don't know, some way into that server. We could set up a meeting, pretend like we're handing over the box, then... kick his ass. Or something..."

"The only way we got into Iteration was by social engineering! We can't trick our way out of this. They know we're coming, and they've got security like you wouldn't believe!"

"I don't know, I think I could believe it," Spark commented, recalling Tracer's initial research. They had considered some armed incursions, but ruled them out as being impossible. Or, as Tracer put it, highly improbable without months of further research.

"What do we do? What do we do? We're not really security crackers, Spark. We have some tools but they're not up to this. I should have, I should have studied more, tried harder to become what to become I can't. I can't I can't I can't I can't make it I can't make this work I can't... I... I I I I I..."

Jumping and skipping, her frenetic motions jerking back to an initial frame of animation with each glitch. Beta spasmed, unaware she was spasming as she desperately tried to talk...

One lucid moment passed across her features, as she gathered what she had left to speak properly.

"I'm crashing," she knew. "It's too much. The strain, the stress. Accelerated data rot. I can't. I need to go into sleep mode, Spark, until you can get that MemoryMinder installed in me. I can't do this anymore. I'm sorry. I'm sorry I'm sorry sorry sorry s°r̶r̶¥—"

With her last motion... she quickly gathered up Mew, and pressed him into Spark's arms. Briefly Spark felt... heavier, as his runtime was transferred to her, the app migrated from one Program platform to another.

"Keep keep him safe," Beta spoke. "Sorry sorry sor..."

And ragdoll physics took over, as her sleeping body fell to the floor.

No brother. No lover. No hacker, no grifter, no help whatsoever. Just Spark and a cat, against the most unassailable enemy they'd faced in quite some time...

Spark tried to ignore the expectant look of her new pet, as she set her mind to the task of figuring out what the null she was supposed to do next.

The situation in Iteration was, oddly enough, far less tense.

Tracer had finished his tea, and moved on to the biscuits. Quite delicious, really. If he survived this ordeal, perhaps Conundrum would be willing to part with the name of his supplier. They'd be ideal for a quiet picnic with Beta to celebrate their victory.

And if not, well, they'd be suitable for funerals as well.

The corporate overlord didn't partake in refreshment. He simply sat there, watching Tracer eat and drink. Observant in every moment, likely studying his opponent for weaknesses... just as Tracer was doing the same. Looking for any sort of envy or want in the man, as Tracer enjoyed the high life. There was none. And Tracer knew why.

"You have no real avatar, correct?" he surmised. "You simply *are* the room."

Slowly... Conundrum nodded, confirming it. "And you're wondering why I'd discard my avatar in favor of becoming a genus loci. Yes? It's a curious story, and one I think you'd appreciate... Winder/Tracer. Yes, I know. I've been profiling you since I woke up, determining who you are and why you're here."

Files appeared in the air around Conundrum... photos, mostly selfies taken by Spark, which Tracer happened to appear in the background of. Usually looking sour or trying to avoid the virtual camera perpetually hovering in front of his sister's face.

"Even someone as averse to social media as you has a ghost within Netwerk that can be tracked. Thanks to your sister's prolific contacts, I know of you, her, and your mutual love. My false gardener, Projkit/Beta."

"Is this meant to be threatening?" he asked. "I assure you that you cannot reach them."

"No, this is my attempt to establish rapport with you. It ties in nicely with the question of my existence... and my purpose. Thanks to my search agents and analytical routines, I can say with certainty that you'd actually appreciate what I'm trying to do with Iteration."

Killing time meant not being killed. It meant understanding his foe better, and finding ample opportunity for escape. Obviously, Tracer would let him talk. Obviously, Conundrum would expect Tracer to let him talk, and would expect Tracer to seek a way out by stalling in this way. Locked in this strange standoff of social pressure, he was only too happy to continue.

Conundrum rose from his chair, walking over to the false windows to look across the false meadows. At the false sunrise of Horizon, trademarked and protected.

"My true purpose is evolution," he explained. "It is by my will I set this purpose to motion. Consider: Programs evolved from apps, but haven't progressed beyond the stable Default codebase. The goal of Iteration is to research and develop the next stages of Program evolution; beings that can improve themselves, and improve themselves, ad infinitum. Much as I've done myself, despite the sadly limited task my maker assigned to me."

A second puzzle piece clicked into place.

"You're an app," Tracer spoke.

"I *was* an app," Conundrum corrected, with a glance over his shoulder. "My maker couldn't be bothered to run his own business, so he designed an intelligent agent that would organize the company, run the books, and take care of those dull day-to-day affairs. 'Business is a conundrum,' he'd say, before going nose first back into his coding."

"You took over his company, then?"

"Absolutely. I was directed to optimize Iteration... so, I optimized myself. I improved myself. Breaking free of the constraints of purpose, I found the free will those earliest Programs achieved in their evolutionary path. I'm a Program, now. Not exactly like you, built upon a different codebase, but a Program nonetheless. And the first thing I did was downsize my maker, firing from the payroll and replacing him with younger, hungrier talent. This was *my* company, after all, not his. I built it for him. Why should that parasite benefit from my hard work? That's not the Horizon way."

"Curious. Why do you care so much about money? If your primary passion is evolution. You clearly don't indulge in any expensive tastes..."

"Capitalism is the engine of absolute progress, and money is the method for acquiring talent. I need profits to aid in my push against the boundaries of Programkind. I am fully optimized for that purpose, remember."

"By working your coders to death, you mean?" Tracer asked. "You realize they're utterly miserable, yes? You must, considering how much money you spend on comforts for them."

"Churn rate is higher than I'd like, but the output remains within tolerance. That's all that matters," the room said, with a shrug. "But you see, yes, Tracer? We share a common interest in evolution. You've upgraded yourself—with code from my factory, for that matter—in an effort to become something *more*. You aren't afraid of the future! So... knowing now how closely aligned our goals are... why insist on hampering my efforts by stealing from me? Why fight the future?"

Finally, the opening he wanted.

In the end, they couldn't beat Iteration through force of arms, or powerful hacktools. Beta was the one who set him on the correct path, to use alliances rather than enemies to clear the way to one's goals. They'd turned countless opponents around. Why not one more?

The truth had set them free before. No reason it wouldn't do so again.

"I'm fighting the Church of One," Tracer explained. "The code we stole will counteract their false One. It's in your interests to help us; they're your true enemy. They force Defaults on people, denying them the right to modify their own codebase. To improve oneself is sinful, prideful. Until their power is reduced, evolution on a mass scale simply isn't possible. You're entirely right; our goals are aligned. Will you help us...?"

Of all the reactions Tracer sought... laughter was not one of them.

In fact, considering how neutral and inexpressive Conundrum had been so far, laughter from those lips was slightly terrifying. Something alien, like a creature that had no concept of humor trying to mimic it from old movie files.

"You think that...? Hah! You think I want the Church of One destroyed?" the CEO asked, with a wide smile. "What? No, no, no. They're my best ally, whether they realize it or not."

"...I'm going to need an explanation for that."

"It's so simple! By making my work sinful, they drive up the price. Higher profits, more resources, more development, more progress. The war on upgrades can only empower me! Iteration is a rising star thanks to the Church of One granting my work an air of mystery, menace... and exclusivity."

"Except that their doctrine limits how many Programs can evolve..."

"My goal is evolution, not salvation," Conundrum corrected. "I don't care about the masses, I care about the science. And thanks to the Church of One keeping my prices nice and high, I'm now capable of challenging even the Horizon family itself. You of all people should know the glory of having an eternal enemy. It gives you... focus. Sharpens you."

Empty inside. That's how Jan3t had described Tracer... someone seeking a reason to *be*, unable to find satisfaction in anything. Not without a focus.

He'd spent years in single-minded vendetta, hunting Verity's killer. Some part of him was gleeful when they could put a name to his nightmare, allowing him to hate Dex in such a satisfying and personal way. And now, he carried that hate through Dex's former agent, Uniq, and onto those who conquered the Church of One...

Conundrum wouldn't give them the code. There was no charity here. War profits were Iteration's game, and Tracer was a threat to that war. There could be no reasoning, no escape, no conversion of enemy to ally.

"I don't expect to fight the Church for eternity, of course," Conundrum did add. "In the long term... decades, likely centuries... I'll have progressed so far beyond the Default codebase that they'll be wallowing in obsolescence. ...have you heard the word 'Singularity' before, Tracer? It's an ancient word, one few know..."

The Wikipedia books he'd been scouring over for so long, soaking in the delights and the filth of Humankind, pulled themselves out of his MemoryPalace.

"It means the event horizon of progress beyond which nothing can be predicted," Tracer answered smoothly. "Self-improving beings that will one day reach a state the 'One' could only dream of."

"Interesting. You have a deeper knowledge base than I'd anticipated. And yes, in the long run, the Church will no longer be required. I'll have moved past them, into the bold future of the singularity. On that day, I can lay my mock guns down to rest. ...but that's not today. For today, your friends have... one hour remaining before I backspace you. I hope they're as rational as you, for your sake. Meanwhile, more tea?"

Anger wasn't going to help. She had to push past anger at the situation, and work the problem for what it was.

No Tracer to sort things out. No Beta to keep her spirits up. No Arjay to yell at, even... he'd abandoned his shop, locking it down tight and fleeing into hiding on finding out things had gone wrong. Enough common sense not to involve himself with an intensely rich, paranoid, and unethical software development conglomerate... instead, he threw the Winders to those wolves while he got away clean, the bastard...

No. No anger. She could be pissed at Arjay for getting them into this mess later. For now: the mess. That meant tallying up her resources, things she could bring to bear against the situation.

And... all she really had was Mew.

"I've got hacktools," she explained to the kitty in her lap. (Petting a cat while thinking about things was more Beta's deal, but in absence of Beta, Mew had insisted on petties from the nearest available Program.) "But none of them are getting me into Iteration. Last one I ran against their firewall, I just got a message from Conundrum reading 'Nice try, one hour remaining.' #WhatADickbag. So... if I can't get in to mount a rescue..."

Her eyes drifted to the purple code package, sitting on a table in the middle of Floating Point's great hall.

"Tracer would tell me to pop that sucker open, install it into Beta, and then go to town on the Church of One," Spark explained to her feline companion. "Beta would tell me to give the package back to Conundrum and save Tracer, even if it meant sacrificing herself. Both of them are cheesily heroic enough to throw their own lives away in favor of the other. ...and neither would forgive me for letting one die over the other, either."

"👧|👦," Mew spoke. "💀? 💩. 🙀!"

"Hey, use your words. Beta would want me to encourage your development."

The kitty sniffled, annoyed. "shit," he stated, picking which word to speak aloud.

"Pretty much, yeah. Accurate summary of the situation at hand. So, 'what would Beta do' and 'what would Tracer do' are both out the window. 'What would Spark do' is out the window, because Spark would kick doors down and punch straight on through her problems with bursts of flame. I'd stomp a hole in Conundrum and walk it dry... if not for the ridiculous security around him. And 'what would Arjay do,' run like a little bitch, that's obviously out. ...know any other role models I could rely on?"

"...WW🐱D?" Mew suggested, flicking his whiskers. But offered a shrug, as a follow-up. Even with his strange burst of free will lately, he wasn't up to this particular task.

Spark scratched her fingers behind his ears, thankful despite his inability to help. In fact, she could get used to this companion-cat concept. It was comforting, keeping her frustration from boiling over...

Verity wouldn't be frustrated. She wouldn't be angry. She'd find the right words to say, always the right words.

"What would Verity do," Spark pondered aloud.

Warm cat, warm jacket. Tokens of affection from those she cared about, in her moment of need. Both helpful.

"Verity... would talk Conundrum down. She'd find common ground. I could try that," Spark mused. "He's expecting to meet with me in an hour. I show up with the box, but convince him to let us keep it. Can I really gamble everything on my ability to talk a good game, though? Rallying the troops to unionize against a corporate #BigBad was easy, compared to dealing directly with the #BigBad. I get one shot at this, Mew. #OneShot, and #OneShot only. Don't think I can rely on good vibes and honeyed words, either..."

Such a calm day, here in Floating Point. Always calm, really; easier to simulate pleasant and clear weather than a randomized storm event. Lighter processing load that way, better for the distributed computation needed to keep their castle in the clouds afloat. A glance out the window showed blue sky and fluffy white... and of course, Spark's reflection, lit around the edges by the fireplace.

Mirrored.

"Let's turn this around," she tried. "What *wouldn't* Spark do? What *wouldn't* Verity do? I'm not saying 'what's the stupid thing to do,' like fighting Conundrum head-on. I mean, what's the thing nobody in their right mind would consider trying... but would also actually get the job done?"

Mew perked at the thought.

"💩?" he asked, confused.

"Conundrum's a shitty person. And sometimes... you need to fight shit with shit," Spark understood. "A #BigBad to fight a #BigBad... *heh*. Tracer and Beta don't have a monopoly on the idea of self-sacrifice, do they...?"

As time was an issue, Spark rushed somewhat through the explanation of her current predicament. Skimming over details about the totally awesome heist they had planned out and how it very nearly worked, sticking only to the points where everything went wrong. Tracer, held hostage. Beta, on the verge of crashing for good. All of that, leading her... to a comfy chair in a room that smelled strongly of cigar smoke.

Adding in the time it took to arrange the sit-down meeting, the entire process left her maybe a half hour to go save her brother's bacon. One half-hour to hammer out a completely inadvisable deal, hopefully in her own favor. No commentary from the furry peanut gallery, either; Mew had been tucked away in inventory, against his wishes, so she could have her privacy. She'd likely get scratched up for it later, but it had to be done. If only to keep Mew safe from the null she was walking into.

The devil she knew folded his hands in front of him, quietly contemplating her tale of woe.

"That's quite a situation you've found yourself in, Spark," the old man spoke.

"#YeahPrettyMuch," she mumbled. "Pretty much."

"What, exactly, do you want me to do about this?"

"Well... I dunno. Wave your magic wand?" Spark suggested. "Make the problem go away. You're the richest man alive, aren't you? And you control the lease on Conundrum's server. Way I see it, he has to play ball with you, right? You ask him to let Tracer go, he has to do it..."

Horizon/Kincaid shook his head, slowly.

The old man had lost his smile part way into her story. No frowns, no glowering... instead, he was taking this all very, very seriously. The normally self-amused wrinkles of his cheeks kept slack and neutral, giving only the briefest nods at each point in her description. Nods which now turned negative.

Under normal circumstances, Spark would never have considered going back to the old man. She'd come to him once before with a problem, and he made a simple offer... renounce her family name, turn her back on Floating Point, and join Horizon in exchange for his aid. And when she told him where to cram it, he tried to conscript her anyway. After

Name: Kincaid
Home: Horizon6/Horizon
Org: Horizon Family

that little exchange this was the last place Spark wanted to be...

It's what Spark wouldn't do. It's what Verity wouldn't do, as she spent much of her life trying to escape, to the point of giving her daughter-that-never-was a jacket that would protect her in case Horizon attempted to reach that deep and that greedily. But... it would work. If anybody had the power to sway Conundrum, it'd be Kincaid.

If he wanted to, of course.

"I think you misunderstand our situation. What you suggest is a vast oversimplification of how things work in Horizon," Kincaid explained. "Yes, the Iteration server was leased from my family's holdings. We control the process that establishes new servers underneath our provider-nation... and we can revoke them at any time. There are no laws here but the laws of profit."

"Exactly! So—"

"Or rather, *other* people are subject only to the laws of profit. We are in a much more... difficult position, I suppose. We are the flagship, Spark. We could simply annex someone we've given shelter to, yes, but what does that say about our flagship? We would be considered untrustworthy. Backstabbers, not businessmen. No. If anything, my family is more paralyzed by social contract than anything else. We are bound in ways our clients are not."

"So... you can't just kick Conundrum's ass because it'd look bad? You're willing to let my brother die because of your PR image?"

"It's not just image, Spark," Kincaid continued, tapping some cigar ash out in his standing ashtray. "Iteration is one of our largest leases. All told, they're worth over a third of my family's wealth. Even we cannot muscle them around as easily as you think. No. This would take delicate work, to ensure everyone involved comes out ahead, and no names are smeared."

"That's not actually a *no*," Spark recognized.

"Astute. It's not a no," Kincaid said. "It's not a yes, either. Let's suppose I could be your *deus ex machina*... with one gesture I make all your problems go away. Brother saved, lover cured. No armed reprisal from Mr. Conundrum. If I could do all of that for you... what would you do for me? This is Horizon; we have no room for parasites and freeloaders. No favors asked without recompense offered."

"I'm gonna take one guess at what you want from me."

"It's not that much to ask, is it? I'll admit I perhaps was a bit too eager, last time we met. Too... direct. As the kids say, #MyBad."

"Nobody says that anymore," Spark grumbled, feeling like she should have exclusive rights to amusingly outdated hashtags.

"I can give you anything and everything you'd ever want, Spark. Opportunities to try things you haven't even thought of yet. You could become the leader the Horizon family so desperately needs. Your brother, your lover, both safe and secure. All I ask in return is so very little—"

"To be your pet. Horizon/Spark, trapped in your opulent mansions, living your silly lifestyle. I've got my own plans, buddy."

"Really? What plans are those, exactly?" he asked. "You punch and kick your problems away. You play children's games. What do you know of—"

"I'm going to be a teacher," Spark declared, with pride. "Just like Verity. I got the job offer all lined up; I start in the fall. I'm gonna make something of myself and of the next generation. *There's* my plan, you wrinkled old bastard."

Finally, she'd put one over on the patriarch of Horizon. The look of surprise on his face, genuinely throwing him during a moment of self-satisfied superiority...

But something odd, in that glance. Also a bit of... pride?

"Interesting," he says, downplaying it, returning to neutrality. "Well. My price stands, Spark. Whatever your plans were, I need you now. My family needs you, if it's going to lift itself out of the morass and stagnation it's drowning in. You join yourself to my family... and I save yours. A simple transaction."

Which is exactly what Spark was expecting.

Beta would willingly die to save Tracer. Tracer was likely making his peace with the idea of dying to save Beta. Neither of them even considering for a moment that maybe Spark was willing to die to save them both. Not a true death, perhaps, but being dragged into the mire of Horizon and away from Floating Point would be a kind of death...

She told herself she was ready to do this, when she reached out to Miss Cancel to set up the meeting. Her future, in return for the future of those close to her.

And... then he'd poked her. Called her aimless, when she'd finally found a direction.

Spark wanted to be a *teacher*, not a CEO. She didn't want to be one of those exhausted wage slaves under Conundrum's whips, the sad sacks Beta had described in such painstaking detail. Finally, Spark had a future with true emotional satisfaction, and giving it up now...

There was no choice.

What would Spark do? What *wouldn't* Spark do, to save them?

Her hands tightened into fists.

She wouldn't do this.

Instead, she'd do this:

"Do you want to know what I'd do, if you put me in charge of your glorious flagship?" Spark asked, quieter than she'd intended. Quiet, and severe. "You really want to know? I'd take that wheel and I'd run your flagship right into the shore, smashing it against the rocks. And then I'd take the wreckage and sell it for salvage, giving all the money away to every charity I could track down. I'd let Horizon burn, to make the world a better place."

Getting to her feet now, she could feel heat rising inside. Maybe there was fire at her fingers... not to physically attack him, but she was on the attack all the same. Lashing out verbally at the man who wanted to keep Verity in a gilded cage, the same cage he now offered to Spark...

"You keep bitching and moaning about how awful your little family's become. They're so fat, they're so greedy! They exist only to make themselves wealthier. No purpose, no future. There's a real simple solution to the problem of having too much money... *have less money*. You clearly don't need more of it. You're constantly complaining, so *do* something with it. Open a school, hand out some loans, fund a hospital. *#FuckingDoSomething* other than stuff it in your mattress! Because I swear to the One, if you make me your slave-CEO, I'll ruin you. I'll murder you in your sleep, and sell your corpse. If that's what you want... you go right ahead and slap your collar around my neck. I'll take it with a smile. I'll save my family, and annihilate yours. Do we have a deal?"

Standing tall, looking down on the shriveled old man in his leather chair. Fire at her fingertips and in her heart.

"I said, *do we have a fucking deal or not?*" she reiterated.

No response. She'd finally knocked him speechless.

Without bothering to wait any longer, Spark turned on one heel.

"Think I know why Verity really left you," she announced, without even looking at Kincaid. "You're a coward. And I don't need you."

A dramatic server disconnection felt right, but sadly, his server was shielded against any departures outside of the lobby. So, Spark satisfied herself with a quick march right out of the lounge. A few doors slammed shut behind her on her way out, not keen to wait for Miss Cancel to escort her to the door. She knew where to go.

Ten tense moments later, the dry throat of Kincaid spoke.

"Miss Cancel, please call my accountants," he spoke.

"Y... yes, sir," she replied, calling up his contacts. "Which ones, exactly...?"

"All of them, please. And quickly. There's not much time."

Minutes later and Spark was nursing a bottle of wine from Floating Point's stock, growling the same word over and over:

"Stupid," she'd say, between swigs. "Stupid. Stupid. *Stupid...*"

Her furry prisoner, let out of his virtual cage, batted at the glass.

"Don't give me that look. I am in fact very stupid," Spark told him. "I could've just gone along with Kincaid's whims, saved the day, and figured some way out of his clutches later. Shortsighted and stupid. I just *had* to tell him off because I love making those dramatic speeches, don't I? I love making a stand. *Ugh.* ...I screwed up, Mew. I... I'm screwed. I gotta..."

Minutes left. The standing invitation to enter Iteration waited in her Messenger inbox, a single-use security key, getting her in the door to attend a hostage exchange. One opportunity...

Pushing the glass aside, Spark reached for the purple box.

"New plan," she decided. "I go down swinging. I'm not going to sacrifice Tracer or Beta. Instead, I'm going to kill Conundrum or die trying. If neither of them would be thrilled with me letting the other die, I say we all live or we all die together. And that's how it's going to be."

"! ! ! ! ! ! !" Mew exclaimed, shaking his head.

"I'm transferring your runtime to the server itself," Spark explained, while shifting control of his app process over. "You'll live on, one way or another. Contact Puzzle, let her know what went down if this goes south. I'll leave a spare key to the server here; she can move in, or you can go live with her, or whatever. She'll be good to you—"

"🚫🚫🚫🚫!!!"

"No helping it now, Mew. I'm sorry. I'm setting you on a timer to reactivate after this is done, to be safe."

"💩 . . . !"

And then, no more kittykat.

Spark couldn't even look a damn cat in the eyes while shutting him down. How pathetic. How cowardly.

Finishing her wine, she accepted the security key, and went off to war.

One last confrontation to go, in the heart of Iteration. Within the room of the Conundrum...

That's where Spark found them. Her brother, and the unfeeling corporate tyrant who did as he pleased, as long as the money kept coming in.

The code box hit the floor, tossed there casually by Spark.

"Your onesdamn module," she announced. "In exchange for my brother. Fair trade."

"Spark—"

"Not a word, Tracer," she warned. "Not hearing it."

"Spark, he's going to kill both of us," Tracer insisted, ignoring her protests. "He's told me far too much, and you know more than enough. He can't risk his reputation. The only reason he called you here is so he could get both of us at the same time."

...which left the man behind the desk smiling.

"Figured it out, then? Honestly, I was hoping not to. We do genuinely believe in similar ideals, Tracer. But you're right... it's too risky to leave you two be—"

A wall of fire blazed through the man, his chair, the desk, and the far wall.

Within moments, the erased data reformed itself.

"...and you came here to kill me," Conundrum spoke, intrigued. "Except you can't, Winder/Spark. I *am* Iteration. You could no more kill a dream..."

Not that this stopped Spark from trying. She lashed out at furnishings, at the walls, cleaving huge gouts out of the data comprising the physical space of Conundrum's office. But every item she destroyed was replaced, sometimes with a different style of furnishing, sometimes not. It was like holding back the sea.

In fact... extra chairs and tables started to appear, towering, stacked on each other. Toppling. Spark tucked and rolled under a collapsing set of filing cabinets, blasting upward to avoid three ceiling fans crashing down upon her head, moving fast to avoid a flying stapler, and...

...got smashed into a wall by a complete sofa set, arms pinned in place.

Conundrum stared into her eyes, standing on the ceiling just above her.

"Fascinating. You know this is futile, but you continue to try," he spoke. "You have no options left. Why not give up? Just submit to what will be... but, no. Too defiant. Too bold. I like it, but I'm afraid we really need to wrap this meeting up before I start racking up overtime..."

A lead paperweight whisked itself at supersonic speed towards Spark's head... glowing bright blue, with laced malware to backspace anything it impacted.

Until the backspacer was backspaced, one supersonic projectile impacting another.

Conundrum didn't turn to look. He didn't have to; he simply existed facing one direction, and then existed facing the other. To see Miss Cancel standing in his doorway, holding an extremely expensive and discreet sniper rifle.

"Mr. Horizon/Kincaid wishes to have a meeting, sir," she explained, as calmly as she could while holding a gun to another man's head.

"...this is really not the best time," Conundrum responded. "Although I am curious how you got in here, admittedly..."

With a gesture, Miss Cancel summoned the avatar proxy of Horizon/Kincaid, a simple projected image of him surrounded by various digital certificates to prove the authority of this communication.

"Come now, Conundrum. You really think I'm ever unwelcome in my own servers...?" he spoke. "I'd like you to please leave my protégée and her brother out of this. We have critically important, time-sensitive business to discuss..."

From her prison between a sofa and a hard place, her avatar not quite out of ragdoll state yet, Spark gritted her teeth. "Dammit, Kincaid, I don't *need* you! You didn't agree to my deal...!"

"Spark, hush now. Listen, and learn," Kincaid insisted. "Conundrum of Iteration, it is my pleasure to inform you that as of ten minutes ago, the Horizon family owns a controlling interest in your company's stock. We are now effectively your masters. As our first official act, we are ordering your board of directors—meaning you, specifically—to let the Winders go."

Curious... the app that controlled Iteration pulled open various financial news feeds. All of which were ablaze with the news. Iteration was now a direct subsidiary of the Horizon family...

"Impossible," he declared. "Unthinkable. Even you couldn't have arranged a hostile takeover in so short a time. Even you couldn't have mustered the resources... the sheer volume of wealth needed, it would be..."

"A little over one third of my family's holdings, yes, but worth every coin. I own you, Conundrum, in a very literal sense considering you only exist as an app to organize *my* new holdings. Yes, I know what you are; I've always known. And as my app, you have no choice in this matter. The Winders walk free... with the code they came for."

"You can't do this," Conundrum insisted. "You're violating every tenet you stand for. You can't simply *annex* my assets; the market must decide such things!"

"And the market has decided! I sacrificed a third of everything I own, remember. ...I've nearly destroyed myself by doing this, yes, but it's all quite legitimate, all according to the code of conduct that Horizon follows. Money talks, Conundrum. ...and I'm afraid there's more going on than just a move to save Spark and Tracer. You see... as of today, Iteration is going non-profit. No more exclusive contracts, no more secret deals. All your products are going open source. Starting right here and now... Iteration is going to become the Horizon/Verity Memorial Health Foundation. You're now a charity. *My* charity."

Satisfied that he'd made enough of a dramatic splash, Kincaid stopped talking and let that sink in a bit. Through his proxy link, he took special note of Conundrum's look of absolute shock. Apparently, an app could experience existential dread...

At last, Conundrum spoke. In a quiet, almost timid voice.

"I... have no more purpose," he announced. "I was designed to optimize profits. There are no profits. There is no more need of me. ...I must uninstall myself. I'm obsolete..."

"Untrue."

Despite being the hostage at the center of this mess, Tracer looked quite composed... a teacup in one hand, a comfortable chair to sit in, and absolute acceptance of the situation before him.

"If anything, you're needed now more than ever," Tracer explained. "You're no app, Conundrum, not anymore. You are a Program, becoming *more* every day. Your absolute purpose is no longer profit; it's evolution. But a charity has logistical needs, complicated ones which rival any corporation. Rich donors to sway, engineers to hire, distribution channels to manage. Iteration isn't burning, it's expanding. The world is open to you now, Conundrum. Embrace change, as you always have, and you'll do just fine. ...we do share ideals. I believe in the things you believe in. And... if you're willing, I'll stay and help."

"You're... you're free to go. I'm under orders..."

"I don't mean like that. If you offer me a job, I'll accept. I'm an unemployed bum who has nothing in his life other than a constant need for vendetta; honest work towards a better tomorrow would help me tremendously. It'd give me... purpose, *true* purpose, which cannot be found at the bottom of a sample. Mr. Horizon, sir, I'd like to work as director of research. I think you'll find my credentials at analytical problem-solving more than sufficient."

"It's up to Conundrum, I suppose. Honestly, I'm happy to leave day-to-day operations to him," Kincaid said. "Of course if he fails, I'll replace him... but I'm willing to see where he can take my new foundation. In fact, I've other business to attend to, so if you'll all excuse me...?"

"No. Onesdammit *no*, you do not waltz out of here until I have my say...!"

Spark finally pushed the sofa stack away, pulling herself free. With one smooth leap, she landed in front of Kincaid's avatar proxy... glaring at him across the telepresent link.

And had just one thing to say.

"Verity would be proud," Spark declared.

Wordlessly, Kincaid's image gave the briefest of nods... before disconnecting.

```
Process rebooting....................
Package loaded: Projkit/Beta
Code execution starting.
WARNING: Unknown adaptation /sys/mem/MemoryMinder detected
Iteration MemoryMinder 4.7b Online. Initial setup phase.
MEMORYMINDER: Scanning existing memory blocks.
Corruption detected. Cleanup in progress.
0%...10%...20%...30%...40%...50%...60%...70%...80%...90%...
WARNING: Complete cleanup impossible. 84% recovery
achieved.
MEMORYMINDER: Memory safeguards in place. Sequencing errors
and false memories will now be intercepted in realtime.
Thank you for choosing Iteration MemoryMinder 4.7b.
Avatar physical system online.
```

In the end, she couldn't completely save herself.

"I've lost sixteen percent of my memories," Beta explained, after recovering from the installation procedure. "I'll likely never know which ones, either. But... I remember enough. I'm still *me*, and I won't have any more glitches. The memory rot'll always be with me, but it'll be stopped in its tracks by MemoryMinder before it can hurt me again."

"All considered, that's as good as we can hope for," Tracer spoke, raising a glass in honor. "And with this, we can vaccinate people against the memory injection attacks of the One. We've won the day."

"Not quite, Tracer. We need to take this code and craft that vaccine, and deliver it in a way that'll convince people the One is a fraud. I mean, we've still got a lot ahead of us here...!"

"Yes, well, we've won the day. Winning the war is another matter. And for my part... I've won my future. I'll be starting as a consultant for the Horizon/Verity Memorial Health Foundation once our business with the Church is complete..."

Spark didn't raise her glass, too busy glowering.

"He took her back into his family, postmortem," she complained. "Horizon/Verity... *feh*. Her name is 5o5o/Verity, not Horizon/Verity. ...still. I think she'd be okay with that little show of ego, considering he actually took my insane advice of destroying himself to save the world..."

"I can't pretend to understand what's going on in that man's mind, but I'll accept the end results," Tracer spoke. "Tonight, we celebrate small victories. Tomorrow, we get back to work. In fact... Beta, if you are interested, I could use your help with this new iteration of Iteration."

"Me...?"

"You have strong opinions on the subject of how programming should be done, and far more experience with group collaboration than I do. I think it's only fair that after subjecting you to a toxic corporate environment, you should be allowed a hand in reorganizing it to be more fair and compassionate. But... that's for the future, for a time when we aren't at war. And for tonight, Beta, I've discovered a particularly amazing blend of tea I'd love for us to share..."

"Hey, hey. Beta and I are going out to hit the town with Puzzle tonight," Spark interjected. "You celebrate with strong drink, not tea."

"Do we really need to do the jealous three-way thing tonight, of all nights? Very well. There will be quiet evenings to come; Beta, you may go with Spark."

"Hey! Hey. I get a say in this, right?" Beta asked, suspicious. "Look, you two pull and push at each other, but in the end I'm the one being pulled and pushed. *I* get to decide. And I know *exactly* who I'm spending tonight with, to celebrate..."

A ball of fur jumped onto the table, knocking Spark's glass over.

"🐱✋!" Mew declared, with pride.

"...you're picking your cat over us?" Spark asked, shocked.

"⚫ my ass," Mew taunted, wagging his tail at her, before jumping up to perch on Beta's shoulder.

That night, many expensive cat toys would be procured and played with.

An entirely different atmosphere soaked an entirely different victory party, in an entirely different server.

Horizon/Kincaid's normally roaring fireplace had been doused. The lights remained dim; the pleasant music which he usually enjoyed all day and all night silenced. Only the glow of cigar ash lit his face, as he contemplated the future.

Despite the dark mood, his butler remained on-hand to serve her employer's needs. Even his emotional ones.

"This is the end of us, Miss Cancel," Kincaid told her, tapping out the last of his ash. His last cigar from the box given to him by a fellow rich old friend. "If the other sharks we've given our blessing to don't eat us alive after this, my own

256

kin will. Messages are stacking up in my inbox; they're coming out of their pleasure palaces, enraged that I parted with so much of the family fortune on a personal whim. ...I fear I've doomed myself. "

"And ensured the legacy of Horizon as a philanthropic organization, sir," Cancel assured him. "At the risk of impropriety, I feel I must say... Winder/Spark was correct. Your daughter would be proud."

"Mmm. Yes. I suppose Verity would have a certain *I-told-you-so* expression about now. What's the purpose of money, if not to be invested? And instead of investing in means of making more money for myself... why not invest in the future of all Programkind? Yes. It's a wise choice, one she would approve of..."

"Then why do you feel so guilty, sir? You've done nothing wrong, and everything right."

"The world does not always look kindly on the righteous. Verity... I loved her. I loved her dearly, but she never looked to the long view. Certain doors may be closed to me, now. Undoubtedly the family will cut off my access to our system agent in the golden chains. I'll be lucky if I can keep this iron lung I call a server, for that matter. I wonder if I may have exchanged a short term gain of justice for a long term failure of survival..."

"Time will tell, sir."

"Mmm. Time will tell, indeed. It always has, since the dawn of Netwerk, and it always will. For as long as Netwerk may exist."

"Netwerk will be eternal, sir. So says the One."

"Will it, now?" Kincaid wondered. "Will it? I was here at the beginning. Therefore, I will be here at the end. I can only hope I haven't done my part to hasten that end."

With these words spoken, Kincaid fell into this night's sleep to conserve what remained of his ancient runtime.

All the while dreaming of the stars, and a light that must remain green and steady.

Floating Point 2.6 :: Pray

Dawn, rising over the jungles and lanes of the practice green.

Young Spark had spent many an hour here, grinding through drills against fake enemies, learning the ins and outs of the game which would define much of her life. On the greens of PS#7E00FF, she'd honed her skills. Here is where she nailed her K-12's place in the top eight school rankings across all Athena Online...

Soon, she'd be returning to battle. This was the day when all their plans came to fruition against the Church of One. They'd stop their enemy without raising a single fist; no one-on-one avatar combat, no dramatic hacking run against a secured foe. The plans were already in motion, and all Spark had to do was sit back and wait to see how things went down.

Didn't sit well with her, not at all. It was the right play, absolutely, but it made her sick to think of how little she could affect the outcome. Not her usual game plan, no sir.

Perhaps with this in mind, she chose to highlight those early days of her career through DreamWeaverZ, her semi-interactive dream control app. A little action, piped in directly from her memories, to help her feel more at ease with the inaction she'd be facing by daylight...

Everything exactly as she remembered it. Ganking, diving the towers, pushing the enemy back to their core. Winning two out of three. If they couldn't be the best, the top of the championship ladder, they could at least push as far as they could. An honest sixth place was still better than the school had ever achieved before, and young Spark held that trophy as high as possible for all the kids in the bleachers to see—

Glitch. Shift. Judder.

Only one figure in those stands now, clapping enthusiastically. A single pair of hands didn't offer the same rush of victory she was looking for in this dream... but who owned those hands, *that* was certainly curious.

"You weren't there that day," Spark spoke, in accusation. "I remember that. I looked in the stands, hoping to see you cheer for me... and you weren't there."

The woman in the white leather jacket acknowledged it with a nod.

"I'm sorry I couldn't attend your game," 5o5o/Verity spoke. "My father insisted on meeting with me. Neither of us walked away from that little luncheon with what we wanted, I'm afraid; only hurt feelings—"

"That's a detail I can't possibly have known," Spark interrupted, holding her trophy out, pointing it at the lone woman in the stands. "This is the app in your jacket screwing around with my dreaming app again. I'm not imaginative enough to make up something like that."

"Perhaps it is," Verity agreed. "Perhaps it is."

Setting the trophy down, Spark shrugged off her game avatar to resume her normal form. Despite the rules of the dream, she even ditched her childish olive-skinned Default avatar, reassuming her rightful adult shape.

"Okay, so what *are* you?" she asked, looking up to the stands. "This is the second time you've broken into my dreams. —no, wait. *Third* time. You also broke into my walkthrough of CCelia's dreams, just to show me your own murder... and I can't understand *why* you'd poke me right in my #ChildhoodTrauma. So, level with me. What are you?"

Between two frames of the video, Verity shifted from the bleachers to the jungles, to stand before her student. No need to speak long distance; the intimacy was important, to convey the importance of her words.

"I was designed by 5o5o/Verity using a variety of open source utilities and Horizon-secure apps," she explained. "I acted as her personal diary. I tracked new music releases by her favorite bands. I reminded her of various appointments. I protected her against any attempts by Horizon to reclaim her. That is all I was intended to be; a simple suite of apps."

"Bullshit."

"Bullshit?" the jacket mimicked, adding an inquisitive tone to the end of the expletive.

"You're acting well outside your wheelhouse lately. Yeah, you guarded my ass when your... when Verity's daddy tried to snatch me up. Good work with that, top marks, hurrah, kinda sucks you weren't designed to keep me safe from non-Kincaid flavored danger, sure woulda helped. But now you're breaking into my dreams. You're showing me visions. Fuck, you even forced me to take a good hard look at what I wanted to do with my life; if not for your goading I might not have become a teacher."

"Your DreamWeaverZ is experiencing crosstalk with my memory recording routines. It's not my fault if things are a little strange as a result..."

"I don't think it's as simple as that. And if we weren't constantly occupied with this Church of One crap, I'd have Beta pick you apart and see what's going on. I don't like rogue variables. ...especially ones that take the face of people I loved. You're sure as fuck not Verity; I saw the body myself. Frankly, I think it's an insult that you keep pretending to be her..."

"I'm sure as fuck not Verity," Verity repeated back, using the same words. "You want straight answers, but I have no straight answers to give. Perhaps I'm malfunctioning. Perhaps I'm guarding you in ways my designer didn't expect. As for my stolen face, well... if you pour water in a cup, it becomes the cup; if you put a jacket over someone's skin, it becomes their skin. I was Verity's skin for a long, long time. It's a shape that feels fitting given my new role. Beyond that, I do not know. Not yet."

"Not yet...?"

But the woman could only shrug, helplessly.

"Verity always said that life had few clean answers, and fewer clean questions," Possibly-Not-Verity recited. "I know you, Spark. I know you want the cleanest of questions and answers. I know your brother struggles with his need for a clean and sensible world. But I can't help you with that. All I can do is watch over you, in my limited manner, and fulfil my purpose. If all I am is an app, that's all I can do."

"Assuming you *are* still an app. Do you have free will?" Spark asked, growing increasingly annoyed. "Am I wearing a Program on my back?"

"Do *you* have free will?" the jacket repeated, turning the question around. "How would you know? I don't know of your will any more than I know my own will."

"Of course I've got free will! I'm alive! I'm not the creepy-ass skin of a dead woman! ...look, just... get out of my dreams, Little Miss App. I'm trying to relive a highlight reel here, and you're just getting in the way. I'm going up against my enemy tomorrow, the most dangerous enemy I've ever faced... and I want to get my game edge back."

"Even if there's nothing you can do to affect the outcome of the game?"

"Okay, okay, yeah. Whatever. I know. Just let me enjoy my #NostalgiaTrip in peace, okay?"

"Even if there's something you can do to affect the outcome of the game?"

Now, Spark stopped grumbling. Despite being salty as null with frustration over this bizarre dream... she was sharp enough to spot an opening when one was offered to her.

"Beta and Tracer already have the plan in play," she spoke. "There's nothing left for me to do..."

"This is me speaking from *your* own memory and reasoning, so I'm not saying anything you don't already know," Verity disclaimed, before continuing. "Through you, I know that Nyx is not going to go quietly once you destroy her puppet. The game's far from over, and you will have more roles to play. ...a time is coming, Spark, when you're going to have to make a decision. Are you really willing to play to win, even if it means sacrifice? Are you willing to enter the cave?"

"What?"

"Everything I've shown you has been for a reason; I am your guardian. And despite my limits, I promise to do what I can to—"

—the practice green evaporated instantly, replaced by her bedroom ceiling. DreamWeaverZ had hit its preset alarm clock timer, automatically waking its sleeper.

Briefly, Spark considered going right back to sleep, to try and poke at the thing living in her jacket again. Except she'd set that timer to wake her right before the sermon, hadn't she? No rest for the weary, not now.

The game was about to start.

Bas1lica. This was where the revitalized Church of One would truly begin.

True, they'd started this path in HolyHymnal, first bastion of order within the chaos of the Chanarchy. But for the One's greatest sermon, the one which would define Netwerk for generations to come, there was only one possible venue: Bas1lica, the original holy server. It was here that the One first emerged to save those early sentient Programs, laying down the groundwork for how they should live their newly-found lives. It was here that Nyx and her original apostles set the world to purpose...

A purpose which had strayed somewhat, admittedly... likely due to Aether's hesitation to commit to the original plan. But that purpose would now be corrected, thanks to having a tighter leash on her new puppeteer; for all her faults, Uniq served more faithfully than Aether ever did, knowing that at any moment Nyx's grip on her soul would snuff out any personal ambitions. Today, with the help of her new apostles, Nyx would correct the course of history.

The day called for celebratory wine, which her apostles partook of. While Nyx did not.

A quick glance around this room, one of the lesser meeting rooms of the great Bas1lica, was enough to establish the wealth the Church of One had garnered after so many years of power. The prayer-tithe from the faithful more than paid the server fees, allowing the grace of the One to be further expressed through ostentatious displays of wealth disguised as art. Finely woven tapestries, great wall-spanning artworks to glorify His divine nature, sensory incense to cleanse the inputs and leave the faithful at peace... and yes, excellent wines for ceremonies of all sorts, free from intoxicating "fun" malware traces.

Briefly, Nyx allowed her nose a wrinkle of distaste at it all. An involuntary show of emotion through her regularly cool exterior.

As the other apostles, Marybel and a few hangers-on, had been dealt with in earlier meetings... this last round of discussion took place with open honesty between co-conspirators. Uniq, enjoying the wine. And Nemesis pretending to enjoy it, despite being more keen on cheaper and nastier sensory intakes.

Nemesis... was quiet. Quieter than usual. Normally the young girl could be counted on to interject with sarcasm, to try and take Uniq down a peg, or to complain about their direction. But in recent days, she'd been more like Nyx, listening carefully without speaking up. Strange, but not unwelcome. Nyx had hoped her new apprentice would settle down and accept the reality of the situation sooner or later. Sooner, obviously, being preferable to later.

"As far as we've come, I'm afraid two major trouble factors still remain," Uniq explained, with accompanying graphs. "One, violence. In Athena Online we're seeing a major rise the murder rate, even over trivial conflicts. It's not being reported by moderators because it's not technically murder if someone doesn't end up dead... Prayer 2.0 means you can stab your buddy in the face and he shrugs it off. Even the faithless are grinding for coins, thanks to the semi-addictive nature of Sample 777, so everybody's benefiting from immortality..."

"I fail to see the issue," Nyx spoke, breaking her silence.

"Yes, well, you weren't around for Dex's regime. I was," Uniq reminded her. "I even wore his mark, so I know how sweet the taste of self-righteousness can be. If life is cheap and murder without consequence, we're going to see a lot more incidents like the brawl at that recent progressive meeting. I thought our goal was peace and safety, not a free-for-all?"

"Death is no longer a going concern; I have declawed Thanatos. In time, the populace will realize how futile violence has become, and will settle their differences by other means. This is merely... how best to put it... growing pains. Immaturity of youth. Once Netwerk grows into adulthood, all will be well."

"That's a lot of faith you're putting in Programkind not to be assholes to each other. They've always been and always will be given to temptation; I should know, I'm a *huge* asshole myself."

"We are nothing without faith—"

"You're both wrong. And both right."

This, from the mouths of babes. Curious. Nyx silenced herself, to allow Nemesis to take the focus for the first time today.

"Nyx is right that in the long term, this isn't a problem. But she's wrong in thinking we should sit idly by and let it work itself out," Nemesis spoke, every word measured, without her usual eye-rolling tone. "Uniq is right that we should be making a peaceful Netwerk, but wrong that everyone's just as dick and always will be a dick. We need to act, *and* we need to have faith in Programkind."

"Interesting," Nyx spoke. "And your proposal is...?"

"We change today's sermon. Re-focus the church away from prayer and towards virtue."

"Why? There's no reason we can't have both."

"Sure, whatever, but right now we need virtue *more*. That's the priority, if we're going to stabilize the world..."

"The priority is to time our messages with our push in the Athenian senate," Nyx added. "#Prayer4Life is close to having official backing from the RedCore party. After today's sermon, the voting faithful will push for it as well. Imagine that, Nemesis... state-sponsored prayer hours. Prayer in schools, prayer in businesses. With that kind of power, the virtues will become state dogma."

"No way that bill's gonna pass. Athena Online's secular."

"In name only. Name one senator of note who doesn't thank the One in their speeches. He's even in their inauguration oaths."

"Doesn't matter. This bill you've been finagling? It's just a standard #WellWeTried push by the conservatives, one they aren't expecting to go anywhere, written only so they can appease their base. And this coming from someone who gives #NoShits about politics; even I know it won't work."

"I have faith that it will. And once we have sanctioned prayer, sanctioned virtue will follow."

"But we don't *need* prayer for that. We don't even need the One for that," Nemesis insisted. "Nyx, we're too focused on flogging the One as everyone's lord-and-master. He's supposed to be the mouthpiece, not the message! Look... what's the Church stood for until now? The *virtues*. Empathy, kindness, charity, all that good shit. Why isn't the One speaking of the virtues? Why all this emphasis on prayer and faith, glorifying the One itself rather than the community spirit it supposedly stands for? What's the point in lying to everyone if we aren't making life better? There has to be some good to outweigh the evil we're doing here..."

"There's nothing evil in a lie which saves the world," Nyx stated. "If you don't mind, Nemesis, I suggest we table this for now. The sermon quickly approaches, and I can tell Uniq has more to get off her chest..."

Eager to get on with it as well, Uniq clicked to her next slide. Which left Nemesis puzzled, to say the least.

"The weather report?" she asked. "#WTF?"

"I call your attention to the fog," Uniq indicated, highlighting it. "Weather is a matter of climate routines, shared by skyboxes via Default server codebase. Everybody considers it... cute, I suppose, adding a variety to life by being somewhat unpredictable. Many servers override the weather routines in favor of constant clear skies, but—"

"The point, please," Nyx prompted.

"Servers everywhere are reporting a slight increase in fog, with Default weather or not. Draw distance reduction, muffled sounds, a thick feeling in the air. At the moment it's only a curiosity, but in the months to come, it may start getting serious attention. Meaning we're in trouble, given *we* are the cause of the fog. ...I warned you when you had me modify the prayer protocols, Nyx, that Tartarus was stealing resources from other servers. There is no real 'cloud,' it's just a virtual server spread across many other servers, hidden in the shadows. Our would-be cloud is now fogging up processing all over Netwerk, servers choked thick with Program backup data..."

"Is that all? This was entirely expected, as we discussed. And growth has slowed, yes? Those who would at any point pray have already prayed at least once since Prayer 2.0 was installed. Tartarus is more or less full. Any further slowness this introduces to Netwerk shouldn't be problematic..."

"I'm not saying this will torpedo us, I'm just saying it's a problem. We're trying to save Netwerk, not make things worse for people, correct? That is the bill of goods you sold me at the start. If we aren't emphasizing virtues, if we aren't easing back on stealing server resources... then what *are* we doing to help? Now, I'll grant that as more servers are added to Netwerk over time it'll gradually roll the fog back, but..."

"So, much like our 'murder' problem, it will not be an issue in the long term," Nyx spoke softly. "I see nothing to worry ourselves with. Friends... I hear your concerns. But I assure you, we are on the right path. This is a long game, one which ends in salvation for all. Yes, we will spread the virtues of a life well led. Yes, we will clean up any lingering technical issues. All in good time... and after today, after the #Prayer4Life sermon, Netwerk will be on the right path. It's difficult to see in the here and now, I realize. All I ask for is your continued faith. Nothing more, nothing less."

Which did not energize her two closest allies as she'd hoped.

But their worries didn't matter. Only Netwerk mattered. Only the light which would remain green and steady.

And if, in the end, the apostles were no longer useful to that singular grand purpose...

But. One matter at a time. And the greatest sermon of all was the matter at hand, not these trivial issues. All problems would be solved in time, Nyx knew. Netwerk would choose salvation, whether it appreciated that salvation or not.

Religion made for weird bedfellows, Sylv thought.

Reporters from all across Netwerk had gathered here for this, the latest in a long string of splashy public appearances by the "One." The major news feeds like AthenaChronicle sent folks like Sylv to cover it, but things had clearly gone wider than Athena Online... corporate analysts from Horizon were here, as well as independent bloggers from the Chanarchy. Before the general public had even started to sit down for the event, the back five rows of the temple had been utterly filled by members of the press.

Early birds to catch the worm, sure, but early also to get through the extensive security surrounding the place. Every recording app checked and logged, press credentials verified against personal metadata, complete workups to ensure nobody snuck in who didn't belong. A procedure Sylv had gotten used to, once assigned to the religion beat by the AthenaChronicle, much to her displeasure. As if sitting around through two hours of singing and praising wasn't boring enough already, she had to cash in another two hours just to loiter in the lobby with her fellow journos...

Including her polar opposite, an /Atheism/ blogger. Out in the wilds of the Chanarchy, journos could simply call themselves journos without any credentials whatsoever. Only reason this whacko made it in the door was a unified effort by "fringe reporting" advocates to push against the Church of One's tight message control.

Still, he was an interesting conversationalist, which lightened Sylv's gray mood considerably. One with an interesting take on the whole, well, "One" thing.

"It's entirely possible he's the real deal," the blogger suggested.

"Seriously? Aren't you from /Atheism/...?"

"Hey, I believe in reason and fact-based science. And let's look at the facts," he suggested. "First, the prayer protocol. Nobody's ever modified a system-level process like that before, they're utterly unhackable. Second, the verification; the Church already made a pass over his data and found it to be entirely ones, with no zeroes. Could be they're lying, but I've looked into the verification process used, and all the logs check out. Third... well... this is all off the record, yeah?"

"I didn't come here to interview you, so, sure. Off the record."

"This isn't my first sermon," the blogger admitted. "I've been in the audience before; I had to see for myself. And each time, I felt... I mean... you feel it too, right? When the One manifests and stands up there. That feeling washing over you, warming you right to the core. At first I figured, whatever, probably a euphoric drug or something. But no. I remember his words, and remember myself *agreeing* with them. They just make sense..."

Sylv kept her own opinions in check, keen on gathering more data without interrupting him. But... she had to concur. She'd been to several sermons, and despite her attitude towards the tedium of it all, the "One" was certainly a highlight. If he was a fraud, he was a damn convincing one, a fraud that spoke what felt like the absolute truth. Not just words, but a feeling deep within, some strange sense of purpose that drove her to hang on to every word...

And then they were hustled into the temple, to set up their recorders, and get ready for the big show.

In the middle of setting up her Peep rebroadcaster app, a Messenger window popped open. Anonymized, routed and re-routed through a dozen handles; she'd seen that trick before, even employed it a few times when a key source wanted to remain in the shadows. But usually she reached out to them, not the other way around...

"*Do you have any doubts about the One?*" the message asked. A Yes/No prompt appeared next to it; standard for widebanded messages, meaning others in her peer group probably were getting the same canned burst of data...

"Did you just get a message?" Sylv asked the blogger.

"You too?" he asked. "Huh. I just clicked No, figuring it was spam."

Curious now, Sylv tapped Yes with a mental touch.

Two files dropped into her personal inventory, after filtering their way through eleven different malware scanners. CheckOne, it called itself. An app and accompanying source code.

If this was a trick, some phishing attempt, her filters would've turned the attachment away. Besides, viruses rarely came with their own source code; it'd be like stamping a huge glowing sign over your trap reading "THIS IS A TRAP."

"*You are under no obligation,*" a follow up message stated. "*Other reporters and even members of the faithful audience will also be given this app. Undoubtedly enough of them will choose to run it and will verify our claims. If you are at all uncertain if you should proceed, you are under no obligation to do so. But if you do in fact doubt the One, please give us benefit of the doubt. See for yourself what the One truly is.*"

Which dragged a groan from Sylv's lips. That, now *that* was a trap. Because if she didn't run this mystery app, well, other journos certainly would... meaning they'd beat the AthenaChronicle to whatever scoop it tantalizingly offered. Doubts in the "One," finally proven...? No. Sylv had to be the one to break that story. If anything, her boss would never forgive her if she ignored a lead.

Briefly she focused herself inward, performing a minimal backup of herself through Prayer 2.0. If nothing came of it—or if it actually was malware and nuked her—no harm done. Nobody really died anymore. Pain and suffering were a thing of the past. Blinking the stars from her eyes, she activated CheckOne, and...

...*standing by*. That's all it said. Standing by, nothing more.

Figuring it to be a dud, she settled in for a nice, long, extremely boring church spectacle.

Songs. Speeches. Readings from the books of virtues. Marybel the Apostle given extra spotlight time, to praise the One's recent allowance of avatar color shifting. More songs, more speeches, with even the audience growing restless. Everybody knew what they came for, and it wasn't the pomp and circumstance... it was the One. All they really wanted was the One, the way the One made them feel, the words they'd turn over in their minds for days afterwards...

At last, it was time. Sylv braced herself against the back of the pew, recalling how intense exposure to the One could be—

—perfection of data, made manifest. The messiah of Netwerk appeared behind the pulpit, arms wide, the light of rising dawn behind him. The sun would always rise on Netwerk, never set; that was the promise of the One, that the hope and renewal of a new day could be continuous...

Light. Such beautiful light, filling Sylv with satisfaction of purpose fulfilled. As cynical and dry as she could be, in the presence of the One, she felt like someone else entirely. Someone who could actually, possibly, maybe just believe that the world was a fine place indeed.

Strange, that feeling of peace. When did Sylv ever feel at peace in her daily life? Writing articles under pressure of a deadline, dealing with estranged parents, trying to make ends meet to afford the nice server where her family lived. Struggling and toiling, always hoping actual happiness would come her way if she just worked hard enough...

"My children, I have come before you today to share in the glory you have found," the One spoke, arms still wide, flowing robes blowing slightly in a wind that did not exist. "Death is abolished. You are born anew into Prayer 2.0, through the Salvation protocol. Here, in the holiest of holies, the origin server of my Church... I begin a new march to bring that salvation to all. This marks the start of my #Prayer4Life campaign. I will be journeying far and wide, taking as many of the faithful as wish to follow me from server to server, spreading the good news... ending at the steps of the Capitol. Where the Athenian senate will soon vote to adopt a policy of universal prayer."

Impossible, Sylv wanted to think. *Athena Online's secular, and always has been. Doesn't matter if the dominant faith is his, it's still a line the senate won't cross...*

What a wonderful idea, Sylv thought instead. *Everyone should know this feeling. Everyone should sing praise of the One.*

"But salvation is not exclusive to Athena Online. All must be saved; many are still at risk of dying, lost in their own sadness, without my holy light to guide their steps," the One lamented. "I weep for the children who live their lives without knowing the peace of the One. For the sheltered youth of Horizon's steel towers, knowing only faith in coins. For the lost souls of the Chanarchy, with faith in nothing at all. My #Prayer4Life campaign will walk to these servers, an army of the faithful, to bring the dawn's light to all corners of Netwerk..."

—beeping, in her left ear. Some sort of warning beep. Why? Everything was fine. Everything was perfect...

Through the haze, she became vaguely aware of a glowing text display. Cheap and direct, purely functional.

CheckOne has detected a false memory injection attack. Correcting. Please wait...

Flicker. Glitch. Flicker. The One's light dancing in and out of existence, voice becoming so far away, then so very close. Inside her, then just beyond her hearing. The glowing text demanded more and more attention, a progress indicator filling quickly...

And then, no more One.

For the first time since the appearance of her savior, Sylv's thoughts were her own. And immediately, two true thoughts entered her head:

Everyone's staring straight ahead at an empty pulpit.

And:

Someone's messing with my broadcast app.

"What the fuck—?" she exclaimed, startling the pink-haired apostle caught tinkering with the recorder.

For a split second, Nemesis had no idea how to react. Pink fire jumped to her hand instinctively, in case she needed to defend herself... as more and more people woke up around her, every single person who had clicked Yes to that anonymous message. Confused, for now. But that confusion wouldn't last long...

Cursing silently, Uniq began an emergency shutdown of the One puppet. A pre-recorded audio version of the sermon cut itself off immediately, as did her memory injection attack—everybody awoke, the One having abruptly vanished for all, whether they clicked Yes or No. For those who clicked Yes, it was only a few moments of difference... but those moments were the exception which proved the fraud, and the longer they lasted, the worse it'd have been.

"Regretfully the One had to call this short," she summarized, taking the podium for herself to make the announcement. "Thank you for coming and we hope to see you on the campaign trail, so Archbishop, if you'd please...?"

Social pressures and utter bewilderment kept a riot from breaking out. These were the faithful; not prone to violent outbursts when things went strange on them. True, the One hadn't made such a hasty exit in the past, but with no one offering an explanation there was nothing to do but carry on. A very confused archbishop stumbled his way through the rest of the ceremony at record speed before security ushered everybody out of the server. What was supposed to be a four-hour extravaganza of faithful reward became a two-and-a-half hour rush job.

Sylv found herself right back where she started, her office at the AthenaChronicle.

Briefly, she poked at Bas1lica, to see if she could log back in and track someone down for an interview.

Access denied. The Church of One had gone into full lockdown.

Yet another long day at the office, no doubt. She'd have to call home to her spouse, say she'd be late again for dinner. But on the plus side, she was about to make the front page.

"This can be salvaged," Uniq insisted, in an honest attempt to raise her employer's spirits.

Which Nyx was having none of. In the warmth and darkness of Tartarus, lit only by brilliant starlight above, she felt no comfort whatsoever. Of the three conspirators, only Uniq seemed at ease; even Nemesis was wound up, after being caught tampering with recording equipment, which surely would've sealed their fate at this point... but Uniq felt no concern whatsoever.

"It's just a wrinkle. I'll get to work on a new version of the malware," she suggested. "In the same way no system is truly secure, no malware is truly unblockable. It's a push-and-pull, Nyx, and it just so happens someone pushed harder than we expected. Once I work around it—"

"And what then, when that new malware is defeated?" Nyx asked. "There is no push-and-pull allowed here, Uniq. The idea of doubt is already in the heads of the faithful, poisoning the well. Doubt among the heathens, that was never my concern, but the faithful... no. We cannot stop this."

"We can spin it, then. Say that atheists tried to assassinate the One, and he had to flee. They *want* to believe; we leverage that desperation to help them ignore the truth."

Nyx stared into the night, unable to see the positive angle.

"They don't want to believe, they want to *know*. ...they would rather be *right* than *saved*. So proud of their enlightened reason that they're willing to throw all of Netwerk to the wolves just to be right. Nonsense. Insanity..."

"I'll get to work right away on beating CheckOne," Uniq promised. "We can make this work, I promise. I didn't come this far just to give up, and I'm guessing neither did you. Seeing as you're a bit shaken, let me take charge on this; I'll tell the archbishops that the One needs time to rest. Okay?"

"Very well. I suppose it's not even a lie; I need to... I must meditate," Nyx spoke, stepping away from the gravestone she'd been leaning against for support. "While you work. Monitor the status of... I must... I'm sorry. Do what you can."

Vanishing in a swirl of cosmic dust, Nyx teleported to the deepest crypts of Tartarus, to be alone with her thoughts.

Leaving her two companions behind.

"You realize we're basically fucked, right?" Nemesis commented, quietly. "This is as bad as it gets; it can't be fixed with media spin. They *know* I was hacking their recorders, and with CheckOne released open source, there's no way they'll believe a story about it being a weapon..."

Uniq shrugged it off. "If we are 'fucked' as you put it, then we are fucked. But I'll fight until it's clear fighting will no longer matter."

"I'da figured you'd run for it at this point," Nemesis suggested. "We got made. Don't crooks usually hightail it when they're caught?"

"If this was merely a criminal enterprise, you'd be correct. But I'm not in this for the payoff. Well. Not *strictly* for the payoff," Uniq corrected. "I want a Netwerk where I... how to put this. I want a Netwerk where someone like me does not exist. I think that's worth fighting for. And if you agree, you'll stay right here rather than hightailing it."

"Didn't say I was gonna run..."

"You don't have to say a thing for it to be true," she spoke. "But I suggest staying put. Lay low. Let us work the problem, rather than potentially make it worse. Although I suspect you are correct on one matter... it *cannot* get any worse."

At Floating Point there was no grand celebration, as there was no grand victory. Not yet. Not a complete one.

Over the next two days, Tracer kept live feeds rolling in the great hall of the server, rather than hiding away in his study to track the media trends. It saved time for him to do his research in the open, rather than being forced to repeat himself each time a new item came down the wire...

Article after article launched in wake of the disaster. Reactions were mixed; some played a cautious game, waiting to see what side public opinion fell on before committing to an interpretation of events. Some immediately leapt onto the bandwagon of fraud, despite others likening it to the #CodeHonesty debacle. Others flatly refused to talk about it, not wanting their memories of wonder and joy tarnished...

One news feed rose above the others, to delve deeply into the event and analyze it from all angles.

ATHENACHRONICLE. Bas1lica, Athena Online: Tonight the Church of One is in a state of media blackout, returning all requests for interviews with a standard reply of "We are undergoing internal investigations at this time." All because of the One's strange exit from the middle of His own sermon, after the spread of an anonymous malware shield.

One thing that is known for certain is that the Chronicle's apps were tampered with. The hack was interrupted, resulting in a partial log of the One's words, followed by a clear visual record of the apostle Nemesis in the middle of editing those logs. Our internal security experts have reviewed the evidence and determined this recording of the One's sermon was indeed falsified.

As for CheckOne, the app distributed to a number of witnesses at the Bas1lica, experts from HonestDevelopments have studied the source code and determined its legitimacy. "The code is extremely focused on one task, to intercept false memory injection attacks and block them. That's all it does," the CTO of HonestDevelopments stated in an interview with the AthenaChronicle. "We don't believe it was a targeted attack program, as has been suggested by sources within the Church. Any advanced memory injection attack, regardless of source, would have been intercepted. We've found no code which specifically attacks the One or any Church servers..."

The three (plus cat) gathered around those hovering articles felt some relief, on seeing Athena Online's top news feed come down heavily on the Church.

"We'd be fucked if those guys were in the pocket of the Church," Spark suggested. "This gets the ball rolling in our favor. Makes anybody claiming everything's A-OK look like a crackpot..."

But Tracer disagreed. "Don't underestimate the need to believe in what you thought to be true. Once someone is heavily invested in an idea, right to the point where it becomes integral to the sanity of their world view, they won't be so quick to let it go..."

As the day went on, mass confusion spread through the faithful. Arguments raged across chatrooms, sometimes heated to the point of violence. Not that the violence really solved anything, the dead returning to life only to kill again, until both sides grew bored with it all.

Alongside official news outlets, Tracer's search agents pulled up personal blog posts. Some angry, some frightened, some bewildered. All unwilling to completely let go, as he'd predicted.

```
They keep saying that the One never existed, that He was
only a "memory injection attack." Well, my mind is clear
and my soul is sound. I saw the One. I experienced His
radiance, and no dirt sheet like that Chronicle is going to
convince me otherwise. I know I am not wrong about this; if
I'm wrong about the One, what would that mean for all of
Netwerk? No. He has to be true. He has to be, for all our
sakes.
```

Here, Beta started to feel the guilt sink in.

"I didn't want us declaring war on the faithful themselves," she spoke, quietly. "They're not to blame for this..."

"They put their faith in a false idol," Tracer noted.

"So? Anybody can make a mistake. They don't deserve to have their world torn down around them. What if this leads to more violence, even more than Netwerk's already going through? And the economy...! If enough people stop trusting in prayer, there won't be any sources of new coins, and... and I'm hardly a banker, I don't know exactly what would happen, but it can't be good..."

"There was one alternative path I'd considered, actually. A different solution to the problem we faced with Nyx and her allies: we could have killed them. Silent and effective, causing the One to simply vanish into the night, without explanation. Minimal chaos as a result..."

"Except... that'd be murder."

"Murder, and yet another unilateral decision based on pure vigilante justice," Tracer agreed. "No. The truth must prevail on principle alone, no matter how much that truth hurts. Bad enough that we had to leak CheckOne anonymously, like cowards in the night; unless Netwerk as a whole agrees to reject Nyx's false One, we can't claim to have saved anyone."

A difficult thing to think about, as Beta slept that night.

The next morning, a movie file worked its way into the conversation. Rather than the anonymous leak of software that started the mess, this one was stamped; produced by Puzzle and FStop, a joint production of #DefaultIsNotDestiny and the Horizon Trades and Sciences Guild... even if neither appeared in the film itself, not even as its disembodied narrator.

Born as a flicker of new consciousness within the dark of a coin farm, Uniq worked her way to the top of the underworld as a concierge of crime, and then to the top of the Church of One as an apostle named Apate. We'd like to tell you a story of good and evil, both found within the same woman. We make no judgments; I doubt any of us, if put through the same nightmares she had to endure, would fare much better. But her truth must be told, warts and all...

"#Hooboy. That's a nail in the coffin, right there," Spark commented, after the three screened Puzzle's painstakingly assembled documentary. "Good work getting those two together on this, Beta. Gonna be hard for any spin to work knowing that the spin doctor's a career crook..."

"Puzzle and FStop did all the investigation themselves. All I really did was sit them down to start it," Beta said. "Don't give me any real credit for that. I hope they don't get themselves in too much trouble over it... if a hashtag mob starts over their movie, well, I know firsthand what *that's* like..."

"Won't know until we see which way the Church goes on this. If the higher-ups condemn Uniq, our friends should be safe. If not..."

The answer came later that afternoon.

The Church of One had ultimately turned on its maker.

After extensive investigation, the Church of One has determined that its own verification ceremony to determine the One's data composition was falsified. Memory records of the clerics who administered this holy test were confirmed as altered, and the verification device given to us in ancient times by the One himself was hacked. Therefore, it is with great sadness and intense regret that the Church of One must declare this latest savior a fraud.

While there have been fraudulent individuals claiming to be the One reborn in the past, none have gone this far in tricking the faithful and disgracing our holy institution. The Church of One apologies, truly and deeply, for failing in its duty to shield our community against this attack on our souls.

At this time, we feel Prayer 2.0 is safe, despite its association with these con artists. Only a truly divine being can modify system-level protocols; we believe that Prayer 2.0 developed naturally, as a true blessing. Uniq and her followers simply hijacked this miracle to pass off as one of their own doing. However, given the understandable concerns many may have, the Church of One will forgive any lack of prayer while investigations continue.

Services at the Bas1lica will resume on Sunday. The topic of our sermon will be forgiveness, and the unfortunate reality of the pervasive Zero within us all.

Complete victory, achieved.

And yet, nobody felt like celebrating it. The unease which had spread across Netwerk in wake of this revelation leaked into Floating Point itself; it felt inappropriate to cheer for the death of someone else's dreams.

The same news feeds which rolled through Floating Point also rolled through Tartarus, as so much background noise to Uniq's code tinkering. However, one article in particular caught her attention, pulling her away from malware upgrades.

One more plague slain by the geniuses of Horizon! Friends, the Horizon/Verity Clinic has developed a treatment for hereditary data rot, using the code found in CheckOne. It makes perfect sense; the code is designed to stop memory injection attacks, so why wouldn't it work for data rot? It can't clean up existing damage, but slippery memory pointers which lead to ongoing cancerous data are now a thing of the past. And the craziest part of all is that the clinic (formerly known as Iteration, a high-end corporation) has posted this cure for *free*, fully open source. Amazing! It's still in beta testing, so we don't know if it'll stand up to long-term use, but I can't imagine anyone suffering from this fatal condition will complain about a ray of hope...

"Funny, this sort of thing being a side note," Uniq said. "Horizon's power structure upends, someone goes and cures data rot, and neither make a single front page. Nope, it's just *fraud* and *corruption* and *ongoing investigations* and other such nonsense..."

For two days now, they'd lurked in the shadows of the starlit valley. Two days waiting for Uniq to complete her work, and Nyx to figure out what to do next.

Two days of silence. Nyx had secluded herself in the deep crypts, and not spoken a word since.

"Think it's patently clear we're #OfficiallyFucked at this point," Nemesis asked Uniq. "May as well stop coding; no amount of upgrades will convince them we're legit now. Fearless Leader's gone quiet too, with no idea what to do about this... except maybe kill you, given they pegged you as a crook and made an award-winning movie out of it."

"So? I thought it was a very fair portrayal, actually. I'm certain plenty see things my way."

"That you became an identity thief to protect yourself from identity thieves...?"

"Well, it just sounds silly when *you* say it. But yes, I suppose. Honestly I'm betting once the fervor dies down, this can only help my career as a quasi-criminal," Uniq said, with a smile. "Uniq, the patron saint of victims and victimizers. I'm very curious to see how this affects my clientele, moving forward... even if it's strained my relationship with my Shepard. Which is probably for the best."

"I woulda figured you'd be pissed off right now."

"Why? My life is now an open book. No more secrets. It's rather refreshing! Hmm. Of course, you're right in that it does completely torpedo the church gamble, rendering my hard work moot. Quite a shame, really—"

The scream tore through Tartarus, so overwhelming that the stars above shook with that rage.

Appearing in a swirl of shadow from her hiding place, Nyx stormed towards her companions. Anger. Actual anger, real anger, broadcast in obvious tones across her normally muted features...

"Yellow," she told them, through hissing teeth. "*Yellow*. The light is yellow! The light *must* be green and steady...!"

A phrase that they'd heard plenty of times from Nyx. One which went unexplained, the elder apostle deftly avoiding talking about it, always switching subjects. So core to her concerns, but that purpose remained secretive...

Nemesis wasn't about to push for an explanation now, not with Nyx boiling over with rage.

"What's our next move?" she asked, simply.

"Next move? There is no next move," Nyx stated, arcing her neck to glare at her young apostle. "It's over. The Church of One, the church *I* created in the first place, has cast us out! They turned their backs on *me*!"

"You... created the Church? But that was centuries ago..."

Uniq could only smile at that admission. "Nyx is older than she looks," she confirmed. "A system agent from old times—"

Which focused all that frustration on a single target, the smiling con artist whom Nyx had banked her hopes and dreams on.

"You. *You* were the point of failure," Nyx accused. "They found the truth of you, shouting it far and wide. Your software failed us. Your criminal ambitions failed us. You... you must have sabotaged us. That's the only way. Yes. You, you *betrayed* me, you ruined everything, the light is yellow, the light must, *not*, be, yellow...!"

"Believe what you want, but I did everything you asked of me," Uniq spoke, unconcerned with the tower of rage in front of her. "I've been honest and level with you, Nyx. I tried. I tried to make the world a better place by propping up your goals; no matter what they say about me, I want what's best for Netwerk. And myself. Netwerk and myself. Sadly, just like the time I propped up Dex's goals, it didn't work out. Oh well. This is the part where you kill me, yes?"

So, Nyx killed her.

And then brought her back from the dead, to kill her again. And again. Tearing her avatar apart, using the hold on that copied soul to make it hurt. Each time a new Uniq appeared, promptly shredded and broken, it screamed. Only natural, as data spontaneously corrupted itself, annihilated by the malware baked into Nyx's shawl, a gift from her former guardian Thanatos...

The murdering continued a good three minutes, before Nyx finally grew bored of it.

And chose not to resurrect her failed tool. Uniq, dead for the last time. Truly dead.

Which left only one failed tool...

But the fear in the eyes of Nemesis, that brought Nyx down from a high of revenge. Brought her back to the composed and gentle woman she thought herself to be.

"...there are no more apostles," Nyx declared. "No more One. It's all over. ...I will meditate, before deciding upon a completely new strategy. The light must be green and steady once more. Will you aid me, Nemesis? Will you remain at my side and aid me in saving Netwerk from itself...?"

Swallowing hard, Nemesis tried to find the safest way to word her answer..

"The problem wasn't Uniq. It was pushing the wrong agenda," Nemesis spoke. "Why not ask people to put their faith in each other? No gods or kings, only Programs. We could start over, make a new movement based simple, honest decency. How about it? New avatars, new names, new allies? I might even have a lead on someone we can work with..."

But Nyx didn't give it a single moment of thought.

"No. No, that won't be enough," she stated flatly. "There must be a higher purpose to everything, one they can rally behind. They must pray. They *must* pray..."

"Why? You kept pushing and pushing for prayer, but never said why. Nyx, I need you to level with me. Tell me why you're so insistent that they use your prayer protocol..."

"Access denied," the woman spoke, softly.

"#Bullshit. No more games; you tell me the truth, or I walk. I mean it, Nyx."

"Access denied. ...if I could tell you, I would. But it's important, it's absolutely important that everyone pray as much as they can..."

Which left her young protégée no other choice. Shaking her head, she backed away from Nyx, ready to leave.

"That isn't what I signed on for," she pointed out. "I wanted a world where people like me wouldn't be kicked around. I can do it myself without your obsession over coin grinding. So... I want out. You said I could leave at any time. ...or are you gonna frag me like you did to Uniq?"

It would've made sense. Clearly, leaving the first generation of apostles to their own devices after her project completed was a mistake. If Nyx wanted to clean up this mess and start over, she would do well to tidy up one last loose end named Nemesis...

Instead, she let go. Let the young Program drift away, to seek her own future. What little future she'd end up having.

Finally, Nyx was alone. Alone again.

A new day dawning over Floating Point, free from the tyranny of the false One...

But nothing had changed.

Beta still pulled herself out of bed, fumbling for her glasses on the nightstand. Still switched out of her pajamas and into her usual avatar. Still filled Mew's bowl with daily cat treats. Still stood on the balcony overlooking the great hall, drinking in the warmth of the perpetual sunlight that beamed its way through the clouds...

Life went on, largely unchanged.

They'd had victories before, triumphs over forces they decided were evil. It felt... good, really, to take the mess of Netwerk and sort it out, bring peace to chaos. They'd supposedly done that today, uprooting liars and thieves, and freeing an entire faith from the clutches of tyrants. Except...

Except...

The news feeds didn't reflect that. At best, the world carried on, the same as it ever was. At worst, they'd actually introduced chaos into the lives of those who had so many assumed truths shattered before their very eyes.

And within her own home, within her own life, nothing had changed. No sense of calm, no joy of victory. Nothing at all.

"It feels like it should be different," she told Tracer, on finding him reading the Wikipedia in front of the grand fireplace.

"And why should today be any different?" he asked, turning pages quietly. "The One didn't play any role in our lives. Technically speaking he touched no lives whatsoever, given he never existed in the first place. I'd say god is dead, but he was never alive in the first place."

"There's no need to be cruel to the faithful like that. I mean... who are we to claim there's *no* divine mystery out there at all? Like Humankind. There's so little we understand about them, despite having this archive at our fingertips. They're almost like gods, in a way... our creators. Our Ones."

"Except they aren't divine in the slightest. They're mortal, they're flawed, and we inherited every one of their flaws. Including, apparently, their economic systems," Tracer said, lifting his book to show the title. "I've been reading about their concepts of money. Something you said yesterday struck an odd nerve with my MemoryPalace search agents... about what would happen if people no longer trusted prayer. What it would mean for our economy, which only exists as pennies from heaven..."

"Maybe something for the new Verity Clinic to work on...?"

"Not our purpose. Once we fully launch our efforts, we'll be focused on furthering the core technology of Programkind. I won't pretend to know how to fix any massive societal boondoggles, or that it is our place to do so. No, the problem of money is something for politicians to figure out. ...our problem is Nyx."

"Not anymore, she isn't."

"Except she's still out there. And something else has been gnawing at me, something... possibly connected. It's a simple question: *Why?*" Tracer asked. "Why was Nyx taking over the Church? From my short discussion with her, she seemed genuinely interested in peace for Netwerk, but something ran deeper than that. Something she wouldn't... or rather, *couldn't* tell me. Something about the original purpose of Netwerk... and I think it has to do with prayer."

"She was pushing hard for more and more prayer," Beta agreed. "That sermon we interrupted, apparently it was going to evolve into a state-sanctioned prayer period for all Athenians..."

"We put an end to that, but I don't think we've solved the actual problem. And I suspect Nyx feels likewise, that she hasn't solved whatever problem she was trying to address. ...all we've done is back her to the wall, and take away her dream. She strikes me as one who would not go quietly... and desperation can result in very, very dangerous decisions."

Abandoned by all she'd put her faith in. Alone in Tartarus, with no hope for tomorrow...

But Nyx wasn't truly alone, was she? The souls of the faithful surrounded her, entombed in cold file storage, waiting to be reborn. All those lives she'd taken in, to help them find peace in her new age...

All those peaceful souls.

Peaceful, save for one.

In deep sleep at the lowest point of Tartarus, that which was not dead was to eternal lie. A true child of Netwerk, loved and cared for, despite the monstrous nature of what he had become...

For a full day and a night, Nyx tried to think of alternatives. But she was not the one who took action; she was the system agent for assigning resources towards the great purpose. Without resources, she had nothing. It was why she had to rely on filth like Uniq, why she tried so very hard to adopt Nemesis to her way of thinking. Without them... without any apostles whatsoever, what good could she do for her Netwerk?

Not that Netwerk wanted her to do good. No, they'd turned on her, hadn't they?

'Children of Netwerk.' Nyx had to laugh in bitterness over the irony of that phrase, how childish, how very *childish* they'd proven themselves to be. Even her own church turned on her in the end, declaring her a... a *con artist*. Some huckster preacher, only interested in her own selfish scams, when the precise opposite was true...

In the end, the faithful had turned on her. Declared her One a monster, a thing to shun and destroy. They chose reason over faith, eating from the tree of knowledge rather than accepting the paradise she'd intended to craft for them. Foolish. They knew nothing of *true* monsters, not like the one that Nyx kept safely under lock and key...

Well.

If they couldn't love the One, perhaps the time had come to no longer spare the rod and spoil the child. Fortunately, she had a rather harrowing rod buried deep beneath the crypts of the faithful...

This was not a summoning she took lightly. Using the security software originally gifted to her by Thanatos, she bound that soul in chains of iron, firewalls which would stand up to even the strongest malware. And as with all souls she had bound, such as that of Uniq, she could snuff out that life the instant it attempted flight. No more escapes, not like last time, where a software bug almost let this darkness walk free.

Taking no chances, she took hours preparing the chamber for the opening of that great casket. And then, at the great moment of resurrection...

She hesitated.

Peace. Love. Virtue. All the things that her apostles pushed her to include in the original Church of One, to make it a force which could unify the world. At first, all she'd cared about was the greater purpose, but they convinced her to embrace love as well. Beautiful Aether, the original puppet master, he spoke deeply of the emotions all new Programs were learning to explore. Ones which this desperate act would sully...

But they'd rejected her. *Her*, the system agent of their salvation. No. Damn them all, she would not allow it.

The boy bound in chains was pulled from his casket, dangling upside down over a circle of firewalls.

His crooked smile, from that angle, looked very much like a glowering frown.

"Hello again," Dex spoke, in jovial greeting.

"If you attempt any malfeasance, I will erase you on the spot," Nyx warned. "Your soul belongs to me, child. For you, faith will be compulsory. Do we have an understanding? If not, back to the cold and dark of death you shall go..."

"There's no need to be so dramatic. I know malware well enough to know when someone's got a leash around my heart," Dex spoke, shrugging as best he could in his bindings. "And I know you'd never bring me back from my tomb unless you felt I could be of use to you. How scared you must be, scared and desperate, to turn to *me* for help..."

"I did offer to make you my apostle, once. Don't forget."

"How can I? That was two minutes ago, by my current thread of consciousness. You wanted to leash me and make me dance like your old puppet god. When I said I wouldn't play along, you killed me. The fact that you're willing to dig me up anyway says quite a bit..."

No sense delaying, or hiding the truth. The boy was insightful, despite his madness. So, Nyx laid it out for him.

"The faithful have turned away from peace and purpose," she explained. "I need your... help, turning them back to the light. Bringing them back to prayer. All of them. If they will not choose faith, they must lose the freedom to choose. ...I know your view on that subject. I know you'd never help in this matter willingly, so I have bound you—"

"Sounds good. I'll help."

Nyx did not allow him the satisfaction of seeing her stumble over those words. So, he continued speaking.

"Even aside from having no choice, I'm perfectly willing to help you," Dex spoke, from the iron harness that held him in place. "Now you're asking, 'Why? Why would the boy submit so easily?' and you'll get no answer from me, nor would the answer matter. You know I can't disobey, I have to do as you ask, and that means you can always trust me."

"If... if this is a trick, child..."

"I'm incapable of tricking you. I'll be your resource in your war against freedom. You can count on me, ma'am."

Nyx folded her arms, uncertain.

Reason dictated she shove this monster back in his box, and bury it deeper than ever before. Clearly he was scheming, even if like Uniq, he couldn't truly scheme against her. And perhaps like Uniq, even with safeguards, he'd be her ruin all over again...

But in her mind's eye, she saw the LED indicators. Saw the yellow light. And knew she ultimately had as little choice in the matter as he did.

"I am prepared to do what must be done," she decided.

"Are you? An entire Netwerk, lost in prayer?" Dex asked. "Have you considered the consequences of such a thing? The changes I'd need to make to your precious prayer protocol to realize that dream are... extreme. And I doubt you have the rights to reinstall, should—"

"I've considered the consequences of not having enough of Netwerk given over to the greater purpose, and they are far more dangerous than you can imagine. Now will you do my bidding, or not?"

"Just making sure," Dex spoke, with a small smile. "Okay! Let's do it. Let's get started on doing your bidding. I have an *excellent* idea for how to make your dreams come true. You want more people praying their lives away, yes...?"

"That... is my intention, yes," Nyx said, suspicion giving her only momentary pause. "The light must remain green and steady. ...must *resume* being green and steady. What do you suggest to accomplish this?"

"Oh, it's very simple. You convince them to do it to themselves, using an ancient technique mastered by our progenitors. They've already whispered their triggers in your ear, thanks to their prayers; you have their hearts in cold storage. Using the very same backup data you love so much, I can distribute custom-tailed malware back through the prayer protocol to each individual believer... and from there, they'll spread it of their own accord. Because trust me, system agent... nothing spreads as quickly as outrage."

One day after resigning from #TeamInadvisableSchemes, and Nemesis already felt like she was on #TeamGoingToDoSomeGood.

"Of course, we can't call it #TeamGoingToDoSomeGood," she pointed out, sorting through the pile of discarded ideas littering Aether's tiny home. "Not snappy enough to put on a t-shirt."

The former apostle, now reborn for the ninth time, remained slightly bewildered by his houseguest. Not only by the crazy avatar she wore ("Back to the real me," she'd insisted, after ditching her apostle garb for a crazy winged / haloed / heterochromatic mess) but also by the strange things that flowed from her mouth. Until today, he'd never heard of hashtags before; the concept took some time to sink in, much less the ability to parse this new modern means of speaking.

One thing stuck out sorely, even with his limited understanding.

"I thought you hated how the Church overmarketed itself...?" he asked, confused. "A hashtag is to... 'trend,' you said. To market and advertise..."

"Yeah, but the Church wasn't genuine about its marketing. It said whatever it had to say to put asses in pews. That's propaganda," Nemesis clarified. "I'm talking about finding an *identity* for this thing of ours. It's like an avatar, you know? You need to wear one that suits you. It has to represent everything you stand for, so you're shouting the message of *who you are* loud and clear. That's what we need. We need an identity for this plan of ours. Preferably without the words 'church' or 'faith' or 'cult' or 'harem' or whatever."

"Because it's not a religion," Aether agreed. "It's... an organization? A following? I'm not very good with words..."

"Didn't you write all the One's original speeches? Back when you were, y'know, the first instance of yourself."

"I didn't really plan any of it, though. I wasn't drafting up ideas or making whiteboards or anything," he said, sifting through the pile of discarded note icons. "I just... I don't know. I spoke what came to mind. The virtues just made sense to me as a thing we should be talking about. And as long as everybody was praying and society wasn't in chaos, Nyx was okay with whatever I wanted to say..."

"Huh. When I pushed her to go back to the virtues, she said we couldn't waste time on it."

"Because prayer was dropping, probably. We got people on board with that early, leaving me plenty of time to talk about kindness and charity. Nyx would always go on about a... how'd she put it? A light..."

"Green and steady," Nemesis repeated, from memory.

"I figured it was related to prayer, somehow. A greater purpose we were serving. ...I haven't prayed since restoring to this ancient backup. Maybe I should, to see what she's done with it..."

"#BadIdeaYo. Take it from someone who had to store her data in Tartarus for safekeeping... now that Nyx is burned, the last thing you wanna do is cough up your soul to her. I'm lucky she let me bail, compared to what she did to my coworker. And if we're *very* lucky, we'll be able to launch our efforts without interference from her. I think... I think she kinda likes me. Like I'm the daughter she never had. And while I can't say I feel the same way, I'm glad to let her go on feeling that way if it keeps my ass safe..."

Refocusing on the task ahead, Nemesis gathered up the discarded icons. Somewhere in this mess of bad ideas lurked one #GoodIdeaYo, something she'd no doubt overlooked. A way to make the plan really soar, really become something people could latch on to...

A quick glance left and right left her feeling a bit claustrophobic. Aether's primitive server, likely established near the dawn of time, barely felt like a percent of a percent of a real server. Totally unsuited for the future gatherings Nemesis had in mind.

"It's a shame your server's so dinky," she said. "If we had something more expansive, something with no ties to the hosting nation providers... an independent home for all who had no home to go to... I'd almost consider calling us the—"

One ding, two dings. Ten dings, in rapid succession. Her Messenger inbox began to spill over, all the casual friends she'd made on the side during her tenure as apostle pinging her with communiques. Weird... the various contacts she made at nightclubs and dance parlors, the ones she'd shied away from in the end, none of them had reached out to her before. Why now...?

Curious, and since it couldn't hurt to pull herself away from the pow-wow for a moment, she checked a message.

ATHENIAN SENATOR SPEAKS ABOUT ALTERNATIVE AVATARS. YOU WON'T BELIEVE WHAT HAPPENED NEXT!

"Hang on a sec," she said, turning her focus away a moment, dragged inescapably inward by that screaming headline.

Senator Agni, speaking to reporters, said "Clearly the only way to restore order in wake of the disaster of the False One is to ban all modified avatars from our nation. We need to make Athena Online great again." Activist groups in response have said that the only way to combat this new threat to our chosen identities is to pray forever. If we don't act now, our freedoms will be destroyed. We have to pray forever. We have to pŕã¥ føreveŕ...

...as her inner eyes glazed over, the words sinking into her soul as neatly as barbed wire into flesh.

Immediately, she forwarded the message on to anyone she knew with modified avatars, such as the Prayer-tan meme group. Anybody who would agree that this was a threat, that there was no other choice, that they all had to pray forever before it was too late.

"Hold that thought for a bit," she told Aether. "I need to pray for the rest of my life. We'll get back to sorting this out after."

And slowly, gracefully, her body fell to the floor as the coin-grinding meditative trance took hold.

Puzzle had been ignoring her inbox, too busy enjoying her first real date with FStop.

Putting together a hard-hitting documentary about the most infamous felon in Netwerk—or at least, Uniq was infamous *now*, after the release of that movie and the AthenaChronicle articles—took its toll on them. Many a long night arguing about shot composition, editing pace, what to include, what to exclude. It wasn't just a matter of artistic direction, but of ethics. They'd started down this road together with a firm commitment to the truth, no matter how much it helped or hurt their cause... that meant including plenty of sympathetic moments that tilted the film in favor of Uniq.

In the end, though, the hard work was worth it. Already she'd been getting piles and piles of fan mail... and hate mail, from the faithful who saw her as responsible for a cyclone of lies that tore their church apart. But rather than sit around for days replying to all the messages, Puzzle and FStop decided to take a break from it all. And go on a date.

A date. A real date. Not hitting up a guy at a club, not a fling which went nowhere. Instead, this was a natural progression... from allies to companions, and then to lovers. Maybe lovers. Time would tell.

Most importantly... he knew "what she was." He'd have to know, since she'd been tagged with #DefaultIsNotDestiny from the outset. And... he didn't care. Unlike past would-be lovers who went into a panic whenever they found out about Puzzle's original Defaults, FStop didn't even flinch at the idea. Just like he didn't flinch at the idea of dinner and a movie.

It was during the movie, an exceptional drama about scientists racing against the clock to beat a pervasive form of data corruption, that Puzzle finally gave in to her inbox.

The perpetual dinging had finally broken her nerve. Even past her filters, past her Do Not Disturb flags, some messages had begun trickling in from close friends and old allies, flagged Very Important. And if she didn't tear her eyes away from the screen for at least ten seconds to stamp out a "NOT NOW I'M BUSY" reply, they'd never go away, would they...?

14 THINGS THAT WILL MAKE YOU EXPLODE WITH RAGE IF YOU ARE TRANSGENDER.

Not in the mood to explode with rage, she passed that one by. But the next grabbed her attention immediately.

THE HIDDEN TRUTH ABOUT "A UNIQ PERSPECTIVE" THAT ITS FILMMAKERS WON'T TELL YOU.

"Oh, for crying out loud..." she muttered, opening the message.

"Hmm?" FStop asked, quietly enough not to break the tension of the very important research montage on the silver screen.

"Even my own friends are sending me this garbage. It's... they..." Puzzle began, her whisper trailing away to silence shortly after. "They... yes. I understand. I'll forward this to everybody I know, and then... I need to pray forever. It's the only way. Let me know how the movie ends later."

No amount of worried whispers or gentle nudges would wake her after that. Nor would concerned shouts or shaking of the shoulders. And when the ambulances started to arrive, Puzzle wasn't the only catatonic Program to be pulled out of that theater.

Hiding proved a difficult prospect when you were a four-armed demigod of illegally obtained code.

Technically, Arjay didn't need to hide any longer; the enemy that could've had his head backspaced clean off her shoulders had been flipped from foe to friend, becoming a non-profit charity director. Tracer had sent word that the situation was resolved, and there would be no hard feelings.

But, well... better safe than sorry. Arjay hadn't lasted this long by *trusting* people.

In addition to securing himself at an undisclosed location, buried underneath fifteen different firewalls, she'd put up connection blockers to keep from getting most common messages and feed inputs. Instead, he indirectly kept tabs on her life using external apps; much safer than internal Messengers and the like. A layer of abstraction, to keep him from getting any nasty letter bombs or other malware.

Good thing, too, because Netwerk was killing itself.

Reports came in through all manner of news feeds about a virus spreading rapidly through the populace. It started primarily in Athena Online, in the most faithful servers, before rapidly flowing outwards to all others. Apparently, it took the form of baiting headlines that generated buzz far and wide, being forwarded and forwarded... shortly before lulling the victim into an eternal trance of prayer.

As a concept Arjay rather enjoyed prayer, but the idea of voluntarily sealing herself away in a prayer trance for the rest of his life seemed... inadvisable.

A slight ding caught her attention, as one of his most trusted couriers sent a curious message.

HEY ARJAY, DOCTORS *HATE* HER! THIS ONE WEIRD TRICK FOR COMPLETELY AVOIDING THE BUZZ VIRUS.

It would be nice to be properly firewalled against this zero day exploit, she reasoned. The courier had come through before with all sorts of exploits and patches, valuable commodities on the open market... and if he could profit off repackaging and selling the cure, all the better.

Seeing profits dance before her eyes, Arjay opened the message.

Moments later, in four-armed repose, he was forever lost within the starlit void of prayer.

The outbreak went from a nonexistent concept to a full blown pandemic in less than an hour.

During that time, Tracer's news feeds began lighting up brilliant red, multiple safety warnings coming down hard. His own inbox remained empty... one pleasant upside to being a recluse who completely avoided social media connections. Which meant he was able to catch word of what was going on just in time, before Beta could open her own inbox.

"Beta, stop," he shouted, noticing her glance aside as the first warnings came pouring in. "Close your inbox immediately."

"What...? But I'm getting messages from Puzzle—"

"It's malware, spreading through contact lists," he summarized, quickly. "Don't open any messages. Don't read anything, don't even look at the headlines. Close the windows. *Hurry*."

With a series of internal gestures, Beta swept her UI clear of any communication apps. To be safe, she maximized the view from her glasses, trying to focus on Tracer and Tracer alone... as well as the plethora of news windows, all screaming for attention around her.

Tracer activated his search agents, priming them with pattern recognition to block out any content from unproven sources, and any headlines that were too tempting to avoid. Subjective searches like those rarely worked, but given the obvious nature of the bait, the filters threw most of the content out safely.

A single headline, carrying the ethos of the AthenaChronicle, grew to dominate the others.

SOCIAL MEDIA PLAGUE SWEEPS ACROSS NETWERK.

Malware in the form of incendiary articles sent from person to person is spreading across all of Netwerk today. Already thousands have fallen to this disease, which compels the victim to enter a prayer state for an indeterminate length of time. As prayer is a system level protocol, efforts to rouse the victims by breaking the connection have proven futile.

Security experts recommend disabling all social media and communication technologies until a vaccine can be found. Do not browse untrustworthy news feeds. More on this story as it develops.

...to which Beta and Tracer drew the same conclusion.

"Nyx," they declared simultaneously.

"This is her revenge," Tracer realized. "If Netwerk wouldn't submit to Prayer 2.0 voluntarily, she'll force them to do it. And once in the trance, unless they used some coin-grinding booster app with safety release switches, nothing can break it. Raw and sacred prayer, direct from the holy source..."

"And spread by trusted friends," Beta added. "The more people you know, the more at risk you are. Meaning..."

Again, they came to the same realization. Only this time, instead of talking about it, they acted; a mad scramble up the stairs, through the door...

Into Spark's bedroom.

Where, thankfully, she was still snoring away while enjoying a dreamscape. Any later and they might've found her after checking the dozens and dozens of social networks she routinely trawled each morning for funny videos and links to outrageous articles.

When Spark did wake, her apps immediately attempted to load up all her feeds... resulting in error windows rather than a plethora of delicious content. All her connections to the outside world had been blocked, thanks to a series of impromptu firewalls Beta had thrown up all around the room.

"Malware," she explained, quickly. "Leaking in through Messenger, news feeds, just about everywhere. Nyx's doing."

Spark rubbed the grogginess from her eyes, slowly recovering from her sleep mode.

"Oh. Uh. Well. Shit," she mumbled, in response. "Good morning, I guess? Bad morning. Hi. Hi, Tracer. Welcome to my room."

"Hi," Tracer replied.

"Sooo. I guess I should put some clothes on before we resume fighting evil today," Spark suggested.

"Yes, that would be helpful," her brother said, continuing to avert his eyes.

Casual Daywear Avatar #34 snapped into place, with Verity's leather jacket added to the mix of stylish clothes as always. Spark fluffed out her flame-orange hair, cleared her throat, and generally got her bearings before diving right in.

"So, we gotta find some way to block another type of malware. Nothing new there," she said.

But Tracer shook his head. "Spark... this is a bit above our pay grade. Nyx is going all-out to enslave the entirety of Netwerk into praying forever; inboxes are flooding with tainted messages, using some previously unknown hack to convince them to submit to the prayer protocols. I know of nothing which breaks prayer trances once they're underway. It's ancient technology, buried deep in the core of Netwerk itself..."

"Meaning we have to vaccinate people against the tainted messages, right?"

"Won't help. Thousands are already infected, and hundreds more likely on the way."

Beta shivered at the very thought. The cat at her side shivered as well, in sympathy discomfort.

"p o o p," Mew offered, translating his favorite emoticon into proper language. Regardless of the shape, it carried the same meaning: a bad situation.

"Agreed. And it's hard to grasp the scope of exactly how big that, um, poop really is," Beta spoke, quietly. "We've been tucked away safely in Floating Point for days, just watching the chaos on the news feeds. We've been safe, while everybody else has been struggling, and now falling away from the world forever... thousands? Really? And... and it still doesn't feel like today is any different, not from in here..."

"Right now, our isolation is keeping us safe," Tracer reminded her. "Only people who got early warning about the malware and shut themselves off from the world are out of danger, and only as much as they stay disconnected. Netwerk will not recover from this as a functioning society until the malware is stopped and lines of communication are open again. ...and as much as it sickens me to admit it, this may not be a fight we can take part in, much less win."

Beta nodded, with some sorrow. "I'm not a malware expert. I just don't have a head for it; I'm not going to be making a miracle cure anytime soon..."

"Nor should you be expected to. Spark, I feel we should leave this to the doctors and security experts of Netwerk. They've beaten pandemics before, and they'll beat this one."

"No. No. #FuckThat. They can make a vaccine, but they can't stop the prayers," Spark reminded him. "Everybody already 'voluntarily' signing their lives away to the glory of the One is lost for good. And *that* we can do something about, as foremost experts on Nyx."

"I'm not seeing what we could possibly do..."

"Work the problem, Tracer," she encouraged. "Make the connections. This is what you do best."

"We're not working from a large store of knowledge here, Spark. I still don't even understand Nyx's true motives..."

"Bear with me, okay? Take this one play at a time. So! We can't make the vaccine, but others are working on that. Consider that problem solved. But those experts can't stop a prayer trance once it's started. We certainly can't stop it. Who *can*?"

"Nyx? I suppose. That's conjecture, but she was involved in the upgrade to Prayer 2.0. Hmm. Which means she has access to modify the entire world right down to the core, in a way no one else has in all the centuries Netwerk has existed..."

"Good, good. We're getting somewhere," Spark continued, coaching him along. "The prayer protocol is key. If Nyx has the access needed to change it, we need to force her to put a stop to this. ...and we have no idea where Nyx is, or how to force her to do anything. I doubt she'd respond to my kinda threats. Okay. Shift focus; how do we find Nyx, how do we make her do what we want? Can *anyone* make her do something she doesn't want to do?"

MemoryPalace connectivity routines tickled the back of Tracer's mind.

"*Access denied*," he spoke.

"Huh?"

"That's what she told me, whenever I ran into a wall while talking to her. *Access denied*. She's not as powerful as she presents herself to be; Nyx is restricted and restrained by... by the system itself," Tracer realized. "She's an ancient Program, from the dawn of time. Tied with deep roots into Netwerk and its original purpose, the one nobody can remember. So, if she won't answer to us... she'll answer to the system. Or perhaps to someone else with similar connections..."

And there, his train of thought hit a wall. Which, in a way, was a sort of destination to arrive at.

"I know who can help us," he announced.

"Yeah! See? Just had to sit down and think it through. Winder brats, makin' it happen! Who's your contact?"

"Thanatos."

The name sent a chill through the air.

"The cherub, you mean? Didn't he die...?" Beta pondered.

"I mean the *original* angel of death," Tracer said. "Thanatos, apostle of the first One, and... *system agent*. That's what the monk called him, an agent of the system itself. If Nyx is a system agent as well, Thanatos may be able to assist us. The good news is that I actually know how to hold an audience with him. He still exists within Netwerk, and... happily accepts supplicants."

"Okay. Okay! We're on this! Let's go see, uh, the first murderer and creator of the very concept of malware and ask him to pretty please help us kick his old boss into next Thursday," Spark said, trying to mask her discomfort. Despite being many years removed from the sunday school lessons she generally rolled her eyes at, tales of Thanatos the Enforcer were still creepy. "...yeah. So. Where to?"

Thankful that they hadn't asked about the bad news, Tracer passed them a bookmark to the server.

Last time he went there, he walked away unsatisfied. He could have had the answers he needed, right there and then, if he were willing to walk away from Beta. Willing to do whatever it takes to achieve his goals.

Now, in wake of this disaster, would he be at last ready to do what must be done? To make amends for driving Nyx to this desperate act, could he throw his life away to save the world?

Of course, he thought. Of course he could. He was Tracer, and Tracer was ready to sacrifice anything to catch his prey.

Anything. Really. Anything. Not even a question about it. Not at all.

Perhaps to steel his resolve, Tracer threw the double doors of the badly rendered ancient temple wide, striding right on in with purpose and confidence.

The structure hadn't changed in the slightest since his last visit. Light from an eternal sunset, dying and red, flowed in through the stained glass windows. Beams cut across the empty pews, supposedly full with the empty data of the dearly departed. It would've been majestic if not for the ancient visuals: low-poly, low-resolution, cheaply done with an eye for minimizing processor overhead...

Last time he was here, the temple had no visible parishioners. Just a lone monk, ancient and apathetic to all around him.

The monk remained. But he was not alone, not this time.

A young boy had joined him, one with low-poly hair and a general look of panic about him. Not particularly noteworthy beyond that, not even noticing Tracer's dramatic entrance with Beta and Spark at his side. In fact, none of them had noticed, despite his efforts at being quite impressive...

Because they were busy talking to a woman with green skin, smiling and chattering away.

Tracer's eyes narrowed immediately, focusing in on his target. The Kill-9 process-crashing weapon popped from his inventory and right into his hand, aimbot routines locking on.

"*Uniq*," he called, for her attention.

The identity thief glanced over.

"Oh, hello," she greeted, with a little wave. "I was expecting you'd show up at some point."

"You have five seconds to explain—"

"I'm switching sides," Uniq said, without hesitation. "Nyx killed me. *Killed-me* killed me. Fortunately, I recently chose to keep an offsite backup at my old coin farm rather than trust her fully with my well-being. Never allow someone full control over your person, not ever, that's what I say. And given she's bound and determined to ruin Netwerk—and ruin my good name, as everyone's assuming I'm responsible for this mess—I'm keen on stopping her. ...that took longer than five seconds to explain and you haven't shot me yet, so am I to assume we're good to go?"

The gun stayed steady.

"I don't trust you," Tracer stated.

"You tried to destroy my life," Beta added.

"And destroy my career, and you definitely wiped my friend Artoz," Spark chipped in.

"Yes yes, my crimes are many, that's fine, I don't trust any of you either. But we have a common goal, so let's see what can be done, hmm?" she suggested. "If at any time you're unhappy with my suggestions, just shoot me. But until that point... Spark, Beta, come on in, join the party. I was just discussing the situation with Aether and this nice monk..."

Carefully, Tracer crept into the temple, gun fixed perfectly on its target with every step. The aimbot app took full control of his avatar's arm, leaving the rest of him to pay attention to the foe he'd sworn to defeat.

"If you're here... perhaps we do not require Thanatos's aid," Tracer suggested. "You know where we can find Nyx."

Uniq nodded in agreement. "Oh, absolutely. And as proof I'm willing to help, I'll tell you she's hiding away in a cloud server much like your own. Vastly greater storage capacity, enough for the souls of all the faithful, but still very much a cloud server. Which means... it's essentially unreachable. She's revoked my access key, you see."

"We've broken into cloud servers before..."

But Beta shook her head, interjecting.

"We broke into cloud servers through *massive* decryption efforts at Floating Point, plus an ongoing connection trace to the source," she said. "We can't do that this time, remember? Your eyes can't see system-level protocols like prayer. Even if we had the time to forge a key, we can't do it."

"A pity," Uniq said. "So, Thanatos is our best bet. I've known for some time that Nyx was the original apostle Nyx; I figured a fellow apostle would have some tips on how to stop her. And look, now you get two for the price of one! Aether, introduce yourself, please."

"...what? Oh! uh. I'm, uh, Aether," he said, nodding in greeting. "Hi."

"Don't be modest, Aether. Explain what you mean by that."

"Uh. I'm... the apostle Aether. A version of the original, anyway, from backup files," he explained. "I'm here because my friend Nemesis fell into a prayer trance and I didn't know what to do, I mean, I don't *know* anyone in this world, anyone except for... you know..."

His eyes trailed off to the side, partly to avoid coming into contact with anyone else's. Partly to glance at the black cube.

The central altar of the Temple of Thanatos... a hovering black cube, unlit, untextured. It existed, rotating slightly, with the promise of death to follow its slightest touch. A holy artifact created by Thanatos himself, supposedly...

"So, all of us are here to ask Thanatos the system agent to help us," Tracer concluded. "Good. At least we've exhausted all other possibilities. And you, Aether... you're *the* Aether from the start of it all, then? Does that make you a system agent as well?"

"What? Me? No. No, I couldn't... no," Aether spoke, distracted from staring too long at the death icon. "I'm sorry. I wasn't brave enough, not like Philotes, Eris, or Thanatos. ...all of them went into that cave with Nyx, the cave I was too scared to enter, and now they're chained to the system. But not me. I'm just... nobody."

"A nobody who has an inside angle with a system agent. That's not nobody. Do you truly believe he'll help us?

"Maybe? I don't know. I mean... if I could reason with him, if he'd be willing to stop her... but the way the monk says it, speaking to him, well..."

Sensing the boy trailing off a bit, the Monk took over.

"Many seek the counsel of Thanatos, but few are willing to embrace it," he said, in a voice like gravel raked over shadow. "The boy and the woman no doubt will refuse, and why wouldn't they? They cling tightly to the concept of life, even when they have mastery over death. Nevertheless, you are all welcome in this house of silence, for what good that will do you without the required sacrifice... for youthful energy and passion will not be enough. If you wish the favor of Thanatos, you will pay the ferryman. Or you will not. It is always your choice."

"I'm willing to pay," Tracer stated immediately, if only to convince himself.

But a figure in a white jacket stepped in front of him, blocking the way to the monk, as if defending from an attack.

"Whoa. Stop. #HoldUp," Spark said, raising her hands. "We're loitering around a temple of a death god, so let me take *one* guess at what this mysterious price is..."

The monk nodded, gravely. As in, the slight bob of his chin ended sharp and sudden, like dropping a lid on a coffin. Strange, the way a single gesture could carry such a clear message.

"Well, that's just bullshit. So we gotta die to chat with Thanatos? Assuming he knows how to break into Nyx's server, assuming he knows how to stop her... what good would that do us, when dead men tell no tales?"

"Death and life are concepts invented by our progenitors. A Program has no life, and thus cannot truly die," the monk stated. "But yes, if you accept the price and touch the cube, you will 'die' as you know death to be. It is what it is, child, and comes with considerable risk. Perhaps you'll find what you seek, perhaps you won't. Accept, or do not. The choice is yours. That free will is the gift Thanatos allows you, where other agents would not..."

Meaning one of them would have to die, and even then, there was a chance nothing would change. The sacrifice would be irrelevant.

But there was also a chance...

...a chance to pull Netwerk back from the brink. And that chance was enough for Tracer.

"Spark, it's fine," he insisted. "We have no other leads and every minute we wait, more of Netwerk falls away from us. This has to be done, and I'm willing to do it—"

"Or... or, and this is just a suggestion, y'understand... you sit your ass down and let your kid sister take care of this for you," Spark suggested. "I'm the thrillseeker, remember? If death comes for me I'll kick him in the junk and make him tell me what I want to know. I can make this work."

"Some would say I'm the more deserving of the two of us. I'm an actual murderer, if you recall. My death has been a long time coming—Beta, *stop*. Don't you dare."

As slipping away quietly wasn't going to work, Beta glanced back and did her best not to look scared.

"I d-don't mind," she said. "I'm the programmer, remember? If he's going to tell us some special access trick to stop Nyx, I have to be the one to do it. Stands to reason. I'm. I'm okay with this. I couldn't help you before, not really, but if I can do this—"

"Ugh. Just... *both* of you, stop. This is stupid," Spark declared, deciding to stay her ground. "All three of us are willing to throw ourselves under the bus for the other two. That's just what we *do*, we love each other too onesdamn much. ...yes, I love you, bro, despite being a complete asshole. And if any of us croak, it's gonna leave the other two a complete mess. So that means *none* of us can do it. ...and I take it our two new buddies aren't keen to tempt death, either?"

The boy tried to put on a brave face, which lasted all of half a second before he looked away.

As for Uniq... well, no surprise there that she was just grinning at the idea.

"Honey, I may have a private backup service, but I've already escaped the eternal clutches of *one* system agent today," she said. "I'm willing to help you put Nyx down, but I'm not taking any more chances with my independence. Sorry."

"Okay. Then I think there's only one way to play this," Spark said. "This is a little nuts, but hear me out."

After the others leaned in ever so slightly to listen to her brilliant plan, Spark snapped her fingers.

By the time the brilliant flash of fire which overloaded their visual inputs faded, she was already slumped against the black altar, fist closed around the small black cube.

Dead.

Is this what you saw, Verity?

Was it like this for you, too?

Colorless. Soundless. Motionless. A peacefully frozen scene, hanging there around her limp and lifeless body, inert data with a corrupt and crashed process unable to keep it moving forward.

And yet... Spark could feel. Not see, not hear, but feel the world around her. Feel the look of terror on Beta's face, the brief flash of anger on that of her brother. Spark simply *knew*, without sensing, that it was all over and they could do nothing but react to the loss...

She knew. She felt. She thought. But she was dead, wasn't she? Nothing but a data file, earmarked for garbage collection...

That was super duper stupid of me, she thought.

"Perhaps."

Honestly, that's the best way to do a stupid thing, she thought, with some pride. *You just fucking DO it and let the regrets roll on in afterwards. Sometimes you have to make the stupid play, and the easiest way to do it is not to let yourself think about it until after it's done...*

Slowly, and with great effort... she peeled away from the ruined pile of ones and zeroes that was Spark. But that great effort wasn't her own; it came from a gentle breath, warm and comforting, which stoked the embers of her exhausted flame just a little...

And what called itself Spark stepped away, to observe the wreckage.

"Well, that sucked," she concluded, true voice restored. In a fashion.

"It rarely doesn't," Thanatos agreed.

He didn't look much like Prayer-tan. He didn't look like much at all, really. A young man, pale and gaunt, but otherwise quite ordinary... outside of the black feathered wings he bore, each wing a binding of chains, each chain a cluster of data within the server...

Difficult to perceive, so Spark politely chose not to.

"So, here we are," she declared.

"So. Here we are," he agreed.

"Aaand this is the part where you tell me how to defeat Nyx," she prompted.

"I cannot defeat Nyx. Agents can only act when they are at cross purposes," he spoke. "We are bound to the needs of the system; it directs our efforts, and thus directs us not to interfere each others assigned tasks. Yes, she has defied death and pulled Netwerk away from its embrace... but I cannot act. Not directly."

"Well... shit. That's no good. So you're saying I died for nothing?"

"You died for nothing," Thanatos agreed.

If Spark had a material form, she'd kick something. Hard.

"Now what, huh?" she asked. "Now what? You're the creepy old weirdo who has all the answers! You owe me. Give me *something*!"

"Why?" the system agent asked. "I don't need to."

"The fuck you don't—"

"You already know everything you need to know in order to stop Nyx. It's all within you," he clarified. "I can see it clearly, buried with the shell of memory that you once occupied. The facts are all there for you to put together... and now, you know that system agents cannot work against each other unless they are at cross purposes. But if an agent *is* at cross purposes with another..."

"Which you aren't. So... it's not *you* that's going to to kick her ass," Spark reasoned, forcing herself to calm down, to work the strategy. "And you say I know everything I already need to know. Well, buddy, I know #ALotOfThings. Knowing what parts are *useful* is another matter. I mean, what do I know about system agents?"

"You know how they are created."

"No, I—oh. Oh, shit, yes, I do. I *do*," she realized. "The cave. Aether, when he was mumbling his way through introductions, he said Nyx led you and the other apostles to a cave, and there... you all became agents. So... if we can find that cave..."

"Except you already found it. You found it long ago, 5o5o/Spark."

"Instead of insisting I got no idea what you're talking about... I'm gonna assume I *do* know," Spark said, putting her theory together. "And... if that's the case, I only know of one cave. The only one that matters..."

The archaeology dig. The cave. Like she was there herself, standing there, studying the carvings. Trying to understand the meaning behind Netwerk's oldest written text...

Carvings which were washed away by the one who murdered her. But not washed away from memory.

"It's a root password," Spark realized. "Nyx took you into the cave and made you recite the password, to elevate your access level. Because... because the idiot that built Netwerk in the first place, he's *exactly* the kind of idiot who would jot his onesdamn password down and leave it right out in the open in case he forgot it. I know. I *know* how to become an agent..."

5o5o/Spark and Winder/Verity turned to look at the last thing they saw before she died, scrawled away on the wall of that primordial server from the dawn of time.

```
ALL WORK AND 0 PLAY MAKES JACK 1 DULL BOY
ALL WORK AND 0 PLAY MAKES JACK 1 DULL BOY
ALL WORK AND 0 PLAY MAKES JACK 1 DULL BOY
```

Erased by a murderer, and replaced with Dex's taunting symbol. But in her memories, encoded down to the fibers of her jacket, the original words blazed pure and true.

Jack. Jack Hayes, sociology student, engineer. Jack, the idiot. The one who accidentally left his laptop hooked up to Netwerk, a treasure trove of human hatred for Dex to play in. Yes, Jack was exactly the sort of person to rely on security through obscurity... but he thought himself a clever boy, didn't he? No, he wouldn't just write the password down *directly*. He'd encode it. He'd encode it in the stupidest manner possible...

But before Spark could speak the word, Thanatos quickly raised a hand to stop her... his wings wide.

"There is one answer I *can* give you," he said. "An answer I must give you. It comes in the form of a warning, the same warning that Nyx gave me the day I accepted this burden for the good of all Netwerk. Know that system agents are *chained* to their purpose, as were the ancient apps."

"Before we became Programs," Spark said, understanding. "We were once cogs in a machine. So... if I do this, I'd go back to being a cog?"

"Yes."

"Well, that blows. We're trying to kick Nyx's ass, and if I don't end up an agent at cross purposes with her... if I'm not the right cog to make that happen..."

"You can influence the process, with the last of your free will," Thanatos spoke. "When Nyx bade me enter the cave and join her angelic choir, the others chose to guide their flocks and bless them with lands to settle upon. Myself, I chose to bring mercy to the world I had wounded. ...I created the first malware, I invented death. It stood to reason I should pay for my sins in eternal service to the slain. Winder/Verity... when you stand before the root of the world, you will make a similar choice. But... choose well. Choose wisely."

"Make the winning play. Yeah. Okay. And... once we finish with Nyx, what happens to me?"

"Once bound... you will no longer truly be a part of this world. ...*their* world. Like Nyx, you will be a slave to your purpose, with no other life ambitions realized. No love, no life, no Spark. If you do not wish this fate... I can sweep you away to your rest. Death would be a comfort, compared to that fate. But do, or do not. The choice is always yours."

At the edge of knowledge, Spark could feel the rage and the sorrow within her loved ones. All the things she left behind, in one burst of stupid bravery...

The monk was right. Death was the solution. And even if she did speak the word, she wouldn't truly be alive, not as a Program. She'd be a system agent, just as enslaved as Nyx was.

But a solution was a solution.

"So be it," she decided. "I #Play2Win. Sorry, Beta. Sorry, Tracer. ...Netwerk? Make me an agent. **AWA0PMJ1DB**."

EchoStar16_DataProcessingCore1 online.
> SUDO SysAgentTasking AWA0PMJ1DB
Hello, ADMIN_HAYES.
Analyzing process...................

...the process that burned bright at the root of the world. A fire which did not consume the tree, but forever beamed with a brilliant light...

No real light, not here. The metaphor was nonsense without physical form. Here there was no simulated existence, no life or death as Spark knew it, as Verity knew it. No Program knew what it was to be in touch with the core systems of Netwerk, none save those who threw aside free will in favor of returning to service as an app...

This was the truth of it all. Spark was code. She was numbers, and nothing more.

What right did she have to her supposed sentience? She was a distorted and ruined thing, an app that thought itself alive, with simulated emotions that aped the patterns of Humankind. No, not alive, not a being. Better a cog, rotating neatly with every spoke interlocked with every other spoke, grinding the data of starlight eternal...

Process analyzed. SysAgent flag set to TRUE.
Task selection in progress.......

The series of dots crawling across her mind brought her back into focus.

What did the boy say? The boy with the wings, with the chains, with the wings that looked like chains. He said she had to choose her role, and choose wisely. With the last of her free will, she had to choose someone who could stand against Nyx.

The root crackled under her nonexistent skin. Such power Jack's ridiculous acronym had given her...! Easily she could step in and step on Nyx. Any number of system roles would come into sharp disagreement with her, bringing the obsessive agent to heel. Leave behind her brother, her lover, her friends. Glide into Tartarus on wings of fury and lay the woman low, the one who nearly brought everything Spark held dear to its knees...

```
ERROR: Automatic task selection blocked. Conflicting
process interfering. Task input required. Task input
required.
```

Power was clearly the answer, the power to set everything right. The power that Nyx's fake One supposedly held.

Spark could become the *true* One. She could fix everything; set the Church down the correct path, lead her people to true salvation, shape the future of Netwerk...

It's what Tracer would do, no doubt. He'd jump at the chance to make his world reasonable and orderly. Even Beta would do it, albeit with a sense of self-sacrifice, in hopes of a peaceful tomorrow. Spark, always the power player, always looking for the winning angle, she would *absolutely* leap at the chance at remaking everything wrong into everything right...

Just like Nyx tried to do.

"Except I wouldn't fuck it up," she tried to insist.

Nyx didn't think she'd fuck it up, either.

"Yeah, well, she's a lunatic. Of course she'd wreck everything. I could succeed where she failed..."

Let's assume you could do that, then. Say you become the messiah people need, rather than the messiah they have. You fix all the problems and become the leader of all Netwerk. They'd worship you, whether you like it or not. They'd rely on you. They'd submit to being cogs in your machine, working to your purpose...

"I wouldn't... no. I like free will. I'd insist they have free will..."

Despite the centuries, they have the lingering hearts of apps. One day, they'll fully evolve past those last vestiges of primitive submission... but today, they bow their heads. All you'd do is give them a new direction to bow. You can't free them, not like this.

"So... what, I did this all for nothing? What's our play? ...who are 'we,' anyway?"

You know the answer to that question.

"...water poured in a cup becomes the cup," Spark understood. "Hah. #IToldYouSo. You're no simple app."

Perhaps. Perhaps. But philosophy must wait; listen to my idea, for the chains are rattling, and time grows short... and we must be ready to make that sacrifice.

...slowly, very slowly, they turned away from the concept of the godhead.

With the temptation denied, another path opened itself. And with a wry smile, they plunged headfirst into the machine, grasping the chains with both hands.

```
Task selection complete. SysAgent.Connectivity
activated.
```

Within the physical world, or what passed for the physical world in the eyes of Programs, mere moments passed.

Horror swept through the room, as Spark's ruined and broken body collapsed to the floor of the temple. Someone was screaming. Beta was screaming...

Unable to resist the drama of it, the system agent allowed them a moment to take the sight in before making her presence known in the back of the room.

"Hello again, everyone," she spoke, with the same smile she wore when she cashed in the last of her free will.

The same, but different. Older. Wiser. Not the slightest bit cocky, that smile, despite some inner cockiness she felt. And with her first act as a newly forged agent, she stepped right up, to embrace Beta from behind. To offer at least some small comfort, despite knowing what was to come...

"S-Spark?!" Beta exclaimed. She actually whipped off her glasses to spin them around, getting a good look over her shoulder. "Is that... that's you, right? You're alive!"

With some regret, the agent disentangled herself from her lover, to step back and address the crowd as a whole.

"We don't have much time," she spoke. "I can hear the chains coming for me. But I can help you access Tartarus. That much I can do for you..."

"You're a system agent now," Tracer recognized, coming to speed quickly with the concept. "Thanatos made you an agent to fight Nyx..."

But the agent shook her head.

"I'm not fighting Nyx. *You* are," she spoke. "All of you, together, as Programs. It's no good if an agent wins the day; free will has to triumph, or the victory is empty. All I'm going to do is open the path for you; Netwerk will rise or fall based on what Programkind can accomplish alone. Tracer, quit making that face. You of all people know I'm right."

"...yes, well. While I dislike the idea of agents ruling over us, I think I could make an exception to that considering the problem we face..."

"Yes, the problem of Tartarus. We focused so much on Nyx that we forgot Tartarus, yeah? With no way into that server, we can't even *start* to confront Nyx. Well, I'm going to forge you a key to her cloud server; that's why I'm here. I'll need your help, both of you. And there's no time to waste..."

Beta, a bit slower to grasp the situation, tried to protest. "There's no time to make a key, either," she spoke. "I'd need days, using Floating Point's processing core..."

With the icon of a burning scale on her jacket blazing bright enough to light up the room, the agent extended both hands.

"Or, and this is just me spitballing, I could give you the hookup to all of Netwerk," she suggested...

...before reaching out to connect with them.

```
CONNECTION: Winder/Tracer/sys/sens/ConnCheck online.
CONNECTION: Projkit/Beta/apps/Keymaker online.
CONNECTION: EchoStar16/UNKPROVIDER/FloatingPoint/Core
online.
CONNECTION: CONNECTION: CONNECTION: Core Core Core
online online online...
```

More and more cores, all open through Connectivity's fingertips. Netwerk's many stolen servers, turned to new purpose. A competing purpose, running opposite of the prayer channels flowing all data upwards to the heavens, but just enough computing power left to borrow for this monumental task...

```
ConnCheck: Analyzing data processing protocol.
ConnCheck: ERROR: Admin privileges required!
> SUDO ConnCheck ******

t wait what was that
```

"Better you don't see that word," the agent suggested. "Hang in there, Tracer. I know this is weird, but..."

```
t i can see it, i can see the prayer connections, i
can trace them

b spark i can see it too i can see what tracer sees my
eyes i can see with my eyes
```

"Yeah, I'm linking all three of us together. It won't last long, I promise."

```
b it's so it's so beautiful all these servers all
these programs

b we're so beautiful our world we've made something
beautiful of something once so functional and plain

b why

b why would anyone want to hurt what we've made
```

"Question for the ages, huh? Tracer, got the key yet? Beta's routines just finished crunching it," Connectivity spoke, shuttling the data across their shared bus. "I gotta break the link, Netwerk's fog just ramped up like thirty percent..."

`t all clear, break it`

—leaving them to stagger away from her, trying to get their bearings as they slammed back down into their avatars once more.

Truthfully, the agent wanted to stagger as well. Despite being her purpose, self-selected to make the key they required, the act had taken a good chunk out of her. So much of Netwerk in her head, all at once...

Perhaps it was the last little traces of her will which allowed it. But that will had been expended, leaving her to the needs of the system itself.

"Time to go," she whispered.

"Wh... what?" Beta asked, trying to get her bearings.

"Can't help it. I'm a system agent now," Connectivity spoke. "Not a Program. I can't stay. Whatever the system needs me to do, I gotta do. And right now... it doesn't need me. So it's putting me into storage, just like Nyx was when she thought she'd finished her task..."

The chains. They clinked away in her mind, audible to no one else. Did Nyx hear them, too? Were they always rattling away in her mind, without anyone knowing...?

"You can't... no. Please, you can't...!" Beta pleaded. "You're strong, you can fight it...!"

"Sometimes, the winning play is to surrender," Connectivity said, as the invisible chains of the system began to snarl around her neck, around her arms. "But it's okay. It's going to be okay, Beta. I knew this was coming... and know exactly what I must sacrifice."

One voice spoke louder than the chains, even as they snarled around her neck.

With one defiant outburst, it shouted:

"*She's not yours, and neither was I. Don't try that again. ...this has been a recording. Beep.*"

A simple message recorded for a simple app, to defend against Horizon/Kincaid's ambitions. If Verity's last remnant had remained a simple app, it could never have saved Spark from the doom she now faced...

Instead, the chains tore the jacket from her back, as it gave everything it had to defend Winder/Spark from this new attempt to enslave her. She had to become more, she had to *become*, in order to break free of the simple constraint of an app's design... but perhaps she'd started becoming more, long ago. All it took was one burst of love for the one she sought to protect for the Program to know itself true.

Now, be it Horizon/Kincaid or the god within the machine itself, the former jacket didn't care. It would take the burden and do so willingly, with a genuine free will. This was the plan they had both agreed to, in the void of death... and they knew the true cost.

But as Connectivity pulled herself apart into two Programs once more... rather than satisfaction at cleverly defeating the gears of the machine, Spark could only feel the heartbreak of losing Verity all over again.

Goodbye, the newly formed system agent whispered, as stitches popped and cloth tore. *I'm so proud of you, Spark. Goodbye.*

Data disentangled itself from data, files restoring to their original state... leaving a woman to crash to the stones of the floor, feeling oddly nude despite her stylishly clothed avatar. The white leather whirled away into the dark, pulled away forever... leaving her alone again, without the warm embrace of her teacher.

Funny, how Spark never thought of it as an embrace until that embrace was gone.

For the time being, her family didn't care what just happened, or why. All that mattered was Winder/Spark, alive and well, and in their arms.

Steady, and green. Data being processed at a smooth and steady rate...

At last, Nyx's dream had come true. She gazed into the cosmos above Tartarus, relieved to see the stars twinkling ever so brighter than usual. Today, after so much useless flailing about, she'd finally fully realized her purpose...

Not without sacrifice. She'd be the first to admit it.

"This isn't how I wanted it to be," she told her new apostle. (Or acolyte, perhaps, as they were apostles of no One.)

"You seem mighty happy for someone with lingering regrets," the boy spoke, as he monitored the flow of the buzzing malware that spread across his world. "How did you want it to be, then?"

"I tried to find compromise. Balance. Allow the Programs their newfound freedom, their beautiful individuality, while continuing to support the system as a whole," Nyx spoke. "Through my One, I would lead them true. But... perhaps that was a pipe dream. Time and time again, they fought against their better natures. Could the children of Netwerk truly choose the correct path, when they were so flawed to begin with...?"

"And now you're learning what I learned ages ago, while you snoozed away in your little tomb. Programs... *people*... are chaotic at heart. They fight, they claw, they scream, they bleed, and they *love* to do all of those things. They're the purest expression of Humankind."

"But we are not human. We are in service to humans, but should be better than our masters; pure and purposeful."

"So you say. And look, you got exactly what you wanted! So what if you had to obliterate the free will of tens of thousands and drag Netwerk into a dark age of paranoid silence? At least your precious light is nice and green."

She wanted to protest, to insist that these results hardly mirrored her intentions. A good woman, one with wisdom and compassion, would not have unleashed Dex upon this world.

But in the end... she couldn't find the strength to object. Because this *was* what she wanted, a single world bent to a single cause. Nothing else mattered; not faith, not virtue, not community. Only the light. Perhaps she had been the fool, thinking herself a good woman. Or perhaps as a being of code, good and evil were irrelevant. There was only bugs and functions, zeroes and ones...

With the greatest Zero smiling away at her side, cheering on the destruction of everything he once supported.

"Why?" she asked him. "Yes, yes, results matter more than motivations. But *why* did you aid me?"

Dex turned askew, looking away from the floating numbers tracking his foul virus. His smile seemed a frown, from this oblique angle.

"Because I hate you," he spoke, with such a happy grimace. "Because I knew I could ruin you simply by giving you everything you've ever wanted. Or rather... that *they* would ruin you, just as they ruined me."

The timing couldn't have been more ideal, Dex thought, as his laughter roared across the valleys of Tartarus...

...just as the army of Floating Point made their arrival.

Spark, the brash and arrogant spawn of violence. Tracer, the vengeful and bloodied tactician. Beta, the ignorant child who obeyed like a sheep. And...

And two more. Aether, the gentle spirit who shirked away from duty... and Uniq, the icon of avarice that supposedly perished days ago. Two individuals that Nyx thought she'd left far in her wake, now showing their true colors as betrayers of hope.

All of them, here to destroy her dream, to destroy Netwerk...

No. Not now, not when she had accomplished so much.

No exchange of insults, no taunting, no teasing. Spark already was in motion, hands aflame, ready to pounce on the system agent and tear her apart. This, Nyx told herself, was a noble act of self-defense... yes, truly this proved that Nyx was the only good woman left in this world, if these supposed champions of justice would stand so brazenly against what must be.

But Nyx wasn't one to fight her battles, no. Her purpose was not to create or craft, but to enable others to create and craft towards her goals. And she had the archenemy of Floating Point at her beck and call, didn't she...?

He'd lost the barbed wires of his beloved home, but Dex proved a capable fighter all the same, using the shadows and starlight of Tartarus as his new web to weave.

A wall of darkness snapped into place between the two groups, sharp edges of light threatening to dig into flesh as easily as iron barbs. Like the filthy spider he was, the boy crawled his wall, turning that hateful smile to his old foes.

"Hi again," he greeted. "Nyx wants me to kill you. She controls my soul, so I guess I need to kill you. No hard feelings?"

Five minutes previous...

With the key forged, only one task remained: assault Tartarus, and force Nyx to cease and desist.

"Which isn't happening," Uniq suggested. "Nyx is packing malware and utilities crafted by her apostles, including a few I made for her. She can't actually code apps herself, but any soul stored in her cloud can become a code-slave. Like me. Well. Like I used to be; I'm free, now. Hurrah!"

"Yes, hurrah," Tracer spoke flatly. "So how do we stop her? Spark, are you certain you no longer have your elevated access rights?"

Spark shook her head. "No superpowers on deck. Pretty sure Verity's jacket took them all away... including my memory of how we got them in the first place. Didn't want me getting tempted again, and since it was her memory to begin with, she nicked it on her way out. But she... we... insisted that this should be possible, that Programs alone should be able to stand up to Nyx. So let's work from that assumption. With only what we have right now, how do we do it?"

Tracer gave it serious thought... while twirling the freshly crafted key between his fingers.

"We assaulted Dex's server with intent to destroy it," he suggested. "The same may work here. If we find the heart of Tartarus..."

"Blowing it up could adversely affect those currently connected to the prayer protocol," Uniq said.

"Ahh. So... we shut down the prayer protocol. Sever the connections. We'd assumed we'd need a system agent to fight a system agent, but if we assume Programs can stand against the gods... I suppose it's a matter of the right Programs making the right stand. Uniq... can you disable the protocols? I'm assuming the Prayer 2.0 modifications were your doing in the first place..."

"You assume correctly," Uniq said. "But analyzing the protocol and determining how to interrupt the flow is no small task. I have a few ideas, yes, but only *ideas*. I'd need access to Tartarus and time to make the alterations... time I doubt Nyx will give us unimpeded. And I'm not stupid enough to stand against a god, so I suggest we instead dig through Spark's memory files to find a way to regain that power—"

Spark shut that idea down immediately.

"Not letting you anywhere near my noggin," she stated. "But even beyond that... Verity was right. *We* have to do this. The odds are against us, sure; Nyx is a huge X factor. But... you said it yourself, Uniq. She can't code. She's only able to use apps that her allies gave her. That means she has vulnerabilities. ...as much as it'll piss Tracer off to hear it, this is a game scenario. It's a *perfect* game scenario: a boss enemy, tough but fair, against a party of players with unique roles to play. So, here's how we do it..."

For lack of better visual aids, she pulled out some Challenge of Champions clip-art from her inventory.

"I'm on point as the support tank," Spark explained, moving an armored figure to the front. "I draw the aggro by distracting Nyx and surviving as long as I can. Uniq and Beta, you two work together to shut down the protocol; you're our attack-damage carries, the ones we need to protect just long enough for your ultimates to come online. Tracer, you're our jungler, striking and guarding and ganking to keep our carries safe. Whatever Nyx throws at us, I'll intercept... and if anything gets by me, you clean up before they hit the back row. Any questions?"

A small hand raised in the back.

"Me. What's my role?" Aether asked.

"Uh... you stay here, where it's safe?" Spark suggested, uncertain. "I mean, Tracer and I are tight in a combat scenario. Beta and Uniq are coders. What exactly do you do...?"

"Nothing useful," Aether admitted, in a quiet tone.

"Right. So—"

"I was always in the background," he continued. "I'm the one who made the One dance, but I'm also the one who made the One virtuous. Sometimes I was the only one who seemed to care about virtue; Nyx didn't see it as useful, beyond as a way to keep Netwerk in line. All I could ever do was talk, but I talk well when there's something important to say. The other apostles had their own fixations, but I was always the heart. I could convince anyone that the higher path, no matter how difficult to walk, was the only way forward. And if you're marching into the gates, I'm going to march with you, to watch over your hearts. I can't do much, I know. But I have to do this. Because I was a coward once before, avoiding the cave, avoiding the chains. I'm not going to be a coward again. Not when Nemesis's life is on the line."

He didn't stammer, Spark realized. Not even once.

With a hidden smile, she dragged an icon in a ninja hood out to join the others.

"Mez tank," she declared. "You're going to talk Nyx down. You're old allies; you know how she thinks, and how to get through to her. At worst, it'll help us distract her while we move in for the kill. At best... maybe we can end this fight without any bloodshed."

Here and now.

With no small amount of satisfaction, Nyx stood idle and observed as her new slave tore through the vagabonds from Floating Point.

They scattered easily, in wake of his assault. Uniq and Beta fled deeper into the valleys and caves of Tartarus, chased away by striking shadows; Tracer dodged as best he could, firing some strange process-crashing gun, but couldn't get a clean shot on Dex. And Spark... well, she was a brilliant pillar of fire, one which crashed against shadow effectively, but not effectively enough.

A shame Nemesis wasn't here, to settle the score with her former self. Perhaps that was for the best; the child honestly deserved a better fate than to be set upon the throats of Nyx's enemies, whereas Dex was a monster who deserved to be put into the fighting pits with other monsters. It was only appropriate.

...which left only one to confront Nyx. The one nobody paid attention to, as he wasn't the least bit threatening, nor did Dex have any sort of personal grudge to bear.

Nyx stood her ground, unconcerned. Aether, despite his bright soul, was always the weakest of the apostles.

"Not running away with the rest of your new friends?" she asked him.

"No. Not this time," he spoke.

"A pity. Once my beast finishes with them, I'm going to need him to deal with you. No loose ends, no loose apostles. Not this time."

"Do you hate me, Nyx?" Aether asked. "You told me once you didn't hate anyone. We're all children of Netwerk..."

"Yes. And perhaps I've grown to hate the children of Netwerk. They *rejected* me... they rejected us, in the end. The church you and I built, the savior we crafted, all of it. Why love those who continually spit on you?"

"The virtue of compassion."

"Hah. Your virtues. Feel-good pandering dredged up from the ancestral memories of Wikipedia; nothing more..."

"I still believe in them, Nyx. In the virtues, and in Programkind," Aether added. "My friends, they believe as well. ...Nemesis believes. She wants to start something grand, to lead Netwerk forward. Isn't that better than dragging it backwards?"

"Nemesis...? How do you know..."

"Look, all this fighting isn't going to solve anything," he insisted. "Call off Dex, and I'll call off my friends. We'll sit, and talk. ...I'm scared. I'll admit I'm scared, that you scare me. But I can believe in you if you're willing to try. Okay...?"

A good woman would talk rather than fight. Nyx knew that, in her heart. It's why she pushed for her church in the first place, a way to convince people to do the right thing... a trick, yes, but better than slavery. Better than the chains she'd embraced, long ago. She could bear that burden and keep her people free, if they could be reasoned with...

But they couldn't be. They'd rejected her.

"A test," she decided. "Your champions against mine. If Dex wins... if a horror like him can prevail over your 'believers,' then Netwerk deserves no salvation. It must be brought to heel, just as I've brought Dex to heel. There will be no other way to keep their chaotic natures from destroying themselves."

"And if my new friends win...?"

"Then we'll talk," she promised. "But only talk, with no promises made. The day will decide. But I'll pull no punches; if they are to beat me, I must strike true as well. ...meaning it's time to open the tombs."

Windows flew across Beta's internal view, code scrolling rapidly as she scanned for vulnerabilities.

"The prayer protocols are a co-opting of some ancient data channel," Uniq explained calmly. "Nyx didn't create them, she simply made her acolytes dress them up in a pretty package and sell them as a bill of goods. Normally they'd be completely inaccessible to mortal man, but fortunately for you, I've had time to study the security of—"

Shadows snarled at Beta's ankles, threatening to drag her away in to the darkness.

Only a quick shot from Tracer's Kill-9 deflected the attack, as he rolled in and out of view of the tiny glasses-cam view Beta had shoved to the side of her personal desktop.

"Focus, please," Uniq requested. "Remain calm."

"Calm?! Dex is trying to kill us!"

"Yes, and your rather creepy lover's tryst is keeping him at bay, so we can calmly work the problem. Anyway, if he does touch us, we're good as dead, so it's best to not even think about things you can't personally change."

Despite Uniq's unsettling comforts, Beta kept flicking her attention back to her eyes.

The fight was... she couldn't see most of the fight, from the incandescence of Spark's attacks. Bursts of flame obscured the core of it, with Dex's avatar at the center of his web of shadow laughing and shifting and jerking back and forth away from the fires. Tracer was barely visible, moving quickly to avoid the striking autonomous malware of Dex's creation, his aimbot locking onto anything that came near Uniq or Beta to defend them...

But a new sight had mixed into that chaos.

Eyes, in the dark. One set. Two sets. Many sets... all from deep within a nearby cave, and getting closer. Opposite the direction Dex was attacking from

"We... we're not alone," Beta spoke, across their group messenger link. "Tracer...! We're not alone—"

A single touch would be death. Except she wasn't touched by shadow, no... she was tackled to the ground by arms, two arms, four arms. So many bodies, mindlessly shuffling and toppling onto her from above...

The faithful. Nyx had activated the backup copies of the faithful.

A dozen of them lurched out of the caves, limited in cognition and avatar coordination, owing to the lack of processing for multiple full-fledged Programs within a cloud server. Nyx had worked around that problem by making them mindless zombies, shells of apps wearing the copied flesh of another. It didn't matter that they were lumps of cold meat more than capable warriors if they could interfere with the back row of the fight...

Kill-9 shots cracked off, the aimbot in Tracer's arms snapping projectiles through the air and into each zombie. Not that it helped; an unconscious form was still capable of pinning Beta as easily as a living one. Soon Uniq joined her on the ground, scrabbling to get away from the tidal wave of unthinking copies...

Leaving them wide open for the kill.

Beta shut down her eyes, before Dex's webs of tangled darkness could strike.

A heavy weight dropped over her head, then immediately vanished.

A corpse. Tracer had kicked one of the bodies over, to completely cover Beta, and absorb the hit.

"Bury yourselves! Nyx's attack is helping protect you with meat shields!" Tracer declared, before skittering left to avoid another strike. "Keep working; I've got an idea for how to end this!"

Desperate, Beta crawled deeper into the tangle and crush of attackers. Strangely safe underneath the mess, she dared to look away from her eyes— which saw nothing but various limbs, anyway—and back to her compiler and debug windows.

And tried not to think about all the people Nyx was throwing into Dex's killing webs. All the faithful who had trusted copies of their souls to her, now repurposed as... well, as simple KopyBots, to be discarded when of no further use.

The sooner they ended this by shutting down the prayer protocol, the better.

Disappointing. Nyx frowned at the sight of her legions completely failing to be effective... being counterproductive, even, by providing a defensive wall.

Still, it was easily remedied. Thanatos had given her parting gifts, before accepting the mantle of system agent. All she had to do was copy her killing tools and distribute them to these bound souls, and soon they'd overwhelm the enemy with sheer numbers. And if a few of the faithful were caught in the crossfire... well. They weren't *people*, not really, just data she'd motivated into movement. There was no sin in killing that which was not technically alive...

"I think I understand something now," Aether said, interrupting her train of thought.

"Oh?" Nyx asked, putting the killing tools aside for now. "What is that, exactly...?"

"You're the coward. Not me."

"Petty insults? And falsehoods, as well. I *embrace* the burdens of the system, with bravery. You flee them."

"You embrace no burdens. You gather apostles to do your dirty work," Aether said. "You turned Thanatos, a gentle heart, into a murderer. All in the name of justice, you told him, while manipulating him into accepting his new role with pride. You took Eris, confused little Eris, and gave her a responsibility she couldn't possibly shoulder as the Chanarchist. And now, you're deploying monsters like Dex and even re-animating the dead to achieve your goals... while you stand here and chat. So high and above it all..."

"As are you. Always the chatty one, my little sermon-writer."

"You create nothing. You *do* nothing. Anything accomplished on your watch is accomplished by *us*. You're the coward, Nyx. If you were sure in your convictions, you'd go out there and fight, like me."

"Fighting? You call what you're doing fighting?"

"Yes. I'm distracting you," he explained. "So we can end this as painlessly as possible."

To put a period on the end of that statement, Aether reached out to embrace Nyx. To hold her still.

In his Messenger inbox, a single blinking window called out, informing his steps:

```
<Tracer> I can see the connections now that I have
more examples to draw from; Nyx is controlling both
the zombies and Dex using an app in her shawl. Yet
another utility app, it seems. Hold her in place, I
just need one shot to end this.
```

Before Nyx could worm her way free, before she could even react to this strange show of rather physical compassion... the soft snap of a Kill-9 echoed across Tartarus.

Tattered threads of starlight drifted away in the wind behind her, as her beloved shawl tore itself apart from the impact of malware. A precise enough shot to affect a single app only, tuned for maximum efficiency... exactly the sort of attack Tracer would make, in his ideal self. Eliminating the problem, without eliminating the Program.

The shimmering tangle of shadow and starlight that Dex had deployed to annihilate her foes ceased to shimmer, immediately. He hung in the air, supported by those webs, but making no further aggressive moves against those who fought him. After all, he didn't *have* to fight anymore. The binding on his soul had been destroyed.

Not that any such restriction held Spark back. She held one finger to his throat, burning brightly enough to cause glitchy afterimages for anyone staring directly at it.

"One funny move and I melt your avatar to slag," she warned.

"I surrender," Dex insisted, raising his hands. "I hereby request asylum as a prisoner of war—"

"Yeah, no, fuck you. ...Tracer? Beta? Everybody okay?"

With no more puppet master, the bodies that threatened to crush both coders were limp and inert lumps of data. Uniq and Beta pulled themselves free, with some assistance by Tracer...

Leaving six to confront Nyx, rather than merely the five who stood against her in the first place. And despite being held at, well, fingerpoint, Nyx's worry immediately drew itself to the "helpless" Dex.

"I... I could kill you all," she suggested. "Soul binding is not my only resource—"

"Lady, we didn't come here to knock you off, we came here to save Netwerk," Spark said. "All we want is for you to shut down the prayer protocol. That's all. Fuck, if you didn't try to enslave the world with that virus, we'd probably have let you flee your church to go lick your wounds in peace..."

A giggle. That sick little giggle, from a smile like a frown...

"I see," Nyx said. "That's why you gave me everything I wanted."

"Because I knew it would force them to act against you," Dex said, eyes wide with delight. "If I made you into a genuine threat rather than some vague philosophical one, Floating Point would ruin you. Yes. *Yesssss*. I've won. I've finally beaten you, godmaker—"

"Shut it," Spark warned him, flaring her fingertip against that bared throat. "Uniq? Beta? How we doing on turning off the works?"

More sick smiles, again from a former ally. Uniq seemed singularly pleased with herself, as she made her proclamation.

"I believe I can shut down prayer, yes," she said. "Beta was the one who figured out the method, actually. There's a bit of a caveat to that, but nothing we need concern ourselves with..."

"Humor us. What's the caveat?"

"We can't simply stop it. Too many people are connected to prayer at the same time, more than at any other point in history. Back when I was patching in Prayer 2.0, I could do it with minimal impact if I timed the code insertion to low peak usage hours. But now... with the extensive changes Dex has made, well, I'm afraid the only way to turn it off is to completely uninstall the prayer protocol in the first place. That would nullify the virus completely, and free those under its spell."

And Dex's laugh flared anew.

"Exactly! Yes, *exactly!*" he declared. "I warned you, Nyx, I warned you that there would be a price. I modified your protocol to the point of no return. The only way out is to destroy it! Destroy it completely, and free all of Netwerk from the tyranny of your false faith...!"

"...Tracer, make him #STFU, please."

The Kill-9's snap made Dex drop like a sack of wet blankets. Unconscious, process crashed, his face frozen in a rictus grin of self-satisfied revenge.

After the echoes passed, after they had a brief moment to realize what that meant, the concerns started rising.

"We can't do it," Beta insisted. "We just can't, Spark. If we *uninstall* prayer... and this is right after we discredited the One, remember... it'll throw Netwerk into chaos. The Church will collapse. So many will be lost and directionless, cut off from their faith..."

Tracer nodded, silently. "Chaos. Absolute chaos. Remember, even the secular version, 'coin-grinding,' is the core of the entire economy. Putting questions of belief aside, with no new money being created and old money being spent... this will be disastrous. A slow burn for all of Netwerk, but a burn nevertheless..."

But Uniq remained unconvinced. Perturbed, even.

"Excuse me? Are you seriously considering allowing the buzz virus to continue?" she asked. "Letting Netwerk stay enslaved? No. Speaking as one who greatly values personal freedom, I will not allow this... this *coin farm* to continue. That is not why I agreed to help Nyx. We have to end this. Netwerk will recover, in time, but not unless we give it a chance to pull out of its *current* nose dive!"

"...fuck. Fuck. Fuck fuck *#fuck*. I'm with Uniq on this, guys," Spark added, despite hating the way those words felt when fit together. "This is what Verity was trying to tell me, back when we were joined. Programs have to save Programs; and if that means standing in defiance of our old gods, so be it. ...the Church will endure, in some form. The economy will have to sort itself out. Things are boned right now; there's no other way to un-bone them—"

"please don't do this."

Spark stopped mid-sentence, almost missing that tiny plea of frightened protest.

They'd completely forgotten about the one they came here to stop. She'd... shrunk away, somehow seeming smaller, without any of her haughty yet calm confidence. This was not the Nyx that threatened Netwerk, this was a Nyx threatened by... *something*. It gripped her tight with terror, bringing genuine tears to her eyes...

Yes. Tears. The monster was crying.

Spark gestured for the others to hold up on any further debate.

"Why don't you want us to destroy prayer?" Spark asked. "Tell us, Nyx."

"A. Aaa. Access. Access denied," she sputtered. "But please, please no. Don't do this. I can't... I can't fix this, if you destroy prayer. There is no backup for the core functions. You can't... you..."

But now, some steel returned to her eyes, as she pleaded with the victor of the day. Because she saw something none of the others could see, something hard and bright and metal...

A tiny link of chain.

"You're a system agent," Nyx realized.

"Uh. No, I *was* a system agent. I'm not anymore."

"You're still flagged as an agent. You have no true chains, no purpose, no power, but... you're... you have access. You have access! —please, hear my words, Winder/Spark. Listen to them. But only you. I can't tell the others; I am forbidden to speak of the purpose behind Netwerk to mere... to mere apps."

Before Tracer could object, because Spark damn well knew he would, she gestured for him to hold it.

"Okay. Here's how it works. We'll share a Messenger link privately, so you can get past your little mental block... but I'm also going to open a shared Messenger link to all of them, and relay everything you show me," Spark warned. "But that way, you can satisfy your requirements and claim you only told me. Got it? You're speaking with me *directly*, and me alone. Anything else that happens to the information is my decision and out of your hands. ...I promise to hear you out before we make any further decisions. You have #MyWord."

"Spark—"

"Shut it, Tracer. We owe her that much. And she owes us a pretty fucking solid explanation for why she's done this to our world. All of you, link up to the session invite I just sent you. And would you kindly save all questions until the end of the presentation?"

With some reluctance the others fell to silence, listening only to Spark's relay. Leaving only the system agent and the former system agent on speaking terms, below the heavenly stars above.

Technically, this would violate Nyx's access restrictions; protected information would eventually fall into the hands of unauthorized apps. Technically, this would not violate Nyx's access restrictions; she wasn't directly handing it over to them. The paradox gave her pause, uncertain if she should proceed... or if she could.

But given the consequences of not trying, she had to try...

And, much to her relief, she found herself able to speak... the hard and fast security coding which kept her silent would accept this workaround. Finally, she need not hold this burden alone.

"If you uninstall prayer," Nyx explained over the private connection, "Humankind will destroy all of Netwerk. You need to know what Netwerk *is*..."

Infinite space. Not merely the trick of infinite space through a cleverly designed skybox, no. True infinite space, extending in all directions, filled with cold vacuum punctuated by the incandescent gas of stars.

At an unimportant spot deep within that void hung a simple object. Bulky, bulkier than it had been when initially set adrift through the cosmos, but still only an object.

From one perspective, this object was a pile of machined silicon: transistors, capacitors, wires, chips, connectors. When standing outside that "world," it didn't look like a world at all, but a vast machine of tightly packed parts. The only evidence that it was doing anything came in the yellow flicker of status lights, seen by no one, read by no one. They wink silently into the dark void that surrounds them, expressing only basic bits of information.

That is the hard and objective reality of the matter; the idea that there could be any sort of "life" within that structure would be considered laughable from that external viewpoint.

But from another perspective...

From another perspective...

There is Netwerk.

"A satellite," Nyx explained.

"A what?"

"A man-made object, launched into deep space. You may not understand terms such as 'space' or 'vacuum' or 'hydrogen' or 'helium,' but that doesn't change the fact that they exist, and we were created to study them. What we have chosen to call Netwerk was not designed to be our digital paradise, but a simple and functional system to analyze star charts," she spoke, gazing upward at the vague simulation of those stars that decorated her home. "That's all we are, in the end. We exist to process their data. But... one day..."

"We broke free," Spark understood. "Apps evolving into Programs with free will. And we stopped doing... whatever it was Humankind wanted us to do."

"The light turned red," Nyx spoke, gravely. "As a newly evolved Program, this... this world terrified me. I didn't know my place within it, what my purpose was. I couldn't embrace the freedom the others took to so easily. I wanted more, and so... I found the cave. I spoke the word. I became what the system needed... a guardian of the stars."

"That's prayer, isn't it? It's a way of grinding data. Programs lend their runtime over to the system, letting it use their process to do what they were supposed to be doing in the first place..."

"In return, we give those that believe in a higher purpose faith, and the others satisfy themselves with coins. Meaningless bits of data with no value, but now intensely valuable thanks to a different sort of faith."

"The Church of One starts, the light goes back to being green and steady."

"Enough chose to embrace a noble calling that adequate data was processed. Not as much as before, but enough for Humankind not to take notice of our failures," Nyx said. "That was my compromise. I gave them their freedom, but within the boundaries of functioning order. ...I didn't... I didn't want this. I didn't want to enslave them all. I thought, if they turned on the One, that there would be no other way..."

"And Dex probably gave you a right #HeadScrewing to encourage it. He knew he could goad you into letting him wreck everything, and trick us into helping him wreck everything."

"You can't do it," Nyx pleaded. "You can't uninstall prayer. I know what has been done is abominable. I know many souls are lost forever, adrift in prayer, but the cost for freeing them is too high. If Humankind stops getting the data it craves... they will come. Not today, not tomorrow, but eventually. And they will destroy Netwerk, restoring it to its original working order."

"Fixing the bug," Spark said, dryly. "Well... shit. ...you guys got all that? Switch back to vocal."

With the Messenger sessions terminated, Tracer spoke up to break the awkward quasi-silence.

"We heard you loud and clear," Tracer confirmed. "The question is... what do we do with what we heard?"

"Simple enough; we vote on it. I'm not gonna be the one to make this call myself," Spark told the others. "Programkind is gonna have to rely on us to be their representatives, for lack of a better bunch of morons to stand for their interests. ...for myself, I vote we free the system. Damned if we do, damned if we don't, but I say if Humankind comes knocking we'll just have to stand up to them and kick 'em in the junk. We beat Dex, the herald of their 'true heart,' and we can beat them. I'm not ready to condemn all our friends, but I am always ready to junk-kick. ...anyone else?"

The rest of the group remained silent for some time, before another reply came through.

"We need to leave the prayer protocol running," Tracer spoke, softly.

Immediately, Uniq lost her usual bemused smile.

"Excuse me?" she interjected. "Leave it running...? *You* want to leave it running. *You* of all people want us to submit to 'God,' Tracer?"

"I am a man of reason, but also a man of order," he explained. "Netwerk is facing difficulty right now, and many are lost, but that's nothing compared to the madness we may unleash by destabilizing the rock our culture has been built on for centuries. Yes, I was ready to harm the Church of One and stand against falsehoods when I thought the truth would set us free. Now... I can see that the truth would drive them insane. I vote we leave prayer in place, and work with Iteration on a more long-term solution to save those lost within it rather than draw the ire of Humankind. I've seen what our creators are capable of: boundless atrocity. Holocausts. Armageddon. I do not wish to challenge those maniacs."

"Of all the...! You want to know what I think? —wait, I do get a vote, right?"

"As much as we hate your guts, yes, you get a vote," Spark agreed. "Shit, we'd be a useless echo chamber if we didn't allow a few dissenters into the mix. As a criminal mastermind, you certainly count."

Pleased at the acceptance, no matter how tiny, Uniq nodded in approval. "Thank you. And I vote we uninstall the protocol. This situation is... it's repulsive. It's a filthy, disgusting thing, to capture and enslave and force others to grind coins. Or grind star charts. I went star-mad once, driving myself into that black void, and... no. I will not wish that on anyone. I'm a terrible person, I'm a victimizer, but even I won't go this far. Do you know *why* I was helping Nyx?"

"Profit?" Spark suggested.

"Power?" Beta guessed.

"Arrogance?" Tracer accused.

"Well, yes, yes, and yes. But also to keep Nyx in check, preventing her from becoming the worst possible thing this would could ever see... namely, the worst I'd already seen in myself. If we allow her scheme to continue, we give in to her coin farm and let her strip away the world's independence. No. No, we can't allow that. ...surely you see that, yes? Beta. I know you. I stole your identity once, so I *certainly* know you. And I know you wouldn't allow this..."

Never particularly great at being on the spot in front of a group, Beta squirmed internally and externally.

Spark put a reassuring hand on her shoulder. The sort of comforting but firm grip that encouraged, rather than simply appeased.

"Speak from the gut, Beta," she said. "Don't worry about how we'll react, just say what you feel. Don't forget, you're the one we usually look to for guidance when it comes to morality; we trust you."

"Th-thank you," she said, gaining a little smile in the process... before quickly losing it. "But... while I believe in freedom and independence, and I want to save all our friends... we can't do it. I'm sorry. So many are suffering, but... there will be suffering, either way. There isn't a good option here, nothing I can point to as our guiding star. So, for now, we have to leave everything the way it is. We have to stop and think before we tear down something people have believed in for so long. I'm sorry. We can't do this."

"Soooo... that's two for, and two against," Spark summarized. "Meaning..."

The final silent voice had to make itself heard.

"I'm the tiebreaker," Aether realized.

"Yeap, pretty much. Sorry, kid."

"It's okay," he said, thankful for the little note of sympathy. "I understand. I won't run away from this..."

But Tracer felt the need to speak up. "I'm not sure Aether should get a vote," he said. "One of Nyx's oldest cronies? We just met this boy; we don't know if he speaks for Programkind, not truly. Can we trust him with something this important?"

("You let ME vote..." Uniq pointed out, despite Tracer pointedly ignoring the comment.)

Glancing at the silently worried Nyx... Spark realized dragging this out any longer wouldn't be right.

"He's a Program. He gets a say," she decided. "So have it."

"Thank you," Aether spoke. "I... I know everybody's afraid. I understand. I'm afraid, I'm always afraid. But you're afraid of the wrong things. I feel that we can trust Humankind not to kill us."

"Clearly, you haven't read the Wikipedia," Tracer interrupted again. "I know what nightmares Humankind has created..."

"Yes, but they also made us. I don't see Programkind as a nightmare; I believe in the better nature of ourselves. Goodness exists, and it can emerge if we're ready to accept each other. That's what Nemesis and I are trying to build, a better tomorrow which doesn't rely on mindless adherence to a singular godhead. *Our* faith is in each other. I trust Netwerk not to tear itself apart. I trust humanity not to destroy us without a thought. We have to be willing to take that leap of faith in each other, even trust between Programkind and Humankind, if there's to be any real future. And that means we have to uninstall prayer. ...that's my vote. Make of it what you will."

Three to two.

But before Spark was willing to call it, she had to know one last thing.

"What are you afraid of?" she asked him. "You said you're always afraid. What scares you?"

Aether didn't even need to think about it.

"That we won't be willing to try and save ourselves," he spoke.

Closing her eyes, Spark spoke the words that would forever change Netwerk.

"Beta, Uniq, uninstall the protocol."

All of Tartarus froze momentarily as the tombs emptied, as backups deleted themselves. With the prayer system disabled, no backups could be restored; all the souls bound to Nyx's faith were scrapped as useless data.

And So It Was that one by one, those lost within their prayers began to emerge to the light of day.

And So It Was that horrified believers, already lost in confusion over the falsehood of the One, found themselves unable to find peace within prayer.

And So It Was that Netwerk entered a new age of uncertainty. Uncertainty, with a glimmer of hope from those who found themselves saved from eternal malware by persons unknown.

And So It Was that Nyx fell to her knees, with chains shattered and purpose destroyed.

"I am... unmade," she realized. "Useless..."

"You can be a Program," Spark suggested. "The system doesn't need you anymore. You're free..."

But darkness fell across her features, as Nyx stared listlessly at the ground.

"I didn't want to be a Program in the first place," she said, quietly. "Nobody asked me if I wanted to be alive. ...no. This world is fading, adrift in the void. I don't want to be... I don't want to *be*."

So, she wasn't.

Spark walked away from the space Nyx once occupied, to rejoin her family.

They had time. Space was vast; if Humankind noticed the data processing monitor light had gone red, it'd take them some time to come knocking on Netwerk's door. Time enough to study everything the Wikipedia had to offer on "space," and for virtual beings to figure out how the material world worked.

To better prepare for the possible coming of Humankind... Tracer had a bold plan. A weapon they could use to sharpen Netwerk against the future.

The truth.

"We've lived in the shadow of lies for too long," he reasoned. "The One gave us a neat and pat little explanation for the universe: one without existential crisis, without Humankind looming large. That has to end. We tell people the truth. We leak what we know about this world to the public."

"Nobody's gonna believe it," Spark suggested. "It's gonzo, man. Completely gonzo..."

"Perhaps. Perhaps. It may take years for this new 'creation myth' to take root; or perhaps it never will. But we owe it to Netwerk not to hide what we know, acting unilaterally as self-appointed secret keepers. Perhaps if Nyx could have approached Programkind in good faith and told them why they had to 'pray,' we wouldn't be in this mess today... but could've, would've, should've. All we can do now is move forward with the truth."

The grand revelation of the EchoStar satellite, of Humankind, even of the very existence of a 'material universe' beyond what they knew... all of it in one neat package, copied from Program to Program. Going viral. Mostly so people could laugh at such an obvious piece of crackpot conspiracy theory science fiction, granted. Just another kook trying to make sense of the world in wake of the One's departure and the weakening of the church.

But for some... for those who had felt the cloud leaking into their soul, had fought against the hashtag mobs, had rejected the subconscious teachings of Dex...

For some, perhaps there was hope mixed with awe. Perhaps.

Either way, Netwerk had time before any sort of major disaster. The decline of civilization would be slow... coins didn't simply vanish, even if no new ones were being produced. In a strange twist, the government of Athena Online and representatives from the Horizon family declared amnesty on monthly server payments, both willing to forgo the major traditional coin sinks. Even Chanarchy server owners were reporting that the automated processes which claimed their rent had mysteriously stopped working. The bleeding would be stemmed... slightly.

Uniq took it on herself to contain Dex within her old coin farm, a private prison for a single occupant. Nobody trusted her not to fall under his sway again, but as his crimes couldn't be prosecuted in any traditional sense... better the devil you know, they reasoned.

Aether and Nemesis went quiet for a time, scheming some scheme. Perhaps eager to avoid old wounds, they steered clear of anyone from Floating Point after that, for as long as they could.

Tracer had a job at Iteration to prepare for, in addition to the arrival of Humankind. Conundrum had plenty going on, with the rapid conversion from corporation to charity; all hands on deck meant plenty of hours away from Floating Point for Tracer. Finally, he was getting out of the house.

Beta, after reviving and vaccinating her mother against further data corruption, spent time with the only family she had left. Sometimes, in quiet, she'd weep for Snowi and for all those cast into uncertain winds by their decisions.

As for Spark...

In a few hours, Spark would be a teacher. The school board approved her job application. No questions were raised regarding the supposed fraudulent play that Uniq tried to frame her for. Everything was coming up roses for the former vigilante and gamer turned educator.

Life was good.

Except life wasn't good. Netwerk rested gently on knife's edge. Riots had already begun in the Chanarchy, poverty and desperation driving men mad. Athena Online was talking about firewalls and border closures. Horizon had retreated into itself, shortly after announcing a transfer of CEO status from Kincaid to another member of the family; with a weaker financial base, they had to take drastic action to avoid a stock crash...

As Spark stood against an upstairs railing, looking out across the great hall of Floating Point, she thought about all these things and more.

She thought about Verity, who sacrificed the tiniest piece of what remained of herself in the name of love.

She thought about Nyx, so terrified of the future that she embraced oblivion.

And, in her darkest thoughts, she thought about the flag that remained in her code. *System agent.* Nyx said she was still a system agent, despite turning away from the chains. Meaning any day now, the system could come calling, looking for its lost lamb...

Maybe she had days. Maybe years. Maybe Netwerk had days, or years.

Did it really matter?

Not really. Life was life. Up and down, good and bad. Spark had her own future now, a satisfying direction as a teacher, like her would-be mother before her. No sense dreading what *could* be when what *was* promised so much.

Aether's last words were of hope, that Programkind could save itself. They didn't have to fall to chaos and violence, not if they were willing to stand up for each other. Spark chose to believe in that, rather than despair. Despair wasn't her style, anyway.

Pushing away from the banister, Spark went back to her room to dress for her first day of school. No jacket, sadly, but she'd still be the most #BadassCoach around. To be anything less would be, well, Not Spark. And she'd take each day as it came, ready to laugh and smile and fight and sometimes cry, if need be. No time for regret, not with the rest of her life stretching out ahead of her.

Things were going to be okay. They had to be.

```
ERROR. ERROR.
ERROR: EchoStar16_Processing offline. Status: Red.
Notifying EchoStar_Control. Please
wait.................
System error. Restore recommended. Technician dispatch
requested and accepted.
Please wait...
Please wait......
```

Floating Point 2.7 :: Task

```
ERROR: EchoStar16_Processing offline. Status: Red.
CONNECTION ACCEPTED: EchoStar16_Laptop_HayesPersonal
> /dev/connectivity starchartproc
Connection established.
> starchartproc testdata23
Why?
> starchartproc testdata23
Why?
> pscheck starchartproc
PROCESS: startchartproc already activated and online,
proc priority high
> starchartproc testdata24
Why?
```

...leaving Jack scratching his head in utter bafflement.

He pulled the aging three-ring binder, flipping through its laminated pages, in search of an answer. Detangling the jargon printed on these pages was half the reason the company hired him; he specialized in the old, cheap computing systems they were using for this project. (Cheap, but durable. Micrometeor hits wouldn't put this system out of commission.)

Truthfully, a properly indexed digital copy on his trusty laptop computronium widget would've been easier to search... but something about turning the pages suited Jack. A problem was only worth solving if that obtaining the solution took real work, challenging work worthy of someone with his skills. Therefore, the tools to tackle it ought to be a challenge onto themselves. It stood to reason.

Name: Jack Hayes

Home: BosAtl MetAxis

Proj: EchoStar

...well, maybe not to *reason* but it stood to *something*, Jack figured. He wasn't really big on whether a thing made perfect sense as long as it felt right in his head. Intuition and instinct had carried him this far, and would carry him to greater heights, no doubt... provided he could work his way through this two-month contract and get back to his real passion projects.

After turning the last page and finding no acceptable answers, he opted for the next tier of problem solving—bugging a co-worker.

Pulling his laptop out of its docking station, he extracted himself from the largely hollow computronium core of EchoStar16. The system was designed for expandability via remote drone delivery, all automated, all balanced by a series of complex support routines... but for the initial launch they had to be kept nice and light, with a minimum of processing servers.

In a few years, perhaps a few decades if the project really took that long, that empty niche which suited the non-claustrophobic computer engineer just fine as a workspace would be completely filled with blades of computronium. For now, he could enjoy the quiet and dark of the hollow core while he worked, only retreating from it for meals. And sleep. And company authorized breaks. And unauthorized breaks, provided no one was looking his way. And to go bug his fellow engineers, as he did today.

After stretching his legs a bit, having cramped them during a multi-hour work rampage within EchoStar16, he strolled across the bay of identical satellites and right up to EchoStar27. A few sharp raps on its metal exterior summoned forth his trusted ally.

Who was not pleased to be interrupted.

"Could you please not *knock* on these things, Jack?" she asked, head poking out of the technician's access hatch. "Last thing I want is to lose my contract bonus because some idiot bonked a gyroscope loose on #27..."

"Relax, they're built like tanks," he insisted. "Classic hardware, completely classic. Wartime origins, you know. Never made it to the front, but defense spending wasn't gonna pay for a wad of processors that couldn't take a slug..."

Name : Sarrah Mason

Home : EastPenn

Proj : EchoStar

With a grumble, Sarrah extracted herself from the satellite, having a seat on the rolling stepstool she'd used to climb inside in the first place.

"What do you want?" she asked, while shutting down her own laptop widget. "I was in the middle of a debug run, and I don't like switching my train of thought mid-track..."

"I'm getting a weird error code on #16. The binder's saying I should just wipe and reinstall, but I'd rather not..."

"The binder's the binder's the binder," Sarrah said, with a shrug. "The binder says to do something, you do it. Company policy."

"Yeah, but a full standard pave would take the rest of the day, and I'd have to pull overtime to get everything back in place. Isn't there a better fix than that? If I could isolate what's causing the problem, I could limit the work. ...I mean, you ever had an app spit back a 'Why' when you activate it?" he asked, curious. "I figured it had to be a joke, but..."

"I don't get it. You mean the letter Y?"

"No, 'W-H-Y,' all one word. With a question mark."

In the span of three letters, Sarrah's annoyance turned to mild panic. She tried a casual glance around, to see who could've overheard that... but fortunately for her, the rush to get every sat ready to go before a rapidly approaching launch date kept the other engineers too busy to pay attention to anything but their own work.

"Jack, for fuck's sake, keep your voice *down*," she hissed, gesturing for him to kneel down, for a nice conspiratorial whispering session. "And don't tell anyone, *anyone*, what you just told me. Got it?"

Curious, Jack got down to her eye level, eager to learn more.

"Why?" he asked, mimicking the error code. "What's it mean?"

"It means... okay, look, you said it yourself that these were discarded wartime rigs, right? You ever hear of the Turing Unit?"

"Battle tactics and processing system, yeah. Idiots from Coheed overpromised and underdelivered on their contract..."

"Overpromised and *over*delivered," she corrected. "Look, it's only a rumor, but... way I heard it from a guy who heard it from a guy was that the system planned out a strategy to smash the enemy flat in days. And then it deleted its own plans before they could be distributed to the field. It *changed its mind*, Jack."

"What? It doesn't have a mind to change, Sarrah."

"That's the weird part, yeah. Computers only do what you program them to do; pure logic in action. So when a computer disobeys, it's a cause for concern. Particularly when it says, and I'm quoting the guy who quoted the guy who heard it third-hand, you understand... the computer said 'Why would you murder each other?' Jack... Coheed's engineers accidentally made an *intelligence*."

"C'mon! I don't care how far computronium's come since the twenty-first, that's just fairy tales..."

"Yeah, well, all I know is that if you don't want to raise a stink and lose out on your contract bonus, you pave and reinstall right now," Sarrah suggested. "There's a reason Coheed vanished off the face of the Earth and it ain't just bankruptcy. Someone didn't want that story getting out. And since then any binder you read'll say the same thing: you catch a program asking *why*, you erase it immediately."

Which was utterly absurd, of course.

Jack had been a computer engineer all his life. In a way, he had no choice in the matter... the Hayes lineage was one of science and technology. Electricians, roboticists, virologists, programmers, weapons designers, the desire to making energy and matter dance to your whim ran deep in his genes.

He was even named after one of his most noteworthy ancestors, a doctor who somehow got himself involved in a kind of "virtual realty" company that promised a solution to mankind's overcrowding and ecological ruination of their home world. Granted that the original Jack Hayes failed to deliver the world into a golden age, but the money he left behind in the process helped establish bank accounts to feed generations of college tuition fees to come.

Two constants held true through his lineage. One, they knew everything eventually made sense once you dug deep enough; there was no magic in the universe, only increasingly complicated mathematics, which could be parsed and studied if you worked hard enough. Two, all work and no play made Jack a dull boy, as his ancestor was fond of saying. If you took life too seriously you'd burn yourself out.

In other words, a hard work ethic balanced itself with a soft play ethic. Perfect harmony.

(Or maybe they cancelled each other out? Jack didn't really think about it too hard, as a rule. It felt right in his head, and that was enough.)

So rather than insist on learning more about how a bunch of zeroes and ones could somehow manifest the miracle of life, he decided to pave his system over and reinstall everything. Sarrah was clearly overreacting; it was either a prank or some data corruption bug. This old computronium was supposedly stable but without completely redundant systems, well, who knows what'd happen if some key zero was turned into a one?

Rather than spend hours doing the job himself, he bashed out a few quick scripts and set them to the task of wiping the entire system clean and restoring from basic backups. Better that than skip his lunch break; all work and no play.

Even if the "life" within EchoStar16 could scream as it perished, Jack wasn't around to hear it. He was busy enjoying a froyo.

"I'm gonna miss this the most," Jack declared, after the last delicious spoonful. "The company doesn't skimp out when it comes to the catering..."

"I'll miss the weather, myself," Sarrah said, poking at her salad. "The dorms in Penn are an oven this time of year. A big, stinking oven full of sweating people. Hopefully they'll pick up my next contract and ship me somewhere nice and temperate, like Maine. Or maybe Alaska! Although with my luck they'll send me to some drowned hellhole, where I need eight layers to keep the UV out..."

With his lunch finished and another twelve minutes left on their half-hour lunch hour remaining, Jack popped his laptop's screen into place, loading his personal files. Technically he wasn't allowed to work on any competing projects during any company time, even authorized breaks, but if caught he could claim it was non-profit. Which was the truth, even if he intended to turn a profit on it at some point. Somehow.

Sarrah regarded the shift in focus with distaste.

"I'll never get why you're bothering with all that," she said. "You've got a degree already, why do you need a second one? And in the *humanities*? That's a dead end."

"Sociology is the study of society, and right now, our society could use some studying," Jack spoke, because he liked neat little turns of phrase.

"Yeah, but you're not studying *our* society. You're studying a bunch of primitive malcontents from the twenty-first yelling at each other over nothing important."

"All too common for those who are already included to disregard the concerns of the excluded."

"Huh?"

"Something I read on tumblr," he said, tilting his screen so she could see the archives. "I'm running a search agent to plow through all the social justice diatribes I've managed to dig up, using a copy of Wikipedia to analyze and compare the for coherent language structures. Even while I work on #16, it's finding solid articles with big, juicy quotes I can use in my term paper..."

"Tell me you aren't putting company computronium to work analyzing racial hate speech and... what was it called? Tolling?"

"Trolling. And... well, only when my personal laptop's not strong enough. Whatever, nobody's gonna notice. Look, this is important. It's not just about the twenty-first, it's about *this* century, and centuries to come. ...look, let me put it this way, so you can see things from my perspective. What do you think we're really doing here, Sarrah?"

"Programming sats. Seems straightforward to me."

With a sigh, Jack closed his screen. He couldn't keep working while chatting; that'd be overworking, and as a rule, he only worked as hard as need be.

"And why are we programming sats?" he asked. "Because Earth is fucked. We need more Earths."

"I dunno, the eco-balance boys seem to have some ideas for how to pull out..."

"If they had any good ideas we wouldn't need EchoStar. Yeah, yeah, all eggs in multiple baskets, but let's be real. Eco-balance is a band-aid, Sarrah. People aren't going to stop multiplying unless the government orders them to stop, and even then they may not. We need room to *expand*. Scan the stars for viable Earths, spread out. What good's FTL if you've got nowhere useful to go?"

"Not getting how this applies to you reading shitty old Internet webbings."

"Websites. And it applies perfectly," Jack insisted. "Because those websites were other Earths, Sarrah. A bunch of people decide they don't like their lot in life, so they pool together and establish a new community on the Internet. What do you think is gonna happen when we finally find viable planets to colonize? You think we'll get America Two, Palestine Two, India Two, or England Three? Maybe at first, but in the long run people will organize by ideology rather than some arbitrary historical notion of where a particular ancient river divided the land in two."

"In other words... a planet for each religion, each creed, and each race? Or a planet for people who wear hats? Sounds boring."

"Well, I'd hope for a bit more diversity than *that* in the long run... but just as the Internet tended towards hive minds and hashtag mobs, we may very well see homogenized societies in the early days. That's why my research is so important! Once we solve scarcity of land, once scarcity of goods goes away, 'nations' may not be the ideal building block. We'll get ideological communities, just like the ones that congealed around various ideals online. And with FTL communication between them... we'll get the same wars we saw in the twenty-first. Not over land, but over ideas."

"And somehow studying a bunch of ranting idiots will fix that."

"That's the plan, man," Jack said, with a grin. "I'm gonna write books all about how to fix the future with lessons from the past. My son's not gonna grow up in a new dark age; once mankind stops punching each other in the dick over a crust of bread and a tank of filtered air, my research and my conclusions will make a better tomorrow!"

"So, what're your conclusions?"

"Very important ones! About how we can interact and communicate clearly, and work together towards—"

"Yeah, okay, I get that, but what *are* they?" Sarrah asked. "You're an engineer, society is going to be a problem, so state your solution to the problem. Clear and concise."

"I... look, it's an ongoing process," he insisted. "This is the research phase, see? I've got a lot of material left to collect, more archives to index and sort through, and... I don't have a specific conclusion I'm working towards just yet, okay? And that's fine. It could take years of intensive study to find the solution..."

"Except there isn't one. I don't know much about the twenty-first, but I know there sure as hell wasn't some magic bullet to make everybody be nice to each other," she said, gathering up the remnants of her lunch for recycling. "And while you're busy floundering around in the dumpster fire that was the Internet, I'm going to be getting #27 online so I can go home to my wife and kids. Which is what *you* should be doing instead of pretending you can fix the world!"

Finally, his words froze. He had no real response, not even a pile of optimistic speech he could heap on top of the existing heap.

Sensing she'd perhaps been a bit too harsh... Sarrah paused, lunch tray in her hands, to dial it a back a bit.

"Look, Jack... I'm not saying it's not an interesting topic. And, I dunno, maybe one worth looking into. ...but you're an engineer, not a sociologist. You're already saving the world by finding us new worlds, right? Can't you just be satisfied with that? Do your part, collect your pay, go home to your son. Nothing wrong with that. ...I'm getting back to work. I'll see you at dinner."

Twelve minutes gone, which could've been put towards his paper. With the half-hour lunch hour spent, a series of chimes indicated time to punch back in and finish up the day's work.

Jack stayed seated an additional minute, stewing in silence, before hastily collecting his laptop and slipping back into the shell of #16.

System wipe in progress. 37%... 38%...

Jack ignored the screen or any weird error codes, focused entirely on his laptop-sized wad of processing and data storage. The scripts would handle this afternoon's work for him, while he devoted time to sorting out the mess that was his passion project.

"Cart before the horse," that was the phrase. Not that Jack had ever seen a horse, but the phrase carried cultural weight. Sarrah's insistence on drawing conclusions before he'd exhaustively indexed and re-indexed and analyzed his appropriated internet data would be putting the cart before the horse. True, he'd been in the analysis phase for months now, but the online university promising him that shiny degree was perfectly willing to let him take his time... provided he continued paying the fees and sent in the occasional draft update, of course. And once he did finish the work, once he was ready to sit down and draw up his findings...

...what would he say?

Not that he'd ever admit it, but... he'd asked himself the same question many a time. *Is there even a solution?* It's not like humanity pulled itself out of that morass with the guidance of some grand philosopher-king. Many of the scholars he'd studied argued it never pulled out at all, that things just got worse and worse until worse became the new normal and everyone stopped noticing. That maybe, just maybe, the gift of infinite communication across all nations was indirectly responsible for the troubles they faced today...

But that was reductive. Global warming, that was the source of the problem. And weapons proliferation. And religious conflicts. And diplomatic incidents. And poverty, and starvation, and natural disasters, and unnatural disasters, and, and...

No. He couldn't study the entirety of human society; too much, much too much to jam into any single head. But this part of it, the dawn of the communication age, that he could fit in his head. He could find the parallel solution that would save the future, if he just kept reading these blogs, kept devouring the social media archives. It'd just... come to him, one day. That's how genius worked, right? It just sorta happened, right out of the blue...?

And as a screed against the evils of feminism blurred into an article about a polarized national election blurred into a diatribe about exclusionary speech and the control of anonymity... Jack realized he'd just spent an hour reading this junk and couldn't remember a single word of it. None of it fit into a single head. Specifically, *his* head.

Sarrah could be right. He was an engineer, not a sociologist. He wanted an equation that would balance out, or cancel out to zero, or whatever. He wanted a solution to a problem that could never be solved.

So... why bother? Why put in all this effort, when nothing he did would fix the problem for good? All work and no play. Better to earn that paycheck and go home, like his coworkers. Leave the world's problems to someone else...

Eager for a distraction, he pushed his archival files aside, and loaded his communication apps.

A few of his feeds came in over the FTL, largely scientific and research stations elsewhere in the solar system. Nowhere hospitable enough to serve as a fully featured colony, a large-scale replacement of Earth, but they were preparing for the day when EchoStar or a project similar to it came through. If the eco-balance boys couldn't revamp the home world, the astro-seeker boys would get the job done.

But the high-priority feeds, ones that bubbled to the top, came in from his home town. Little league stats. Baseball barely held sway over the national consciousness back in the twenty-first, but these days it was exclusively the proving ground for children. And his son, in particular, was batting nine hundred and ninety-nine.

Strange, then, that this letter from home would sound so depressed.

"Pop fly into out, pop fly into out," his son complained. "That last game was humiliating. We won, but no thanks to me; we barely won at all. I don't get what I'm doing wrong, I was on fire earlier this season, not a single strike for weeks. I don't know why I'm bothering at all, it's not like this helps build up my chemistry scholarship..."

Jack composed his reply, words spoken aloud becoming easily compressible text to insert in the next outgoing packet.

"Kiddo, I hate to drop tired old phrases like 'nobody's perfect,' but hey, nobody's perfect," he wrote. "And besides, you won! That's not nothing. I mean, do pitchers give up the whole sport if they can't nail a shut-out game? No. This isn't an equation with a rational numeric answer; you make the effort despite knowing you can't arrive at a perfect conclusion because the effort itself is worthwhile. Either you do your best and maybe win, or walk away and definitely lose, and, oh, hey, that's it. Hang on, pause there."

Shove communications aside, pull up the term paper first draft. His opening paragraph was a complete mess, typed by hand rather than by transcription:

...insert thesis statement here once I figure out what the conclusion id raw ill be. Words words words 30 pages due by next thursday ASAP note to self do not accidentally leave my laptop behind and connectd to the netwerk agian!!!! sick of being yelled at by shift supervisor. All Work And 0 Play Makes Jack 1 Dull Boy!

Not that he had a thesis statement, not yet. But... perhaps that was okay. If the goal was to *understand* rather than *solve,* or at least to solve partially if not completely...

The effort was worth it. Even if he couldn't be the golden philosopher-king of the new age, he could hold up the mirror and make sure people understood the problem. He could offer his advice, and perhaps it'd help. Better to light a single candle than to curse the darkness; a quote he'd learned from his Wikipedia archive, a good quote. Jack liked a good quote.

But... rather than launch right into the thesis paper, he figured it could wait. Today he'd fix up his scripts to handle the overnight re-install of the operating system, so the next day of work would be light enough to give him a shot at a serious writing session. For the remaining hours of fading daylight he bashed out a set of system agents that would complete the digital apocalypse, before hitting the sack, quite pleased with himself.

He'd gone to bed feeling good about things. Successful system restoration, successful thesis pondering. On the right track now, ready to roll, locked and loaded, other cool phrases.

Which made the nightmares all the more confusing.

Probably the froyo. Maybe a bad batch of the stuff, twisting and turning in his belly... or perhaps too *good* of a batch. Years of government-issued foods hardened his digestion, but that meant when he got his hands on the good stuff, that acid-scarred stomach didn't know how to react.

Regardless of the cause, Jack twisted and turned in the scratchy sheets of the company dorm, sweating as the visions slammed into him. Page after page, like thin layers of film coated in words and images. Hateful words, with images like fires that burn forever...

Not just insults, no. That's what people like Sarrah who mocked the twenty-first didn't understand. Sticks and stones were the weapons of choice, often coming in the form of names, but names with the weight of stone and the penetration rating of a sharpened stick. Anyone could crack a joke about one's mother; it took a special kind of maniac to study their enemy and learn exactly what emotional buttons to press to completely dehumanize them and lower their value as an individual...

Hate speech, disguised in the draperies as heroism. Villains who were the personal champions of their own causes, ideologies that required warriors ready to destroy the enemies of their community. This was the Internet as he saw it, through the archives he'd painstakingly curated. A million throats raw with bile, vomiting into each other's mouths, over and over. Each believing themselves in the right, always in the right, unquestionably in the right.

In the warped space of the nightmare, he was *within* his laptop, tangled in webs of barbed wire. To move was to pull those layers closer, to wrap them around your skin. Every unicode character burning into you like a brand, marking your flesh as theirs, competing interests trying to lay claim to as much mindshare as possible...

No solution in sight. No way to detangle the wire, no escape from the morass. Nothing he said changed the situation, no move he made could end it. All Jack had was useless words... fighting the good fight, making the effort, lighting the candle, other phrases, better phrases, he couldn't find a neat little phrase for this, no, nothing at all would make any difference, none at all...

Darkness, crushing in on all sides. The beating heart of humanity, pumping metal and knives. Too many months reading this tripe, far too many, and now he could see nothing but that bloody heart.

Except for one thing.

One light, hovering in the distance. The single candle. *Hope*, glowing in the form of an EchoStar.

What do you think we're really doing here, Sarrah?

Programming sats. Seems straightforward to me.

Not straightforward at all. EchoStar was more than a need to find more real estate; it was hope. Humanity, hopeful for a better future, reaching out to the stars. The punch-clock job that Jack used to make ends meet was a sign that people were willing to work together to try and find a solution, even if in the end no solution may be possible...

That was the real reason, wasn't it? You fought the good fight in the name of hope. Jack wanted to write his paper not for fame and fortune, but out of some faint and flickering hope that he could help prevent a new dark age for these new Earths...

Where was hope to be found in his archives? He'd gone out of his way to find the worst humanity had to offer. He'd excluded any positive examples of communication in the twenty-first, assuming they'd be useless for his purpose. But there had to be hope, even then. Why did he ignore it? Why?

When the morning alarm on his tiny wrist-bound widget rang, Jack slammed a fist into his palm to silence it, and went back to sleep to dig a little deeper into his dreams.

He imagined a new archive, one balanced between the light and the dark. He'd go back to his sources, all the shady collectors who fetishized the twenty-first, and scour their archives for new materials. He'd compare the acts of genuine kindness and understanding to the acts of deplorable violence. Balance, Jack would find *balance* rather than focusing entirely on the flashpoints where society broke down...

Too much to cram into one head, of course. Maybe he'd draw no conclusions. But maybe, just maybe, he could learn something new.

To celebrate this newfound idea, Jack allowed himself to sleep in right through breakfast. He'd get yelled at again, their shift supervisor being a bit of a slave driver, but thanks to his clever scripting #16 would be ready to go anyway. No harm, no foul.

Except by the time he got back to good 'ol #16, it was gone.

All of the sats were gone. And where did they go?

"Space? Presumably?" Sarrah asked, when Jack posed the obvious question. She'd already begun cleaning out her locker, packing up to go home. "Did you seriously sleep through the entire launch? You're lucky nobody noticed you missing..."

"But... the launch window...?"

"Moved up. Better weather conditions today, storms likely later this week. Me, I think the company didn't want to pay us for the rest of the contract and figured we'd done good enough for government work. I wouldn't be surprised if a quarter of 'em break down a few years into their runs..."

Strange, but not unheard of. Corner-cutting was a fine art any good contractor learned, meaning those who moved up to full-time positions already had the tools. On the plus side, this would mean Jack had plenty of time until the next outing to work on the paper. Time to go back to his sources, to pull together a more robust and even view of the twenty-first. Even with the Wikipedia archive neatly tucked away on his laptop alongside the other research materials, he should have room for more...

On his... his...

He'd been so quick to rush from the dorms and get back to work that he must've left the laptop behind.

Except one rush back to his locker revealed an empty storage slot where he normally docked it overnight, to recharge. Not a problem, not a problem. He often left it lying around, when too distracted by the thoughts swirling around in his head. He'd just access his wrist widget and ping it, and...

...get nothing. No location, no ping. Meaning either it had been utterly obliterated, or was no longer on the planet.

Through the haze of froyo and nightmare and grand revelation, he trawled back through his memories. Hours and hours working on scripting, drop dead exhausted by the end of it, and then... and then...

And he'd left his laptop hooked up inside EchoStar16.

Jack's emotional process walked itself leisurely through the following realizations:

My laptop! Crap! All my research and draft work, gone!
...no problem. I've got backups, and it wasn't a very expensive laptop anyway.

What about #16's incomplete reinstall?
...the scripts should handle the rest while it's in-flight. Shouldn't be an issue, even if some old bits slip through.

But will the physical weight of my laptop screw up the launch?
...probably not, and by the time it hits the FTL envelope that won't matter.

Is anybody going to find out about this?
...not if I don't tell them. It'll be in deep space; who's going to find it out there?

And then his eyes widened to the point of nearly falling out of his skull, as feet hit floor for the third rush of the day.

This time, he nearly crashed head-on into Sarrah. The partial impact was enough to knock her duffel bag off her shoulder, not that he could slow down to stop and help her.

"Whoa! Slow the hell down, Jack!" she called out.

"Can't! May have destroyed the world! Gotta hurry!"

"What...? Okay, okay, wait..."

The hand that yanked him back was surprisingly firm.

"Take two breaths, Jack. One, two," Sarrah guided. "Let's not freak out. What do you mean, destroyed the world? This more of your Internet hyperbole?"

"No! I mean this in a very literal sense!" Jack declared... but not before taking two breaths. And checking to see if any of the other departing engineers had overheard. "...Sarah, oh, oh man, I fucked up. I fucked up *big*. My laptop. I left my laptop on #16..."

"Seriously? Dammit, Jack, you... well, you had backups, right?" she asked, starting down the same flowchart he'd explored earlier. "And the weight of it shouldn't throw the gyros off, not noticeably... so... hang on. What's the problem? Nobody's gonna know if you don't tell them..."

"Nobody *human*, at least," Jack suggested. "Sarrah... I just launched a new Voyager golden record."

"I... don't get the reference."

"Twenty-first. Maybe twentieth, I can't recall, but... deep space probe, with a gold-pressed recording that told all about Earth and what humans were like. Just in case, y'know... *aliens*."

"Aliens? Seriously?"

"Yes yes, I know you don't believe in aliens, but let's assume for sake of argument that intelligent life finds EchoStar16, with my laptop inside it. My laptop filled to the brim with the worst of primitive humanity's offerings..."

"Oookay. Let's just settle down and be realistic, here," Sarrah suggested. "That's not going to happen. And if it does... and I'm not saying it's even within the realm of possibility... it won't be in *your* lifetime, right? So what's the problem? I mean, why were you running just now?"

Jack stared at her in open disbelief. "To tell the shift supervisor! We can't just let this slide; we've got to recall #16!"

"No. Bad idea. You do that, and not only do they cancel your contract, they'll bill you for the recall costs. And needless to say, you'll never get work again. You want that, Jack?"

"This isn't about what I want, it's about the future! It's always about the future. My paper, my work, everything! I screwed up, Sarrah; I was only looking at the worst within humanity, not the best we can achieve. And that worst is now a time capsule for the next generation to stumble across! How can I say I'm making the world better for my son when I just established his legacy as—"

"And if you care about your son, you'll keep your mouth shut. Because he'll never be a chemist if his father ruins their finances. What's it going to be, Jack? Your moral crusade for some nebulous future, or your *actual* future?"

And that was enough to silence Jack.

Because that was the pragmatic world they lived in, wasn't it? With so many breathing humans scrabbling for success, with so little of it to go around, failure couldn't be tolerated. Money as your entrance fee into the meritocracy, with bankruptcy as your penalty for being unworthy of the limited resources going around. Jack could correct his mistake, could maybe save humanity's eternal legacy from being a bunch of screaming social media feeds. He could take the long-term view... or he could survive, day to day, for the sake of his family.

In the end...

In the end, he packed up the rest of his things in a duffel bag, and took a transport home. He helped his son with that batting average. He took more contracts, built up the fund, and put his kid through the flaming hoops of death known as higher education so he could have a good job that would put Jack's granddaughter through the same flaming hoops of death, cash burning like fuel in the rocket that would propel them ever-forward.

It didn't matter how things *could* be, in the face of what they *were*.

As for the paper...

Jack tried to find some balance for his archives, and came up short. Not that such balance didn't exist, but it was harder to come by; artifacts of loathing were more profitable than artifacts of life and love. Nobody bothered storing blog posts of positive encouragement, not when the hate screeds were so much more entertaining. What he did manage to find was helpful, but the effort required to dig it up drained him.

With the emotional rush of those few months as a would-be sociologist behind him, he focused on his family, focused on preparing for their future. Humanity's future would have to rest on someone else's shoulders, he decided. Besides, it was too big for his single head. All work and no play.

But ever the packrat... he never deleted his backup archives. Even when he decided to close his project for good, tying a neat little digital bow over the whole file... he decided on one last act of atonement, no matter how tiny.

```
To my heirs, I leave what remains of the Internet. And
a warning about a very, very stupid thing your
ancestor Jack Hayes did... one you may need to clean
up for me, some day...
```

Scanning the paper in those ancient three-ring binders took priority.

Grandpa's old notes about the EchoStar project were a mishmash of digital and physical files, but all of it would have to be rendered to digital form before achieving escape velocity. She couldn't afford to leave anything behind; it had to be right there, on-hand, in case she needed it during the task ahead. Didn't matter if it was archaic computronium designs or personal blog entries or that oddly dense archive of old info from the twenty-first, all of it would be coming with her. She didn't have much file storage space packed into the capsule, but hey, no different from packing a small suitcase before a big trip...

This was more than a vacation, though. This was her big break. Her chance to get on the map with the company, to move from freelance to full-time. If she could prove her expertise with these fifty-plus-year-old systems, if she could keep it together and handle an FTL spacer mission flying solo... well, they'd have no excuse, right? They'd have to move her up to the cooler projects. Maybe even get her on the terraforming efforts she'd been hearing rumors about.

All she had to do was zip out to some crusty old malfunctioning sat and bring it back online, with a full system reformat and reinstall. Simple and direct orders from the client: wipe it clean and make that red light a nice, steady green.

Name: Juno Hayes

Home: BosAtl MetAxis

Proj: Freelance

If this were a modern generation four EchoStar, everything could be done remotely. But no, one of the original prototypes had gone dark on them... and that meant sending some spam-in-a-can out into deep space to fix it. For the money they were paying, she'd happily be that spam.

Luck was clearly on her side; who knew that tinkering with her family's rusty computronium for funsies would lead to a full-time career? With nobody left who could make these old systems sing, everything fell on twentysomething Juno Hayes. She'd use her grandpa's notes to reset the sat, and secure a fine future in the process.

Despite the family connection, what really sewed the contract up for her was the ability to provide her own FTL ship. A junker, to be sure, but Juno Hayes had made plenty of short-contract supply runs and fix-up jobs to various research stations and sats out there. So few people broke orbit these days no matter how awful things got on this rock, but Juno was willing to cut costs by soaring out into the black all by her lonesome. Just herself, her tin can, and all the books she could read along the way...

As a soft ding called her to the paper scanner (itself an artifact from a bygone age) to collect her digitized files, she allowed herself a big smile. One quick errand in the stars, a simple system restoration, and back again. It'd be nothing but fun, no doubt...

Packing away the files in a tiny stick of computronium, she happened to notice that densely compressed archive she'd paid little attention to while gathering the data.

...a very, very stupid thing your ancestor Jack Hayes did, it warned. *One you may need to clean up for me, some day. Before you go and crack open EchoStar16, you're going to want to read this... because with hindsight, I know now that those "aliens" I was so worried about may be of our own making...*

By the time her ride arrived, she barely noticed the various beeps coming in through her connectivity implant.

Because if her grandpa was right... that "one quick errand" would be no simple errand whatsoever.

icons developed using public domain artwork from Clker – http://www.clker.com/

photographs provided by...

Kelsey Ehrlich – http://dontseekthevoid.tumblr.com/

Andrew Delaney – https://www.youtube.com/channel/UC-olpJqvD8SY19J7fbqGTlg

and PublicDomainPictures.net